THE LIBRARY FUZZ MEGAPACK®

THE LIBRARY FUZZ MEGAPACK®

JAMES HOLDING

CONTENTS

INTRODUCTION

James Holding (1907-1997) was a prolific short story author in the mystery field. (He also wrote children's books—including the Ellery Queen Jr. series—but short stories were his true domain.) Among the many series he created, the "Library Fuzz" stories, about detective Hal Johnson who tracks down overdue library books (and often stumbles across crimes) is one of the most unusual…and fun!

This MEGAPACK® collects all of the "Library Fuzz" stories, plus several that feature secondary characters in their own stories…plus a *very* different alternate version of one story.

Enjoy!

—John Betancourt
Publisher, Wildside Press LLC

LIBRARY FUZZ

Originally published in* Ellery Queen's Mystery Magazine, *November 1972.

It was on the north side in a shabby neighborhood six blocks off the interstate highway—one of those yellow-brick apartment houses that 60 years of grime and weather had turned to a dirty taupe.

The rank of mailboxes inside told me that Hatfield's apartment was Number 35, on the third floor. I walked up. The stairway was littered with candy wrappers, empty beer cans, and a lot of caked-on dirt. It smelled pretty ripe, too.

On the third landing I went over to the door of Apartment 35 and put a finger on the buzzer. I could hear it ring inside the apartment, too loud. I looked down and saw that the door was open half an inch, unlatched, the lock twisted out of shape.

I waited for somebody to answer my ring, but nobody did. So I put an eye to the door crack and looked inside. All I got was a narrow view of a tiny foyer with two doors leading off it, both doors closed. I rang the bell again in case Hatfield hadn't heard it the first time. Still nothing happened.

The uneasiness that had driven me all the way out here from the public library was more than uneasiness now. My stomach was churning gently, the way it does when I'm hung over—or scared.

I pushed the door wide-open and said in a tentative voice, "Hello! Anybody home? Mr. Hatfield?"

No answer. I looked at my watch and noted that the time was 9:32. Then I did what I shouldn't have done. I opened the right-hand door that led off Hatfield's foyer into a small poorly furnished living room, and there was Hatfield in front of me.

At least, I assumed it was Hatfield. I'd never met him, so I couldn't be sure. This was a slight balding man with a fringe of gray hair. He was dressed in a neat but shiny blue suit with narrow lapels. I knew the suit's lapels were narrow because one of them was visible to me from where I stood in the doorway. The other was crushed under Hatfield's body, which lay sprawled on its side on the threadbare carpet just inside the living-room door.

I sucked in my breath and held it until my stomach settled down a little. Then I stepped around Hatfield's outflung arms to get a better look at him.

There wasn't any blood that I could see. Looked as though he'd fallen while coming into the living room from the foyer. Maybe a heart attack had hit him at just that instant, I thought. It was a possibility. But not a very good one. For when I knelt beside Hatfield and felt for a pulse in his neck, I saw that the left side of his head, the side pressed against the carpet, had been caved in by a massive blow. There was blood, after all, but not much.

I stood up, feeling sick, and looked around the living room. I noticed that the toe of one of Hatfield's black loafers was snagged in a hole in the worn carpet and that a heavy fumed-oak table was perfectly positioned along the left wall of the room to have caught Hatfield's head squarely on its corner as he tripped and fell forward into the room. A quick queasy look at the corner of the table showed me more blood.

Uinder the edge of the table on the floor, where they must have fallen when Hatfield threw out his arms to catch himself, was a copy of yesterday's evening newspaper and a book from the public library. I could read the title of the book. *The Sound of Singing.*

I thought about that for a moment or two and decided I was pretty much out of my depth here. So I called the police. Which, even to me, seemed a rather odd thing to do—because I'm a cop myself.

* * * *

A "sissy kind" of a cop, it's true, but definitely a cop. And it isn't a bad job. For one thing, I don't have to carry a gun. My arrests are usually made without much fuss and never with any violence. I get a fair salary if you consider ten thousand a year a fair salary. And nobody calls me a pig, even though I am fuzz.

Library fuzz. What I do is chase down stolen and overdue books for the public library. Most of my work is routine and unexciting—but every once in a while I run into something that adds pepper to an otherwise bland diet.

Like this Hatfield thing.

The day before I found Hatfield's body had started off for me like any other Monday. I had a list of names and addresses to call on. Understand, the library sends out notices to book borrowers when their books are overdue; but some people are deadbeats, some are book lovers, and some are so absent-minded that they ignore the notices and hang onto the books. It's these hard-core overdues that I call on—to get the books back for the library and collect the fines owing on them.

Yesterday the first name on my list was Mrs. William Conway at an address on Sanford Street. I parked my car in the driveway of the small Cape

Cod house that had the name "Conway" on its mailbox and went up to the front door and rang the bell.

The woman who answered the door wasn't the maid, because she was dressed in a sexy nightie with a lacy robe of some sort thrown over it, and she gave me a warm, spontaneous, friendly smile before she even knew who I was. She was medium-tall in her pink bedroom slippers and had very dark hair, caught back in a ponytail by a blue ribbon, and china-blue eyes that looked almost startling under her dark eyebrows. I also noticed that she was exceptionally well put together.

What a nice way to start the day, I thought to myself. I said, "Are you Mrs. Conway?"

"Yes," she said, giving me a straight untroubled look with those blue eyes.

"I'm from the public library. I've come about those overdue books you have." I showed her my identification card.

"Oh, my goodness!" she said, and her look of inquiry turned to one of stricken guilt. "Oh, yes. Come in, won't you, Mr. Johnson? I'm really embarrassed about those books. I know I should have returned them a long time ago—I got the notices, of course. But honestly, I've been so busy!" She stepped back in mild confusion and I went into her house.

It turned out to be as unpretentious as it had looked from outside. In fact, the furnishings displayed an almost spectacular lack of taste. Well, nobody is perfect, I reminded myself. I could easily forgive Mrs. Conway's manifest ignorance of decorating principles, since she was so very decorative herself.

She switched off a color TV set that was muttering in one corner of the living room and motioned me to a chair. "Won't you sit down?" she said tentatively. She wasn't sure just how she ought to treat a library cop.

I said politely, "No, thanks. If you'll just give me your overdue books and the fines you owe, I'll be on my way."

She made a little rush for a coffee table across the room, the hem of her robe swishing after her. "I have the books right here." She scooped up a pile of books from the table. "I have them all ready to bring back to the library, you see?"

While I checked the book titles against my list I asked, "Why didn't you bring them back, Mrs. Conway?"

"My sister's been in the hospital," she explained, "and I've been spending every free minute with her. I just sort of forgot about my library books. I'm sorry."

"No harm done." I told her how much the fines amounted to and she made another little rush, this time for her purse which hung by its strap from the back of a Windsor chair. "The books seem to be all here," I went on, "except one."

"Oh, is one missing? Which one?"

"*The Sound of Singing.*"

"That was a wonderful story!" Mrs. Conway said enthusiastically. "Did you read it?" She sent her blue eyes around the room, searching for the missing book.

"No. But everybody seems to like it. Maybe your husband or one of the kids took it to read," I suggested.

She gave a trill of laughter. "I haven't any children, and my husband"—she gestured toward a photograph of him on her desk, a dapper, youngish-looking man with a mustache and not much chin—"is far too busy practicing law to find time to read light novels." She paused then, plainly puzzled.

I said gently, "How about having a look in the other rooms, Mrs. Conway?"

"Of course." She counted out the money for her fines and then went rushing away up the carpeted stairs to the second floor. I watched her all the way up. It was a pleasure to look at her.

In a minute she reappeared with the missing book clutched against her chest. "Ralph *did* take it!" she said breathlessly. "Imagine! He must have started to read it last night while I was out. It was on his bedside table under the telephone." She handed me the book.

"Good," I said. I took the book by its covers, pages down, and shook it—standard procedure to see if anything had been left between the pages by the borrower. You'd be surprised at what some people use to mark their places.

"I'm terribly sorry to have caused so much trouble," Mrs. Conway said. And I knew she meant it.

I had no excuse to linger, so I took the books under my arm, said goodbye, and left, fixing Mrs. Conway's lovely face in my memory alongside certain other pretty pictures I keep there to cheer me up on my low days.

I ticked off the last name on my list about one o'clock. By that time the back seat of my car was full of overdue books and my back pocket full of money for the library. Those few-cents-a-day book fines add up to a tidy sum when you put them all together, you know that? Would you believe that last year, all by myself, I collected $40,000 in fines and in the value of recovered books?

I went back to the library to turn in my day's pickings and to grab a quick lunch at the library cafeteria. About two o'clock the telephone in my closet-sized office rang and when I answered, the switchboard girl told me there was a lady in the lobby who was asking to see me.

That surprised me. I don't get many lady visitors at the office. And the lady herself surprised me, too. She turned out to be my blue-eyed brunette of the morning, Mrs. William Conway—but a Mrs. Conway who looked as though she'd been hit in the face by a truck since I'd seen her last.

There was a bruise as big as a half dollar on one cheek, a deep scratch on her forehead; an ugly knotted lump interrupted the smooth line of her jaw on the left side; and the flesh around one of her startling blue eyes was puffed and faintly discolored. Although she had evidently been at pains to disguise these marks with heavy make-up, they still showed. Plainly.

I suppose she saw from my expression that I'd noticed her bruises because as she sat down in my only office chair, she dropped her eyes and flushed and said with a crooked smile, "Do I look *that* bad, Mr. Johnson?" It was a singularly beguiling gambit. Actually, battered face and all, I thought she looked just as attractive now in a lemon-colored pants suit as she had in her nightie and robe that morning.

I said, "You look fine, Mrs. Conway."

She tried to sound indignant. "I fell down our stupid stairs! Can you imagine that? Just after you left. I finished making the beds and was coming down for coffee when—zap!—head over heels clear to the bottom!"

"Bad luck," I said sympathetically, reflecting that a fall down her thickly carpeted stairs would be most unlikely to result in injuries like hers. But it was none of my business.

She said, "What I came about, Mr. Johnson, was to see if I could get back *The Sound of Singing* you took this morning. My husband was furious when he came home for lunch and found I'd given it back to you."

"No problem there. We must have a dozen copies of that book in—"

She interrupted me. "Oh, but I was hoping to get the same copy I had before. You see, my husband says he left a check in it—quite a big one from a client."

"Oh. Then I must have missed it when I shook out the book this morning."

She nodded. "You must have. Ralph is sure he left it there." Mrs. Conway put a fingertip to the lump on her jaw and then hastily dropped her hand into her lap when she saw me watching her.

"Well," I said, "I've already turned the book back to the shelves, Mrs. Conway, but if we're lucky it'll still be in. Let me check." I picked up my phone and asked for the librarian on the checkout desk.

Consulting my morning list of overdue book numbers, now all safely returned to circulation, I said, "Liz, have you checked out number 15208, *The Sound of Singing,* to anybody in the last hour?"

"I've checked out that title but I don't know if it was that copy. Just a second," Liz said. After half a minute she said, "Yes, here it is, Hal. It went out half an hour ago on card number PC28382."

I made a note on my desk pad of that card number, repeating the digits out loud as I did so. Then, thanking Liz, I hung up and told Mrs. Conway, "I'm sorry, your copy's gone out again."

"Oh, dammit anyway!" said Mrs. Conway passionately. I gathered this was pretty strong talk for her because she blushed again and threw me a distressed look before continuing. "*Everything* seems to be going wrong for me today!" She paused. "What was that number you just took down, Mr. Johnson? Does that tell who's got the book now?"

"It tells me," I answered. "But for a lot of reasons we're not allowed to tell *you*. It's the card number of the person who borrowed the book."

"Oh, dear," she said, chewing miserably on her lower lip, "then that's *more* bad luck, isn't it?"

I was tempted to break the library's rigid rule and give her the name and address she wanted. However, there were a couple of things besides the rule that made me restrain my chivalrous impulse. Such as no check dropping out of *The Sound of Singing* this morning when I shook the book. And such as Mrs. Conway's bruises, which looked to me more like the work of fists than of carpeted stairs.

So I said, "I'll be glad to telephone whoever has the book now and ask him about your husband's check. Or her. If the check *is* in the book, they'll probably be glad to mail it to you."

"Oh, would you, Mr. Johnson? That would be wonderful!" Her eyes lit up at once.

I called the library's main desk where they issue cards and keep the register of card holders names and addresses. "This is Hal Johnson," I said. "Look up the holder of card number PC28382 for me, will you, Kathy?"

I waited until she gave me a name—George Hatfield—and an address on the north side, then hung up, found Hatfield's telephone number in the directory, and dialed it on an outside line, feeling a little self-conscious under the anxious scrutiny of Mrs. Conway's beautiful bruised blue eye.

Nobody answered the Hatfield phone.

Mrs. Conway sighed when I shook my head. "I'll try again in an hour or so. Probably not home yet. And when I get him I'll ask him to mail the check to you. I have your address. Okay?"

She stood up and gave me a forlorn nod. "I guess that's the best I can do. I'll tell Ralph you're trying to get his check back, anyhow. Thanks very much." She was still chewing on her lower lip when she left.

Later in the afternoon she called me to tell me that her husband Ralph had found his missing check in a drawer at home. There was vast relief in her voice when she told me. I wasn't relieved so much as angry—because it seemed likely to me that my beautiful Mrs. Conway had been slapped around pretty savagely by that little jerk in her photograph for a mistake she hadn't made.

Anyway, I forgot about *The Sound of Singing* and spent the rest of the afternoon shopping for a new set of belted tires for my old car.

Next morning, a few minutes before 9:00, I stopped by the library to turn in my expense voucher for the new tires and pick up my list of overdues for the day's calls. As I passed the main desk, Kathy, who was just settling down for her day's work, said, "Hi, Hal. Stop a minute and let me see if it shows."

I paused by the desk. "See if what shows?"

"Senility."

"Of course it shows, child. I'm almost forty. Why this sudden interest?"

"Only the onset of senility can account for *you* forgetting something," Kathy said. "The man with the famous memory."

I was mystified. "What did I forget?"

"The name and address of card holder PC28382, that's what. You called me to look it up for you not long after lunch yesterday, remember?"

"Sure. So what makes you think I forgot it?"

"You said you had when you called me again at four thirty for the same information."

I stared at her. "Me?"

She nodded. "You."

"I didn't call you at four thirty."

"Somebody did. And said he was you."

"Did it sound like my voice?"

"Certainly. An ordinary, uninteresting man's voice. Just like yours." She grinned at me.

"Thanks. Somebody playing a joke, maybe. It wasn't me."

While I was turning in my voucher and picking up my list of overdues I kept thinking about Kathy's second telephone call. The more I thought about it, the more it bothered me.

So I decided to make my first call of the day on George Hatfield...

* * * *

Well, I didn't touch anything in Hatfield's apartment until the law showed up in the persons of a uniformed patrolman and an old friend of mine, Lieutenant Randall of Homicide. I'd worked with Randall when I was in the detective bureau myself a few years back.

Randall looked at the setup in Hatfield's living room and growled at me, "Why me, Hal? All you need is an ambulance on this one. The guy's had a fatal accident, that's all."

So I told him about Mrs. Conway and her husband and *The Sound of Singing* and the mysterious telephone call to Kathy at the library. When I finished he jerked his head toward the library book lying under Hatfield's table and said, "Is that it?"

"I haven't looked yet. I was waiting for you."

"Look now," Randall said. It was book number 15208, all right—unmistakably the one I'd collected yesterday from Mrs. Conway. Its identification number appeared big and clear in both the usual places—on the front flyleaf and on the margin of page 101. "This is it. No mistake," I said.

"If Hatfield's killing is connected with this book, as you seem to think," Randall said reasonably enough, "there's got to be something about the book to tell us why."

I said, "Maybe there was. Before the back flyleaf was torn out."

"Be damned!" said Randall, squinting where I was pointing. "Torn out is right. Something written on the flyleaf that this Conway wanted kept private maybe?"

"Could be."

"Thought you said you looked through this book yesterday. You'd have seen any writing."

"I didn't look through it. I shook it out, that's all."

"Why would a guy write anything private or incriminating on the blank back page of a library book, for God's sake?"

"His wife found the book under the telephone in their bedroom. He could have been taking down notes during a telephone conversation."

"In a library book?"

"Why not? If it was the only blank paper he had handy when he got the telephone call?"

"So his wife gave the book back to you before he'd had a chance to erase his notes. Is that what you're suggesting?"

"Or transcribe them, yes. Or memorize them."

Lieutenant Randall looked out Hatfield's grimy window for a moment. Then he said abruptly, "I'm impounding this library book for a few days, Hal, so our lab boys can take a look at it. Okay?"

"Okay."

Randall glanced pointedly toward the door. "Thanks for calling us," he said. "Be seeing you."

I stepped carefully around Hatfield's sprawled body. "Right."

"I'll be in touch if we find anything," Randall said.

* * * *

Much to my surprise he phoned me at the library just about quitting time the next day. "Did you ever see this Mr. Conway?" he asked. "Could you identify him?"

"I never saw him in the flesh. I saw a photo of him on his wife's desk."

"That's good enough. Meet me at the Encore Bar at Stanhope and Cotton in twenty minutes, can you?"

"Sure," I said. "Why?"

"Tell you when I see you." He was waiting for me in a rear booth. There were only half a dozen customers in the place. I sat down facing him and he said, without preamble, "Conway *did* write something on the back flyleaf of your library book. Or somebody did, anyhow. Because we found traces of crushed paper fibers on the page *under* the back flyleaf. Not good enough traces to be read except for one notation at the top, which was probably written first on the back flyleaf when the pencil point was sharper and thus made a deeper groove on the page underneath. Are you with me?"

"Yes. What did it say?"

Randall got a slip of paper from his pocket and showed it to me. It contained one line, scribbled by Randall:

Transo 3212I5I13 Mi Encore Harper 6I12

I studied it silently for a minute. Randall said, faintly smug, "Does that mean anything to you?"

"Sure," I said, deadpan. "Somebody named Harper off Transoceanic Airlines flight 3212 out of Miami on May 13th—that's today—is supposed to meet somebody in this bar at twelve minutes after six."

"A lucky guess," Randall said, crestfallen. "The *Encore* and *Transo* gave it to you, of course. But it took us half an hour to figure the meaning and check it out."

"Check it out?"

"There really *is* a Transoceanic flight 3212 out of Miami today—and there really is somebody aboard named Harper, too. A Miss Genevieve Harper, stewardess."

"Oh," I said, "and of course there *is* an Encore Bar—could even be a couple of them in town."

"Only one that Harper can get to through rush-hour traffic within twenty minutes after she hits the airport," the lieutenant said triumphantly. "She's scheduled in at 5:52."

I glanced at my watch. It was 5:30. "You have time to check whether Conway had any phone calls Sunday night?"

"Not yet. Didn't even have time to find out what Conway looks like. That's why you're here." He grinned. "What's your guess about why they're meeting here?"

I gave it some thought. "Drugs," I said at last, "since the flight seems to be out of Miami. Most of the heroin processed in France comes to the United States via South America and Miami, right?"

Randall nodded. "We figure Conway for a distributor at this end. Sunday night he got a phone call from somebody in South America or Miami, telling him when and where to take delivery of a shipment. That's what he wrote on the flyleaf of your library book. So no wonder he was frantic when his wife gave his list of dates and places to a library cop."

I suddenly felt tired. I called over to the bartender and ordered a dry martini. I said to Randall, "So Hatfield's accident could have been murder?"

"Sure. We think it went like this: Mrs. Conway gave you the book, got knocked around by her husband when she told him what she'd done, then on hubby's orders came to you to recover the book for him. When she couldn't do that, or even get the name of the subsequent borrower, her husband did the best he could with the information she *did* get—the borrower's library card number and how you matched it up with his name and address. Conway got the name the same way you did—by phoning what's-her-name at your main desk."

"Kathy," I said.

"Yeah. Conway must have gone right out to Hatfield's when he learned his identity, prepared to do anything necessary to get that book-back—or his list on the flyleaf, anyway." Randall nodded approval of his own theory. "Conway broke the lock on Hatfield's apartment and was inside looking for the book when Hatfield must have walked in on him."

"And Conway hid behind the door and clobbered Hatfield when he walked in?"

"Yeah. Probably with a blackjack. And probably, in his panic, hit him too hard. So he faked it to look like an accident. Then he tore the back flyleaf out of your book thinking nobody would ever notice it was missing."

"You forgot something," I said.

"What?"

"He made his wife call me off by telling me he'd found his lost check."

"I didn't forget it," Randall grinned.

I said, "Of course you can't prove any of this."

"Not yet. But give us time. We get him on a narcotics charge and hold him tighter than hell while we work up the murder case."

"*If* it's Conway," I said, looking at my watch, "who shows up here in twenty-two minutes."

"He'll show." Randall was confident. "Likely get here a little early, even."

And he did. At 5:56 the original of Mrs. Conway's photograph walked in the door of the Encore Bar. Dapper, young-looking, not much chin under a mustache that drooped around the corners of his mouth.

He sat down in the booth nearest the door and ordered a Scotch-and-soda.

Randall threw me a questioning look and I nodded vigorously. Then we talked about baseball until, at 6:14, a bouncy little blonde dish came tripping into the Encore and went straight to Conway's booth, saying loud enough for everybody in the joint to hear, "Well, hello, darling! I'm so thirsty I could drink *water*!" She looked very pert in her uniform and she had a flight bag over her shoulder. She sat down beside Conway with her back to us.

Randall got up, went to the bar entrance, and opened the door. He stepped out into the vestibule and casually waved one arm over his head, as though he were tossing a cigarette butt away. Then he came back in and leaned against the bar until three-young huskies appeared in the doorway. Randall pointed one finger at Conway's booth and the three newcomers stepped over there, boxing in Conway and Miss Harper.

It was all done very quietly and smoothly. No voices raised, no violence. One of the narcotics men took charge of Harper's shoulder bag. The other two took charge of Conway and Harper.

When they'd gone, Randall ordered himself a bourbon and carried it back to our booth and sat down. "That's it, Hal," he said with satisfaction. "Harper had two one-pound boxes of bath powder in her flight bag. Pure heroin. This is going to look very good—very good—on my record."

I took a sip of my martini and said nothing.

Randall went on, "You're sure Conway's wife has nothing to do with the smuggling? That she doesn't suspect what her hubby is up to?"

I thought about Mrs. Conway's friendliness, so charming and unstudied. I remembered how the animation and pride I'd seen in her eyes yesterday morning had been replaced by distress and bewilderment in the afternoon. And I said to Lieutenant Randall, "I'd stake my job on it."

He nodded. "We'll have to dig into it, of course. But I'm inclined to think you're right. So somebody ought to tell her why her husband won't be home for dinner tonight, Hal." He paused for a long moment. "Any volunteers?"

I looked up from my martini into Randall's unblinking stare. "Thanks, Lieutenant," I said. "I'm on my way."

MORE THAN A MERE STORYBOOK

Originally published in* Ellery Queen's Mystery Magazine, *February 1973.

I wasn't ready for his violent reaction. He hurled the heavy glass ashtray at me from pointblank range with the accuracy of a big-league pitcher splitting the strike zone.

The tray caught me a stunning blow on the temple and, as they say, I saw stars. Believe me I did. Plenty of them.

While I sagged on the sofa, dazed and groggy, Campbell scurried into an inner room, came out with an oversize brief case, and ran for the door like a beagle after a rabbit.

He should have finished me off. By the time he was halfway down the steps to the apartment house lobby I had gathered my few senses together and was able to stand up and then follow him. My whole life recently seemed to consist of following Herbert Campbell.

I went down the stairway after him two steps at a time. I caught him before he reached the doorway that led outside. When I put a choke hold on him from behind, none too gently in spite of his being an old man, the fight went completely out of him. He dropped his brief case as though its handle were red-hot and began to tear at my forearm across his throat.

I eased up a little as his face congested. "Pick up your brief case," I said and released him. "Let's go back upstairs."

He nodded meekly. He picked up the brief case and we climbed up the stairway to his apartment. I held his right arm in a businesslike grip.

Once back in his living room he collapsed into an easy chair and began to sob weakly. Keeping a weather eye on him, lifted his brief case to the tabletop and opened it up.

It was full of clothing. Shirts, socks, underwear, slacks. Campbell had been about to leave town when I arrived, it seemed. I rummaged around in the case and at the very bottom, under the layers of clothing, I found two books.

I pulled them out and looked at them. Volume I and Volume II. Their half-calf covers were soiled and stained and worn; a corner of Volume I was bent; there was a slight tear along the spine of Volume II.

Not library books, certainly. One look at the title page of Volume I showed me what they were. I turned another page in Volume I, reverently now, and stared at what was written on the flyleaf in faded brownish-colored ink.

That was when I called Lieutenant Randall of the metropolitan police. I suddenly had the uneasy feeling that Herbert Campbell was too big game for a mere library cop to handle.

* * * *

The fourth name on my list for the day was Herbert Campbell at an address on Dennison Avenue. I parked my car a block away and walked to the sleazy apartment house where Campbell lived. The building was a rundown relic of better days.

I went into the vestibule, found out from the mailboxes that Campbell's apartment was number 22, on the second floor, and walked up. I played a tattoo on the door panel of number 22, and after a while the door opened to show me a cherubic, ruddy-faced gent with no chin and a white bristly mustache. He was about 60, I figured, give or take a couple of years, and his head was bald except for an inch of fringe around the edges that matched his white mustache.

Over the raised voices of two women quarreling in a TV soap opera I asked, "Mr. Campbell?"

"Yes," he said, giving me a sharp look out of mild blue eyes. "And who are you?"

"I'm from the public library," I said politely. "I've come about all those overdue library books you have, Mr. Campbell."

"Oh," he said, and his look of inquiry changed to one of guilt. "Oh, yes. Come in, won't you? I'm very embarrassed about those books. I know I should have returned them long ago. I got the notices, of course." He stepped back. I went into his apartment.

It turned out to be surprisingly clean and attractive. There were a sofa and a round coffee table; two easy chairs, one with a tall bridge lamp beside it and a plastic cushion that showed existence of much sitting, and a floor-to-ceiling wall of bookshelves, well filled, opposite the sofa. The TV was in a corner, going full blast.

He switched off the TV, motioned to a chair, and said, "Won't you sit down?"

I said, still politely, "No, thanks. If you'll just give me your overdue library books and the fine you owe, I'll be on my way."

"Certainly, certainly. I have the books right here." He gestured at a pile of books on the coffee table. "I was all ready to bring them back, you see."

"Why didn't you?" I asked. I began to check the book titles against my list. They were all there.

"I've been sick." He gave me another treatment of his mild blue eyes.

"Sorry to hear that, Mr. Campbell. You could have renewed the books, you know."

Campbell was sheepish. "Well, I must confess, Mr.—ah—"

"Johnson," I said.

"Yes, I must confess, Mr. Johnson that there's another reason I'm overdue." He cleared his throat. "You see, I quite literally *hate* to return library books. Can you understand that? I have this fierce love for books, any books, and when I have them in my possession it takes all my will power to make myself let them go. I'd never borrow books at all if I could afford to own enough of my own. Like these." He waved a thin hand toward his bookshelves. "I guess I'm what they call a bibliophile. Are you familiar with the term?"

"Sure," I said. "I work for the library, remember?"

"Yes. Well then, you can appreciate the minced feelings I have every time I am compelled to return books to the library! I know they don't belong to me, but I am terribly reluctant to give them up. You know? Especially, of course, if I haven't finished reading them."

"I know," I said. I'd run into plenty of book nuts. I began to gather his overdue books into a manageable stack. "You owe us a pretty big fine on this batch, Mr. Campbell."

"This is the first time I've ever actually *ignored* the overdue notices," he explained apologetically. "I did *so* want to finish this one, this novel, before I brought them back." He tapped the book at the top of the stack, a current bestseller called *Sexless in Salinas*. "It's so fascinating, so well done, that I can't bear to finish it and end my pleasure. You ever feel that way about a book, Mr. Johnson? Yet I can't bear *not* to finish it, either." He laughed.

I laughed, too. I'd read that particular book myself. "Listen, Mr. Campbell, I'll make a deal with you. Pay your fines on all these other books and I'll leave that one with you so you can finish it. Fair enough?"

"Oh, would you? How very kind!" He took *Sexless in Salinas* from the stack, hugged it to his chest, and asked how much he owed me.

I told him. He dipped his hand into his pants pocket and brought out money. While he counted out the fine I idly ran an eye over his bookshelves across the room. Judging from the few titles I could read from that far away, he had the catholic tastes of a true bibliophile. I saw a book on the flora of Nevada, one on weightlifting, and a home-repair guide, cheek by jowl with numerous fiction titles.

Mr. Campbell said, “There you are, Mr. Johnson. And thanks for being so understanding about my—ah—affliction.” He smiled at me as though at a fellow bibliophile. “I’ll return this one to the library as soon as I finish reading it.”

I nodded and left.

I went back to my car, unlocked it, and added Mr. Campbell’s overdue library books to the others I’d already collected. There were a lot of them. Then I crawled under the wheel, started the engine, and headed for the main library downtown. My morning’s work was officially over now, except for turning in the overdue books and the fines.

After that I hadn’t much to do until lunch except to sit at my desk in the little room, behind the business manager’s office and indulge my curiosity about that old booklover, Herbert Campbell, who had wanted to finish *Sexless in Salinas* even at the cost of paying another few days’ fine.

Well, a phone comes with my office, so I figured it wouldn’t cost anything to feed my curiosity. I picked up the telephone and got on to Ellen Corby, one of our librarians who is currently trying to make up her mind whether she’ll marry me or not. I asked her if she’d give me the inventory record on *Sexless in Salinas.* She said she would.

She called me back a few minutes later. “Twenty-seven copies, Hal,” she said. “It’s a popular item.”

“Yeah, no wonder,” I said. “Have you read it?”

“Of course. Can’t you see my maidenly blush?”

“How are the twenty-seven split, Ellen?”

“Six and three,” Ellen said.

“Thanks.” I hung up. You’re not supposed to engage in social chitchat on the library’s time.

Twenty-seven copies, split six and three. Six at the main library, three at each of our seven branches.

My next call was to the checkout desk. “Inventory says you have six copies of *Sexless in Salinas* circulating,” I said, after identifying myself. “Can you account for all six?”

“Why?” asked the girl, irritated. “Are you queer for best-sellers, or something?”

“Just answer the question, honey.”

“I’ll call you back.”

When she did she said, “Four are out, one is in the return pile.”

“How about the other one?”

“Gone,” she said. “No record.”

“Not on the shelf?”

“No. I looked. You want its catalogue number?”

"Never mind. Is one of your 'out' copies on library card XL-392716?" That was Herbert Campbell's library card number on my overdue list.

"Yes," she said after a minute. "And incidentally, it's long overdue."

"Thanks," I said.

In turn I telephoned all seven of our branches and checked on their copies of *Sexless in Salinas.* Out of the 21 copies supposed to be circulating through the branch libraries four had vanished without trace.

I sat back in my chair and thought about that for a while. Then I had another idea. I walked down the corridor to the room where our card-catalogue cabinets are. There I went through the cards under the letter 'F' and pretty soon I was looking at a card with the neatly typed book title I was hunting: *The Flora of Nevada*. I took down its number and shelf position and searched the shelves for the book without success. Then I asked Ellen to see if she could locate it for me. She couldn't—neither the book itself nor any record of its having been borrowed. Inventory showed the library had bought only one copy of that book, for the main library. None for the branches.

I thought about that, too.

What all this thinking led to, of course, was the conclusion that my friendly bibliophile, Herbert Campbell, was stealing the library blind; and that since I'm a library cop, hired to chase down stolen and overdue books by the public library, I'd better do something about it.

So, after a leisurely lunch at Morris's Cafeteria, I set out again for Dennison Avenue. It was a lovely spring afternoon. Whipped-cream clouds drifted lazily across a delft-blue sky. I caught the delicate fragrance of lilacs through my open car window as I drove. And I wished Ellen Corby would make up her mind to marry me and save me from a lifetime of dreary cafeterias like Morris's.

I parked about a hundred yards south of Campbell's apartment house—the only parking space I could find on the block—got out of my car and started toward the entrance, thinking about what I'd say to him and how tough an act I should put on. Although I'm allowed to carry a gun and make arrests, I didn't figure to need a gun to handle old Campbell, and I hadn't decided yet whether to arrest him or not. That depended on how many of the library's books I could recover and whether he'd be willing to pay the big overdue fines I'd assess on them.

While I was still about fifty yards away, Herbert Campbell came out of the apartment-house entrance carrying a king-size brief case which seemed pretty heavy, to judge from the way he handled it when he unlocked a gray VW at the curb and maneuvered the brief case into the back seat. Then Campbell got into the car himself.

I had to make a quick decision—should I brace him now or let it go until later? His brief case made up my mind. It seemed possible, from its evident weight, that the case contained books. If it did, and the books happened to belong to the public library, I wanted to see where they were going.

So I turned and went back to my car, slid into the driver's seat, and waited until the VW pulled out from the curb. Then I took out after Campbell's car, hanging far enough back so that he wouldn't notice I was trailing him. I hoped.

We played follow-the-leader through light traffic to the South Side. When Campbell pulled up in front of a row of stores on Cameron Way I drove right on by, rounded the next corner, and parked. I ran back to the corner in time to see Campbell and his brief case disappearing into the middle shop of the seven in the row.

I debated with myself for half a minute on what to do next, finally lit a cigarette and sat down on a corner bench meant for the convenience of bus riders. From there I could see the entrance to-the shop and Campbell's parked car.

In about ten minutes he reappeared on the sidewalk, still carrying his brief case. Now, though, from the effortless way he swung it into the back of his car, I figured the case was empty. He started up, drove toward me, and went rolling past without even a glance in my direction. Then he took a left at the next block and went out of sight. I let him go.

I walked down the sidewalk to the store Campbell had entered. A sign over the door said: The Red Quill, Edwin Worthington, Prop. The merchandise displayed in the store window was books and more books. My friendly bibliophile, Herbert Campbell, had been paying a visit to the secondhand bookshop. I opened the door and went inside. The interior seemed very dim after the bright sunshine outside, but I could make out tables and racks and shelves of books on every side.

The man standing at the counter at the back of the shop talking on the telephone must be Edwin Worthington, Prop., because he nodded at me when he saw me come in and mouthed silently at me above his telephone receiver, "Be right with you," then went back to his conversation.

I browsed idly through his stock of books, paying no attention to him until he said into the phone, "Octavo, yes, yes, 1719, eh? Good. That's what I thought it was but I wanted to be sure. Thanks very much, Miss Gilchrist. Thanks *very* much!"

He hung up and turned on me one of the most radiant smiles I'd seen recently. His full beard tended to hide his mouth, but there was no mistaking the full set of white teeth or the triumphant lilt of his voice when he said, "Now, then, what can I do for you, sir?" He was feeling very good about something.

"Just browsing, thanks," I answered him.

He waved a hand. "Help yourself."

I stepped over to the fiction shelves and pulled out a copy of *Sexless in Salinas* and thumbed through it. Then, carrying it with me, I drifted over to Worthington who was leaning against his counter beside the cash register.

I held up *Sexless in Salinas* "Isn't this a best-seller?" I asked.

He nodded. "Second on the list for several months now."

"Is it available in paperback yet?"

"Not yet."

"How come you have best-sellers while they're still so popular?"

He shrugged. "From book club members, estates being settled, people moving away. And of course, from church bazaars, rummage sales, charity book sales of all kinds. Lately I've had a part-time man covering the charity things for me. That book you have there was one of a batch he brought in just a few minutes ago."

I put the book down on the counter beside his cash register. "I'll take it," I said. "How much?"

"Dollar and a quarter. It's a six ninety-five book." Then he smiled that big smile again. He was still feeling very expansive. "I'll let you have it for a dollar today, though."

"How come?"

"Call it a going-out-of-business price. I'm celebrating. I've had a lucky break and I'm going to close up my shop."

"Great," I said. I gave him a dollar. "Happy retirement, Mr. Worthington."

Back in my car I examined the second-hand copy of *Sexless in Salinas* with the help of a good magnifying glass I carried on the end of my key chain. I found what I expected. A slight granulation of the inside front cover's end paper where a solvent had been used to remove the card pocket pasted in the front of all library books. The front flyleaf, where the library's name stamp appears, had been cut out. There were barely discernible traces of the library's name stamp lingering on the closed-page edges after treatment with an ink eradicator. And very faint evidence on some of the page margins that the book's identification number had been removed.

What I'd got for my dollar at The Red Quill was one of the library's missing copies of *Sexless in Salinas*, skillfully doctored by a certain bibliophile named Herbert Campbell.

So now I not only knew that a thief was robbing the library, but I knew the receiver of his stolen goods. An innocent receiver, I was sure, but a receiver, all the same. So I'd know where to find a lot of our library books after I'd taken care of Campbell.

With that information in my possession, my sense of urgency about Campbell subsided. There was no hurry about arresting him now. I decided to finish my overdue calls that afternoon, take Ellen to dinner and the movies, as planned, and get to Campbell first thing in the morning. I felt a little sorry for the old boy, as a matter of fact, even though I knew he was an unmitigated thief.

I was back at the library at quitting time. I walked through the reference department to pick up Ellen for our date and found Annie Gilchrist putting on her jacket to go home. "Annie," I said, pausing at her desk, "you got a telephone call from a Mr. Worthington of The Red Quill bookshop this afternoon about two o'clock, didn't you?"

"Nope," said Annie, "I called him. To answer a question he'd phoned in earlier."

"Whatever you told him on the phone made him so happy," I said, "that he gave me a discount on a book I was buying from him at the time."

"You were *buying* a book?" Annie exclaimed. "With the whole public library system here to supply you with free reading material?"

"I hate to accept charity," I said, grinning. "What was the question you had to look up for Worthington?"

"The date of the first edition of *Robinson Crusoe*."

"1719?"

"That was it. You must have been eavesdropping."

"I was. Did Worthington *have* a first edition?"

"He didn't say. Just wanted to be sure of the date."

"Would a first edition of *Robinson Crusoe* be worth a lot?"

"Depends on what you mean by a lot. And what condition the first edition is in."

"Enough for Worthington to retire on?"

She shook her head. "I doubt it very much, Hal."

"How much do you think it would be worth?"

"I'll look it up for you tomorrow," Annie said. "Right now, if you don't mind, I'm going home." She grabbed her purse and started out.

"Forget it, Annie," I called after her. "I was just curious."

* * * *

I was knocking at Herbert Campbell's door at nine the next morning. He opened at my second knock and recognized me at once. He was in his shirt sleeves, his fringe of white hair tousled, his eyes as innocent of guile as a child's. Holding the door open a few inches he said, "Why, hello, Mr. Johnson."

I said, "May I come in for a minute?"

"I haven't finished that last book yet."

"I want to read you something," I said.

He backed up, puzzled, and I followed him in. "I don't understand," he said mildly, "but whatever it is, read it to me, by all means." He went to sit in his favorite chair, the one with the dent in the seat cushion.

I read him my Miranda card, informing him of his legal rights. When I finished he stared at me. "What in heaven's name does *that* mean?"

I sat down at one end of the sofa. "It means I'm going to arrest you."

"Arrest me?" His gaze was incredulous. "What am I supposed to have done?"

"I'll tell you what you've done. You've been stealing books from the public library for months. You've been using your library card to borrow books legitimately at all our branches and every time you borrowed you walked out with three or four *extra* books under your coat or in your brief case that you didn't bother to have the librarian check out. You've been bringing these stolen books here to your apartment, removing the library's identification marks, and peddling the books for whatever you can get."

Campbell shook his head in bewilderment.

I plowed on. "You keep the stolen books here"—I pointed to his crowded bookshelves—"until you think the heat, if any, has died down, using your apartment as a sort of warehouse for stolen books. And you also use it, I might add, to build up your image of a harmless eccentric who loves books so much he just can't bear to part with them. That's why you held those overdue library books until I came to collect them yesterday—so you could impress me with your eccentricity and establish a bibliophile image with the library authorities."

"Why," asked Mr. Campbell reasonably, his eyes still mild and puzzled, "would I try to establish an image like that?" He was toying with a thick glass ashtray on the arm of his easy chair.

"Because you know that in the normal case of book theft from the public library by a bona-fide bibliophile type, all we usually do is hit him with a fine and take back our books. You figured if we ever tumbled to your operation you would qualify for the same treatment—a fine instead of prison."

"The only thing wrong with your theory, Mr. Johnson," said Campbell with dignity, "is that it happens to be quite untrue. Who, for example, would I sell stolen library books to, for heaven's sake?"

"The Red Quill bookshop, for one," I answered. "I talked to Mr. Worthington yesterday." And that's when he threw the ashtray at me.

* * * *

As it turned out I *was* right to call Lieutenant Randall into the case. He sat across from me in Clancy's Bar and Grill that evening, off duty, and told me about it.

"When we got there," he said, "The Red Quill had a penciled sign on the door saying the shop was closed. But there was a light on in the living quarters upstairs—a lamp we could see through the front second-floor window. So we tried to raise Worthington. When we couldn't, we went in and found him at the foot of the flight of steps that leads down from his rooms upstairs. Dead as a mackerel. With a broken neck."

I murmured, "Did he fall or was he pushed?" I was feeling rotten. If I had gone after Campbell yesterday instead of waiting, I might possibly have saved Worthington's life.

"He was pushed," Randall said.

"How do you know?"

"There was a lump the size of an egg on his head and we found a wrought-iron ashtray upstairs with blood and hair to match."

I sighed. "He likes ashtrays." My temple was still sore.

"Yeah." Randall's gaze was amused. "Campbell admits the killing now. Says Worthington told him about the first edition when he delivered those stolen books to The Red Quill yesterday. The first edition was a lucky break—found among hundreds of old books Worthington bought from an estate. The owners never knew what they had, of course."

"More than a mere storybook," I murmured.

"What's that?"

"*Robinson Crusoe.* That's how Edward Everett Hale described it."

"Well," Randall went on, refusing to be sidetracked by this literary allusion, "Worthington told Campbell if the *Robinson Crusoe* first edition turned out to be genuine, he was going to close his bookstore and retire. So Campbell went back to The Red Quill about one o'clock last night, killed Worthington, and swiped the book." Randall grinned. "Just a harmless, eccentric old book-lover."

I grunted. "He's not a real booklover," I said. "He wanted to be rich, that's all. Did you notice that signature on the flyleaf of Volume One?"

"Yeah. Some guy's name," Randall said. "I can't remember it."

"Button Gwinnett."

"Sounds like the head of the sewing circle. Who was Button Gwinnett, for God's sake?"

"Only one of the signers of the Declaration of Independence."

Randall refused to be impressed. "Well, well," he said. "So he owned a copy of *Robinson Crusoe*. So what?"

“A first edition of *Robinson Crusoe*,” I said quietly, “with Button Gwinnett’s signature in it would sell at auction for a quarter of a million dollars, Lieutenant, maybe more.”

“What!”

It was my turn to grin. “Button Gwinnett signed the Declaration of Independence, all right, but apparently that’s about all he *did* sign during his lifetime. Except for Worthington’s first edition of *Robinson Crusoe*. Button Gwinnett’s signature is one of the rarest—and therefore one of the most valuable—in the whole autograph-collecting field. So you see what a beautiful combination Campbell killed Worthington to get? A first edition of *Robinson Crusoe* autographed by Button Gwinnett. It’s fabulous.”

Randall was impressed at last. “What becomes of the book now?”

“Worthington’s heirs get it, I suppose—if he bought it fair and square from that estate.”

“Some legacy,” Randall breathed, “from a second-hand bookdealer!” He put his opaque stare on me. “What tipped you off to this Campbell in the first place?” he asked.

I told him about the song and dance Campbell had given me yesterday about wanting to finish reading *Sexless in Salinas* before I took the book away from him.

“I don’t see anything in that,” Randall said.

“You’re not a second-hand book expert, that’s why,” I explained. “But *I* am. So I noticed that when Campbell was begging to keep the book so he could finish reading it, he had two *other* copies of *Sexless in Salinas* right there on his bookshelves in plain view.”

THE BOOKMARK

Originally published in* Ellery Queen's Mystery Magazine, *January 1974.

Being in the business I'm in—chasing down stolen and overdue books for the public library—I could almost write a book myself on the crazy things people use for bookmarks. Pornographic postcards, hairpins, dog-show ribbons, stalks of celery, marijuana cigarettes. You wouldn't believe the variety. I even found one teen-ager using the dried skin of a six-inch coral snake. So there was nothing very remarkable about the bookmark I found in Miss Linda Halstrom's overdue library book. At least, I didn't think so at the time.

Miss Halstrom was the third on my list of overdues that day. She lived on the north side in a rundown apartment house that was really an old Victorian mansion converted into a dozen efficiencies. The neighborhood had long since lost its pristine elegance, if any.

I walked up three flights of rubber-treaded stairs to her apartment and knocked on her door, wiping my forehead with an already sodden handkerchief. The outdoor temperature that July day must have been over ninety. The third-floor landing was dark and dreary-looking and smelled of stale cooking, which made Miss Linda Halstrom, when she answered my knock, seem all the more entrancing to me.

She was dressed in white stretch slacks and a man's shirt with the sleeves rolled up, and looked very cool indeed on such a hot day. Her long, straight blonde hair framed a blue-eyed, high-cheekboned face that now wore an inquiring smile. It was downright refreshing just to look at her.

"Yes?" she asked me brightly in a cool contralto.

"Miss Linda Halstrom?" I countered.

She nodded.

I showed her my identification card. "I'm from the public library," I said. "Our records show that you have some library books overdue, Miss Halstrom. I've called to collect the books and the fines you owe."

A lot of book borrowers get quite indignant at me, for some reason, when I appear at their doors to take back the public library's property. Maybe it's because they feel the library is questioning their integrity by sending me around. Or maybe it's because people tend to resent any kind of police these days—even a library cop like me.

Miss Halstrom, however, was hospitality itself. She apologized profusely for keeping the books so long beyond their due dates. "Come in, Mr. Johnson," she invited. "I have the books right here."

I followed her into her combination living room-bedroom. The bed, along the far wall, was neatly made up into a day bed, covered with a gaily striped bedspread and strewn with colorful pillows. Everything in the place was as clean and refreshing as Miss Halstrom herself. She pointed to a coffee table by the daybed. "There they are," she said, "three of them. Right?"

"Three is correct." I picked up the library books and checked them against my list. "You'll have to pay the fine."

She shrugged prettily. "My own fault," she said. "I lent them to a friend and forgot all about when they were due. How much is the fine?"

I told her the amount. "I'll get my purse," she said, and headed for a closet at the other end of the room while I went through my standard procedure of shaking her three books upside down to see if she'd left anything between the pages.

A small slip of white paper fluttered to the floor from the third book, a suspense story called *The Hub of the Wheel.* The paper landed on the carpet face up, and as I stooped to retrieve it I noted automatically what seemed to be a telephone number written on it in black ink. I picked up the paper and put it on Miss Halstrom's coffee table.

Miss Halstrom found her purse on the closet shelf, crossed the room to me, and counted out the money for her fine. I took it, gathered up her overdue books, and left. I was reluctant to exchange her cool presence for the stifling heat of the streets. But a job's a job.

Going down her stairs, between the second and third floors, I brushed past a short swarthy man in a neat gray suit who was going up. Then I was out in the street again, reaching for my damp handkerchief to resume mopping operations.

I negotiated two blocks of steaming sidewalk between Miss Halstrom's apartment house and my parked car, unlocked the trunk compartment, and fitted her three library books into a big carton. Then I climbed behind the wheel, fired up, and went on about my business.

On my next call I picked up four overdue books from the janitor of a funeral home and came panting back to my car once again, fishing in my pocket for my car keys. I stooped to unlock the trunk and only then realized that this time I wouldn't need a key. Because the trunk was already unlocked. And the lid gaped open about two inches.

Since I'm often careless about locking my trunk, this wouldn't have bothered me at all, except that the trunk lock was twisted out of shape, and the lid showed definite evidence that a prying tool had been used to force it.

Well, the rifling of locked car trunks has become a favorite outdoor sport of the "disadvantaged" these days, they tell me, so I wasn't too surprised at becoming another victim. I lifted the trunk lid and saw that my carton of books was still there. To the casual eye it looked completely undisturbed.

But my eye is not a casual one; I have an extremely good visual memory. And I distinctly remembered that I had fitted Miss Halstrom's three overdue books into my carton with a novel called *Brainstorm* on top. Now the top title was *The Hub of the Wheel*, and *Brainstorm* had been demoted to the second place in the stack.

I transferred all the books from the trunk to the back seat of the car, tied the trunk lid down with a piece of cord, and got behind the wheel again, reflecting ruefully that my trunk lock had been destroyed to no purpose. For it was obvious that whoever had broken into my trunk, on finding nothing but a box of library books (used) for his trouble, placidly glanced over some of the titles and then departed in disgust to try for richer spoils elsewhere. A nuisance. But my insurance would take care of the damage to the lock.

At noon I went back to the library and turned in the books and the fines I had collected, ate my lunch in the library cafeteria, and had barely got settled at the desk in my tiny office to plan the afternoon's work when my phone rang. Annie, on the library switchboard, said, "Hal, some girl has been trying to get you for an hour. Where've you been?"

"Eating lunch," I said. "Who was she?"

"A Miss Halstrom. I told her you'd call her back when you came in."

I felt a small thrill of pleasure. "What are you waiting for then?" I asked Annie.

When Miss Halstrom's contralto came on the line it sounded different. Not so cool and refreshing now. In fact, it sounded on the edge of panic. It said, "Mr. Johnson?"

"Yes?"

"Are you the man who collected my overdue library books this morning?"

I assured her I was.

"Oh, thank goodness!" she said. "Will you please do me a favor, Mr. Johnson?"

I said gallantly, "Just ask me, Miss Halstrom."

"Well, there was a bookmark in one of my library books, with a telephone number on it, Mr. Johnson. And I have to get it back, please. It's very important. It was in the book called *The Hub of the Wheel.* Do you remember that book?"

"Sure," I said. "And it did have a bookmark in it. But I left the bookmark on your coffee table this morning."

"The coffee table!" Her voice held the beginnings of relief. "Are you sure? Please, wait'll I look, will you please?" In a moment she was back on the line. "It's there, Mr. Johnson! Oh, how can I thank you? I'm so *dumb*! I put my purse right down on top of it when I was paying you the money for my fine this morning. No wonder we didn't see it. My boyfriend was furious with me!"

"Boyfriend?" I tried to keep disappointment out of my voice.

In her relief she chattered exuberantly on. "I *told* you this morning I'd lent the books to a friend. Well, it *was* my boyfriend, and the bookmark with the telephone number on it was *his*, not mine. I didn't even know it was in the book until he came in this morning right after you left and asked for that book because he'd remembered he'd left an important telephone number in it. And I told him you'd just left with the books, so he ran out after you to see if he could reach you and get his bookmark back, but he couldn't find you, so he told me to get that telephone number back for him somehow or I'd be sorry."

She took a deep breath. "And now I've got it, and the whole silly thing was just because of my dumbness!" She laughed. "I'm sorry I bothered you, Mr. Johnson. But I've never seen Jerry so upset!" She hung up.

I remembered the short swarthy fellow I'd passed on her stairway that morning. He must have been Miss Halstrom's boyfriend and evidently had an ugly temper. And obviously the man was pitifully unworthy of Miss Linda Halstrom, the Scandinavian goddess who had brightened my morning.

It was late the next afternoon before I got around to calling my insurance man to tell him about the broken lock of my car trunk. He said, "Get it fixed and send the bill to me. You've reported it to the police, of course?"

"No. What's the use? Nothing was taken."

"Do it anyway," he told me. "It has to be on the official record before we can pay any claim on it."

"I'm police," I said. "Don't I count?"

"You're just sissy unofficial fuzz," he said. "Report it downtown if you want us to pay the bill."

So on my way home that evening I stopped off at police headquarters and asked to see Lieutenant Randall. I'd worked for several years in the plainclothes division under Randall before I took my library job.

Randall was sitting in his office behind a perfectly clear desk, chewing gently on a stogie and regarding the world sleepily through his yellow cat's eyes. He greeted me with a wave of his hand. "Hi, Hal," he said blandly.

"You run into some crime at the public library that you can't handle by yourself?"

Just as blandly I answered, "No, Lieutenant. And if I need help I wouldn't come here for it. I understand the only good detective you ever had in this department resigned five years ago.

Randall grinned. "So what do you want?"

"To report a break-in."

"My, my! Whose?"

"Mine. Somebody jimmied the trunk lid of my car between 10:30 and 10:45 yesterday morning while I was parked in the 9200 block of Cook Street on the north side."

"Anything stolen?" asked Randall placidly.

"No. But my insurance man won't pay for repairs unless I report the thing officially."

"Okay," Randall said. "You've reported it. You don't expect us to find the culprit, do you?"

"No way."

"Unless," said Randall, very bland again, "the only good detective we ever had in this department can give us a clue to work on."

I grinned and started to shake my head. Then I said, "Wait a minute, Lieutenant. Maybe I *do* have a clue for you." For echoing in my mind, suddenly and for no reason, was the contralto voice of Miss Linda Halstrom saying to me over the phone: "...so he ran out after you to see if he could catch you and get his bookmark back, but he couldn't find you...)

I told Lieutenant Randall about the bookmark business. "So it's barely possible, isn't it," I asked him when I'd finished, "that Miss Halstrom's boyfriend didn't try to catch me at all, but instead followed me in his car until I parked, then jimmied open my trunk, looking for his telephone number? And didn't find it? For the only books that showed signs of having been moved in my carton were two of Miss Halstrom's books."

Randall laughed. "Some clue! Why would this boyfriend do a thing like that? When he could have just asked you for the bookmark?"

"Maybe he didn't want me to notice the telephone number?"

"Why not?"

"How do I know? But he obviously considered the number important enough to come down hard on poor Miss Halstrom for unknowingly giving it to me."

"If he couldn't remember the number, why not look it up again? Or ask Information for it?"

"Maybe it was an unlisted number."

Randall blew smoke. "Do *you* remember it? You used to be good at that."

I closed my eyes and visualized the slip of paper staring up at me from Miss Halstrom's carpet yesterday. "Yeah," I said. I tore a sheet off Randall's desk pad and wrote on it: *Cal 928-4791*.

Randall looked at what I'd written. "What's the 'Cal'?"

"Layman's shorthand for 'Call,' I guess."

Randall put his stogie on a battered ashtray, asked for an outside line, and dialed the number. He held his telephone receiver a couple of inches away from his ear so I could hear the distant ringing.

After only one ring someone picked up the receiver. A woman's voice said, "Yes?"

Randall murmured into the phone, "Is this the Peckinpaugh residence, please?"

"No," said the voice. "Wrong number." And there was a click as she hung up.

"You're losing your charm," I said to Randall.

Unabashed, he waited a moment, then dialed the number again. The same woman's voice answered immediately. "Yes?" This time the question was asked in a tight controlled tone, highly charged with either anxiety or anger.

Randall said, "Who is this, please?"

"Will you kindly stay off this line?" the woman said sharply. "I'm expecting an important call." And she hung up again.

"Why didn't you tell her who you are?" I asked Randall.

"I didn't get a chance." Grimly he dialed the number once more, and when the woman answered he said sternly, "Now don't hang up, lady, this is the police calling."

This pronouncement was greeted by an exclamation that was part wail, part sob. "The police! But we don't *want* the police! Will you please stop tying up this line?" And another click.

Randall's yellow eyes turned thoughtful. "'But we don't *want* the police,'" he murmured. "An odd turn of phrase, wouldn't you say, Hal?"

"I would. And she sounded quite upset."

He pushed his phone across the desk to me. "You try it," he said. I began to dial. He said, "Wait." He was looking at the memo sheet with the telephone number on it. "What if this 'Cal' doesn't mean 'Call'? What if it's a name? Like short for Calvin, or Calhoun, or something?"

That hadn't occurred to me. I nodded. "I'll try it." I dialed the number.

This time, when the receiver was lifted at the other end, I got in first. "Is Cal there?" I asked brightly.

A sharp intake of breath came clearly over the wire. Then, "Thank God!" The woman's voice sounded faint and weak. "Is she all right? You haven't hurt her, have you?" A gulp. Then, with more control, "I'm doing exactly as you said. I'll have the money ready tomorrow, as soon as the banks open...)

Randall was leaning over his desk toward me, listening intently to the small voice at the other end of the wire. I looked into his cat's eyes and raised my eyebrows. He shook his head violently. I said into the telephone, "Isn't Calvin Brown there? Isn't this 928-3791?"—deliberately giving the wrong number.

Her words stopped as though I'd turned off a faucet.

Randall nodded at me and I said hurriedly, "I'm sorry. I must have dialed it wrong. Excuse it, please," and hung up.

Lieutenant Randall leaned back slowly in his chair. "How do you like that?" he said softly.

I said, "Are you going to barge in on it? She was terrified of police."

"Not at her end. I want to know who she is, though. And Cal, too."

An official police demand brought us the information from the telephone company that unlisted number 928-4791 was assigned to a Mrs. Wilson A. Benedict on Waterside Drive.

I whistled. "She can afford to pay the ransom, I guess. She's the widow of Wilson Benedict, the bank president, isn't she?"

Randall didn't answer. He was already calling the Obituary editor of the *Evening News* who informed us, after he located the clipping in his files, that Wilson A. Benedict, when killed in an auto accident the year before, had been survived by his wife, two college-age sons, and a four-year-old daughter named Callie.

"Callie," Randall said, picking up his stogie. "She must be our Cal. Let's go see your Miss Halstrom."

I was already on my feet. "Right," I said, just as though I still worked for him.

Five minutes after we found her partaking of a late dinner in her apartment on the north side, Randall had extracted the following information from a distressed but cooperative Miss Halstrom. Item: her boyfriend's name was Jerry Gates. Item: he was chauffeur-handyman for a wealthy family named Carson on Waterside Drive and lived in their garage apartment. Item: the Carsons were on vacation in the mountains. Item: Jerry Gates was going to marry Linda Halstrom as soon as he got the large legacy he was expecting from an uncle who had died while Jerry was serving as a medic in Vietnam several years ago, before Jerry had even met Linda. And item: the telephone number on his missing bookmark, according to Jerry, was that of the lawyer, name unknown, whom he was supposed to call to find out when he could expect his legacy.

Well, that was enough information for Randall. We left Halstrom weeping into her cold TV dinner and took off for Waterside Drive. En route Randall called headquarters and ordered reinforcements to meet us. He wanted to leave me out of it, but he couldn't waste time arguing, so I went along.

When the reinforcements arrived, there were six of us, counting me, a small army.

As it turned out we didn't need that many, but we didn't know that till later. It was full dark by the time we reached Waterside Drive. A promise of coming coolness was faintly detectable in the overheated July air. We drove past the stone entrance pillars twice before we left the cars a block away and drifted back, in shifts of two, trying to look inconspicuous as we ducked inside and melted into the gloom of the trees that lined the drive.

When we were all there, gathered in the dense shadow of a huge sycamore, Randall looked over the setup. The enormous turn-of-the-century house, covered with gingerbread scrollwork that was faintly visible to us in the starlight, squatted at the end of the driveway like an obscene insect. Not a single light shone in it. Off to the right, maybe 30 yards from the house and placed out of sight from the street, was an old-fashioned two-car garage, originally a carriage house in all probability, with the chauffeur's quarters above it. We could see a light shining from the front windows of the garage apartment.

Randall pointed to the light. "That's it," he whispered. He looked up at the gnarled limbs of the sycamore that sheltered us and said, "O'Neill, get up in this tree with your field glasses and see what you can see."

We waited then in complete silence, broken only by the scrape of shoe leather on rough tree bark, while O'Neill climbed the tree. Every few feet he'd stop and take a look through the field glasses to see if he was high enough to get a view into the lighted windows of the chauffeur's quarters. Finally he settled on a thick branch about 25 feet up and trained his glasses on the windows for several minutes without moving.

"Well?" asked Randall as O'Neill came sliding down the tree.

"One guy," said O'Neill, barely loud enough to be audible. "Sitting in an easy chair reading the newspaper. *The Evening News*."

"Could you see the whole room? Only one guy? You're sure?"

O'Neill nodded. "I'm sure."

Randall shook his head. "One doesn't seem enough."

"Maybe there are guards outside," I suggested.

"You keep out of this," Randall told me. Then, to two of the others, "Jim, make a circuit of the house. And you, Lew, take the garage. No noise, you hear? Just see if you can locate any guards around. And if you do, fade out. Come back here. Don't take any aggressive action of your own. Understood?"

Jim and Lew slid away without a word. We waited again. I needed a cigarette. But then, so did the others, probably. Twenty minutes crept by.

O'Neill was up in the tree again, keeping in view the man reading the newspaper in the garage apartment.

"No guards that we could see," Jim reported when he and Lew rejoined us.

"Huh!" said Randall. He seemed disappointed. "Only one guy. Any other lights visible?"

"None in the main house," Jim said.

"And only in the garage in that front room upstairs," Lew said. "The back windows are dark. Or back window, rather. There's only one."

Up in the tree O'Neill spoke. "The guy's getting up from his chair. Going to a door at the back end of the room. Opening it. Going through. It's a little hallway. He's gone now."

Randall nodded. "Come on down, O'Neill." He turned to Lew. "Any place behind the garage where we can look through that rear window with the glasses?"

"Yeah," Lew answered. "A tree bigger than this one. Except there's no light."

"Come on," Randall muttered, and we followed him a silently as we could toward the garage, clinging to the shadows. At the foot of the outside staircase that led up to the garage apartment Randall said, "Lew and Jim. Stay here in the angle of the wall until I tell you different. O'Neill, take the garage doors—there might be an inside exit. Shenkin. Under the back window. Nail anybody who tries to get out of that upstairs apartment. Got it? And Hal," he said, "you come with me."

I nodded. Randall took the field glasses from O'Neill and led me quickly around to the back of the garage, Shenkin trailing us and taking position under the back window as instructed.

"I want to see what's in that back room," Randall said to me. He gestured toward the big tree Lew had reported. "Climb up there and give it a try, will you?"

"I'm no tree climber. I thought you wanted me out of it?"

"I do. That's why I'm sending you up the tree." His yellow eyes glittered in the starlight. "Get going." He tilted his head to look up at the rear window. "Maybe reflected light from the front room will show you something."

"And if I see anything?"

"If you see enough to show you we're right about this screwy deal, whistle. We'll take it from there."

I climbed up the tree as silently as I could manage it.

I sat with the glasses trained on the small rear window of the garage apartment for ten long minutes before I could report anything to Randall below. Then a door opened and a path of light cut into the darkness of the back room I was watching. The shaft of light began at the opening door and ended at a bed on the left side of the room. A girl lay on the bed, sleeping.

I whistled softly. Immediately I could hear Randall taking off and running hard for tire front of the garage. In another moment the sound of rushing feet on wooden steps thundered in the night, and Randall's voice, perfectly clear to me up in my tree, shouted, "Open up! This is the police!"

I kept my glasses trained on the man who had entered the back room. Randall's shout caught him just as he bent over the sleeping girl. He straightened galvanically. He cast one incredulous look toward the front of the garage, then turned and came charging directly toward me.

With hands and arms stiffened before him to protect his head, he hit the rear window of the room in a long horizontal dive that carried away window glass, sash, and sticks of frame. It was like watching a TV detective leap through a breakaway window. In the midst of the window explosion the man tumbled out into the night air 15 feet above the unprepared head of Shenkin, dutifully parked under that back window.

I yelled, "Shenkin! Watch out below!" But it was too late. Shenkin looked up, jerked right, then left, trying to avoid the falling object. He failed. The man's hurtling body landed feet first on Shenkin's head and shoulders and drove him to the ground as effectively as a pile driver.

Transfixed for a few seconds in my tree, I waited for Shenkin to move. He didn't. He was out cold. And the man who had leaped from the window—Jerry Gates presumably—was in little better condition. He seemed badly shaken by his fall. It took him roughly forty seconds to stagger to his feet, look around him muzzily, and set off again, straight toward my tree.

By that time I was heedlessly removing square inches of hide from my arms and ankles, shinnying down my tree backward as fast as I could slide without going into free fall. The field glasses hung from my neck on their strap and set up a clatter as they bumped against the tree trunk during my hasty descent.

A reverberating crash from the front of the garage informed me that Randall and Jim and Lew had broken down the front door of the apartment. I was aware of this only on the fringe of my attention which was centered strongly now on Jerry Gates. He was running toward me unsteadily as I reached the foot of my tree.

I was in deep shadow there. He didn't see me. So I did the only thing I could think of to stop him. I swung Randall's heavy' field glasses on the end of their carrying strap once around my head for momentum, like a cowboy twirling a rope, and let them fly.

They caught the fugitive just above the right temple, making a thump of their own to add to the assorted violent sounds of that night. And he went down for the count even more gracefully than poor unlucky Shenkin.

When Randall burst through into the garage apartment's back room a moment later, with his gun out, he found that little Callie Benedict had slept peacefully through all the fireworks.

* * * *

The next day the police were heroes in the newspapers and on TV. For when little Callie was returned, unharmed and without payment of the ransom, Mrs. Benedict couldn't say enough nice things about "those marvelous policemen." I was mentioned in the news reports as a former cop who had inadvertently alerted the police to the kidnapping during a routine report of a car break-in. They didn't even mention my name.

Lieutenant Randall called me at the library at noon. "We got the story out of Gates," he said. "I'll fill you in. The only solo kidnapping attempt in my experience. Living next door to the kidnap victim made it almost work for him."

"How'd Gates grab the girl?" I asked.

"She's got a pet rabbit in a hutch by the hedge that forms the boundary line between the Benedicts and the Carsons. Every afternoon at five o'clock the kid goes out to feed her rabbit. So Gates just reached through the hedge from his side, slapped a chloroform pad over the kid's face, and carried her up to his garage apartment. Then he gave her a shot of drugs to keep her out of it until he collected the ransom from her mother. He swears he was going to turn her loose—unharmed, of course. And he was counting on Mrs. Benedict's promise not to call us in. Any questions?"

"Where'd he get the unlisted phone number?"

"Three weeks ago in a bar after a few drinks with a guy who used to be the Benedicts' chauffeur."

"And 'Cal' was a code word to identify the kidnaper to Mrs. Benedict?"

"Yeah."

"Okay," I said. "No more questions. But I've got a big fat complaint."

"Let me guess. Your feelings are hurt because we didn't give you a fair share of glory in the public prints, right?"

"It would have been great publicity for the library."

"And for you, too, hey?"

"You could have given them my name, at least. It wouldn't have hurt you any."

Randall chuckled. "It wouldn't have hurt *me,* no. But it would have hurt the department, Hal."

"For God's sake! How?"

"Well"—Lieutenant Randall was at his blandest—"don't you think it might destroy public confidence in the police department if I let it be publicly known that the only real *good* detective we ever had in the department resigned five years ago?"

THE REWARD

Originally published in* Alfred Hitchcock's Mystery Magazine, *October 1980.

I didn't want to waste my time on another fruitless call at Annabel Corelli's home, so I telephoned her at eight-thirty Friday morning.

After two rings, I heard the receiver lifted and a voice said, "Hello." The voice was unmistakably female and it sounded like contralto coffee cream—rich and very, very smooth. It gave me such a jolt of pleasure that for an uneasy moment I felt somehow disloyal to Ellen Corby, one of our librarians, whom I'd been assiduously courting for over a year.

I said, "Is this Miss Annabel Corelli?

"Yes. The way she said it painted an instant image of a tall, Junoesque creature in a string bikini walking along a tropical beach.

"My name is Hal Johnson," I said, "and I'm calling about your overdue library book, Miss Corelli. I stopped at your house yesterday to collect it, but you weren't home."

"I'm almost never home in the daytime, Mr. Johnson. I'm an Argyll Lady. I'm just on my way out to work now." That figured, I thought, a door-to-door cosmetics lady. With that voice, she ought to be able to sell skin lotion to a porcupine. "I'm sorry about the book, she said. "I'm afraid I let a friend borrow it and then forgot all about it.

"It's six weeks overdue, I said, "and it's a one-week book, so it's costing you a bundle in fines."

"I'm really sorry, Mr. Johnson." Her voice caressed me. "How much do I owe on it?"

I told her.

"Well, how about if I leave the book and the fine in my carport for you so you can pick it up today while I'm out?

I said, "Today? But if you've lent the book to a friend—"

"No, today'll be fine," she said with a laugh. "The friend I lent it to lives here with me."

Lucky friend, I thought as I hung up.

* * * *

I stopped at Miss Corelli's house in the Last End in mid-morning. Sure enough, there was the library book—*The Hong Kong Diagram*—on a shelf in the carport, with the exact amount of the fine neatly stacked on top of it. A cornerpost concealed the book and money from anyone not specifically looking for it.

As I put the book on the back seat of my old Ford, it occurred to me that Annabel Corelli must do pretty well as an Argyll Lady. Her house was nothing elaborate, but it was no hovel either—two-story white clapboard with green shutters and a neat yard attractively planted. And the carport was a two-car job. Maybe Miss Corelli's friend contributed to the budget. I felt a vague sense of regret that I hadn't been able to meet the lady and her exciting voice in person.

That Friday was a busy day for me. By the time I'd made the last call on my overdue list, the hot August afternoon had already gobbled up my usual cocktail hour and was shading rapidly toward dinnertime. I was tired and out of sorts, and I felt sticky. I wanted a long shower and an ice-cold martini, straight up. So instead of returning to the library to check in my hooks and fines before I knocked off for the day I went straight home, luxuriated for twenty minutes in the shower, and had not one but two ice-cold martinis before dining in bachelor loneliness on a double package of frozen chicken chow-mein.

I cleaned up the dishes, listened to the news on television, then turned it off, feeling fidgety and restless and wondering how long it was going to be before Ellen agreed to marry me—or at least let me see her more than two evenings a week, which was my present ration.

Thinking about Ellen reminded me of Annabel Corelli's sexy voice, and that in turn reminded me of her overdue library book, *The Hung Kong Diagram*. It was a relatively new novel of the stolen-nuclear-device-endangers-the-world school, and a suspense blockbuster.

It was full dark now. I went out the back door of my garden apartment into the garage, unlocked the car, and, by the light in the dome, rummaged through the stacks of books in the back seat until I found *The Hong Kong Diagram*.

Have I mentioned that I'm an avid reader? Well, I am. I'll read anything—from coffee-table art books to paperback gothics. I've found that reading's the best way to educate yourself beyond the few basic disciplines you get in college. When I was working as a homicide detective under Lieutenant Randall, before I decided to become a library cop, I d taken courses in speed reading and memory development. You know how an ambitious rookie in any new job can be an eager beaver? That was me. But, as a matter of fact, the speed reading and memory training come in very handy in my present work, which, as you've probably gathered by now, is to run down overdue and stolen books for the public library.

I figured I could probably zip through *The Hong Kong Diagram* in a few hours. At the very least, it would amuse me until bedtime. I relocked the Ford and went back inside, riffling through the book, looking for anything that might inadvertently have been left between the pages. The shakeout is standard procedure with me when I collect overdue books, and you'd be surprised at some of the items I've discovered. I once found a brand-new hundred-dollar bill in a library book borrowed by an offset printer on the South Side. From the alacrity with which he grabbed the bill and thrust it out of sight, I've always suspected it might have been one he'd printed himself.

There wasn't any hundred-dollar bill in *The Hong Kong Diagram*. There was, however, a list of addresses written in a careless scrawling hand on the back of a sales slip that carried the heading Argyll Cosmetics. A memo, I concluded, to herself from Miss Annabel Corelli.

I ran my eye down the half-dozen addresses. They didn't mean anything to me. But they might he important to a door-to-door Argyll Lady. At the very least, I thought, they gave me an excuse for further exposure to Annabel Corelli's golden voice. I dialed her number and waited eagerly for the sound of rich contralto. What I got, after two rings, was a harsh, impatient baritone, "Yes?"

I said, "Is Miss Corelli there?"

"Who's calling?"

"Hal Johnson from the public library. I spoke with Miss Corelli this morning."

"Hang on."

I hung on, reflecting on the sad fact that Miss Corelli's live-in friend, judging from the depth and proprietary sound of his voice, seemed to be a man—and not another woman, as I'd imagined. Probably a Fuller Brush Man, I thought sourly.

"Hello, Mr. Johnson. Didn't you get your book O.K.? It was gone from the carport when I got home."

"I got it, Miss Corelli. And thanks. But I found a memo in it and I thought maybe you'd need it.

"A memo?" she said with a puzzled lift to that gorgeous voice.

"Yes. A list of addresses written on the back of an Argyll Cosmetics sales slip. Maybe a list of calls you plan to make or something."

She hesitated a moment. Then, "Oh, yes, Mr. Johnson. I recognize if. It *is* a call list, but I don't need it any more. You can throw it away."

"OK I just wanted to be sure it wasn't important."

"It was terribly nice of you to call about it."

"Not at all, Miss Corelli," I said. "Good night."

I hung up, tossed the list in the wastepaper basket, and started to read *The Hong Kong Diagram*.

The ads were right; it was a suspense blockbuster. It made me so nervous I couldn't get to sleep until after midnight.

* * * *

Wild coincidences do happen occasionally in library work like mine, just as I suppose they do in other businesses. I was at my desk in the library the next morning, working on my weekly records, when I got a telephone call from my old boss, Lieutenant Randall of Homicide.

"Hal," he said, "do me a favor." It sounded more like an order than a request, but that was in character for Randall when he was in a hurry.

"Like what? I asked noncommittally.

"Like saving me a trip to the library. You can get me the information I need quicker than I can—if there is any."

"What do you need?

"Any information you can dig up about one of your card-holders named Josephine Sloan. A twenty-seven-year-old woman. Single. A live-in maid. One of your best customers, judging by the stack of borrowed library books in her room.

"Who has she killed, if I may ask?"

"Nobody that I know of. She was reported missing on the eleventh of this month by her employers, a Mr. and Mrs. Gaither. When the Gaithers got home from a weekend at the shore on that date, she was missing."

"Along with the family's jewels and silver?"

"No. Nothing was missing except the maid."

I said, "Since when have you been switched from Homicide to Missing Persons?"

"I haven't. Josephine Sloan's body was found yesterday afternoon by some kids playing in Gaylord Park. The body, with a badly cracked skull, was stashed under an overhang along the creek bank. It could be a hit-run, murder, or any other damn thing except a natural death."

"Well, in that case," I said, "sure. I'll nose around for you. But her employers ought to be able to tell you a hell of a lot more about her than any of our people here."

"Her employers can't give us anything that helps. We've tried. Since they were away, they don't know anything about her activities that weekend. To hear them tell it, she was a model maid—industrious, efficient, quiet, honest, no known boyfriends." Randall cleared his throat. "Which figures, I suppose. She was quite unattractive."

“I still don t get why you think we can help you, no matter how many library books she read.”

“The post-mortem shows her death had to have occurred that weekend. And we’ve only got one lousy lead to her movements that weekend.”

A pause.

“Something to do with the library.”

“Right. Apparently one of the last things she did before she went missing was to borrow eight books from your library on Saturday, the eighth—two weeks ago today. You and your people are probably the last ones to have seen her alive.”

“O.K.,” I said with a deep sigh. “What do you want me to do?”

“Ask around about her among your Saturday stall and volunteers, find out if anybody knows her. Does anybody remember her coming in on the eighth? Has anybody ever noticed her with a boy friend at the library. Did she, by some freak of chance, say anything to anybody about her plans for that weekend? Or about her employers being away? You know what I want, Hal. A starting place, that’s all.”

“I’ll try, Lieutenant,” I said, “but don’t hold your breath. I took out a pencil. “Josephine Sloan. Twenty-seven years old. A spinster. Unattractive. Address?”

“Same as her employers’, said Randall. “The R. C. Gaithers. Thirty-four North Linden Drive.”

I took it down. “I’ll be in touch.”

“Thanks, Hal.” We hung up.

That’s when the coincidence showed up. As I looked at the address I’d just jotted down on my pad, I realized I’d seen it before very recently. In fact, only last night. On the call-list bookmark left in her overdue library book by Annabel Corelli, the Argyll Lady.

* * * *

After plenty of questioning, what I got for Randall out of our Saturday staff and volunteers was exactly zero. We have four girls on the check-out desk of the main library, including Ellen, and only one of them had. Anything of even remote interest to reveal about Josephine Sloan, and that was Ellen herself, who, after much thought, said she vaguely remembered checking out some books for the name Sloan on the Saturday morning in question. Beyond that, nobody could remember anything at all. In fact, though two of the other girls and one of our men volunteers were familiar with Josephine Sloan through her frequent visits to the library, not one of them had ever exchanged any more words with her than were necessary to check her books in and out.

Before calling Lieutenant Randall with the bad news, however, I decided, on the basis of that odd coincidence of addresses, to take another look at Annabel Corelli's call list, which should still be reposing in the wastebasket at my apartment. The library closes early on Saturdays. I went straight home, dug the list out, and was pleased to see my memory hadn't let me down on the Sloan address. It was there all right, along with five others—34 North Linden Drive.

There was something else there too, something that hadn't registered with me the night before when I'd found the list and telephoned Annabel Corelli. I stared at the tiny figures for a moment, then reached for my car keys.

* * * *

Twenty minutes later, I was sitting across the desk from Lieutenant Randall at Downtown Police Headquarters. "You got something for me," he asked hopefully.

I shook my head. "I'm sorry. One of the girls remembers Sloan checking out her books on that Saturday, but that's all. And you already knew that."

Randall sighed. Then he shot me a sleepy look from his cat-yellow eyes. "So why are you here?"

I told him about the Argyll Lady—about her overdue library book, her live-in boy friend, her bookmark memo with Josephine Sloan's address on it. He snorted. "Your Argyll Lady probably called on the Gaither woman to sell her some cosmetics."

"Right, Lieutenant. But look at the tiny figures under the Gaithers' address there." I handed him the list and pointed.

Randall peered at them. "Eight dash eleven," he read aloud. "The other addresses all have numbers too. Probably order numbers. Or appointment dates." He paused and his eyes narrowed. "Dates," he repeated softly. He lit one of his vicious stogies and puffed acrid smoke across his desk in my direction. I coughed. "Dates," he murmured again. "The eighth of the month is approximately when the Sloan girl was killed. And the eleventh is when the Gaithers came home from their weekend and reported her missing. Is that what you're getting at, Hal?"

"Could be," I said.

"Let's find out."

Randall was never one to waste time. He called a police clerk into his office, gave him the list of addresses, and told him to get the names and telephone numbers that went with them. While we waited, Randall smoked in silence and I sat on the hard chair and remembered to be grateful I was no longer a homicide cop. Sissy library fuzz or not, it was a lot more restful collecting library books than murderers.

The clerk was back in eight minutes. Randall grunted his thanks, picked up his phone, asked the switchboard for an outside line, and dialed one of the numbers the clerk had just handed him.

After a short wait, a woman answered. "Mrs. Symons?" Randall said. "This is the Police Department." His tone was as bland as vanilla pudding. "Maybe you can help us. We're investigating a mugging that occurred on your street on the night of—" he read the tiny numbers under the Symons' address from the call list "—either the twenty-seventh or the twenty-eighth of last month. Were you at home those evenings, can you remember?"

Mrs. Symons voice squawked in the receiver. Randall held the phone far enough from his ear so I could catch her words. They were heavily freighted with indignation. "A *mugging*!" she said. What's the *matter* with the police in this city? It wasn't a mugging at all, as you ought to know very well since you spent a whole morning here at my house investigating it!"

"Oh-oh." Randall was abject. "We must have our wires crossed here, Mrs. Symons. If it wasn't a mugging, what was it?

"Our burglary here! They stole every bit of sterling silver we had in the house!"

While she paused for breath, Randall repeated his question. "Were you at home that weekend, Mrs. Symons?

"At home? Of course not! If it hadn't been Parents Weekend at our daughter's college, we wouldn't have lost our silver. The house was empty." Her voice went shrill. "But I've already *told* all this to one of your men named Leroy! And we haven't heard a *word* from him in almost a month now! *Some* police department! Lucky for us we were insured!"

Randall soothed her. "I'll ask Detective Leroy to get in touch with you at once. I can't understand this mix-up, Mrs. Symons. I'm very sorry—please believe me." Mrs. Symons gave the Lieutenant an unladylike raspberry and hung up abruptly.

Randall grinned. "Remind you of old times, Hal?" he asked. He picked up the phone again and asked for Detective Leroy in Burglary. While he waited, he talked to me around his stogie. "We'll take it from here, Hal. Thanks for the lead—

It was a dismissal. I stood up. "Thanks aren't enough," I said. "I want a reward."

"Reward?" He glared at me.

"Reward." I repeated. "If you decide to interview the Argyll Lady any point during your investigation, I want to be there."

"What for?"

"So I can see what goes along with that sexy voice," I said.

* * * *

The following Friday night, Randall called me after midnight. I'd just come in from a dinner and movie date with Ellen. Randall said, "You in bed yet?

"Almost," I said. "Why?"

"We've got your Argyll Lady here. If you want to collect that reward come over to headquarters."

"Now? Its after midnight!"

"So your Police Department never sleeps. You coming?"

"What happened?"

"I'll tell you when you get here." He hung up with a crash.

I sighed. I was tired and sleepy. I wanted to go to bed, not downtown—not even to meet the girl with the sexy voice. After Ellen, Farrah herself would be an anticlimax. But I'd asked for it. I put my jacket and tie back on and went out to the car.

The Lieutenant was alone in his office when I got to headquarters. He smirked at me, and waved me to a chair.

"Couldn't this wait till tomorrow?" I asked.

"You said you wanted to meet her. She may be out on bail tomorrow."

"I said, Don't tell me *she* killed Josephine Sloan."

"I won t tell you anything unless you shut up." He was enjoying himself. "O.K.," I said meekly.

"The minute Detective Leroy in Burglary saw that list of your Argyll Lady's, Randall said, we were practically home free. It was just routine from there on."

"Let me guess. All those addresses had reported burglaries too?"

He nodded. Four out of six. All committed when the owners were out of town and the houses were empty. On the dates indicated by the little figures under each address."

"And silver was stolen from all of them?"

He nodded again. "With the price of silver today, did you know you can get several grand at the smelter for a set of sterling flatware that retailed for only a few hundred bucks ten years ago? Silver's very big in the B-&-E business these days."

"Even a library cop is aware of that," I said sarcastically. "So what about Annabel Corelli?"

"In each case, she'd made a sales call at the burglarized house shortly before the burglary took place."

I grimaced. "So she *did* set them up. A crooked Argyll Lady. She makes a call and during a friendly conversation learns when the lady of the house and her family will be away. She notes the best prospects for a large silver haul, and the dates when no one should be at home."

Randall blew smoke. "A neat operation. You got to admire it."

"I do. But I still don't see how it gets you anywhere with the Sloan murder."

Randall treated me to one of his unblinking yellow stares. Then he said "In each of the four burglaries, entry into the house was effected the same way. By means of a hydraulic jack." I must have looked puzzled, because he went on to explain in a patronizing tone.

"You cushion the pushing head and the footplate of a jack with foam-rubber and position it horizontally against the edges of a door frame about the level of the lock. When pressure is applied, the jack spreads the door-posts apart enough so the lock and deadbolt tongues are drawn out of their sockets and the door can swing open. When you leave the house with your loot, you release pressure on the jack and the door frames spring back to vertical again, reseating the bolts in their sockets as though they'd never been touched. And the only sign of a break-in having occurred is a couple of shallow pressure marks on the doorposts made by the jack."

"Well, well," I said, "what'll they think of next? I still don t see—" But as I uttered the words I did see. "You found the same jack marks on the doorposts of the Gaithers house."

"The very same," said Randall. "Exact match of the marks on the other four break-ins. Although nothing was reported stolen at that address, remember. Only the disappearance of the maid. Yet a break-in had obviously taken place. Are you beginning to get it now?"

"Yeah. Corelli set up the jobs, and she and her boyfriend probably worked them together. But when they broke into the Gaithers' house, it wasn't empty, as they expected it would be. The maid was there. She probably caught Corelli and friend at the silver chest and recognized Corelli as the Argyll Lady who called on Mrs. Gaither. So the fat was in fire, unless—"

Lieutenant Randall nodded. Unless something was done to keep the maid from talking. So they did something. They killed her and, leaving the silver behind, they relocked the door, packed the maid into their ear, and hid her body in Gaylord Park, six miles away.

"Do you have any proof of all this?" I asked.

"Some circumstantial stuff. And when their lawyer gets here and we can interrogate them, I'm hoping for more. Anyway, we sure as hell have proof they're silver thieves if nothing else. We caught them red-handed, about two hours ago, burgling the last house on your list." Randall yawned cavernously. "A blackjack in the boyfriend's pocket could be the Sloan murder weapon. It's at the lab now. And the boys have found a few faint bloodstains on the upholstery of the back seat of Corelli's car that may give us something."

Randall noted my sour expression and said cheerfully, "Hal, my boy, you were dead right about your Argyll Lady. She's a real dish. Wait'll you see her."

He picked up the phone and spoke into it.

* * * *

Two minutes later, Annabel Corelli appeared in the doorway escorted by two uniformed cops, one holding each arm. Even without makeup, her auburn hair in a tumbled mess and her clothing in disarray, she was something to see. She was really impressively beautiful—and big. She must have stood almost six feet tall and tipped the scales at a good hundred and sixty-five pounds—every one of them distributed in the proper place.

Randall stood up politely. I also got to my feet. The Lieutenant said, "Miss Corelli, let me present Hal Johnson from the public library. I promised him he could meet you in person if that list of addresses he found in your library book should help us with this case."

She seemed momentarily taken aback when she heard my name. Then she smiled at me very sweetly. In that unforgettable voice, she said, "I *am* glad to meet you, Mr. Johnson."

Trying to hide my embarrassment, I started to mumble something fatuous, I don't remember what. But I didn't get a chance to finish it. Annabel Corelli pulled sharply away from her guards, took two steps toward me, drew back her right arm, and slapped me so hard I fell back against Randall's desk, my head ringing like a church bell.

They hustled her out but I could tell by the frown on Lieutenant Randall's face it was all he could do not to laugh himself sick.

HERO WITH A HEADACHE

Originally published in* Mike Shayne Mystery Magazine, *December 1976.

When I began to come out of it, the first things I noticed were a whirling sensation in my head with an undercurrent of thumping pain, and a very sick feeling in the pit of my stomach.

I knew I ought to open my eyes but it didn't seem worth the trouble. So I kept them shut and went on feeling dizzy and nauseated until, vaguely, I realized that my whirling, aching head and the nausea were familiar symptoms...something I'd gone through before, or thought I had. A kind of *deja vu* feeling, as Liz, on the library's check-out desk, would express it. She always used egghead terms like that. Or was it Kathy on the main desk?

Anyway, I knew damn well I'd felt this way before. Then I pinned it down—or thought I did.

I'd been sapped. Just as I was, once long ago, when I was working under Lieutenant Randall at the Police Department. Sapped by an expert. I'd felt exactly this way then.

My head went on aching, but my stomach began to settle back out of my throat. I forced myself to open my eyes, which wasn't so tough to do after all. They came open with no more than an extra stab of pain as the light hit them...

And there was Mrs. Stout, across the room from me, tied to a chair with a twisted pink sheet.

Then I *knew* I'd been sapped. Seeing Mrs. Stout brought it back to me almost whole. She was watching me, big-eyed and weeping, silently pleading with me to do something.

But what did she want me to do? I wasn't in too good shape to do it, whatever it was, because *I* was tied to a chair, too. My hands were fastened behind the chair back so tightly that my shoulder sockets screamed at the strain. Not with a sheet, though. This felt like clothesline. It went several times around my thighs, waist and chest and fastened me to the chair tight as a politician's schedule.

We were in a den or study or office. It was a medium-large room with a desk and telephone, two deep leather chairs, the two straight chairs that held Mrs. Stout and me, wall-to-wall aqua carpeting, drapes of the same color and a whole wall of books. In a home like Mrs. Stout's, I guess you'd call it a library. Mrs. Stout was tied to the desk chair. My chair was across the room from hers in a corner near the bookshelves.

I licked my lips and was considerably pleased that I could, for that meant my mouth wasn't pasted shut with a strip of adhesive tape like Mrs. Stout's. I figured fuzzily that therefore I ought to be able to talk, so I tried it. My words came out, "Wheewhis Whow," thick and hoarse, instead of "Mrs. Stout" as I intended.

By this time my head had slowed its spinning enough so that I could think a little more clearly. All that got me was a feeling of guilt and embarrassment at how stupid I'd been to get into this mess in the first place. I'd made a fool of myself, and of poor Mrs. Stout, too, for that matter. And nobody to blame but myself. Old Hal Johnson, a trained police officer, acting like any callow Sir Galahad, for God's sake.

Not that I was actually a cop any more, but I'd *been* one. Come to think of it, maybe that accounted for my sticking my nose into Mrs. Stout's business instead of minding my own. My own business nowadays, let me explain, was simply chasing down overdue and stolen books for the public library. I was still fuzz in a way, I suppose, but sissy fuzz. Library fuzz, for Pete's sake.

The first name on my list of overdue library book-borrowers that morning had been Mrs. J. W. Stout, 1525 Washburn Drive, on the West Side. I like to start my day out with a little class as much as anyone, so I was glad the address was in a good neighborhood. The houses were mostly split-levels and spacious, set well back from the street with a lot of manicured lawn around them.

There are a lot of reasons—and I've heard them all, believe me—why people who borrow books from the public library fail to return them on time, and then ignore as well the overdue notices the library sends out to them as reminders. One reason is that the book borrower is just too lazy to bother bringing the books back and too rich to give a damn about the fines he'll have to pay as a result. One-five-two-five Washburn looked like one of that kind to me. Lazy and rich.

It was ten minutes to nine when I pulled up there, parked behind a dark green van that said *Heritage Cleaners* on the sides in sloppy lettering and walked up the-long flagstone path to the front door. On the way, I admired the Indiana limestone facing of the house and the gleaming Thunderbird standing on the left side of i:he open two-car garage.

I rang the doorbell, only it wasn't a bell, it was chimes. I could hear them sending musical notes through the house to announce my arrival. Nothing happened, so after a minute or so, I gave the chimes another thumbing and waited some more. This time, sounds of movement inside the door told me that somebody was at home after all. I could hear a chain rattling, then a bolt being turned, and then the door was drawn open and a handsome middle-aged woman with gray hair and dimples was looking at me inquiringly.

"Mrs. Stout?" I asked.

She nodded, but didn't say anything, although I could see her swallow as if she was getting ready to. I went into my usual spiel. "I'm from the public library," I said, showing her my identification card, "and I've come about all those overdue books you have."

She looked at my identification card suspiciously. Then she cleared her throat and said, "Oh—oh, yes. Those would be the books I took out of the library to amuse my grandson when he was visiting us last month." She cleared her throat again. "I—I'll return them as soon as—as I can, Mr. Johnson."

I said, "I'll take them off your hands right now and save you the trip."

"Oh…well, thank you," she said ungraciously. "Wait there a minute, then." She pushed the door to and went away. She didn't ask me in. Lazy and rich, all right, I thought, and not very polite, either.

I cooled my heels for a couple of minutes before she came back with an armload of children's picture books. "Here," she said in a harassed voice and thrust them at me. She was angry and distraught and I got the feeling that she thought I ought to apologize to her for bothering her so early in the morning. She was obviously anxious to get rid of me and no two ways about it.

As she was about to close the door in my face, therefore, I took a little malicious pleasure in saying, "Wait, Mrs. Stout. You owe a fine on these books.

They're way overdue, you know."

She gave me a strange look. "A—a fine? Oh, *dear*! How much?"

I told her the fine came to six dollars and thirty cents.

"Well—all right. W-wait till I get my purse," she stammered in what suddenly seemed like distress. She went away again.

When she returned, she handed me the exact amount of the fine and I said, "Thank you, Mrs. Stout, you know you can renew library books and avoid the fine," and I turned to leave. Then, to my great surprise, she suddenly reached out a hand and touched my arm lightly. I turned back to her.

She pointed to the top book of the pile I was carrying. "My grandson thought this one was particularly good," she said in a hushed murmur, and tapped her forefinger twice on the title. *The Robber of Featherbed Lane*. Both taps landed lightly on the word *Robber*. Her hand was shaking.

I went out to the street, deposited her books in the back seat of my car, and climbed under the wheel, vaguely troubled about Mrs. Stout. Old police habits of thought don't die easily. I couldn't help thinking that, if I were still a real cop, I'd be curious about the answers to several questions that occurred to me in connection with my visit to Mrs. Stout.

Question one—why was Mrs. Stout, normally a pleasant and light-hearted woman if her dimples and smile lines meant anything, so disagreeable, impolite and, yes, agitated, over my simple demand for a batch of overdue library books?

Question two—how come Mrs. Stout stammered noticeably sometimes and didn't stammer other times?

Question three—where was the driver of the *Heritage Cleaners* van that was still parked ahead of my car.

Question four—why did Mrs. Stout delay my departure at the last minute with a trite remark about her grandson when, up to them, she'd been trying like crazy to get rid of me?

Finally question five—how about that trembling finger tapping the word *Robber* so pointedly?

To tell you the truth, I didn't have the guts to drive away from Mrs. Stout's house leaving these questions unanswered behind me. I knew I'd feel like an all-American heel later on if I did. I've always been a sucker for women in distress, anyway. That's one reason why I'm not with the Police Department any longer.

So, I thought, *let's see if Mrs. Stout is really caught in a pickle.*

I looked up *Heritage Cleaners* in the telephone book and the City Directory—both of which I carry in my car to check addresses when I'm on the job—and you know what? There was no firm called *Heritage Cleaners* listed in either one. Yet not more than four feet ahead of my car's front bumper sat a dark green van with *Heritage Cleaners* lettered on the sides, big as life.

What would you think? What would anybody think? The same thing I thought, I'm sure. Except that what you'd do about it would probably be much more sensible than what I did about it. You'd call the cops. But I used to *be* a cop, so I thought I could handle Mrs. Stout's trouble by myself.

I crawled out of my car and went up the flagstone walk to Mrs. Stout's front door again. I rang the chimes again. In due course, the door was opened again. This time, though, it wasn't Mrs. Stout who faced me. It was a smooth-faced man of indeterminate age with a black mustache, long sideburns and hair cut as short as my own.

I said, "Mrs. Stout, you didn't give me back—*oh,* you're not Mrs. Stout, are you?"

"No," he said, "I'm Mr. Stout. Can I help you?"

"Well, I'm from the public library, Mr. Stout, and a few minutes ago, when I collected some overdue library books from your wife, she must have missed one. She paid the fines on all of them, but I checked the titles and she still has one book."

"Which book is that?" He raised an eyebrow.

I said the first thing that came into my mind. "A picture book called *Cato the Kiwi Bird*."

He nodded. "It's possible my wife still has it. But she's very busy right now. So come back some other time, okay?" He began to shut the door.

I lowered my right shoulder and charged the door with it like a defensive tackle on the blitz. I thought I could use the door as a battering ram to throw him off balance enough, even if he had a gun as seemed likely, to give me time in the confusion to get inside the house where I could handle him.

But no. A split second before my shoulder hit the closing door, he suddenly reversed his field and pulled the door wide *open* instead of slamming it shut. The result was that, failing to encounter the expected resistance to my lunge, I catapulted through the opening, tripped on the doorsill and went down full length on my face inside the entrance hall.

Then Mr. Stout closed the door. I heard it slam. I twisted my head around and caught a brief glimpse of a snub-nosed automatic in Mr. Stout's left hand. He stooped over me and ground the barrel of the gun painfully into my back at about the place where I imagine my right kidney is.

"What was that book again, friend?" he asked in an expressionless voice.

"*Cato the Kiwi Bird*," I repeated, feeling like a fool but also knowing that one little move now without his permission could get me killed.

"It sounds fascinating," he said. "I'll have to read it sometime."

I heard a swishing sound. Then my head exploded in a big burst of orange fireworks.

* * * *

The fireworks were still flashing faintly now as I looked across the library at poor Mrs. Stout, gagged with adhesive tape and tied in her chair with a pink sheet. I tried my voice again, and this time it came out much better.

"Mrs. Stout...)

She widened her eyes. There was still terror in them.

"He wasn't your husband, was he?" I said next. A dumb question.

She shook her head vigorously.

"I'm sorry," I said, struggling against the clothesline on my wrists. "He was too cute for me. Did he hurt you?"

She shook her head again. Tears were rolling down her cheeks.

"Good," I said. "Have I been out long?" My headache was making my thoughts hazy and muddled.

This time Mrs. Stout accompanied her headshake with a frantic cross-eyed look down her nose toward the mouth-sealing tape below it. Only then did it occur to me that the conversation was going to remain pretty one-sided unless I could somehow arrange for Mrs. Stout to join in.

I gave up on my wrists and tried wriggling my feet. They were tied together with more clothesline. Not crossed, and not tied to the chair—but tied together so tightly that I hardly knew they were mine. I was relieved, all the same. Maybe the guy who sapped me wasn't such an expert after all. No tape on my mouth, ankles not crossed, and not even fastened back under the chair seat to keep my feet off the ground. Amateur stuff.

I leaned forward, my weight tipping my chair onto its front legs, my bound feet the third leg of a tripod that made it easy for me to stay balanced that way. Then I straightened my legs, put my full weight on my feet, and began to hop very carefully, a few inches per hop, toward Mrs. Sout. I was hunched over like an arthritic dwarf, I had an antique ladder-back chair strapped to my back and legs, but my feet were on the floor and I was capable of locomotion of a sort. That was the important thing.

Reaching Mrs. Stout's chair, I paused and bent toward her face as though I was going to kiss her on the cheek. Instead, I nipped a corner of her adhesive tape between my teeth and ripped off her gag—far enough, anyway, so her mouth was uncovered. She winced and moaned as the tape came unstuck—all the same, she pulled her head back hard to help me dislodge the tape more easily.

The first sound that came out of her was a sob. The second was a name. "*Jamie*!"

"Who's Jamie?" I said.

Still crying, she worked her mouth painfully. "My husband!" she moaned then. "They took him away!" Her sobs came faster.

"They?" I said.

"Three of them. They had guns! Oh, Jamie…) She could hardly get the words out.

"I saw one of the guns," I remembered. "You said *three* men?"

She wailed, "And it's my fault they hurt *you*, too! That—that man untied me and made me answer the door when you rang. He told me to get rid of you if I didn't want to get shot. He—he pointed his gun at me all the time I was giving you those library books!"

"Forget it," I said. "You were brave to warn me the way you did. I was the dumb one." I tried to make my headache go away by shaking my head.

That made it worse. I said, "Two men took your husband and left one man here with you, the one who slugged me? Is that it?"

She nodded. "The one who hit you left ten minutes ago." Her eyes went to an electric clock on the desk to confirm that. "The telephone rang while he was tying you up, and he answered it, and then he left right away."

That explained my amateur tying job—he hadn't waited to finish. "What did he say on the telephone—could you hear?"

"He said 'Okay', that's all."

I began to see the pattern. "What time was it when they took your husband away?"

"We were still at breakfast—about ten minutes after eight, I guess." She closed her eyes and shivered uncontrollably.

"In your husband's car?" I asked, remembering the empty spot in the garage beside the Thunderbird.

She didn't seem to hear me. She started to squirm around frantically in her chair, trying to shed the twisted sheet that bound her and moaning like a wounded animal.

I tried again. "Mrs. Stout, where does your husband work?"

She sobbed convulsively, her mouth making ugly moues in her tear-streaked face. Her dimples made her look worse, somehow. The strip of adhesive tape was still dangling from one cheek and her eyes were wild. Hysteria was catching up with her.

I shouted to get through to her. "Mrs. *Stout*! *Listen* to me! Where does your husband work? *Work!* Tell me! Don't you want to save your husband Jamie?"

She stopped squirming as suddenly as though turned to stone. The wildness went out of her eyes. "He's the cashier of the Second Fidelity Bank," she said in a dead voice.

"Thanks," I said. I hopped three hops to the other side of the desk, where the telephone was, and set my chair down again on all four legs. Then I stretched forward as far as I could and flipped the telephone receiver off its stand by coming down hard on one end of it with my chin. It was a touch-type phone. The receiver fell face up on the desk, with the dialing buttons right there under my nose.

I took this as a good omen and dialed the police emergency number with it—my nose, I mean. I had to stop and wait, after each jab at a button, to give the receiver time to stop rocking on its spine, but I finally got the number dialed. Then I got my left ear as close to the receiver as I could, and waited for the police to answer.

When they did, I raised my voice in an official bellow and yelled "*Emergency!* Get me Lieutenant Randall!" The cop on the board must have thought I was a captain, at the least, because Randall was on the wire in almost exactly nothing flat.

"Lieutenant," I said, "this is Hal Johnson. Don't say anything, just listen for a minute, okay? I'm pretty sure the Second Fidelity Bank was robbed about half an hour ago by two men with the unwilling help of the bank's cashier, Mr. J. W. Stout. He was probably forced to open the vault after the time lock was off but before the bank opened for business at nine. The cashier's wife and I were held prisoner in Stout's home, one-five-two-five Washburn, by a third man during the heist. We're still prisoners.

"But get this—our guard left us fifteen minutes ago, immediately after getting a phone call here. He was probably going to pick up his pals and the loot somewhere near the bank downtown. He's driving a dark green Chevrolet van labeled *Heritage Cleaners* and should be about halfway to town by now on either Murchison or Cambria Avenue. There's still time to get the van—but don't stop it until it makes the pick-up. You got all that, Lieutenant?" I drew a deep breath.

As cool as a well-digger's shirt tail. "I got it," he said. "Hold on, Hal. Be right back."

He went away, presumably to start a little action. While he was gone, I sent comforting upside-down looks at Mrs. Stout, whose sobbing had now subsided to intermittent catches of breath. Four minutes ticked slowly by on the desk clock before I heard Lieutenant Randall's voice squeaking in the receiver again.

"I've got it started, Hal. We're checking on the bank and the cashier right now. Patrol car three-o-three has your green van in sight on Murchison. And I've got another car on its way to you."

"Fine," I said. "I'll tell Mrs. Stout that help is on the way."

* * * *

That evening, Lieutenant Randall telephoned me at home. "What happened to you," he asked, "after my man cut you loose this morning? With everybody waiting to give you the conquering hero treatment."

"*Hero* treatment?" I said. "Then the bank *was* robbed?"

"Sure. I been trying to locate you all afternoon to tell you."

"What about the cashier, Mr. Stout? Was he hurt?"

"Not a bit. Locked in the vault with the vault guard after the thieves had cleaned out the cash. Then they just walked out of the bank like two customers when the bank opened at nine."

"You nailed them, I hope?"

"Sure. Your green van led us right to them—and to the loot, too, Hal. Don't overlook the loot. Two hundred and twelve thousand dollars. That's why the hero treatment was ready for you, boy. Mrs. Stout told us how you happened to get mixed up in the thing. So why didn't you stick around to take a bow?"

"I had a hell of a headache," I said.

"Too bad, too bad," Randall said. I knew his cat-yellow eyes would be as bland and unfeeling as two egg yolks, even as he sympathized. "The fellow who slugged you was Teddy Thurbald, incidentally. A pro. How's the headache now?"

"I still have it," I said.

"Then why'd you go back to work this afternoon?"

"I didn't. I came home to bed."

He clicked his tongue. "You always were soft-headed, Hal—especially about broads. You haven't changed."

I didn't answer that one. "Well, you'll probably be okay by Monday. Mr. and Mrs. Stout can thank you then."

I said, "They'll have to do more than thank me. They owe me money."

Randall sounded scandalized. "You mean you want a *reward* for helping those nice people and their bank?"

"Hell, no," I said, "but since I took the day off today, I won't get Mrs. Stout's overdue library books back to the library until Monday. So they owe me three more days' fines."

"They shouldn't begrudge that," said Randall, "since you saved the bank two hundred and twelve grand. Matter of fact, this whole thing is going to look good enough on *my* record so that I might even pay your extra fines myself. How much do they come to?"

"Eighty-one cents," I said grouchily and hung up. My head was killing me.

STILL A COP

Originally published in* Ellery Queen's Mystery Magazine, *December 1975.

Lieutenant Randall telephoned me on Tuesday, catching me in my cell-sized office at the public library just after I'd finished lunch.

"Hal?" he said. "How come you're not out playing patty-cake with the book borrowers?" Randall still resents my leaving the police department to become a library detective—what he calls a "sissy cop." Nowadays my assignments involve nothing more dangerous than tracing stolen and overdue books for the public library.

I said, "Even a library cop has to eat, Lieutenant. What's on your mind?"

"Same old thing. Murder."

"I haven't killed anyone for over a week," I said.

His voice took on a definite chill. "Somebody killed a young fellow we took out of the river this morning. Shot him through the head. And tortured him beforehand."

"Sorry," I said. I'd forgotten how grim it was to be a Homicide cop. "Tortured, did you say?"

"Yeah. Cigar burns all over him. I need information, Hal."

"About what?"

"You ever hear of *The Damion Complex*?"

"Sure. It's the title of a spy novel published last year."

"I thought it might be a book." There was satisfaction in Randall's voice now. "Next question: you have that book in the public library?"

"Of course. Couple of copies, probably."

"Do they have different numbers or something to tell them apart?"

"Yes, they do. Why?"

"Find out for me if one of your library copies of *The Damion Complex* has this number on it, will you?" He paused and I could hear paper rustling. "ES4187."

"Right," I said. "I'll get back to you in ten minutes." Then, struck by something familiar about the number, I said, "No, wait, hold it a minute, Lieutenant."

I pulled out of my desk drawer the list of overdue library books I'd received the previous morning and checked it hurriedly. "Bingo," I said into the phone, "I picked up that book with that very number yesterday morning. How about that? Do you want it?"

"I want it."

"For what?"

"Evidence, maybe."

"In your torture-murder case?"

He lost patience. "Look, just get hold of the book for me, Hal. I'll tell you about it when I pick it up, okay?"

"Okay, Lieutenant. When?"

"Ten minutes." He sounded eager.

I hung up and called Ellen on the checkout desk. "Listen, sweetheart," I said to her because it makes her mad to be called sweetheart and she's extremely attractive when she's mad, "can you find me *The Damion Complex*, copy number ES4187? I brought it in yesterday among the overdues."

"*The Damion Complex?*" She took down the number. "I'll call you back, Hal." She didn't sound a bit mad. Maybe she was softening up at last. I'd asked her to marry me 17 times in the last six months, but she was still making up her mind.

In two minutes she called me back. "It's out again," she reported. "It went out on card number 3888 yesterday after you brought it in."

Lieutenant Randall was going to love that. "Who is card number 3888?"

"A Miss Oradell Murphy."

"Address?"

She gave it to me, an apartment on Leigh Street.

"Telephone number?"

"I thought you might be able to look that up yourself." She was tart. "I'm busy out here."

"Thank you, sweetheart," I said. "Will you marry me?"

"Not now. I told you I'm busy." She hung up. But she did it more gently than usual, it seemed to me. She *was* softening up. My spirits lifted.

Lieutenant Randall arrived in less than the promised ten minutes. "Where is it?" he asked, fixing me with his cat stare. He seemed too big to fit into my office. "You got it for me?"

I shook my head. "It went out again yesterday. Sorry."

He grunted in disappointment, took a look at my spindly visitor's chair, and decided to remain standing. "Who borrowed it?"

I told him Miss Oradell Murphy, Apartment 3A at the Harrington Arms on Leigh Street.

"Thanks." He tipped a hand and turned to leave.

"Wait a minute. Where you going, Lieutenant?"

"To get the book."

"Those apartments at Harrington Arms are efficiencies," I said. "Mostly occupied by single working women. So maybe Miss Murphy won't be home right now. Why not call first?"

He nodded. I picked up my phone and gave our switchboard girl Miss Murphy's telephone number. Randall fidgeted nervously.

"No answer," the switchboard reported.

I grinned at Randall. "See? Nobody home."

"I need that book." Randall sank into the spindly visitor's chair and sighed in frustration.

"You were going to tell me why."

"Here's why." He fished a damp crumpled bit of paper out of an envelope he took from his pocket. I reached for it. He held it away. "Don't touch it," he said. "We found it on the kid we pulled from the river this morning. It's the only damn thing we did find on him. No wallet, no money, no identification, no clothing labels, no nothing. Except for this he was plucked as clean as a chicken. We figure it was overlooked. It was in the bottom of his shirt pocket."

"What's it say?" I could see water-smeared writing.

He grinned unexpectedly, although his yellow eyes didn't seem to realize that the rest of his face was smiling. "It says: *PL Damion Complex ES4187*."

"That's all?"

"That's all."

"Great bit of deduction, Lieutenant," I said. "You figured the *PL* for Public Library?"

"All by myself."

"So what's it mean?"

"How do I know till I get the damn book?" He sat erect and went on briskly, "Who had the book before Miss Murphy?"

I consulted my overdue list from the day before. "Gregory Hazzard. Desk clerk at the Starlight Motel on City Line. I picked up seven books and fines from him yesterday."

The Lieutenant was silent for a moment. Then, "Give Miss Murphy another try, will you?"

She still didn't answer her phone.

Randall stood up. My chair creaked when he removed his weight. "Let's go see this guy Hazzard."

"Me, too?"

"You, too." He gave me the fleeting grin again. "You're mixed up in this, son."

"I don't see how."

"Your library owns the book. And you belong to the library. So move your tail."

Gregory Hazzard was surprised to see me again so soon. He was a middle-aged skeleton, with a couple of pounds of skin and gristle fitted over his bones so tightly that he looked like the object of an anatomy lesson. His clothes hung on him—snappy men's wear on a scarecrow. "You got all my overdue books yesterday," he greeted me.

"I know, Mr. Hazzard. But my friend here wants to ask you about one of them."

"Who's your friend?" He squinted at Randall.

"Lieutenant Randall, City Police."

Hazzard blinked. "Another cop? We went all through that with the boys from your robbery detail day before yesterday."

Randall's eyes flickered. Otherwise he didn't change expression. "I'm not here about that. I'm interested in one of your library books."

"Which one?"

"*The Damion Complex*."

Hazzard bobbed his skull on his pipestem neck. "That one. Just a so-so yarn. You can find better spy stories in your newspaper."

Randall ignored that. "You live here in the motel, Mr. Hazzard?"

"No. With my sister down the street a ways, in a duplex."

"This is your address on the library records," I broke in. "The Starlight Motel."

"Sure. Because this is where I read all the books I borrow. And where I work."

"Don't you ever take library books home?" Randall asked.

"No. I leave 'em here, right at this end of the desk, out of the way. I read 'em during slack times, you know? When I finish them I take 'em back to the library and get another batch. I'm a fast reader."

"But your library books were overdue. If you're such a fast reader, how come?"

"He was sick for three weeks," I told Randall. "Only got back to work Saturday."

The Lieutenant's lips tightened and I knew from old experience that he wanted me to shut up. "That right?" he asked Hazzard. "You were sick?"

"As a dog. Thought I was dying. So'd my sister. That's why my books were overdue."

"They were here on the desk all the time you were sick?"

"Right. Cost me a pretty penny in fines, too, I must say. Hey, Mr. Johnson?"

I laughed. "Big deal. Two ninety-four, wasn't it?"

He chuckled so hard I thought I could hear his bones rattle. "Cheapest pleasure we got left, free books from the public library." He sobered suddenly. "What's so important about *The Damion Complex*, Lieutenant?"

"Wish I knew." Randall signaled me with his eyes. "Thanks, Mr. Hazzard, you've been helpful. We'll be in touch." He led the way out to the police car.

On the way back to town he turned aside ten blocks and drove to the Harrington Arms Apartments on Leigh Street. "Maybe we'll get lucky," he said as he pulled up at the curb. "If Murphy's home, get the book from her, Hal, okay? No need to mention the police."

A comely young lady, half out of a nurse's white uniform and evidently just home from work, answered my ring at Apartment 3A. "Yes?" she said, hiding her dishabille by standing behind the door and peering around its edge.

"Miss Oradell Murphy?"

"Yes." She had a fetching way of raising her eyebrows.

I showed her my ID card and gave her a cock-and-bull story about *The Damion Complex* having been issued to her yesterday by mistake. "The book should have been destroyed," I said, "because the previous borrower read it while she was ill with an infectious disease."

"Oh," Miss Murphy said. She gave me the book without further questions.

When I returned to the police car Lieutenant Randall said, "Gimme," and took the book from me, handling it with a finicky delicacy that seemed odd in such a big man. By his tightening lips I could follow his growing frustration as he examined *The Damion Complex*. For it certainly seemed to be just an ordinary copy of another ordinary book from the public library. The library name was stamped on it in the proper places. Identification number ES4187. Card pocket, with regulation date card, inside the front cover. Nothing concealed between its pages, not even a pressed forget-me-not.

"What the hell?" the Lieutenant grunted.

"Code message?" I suggested.

He was contemptuous. "Code message? You mean certain words off certain pages? In that case why was this particular copy specified—number ES4187? Any copy would do."

"Unless the message is in the book itself. In invisible ink? Or indicated by pin pricks over certain words?" I showed my teeth at him. "After all, it's a spy novel."

We went over the book carefully twice before we found the negative. And no wonder. It was very small—no more than half an inch or maybe five-eighths—and shoved deep in the pocket inside the front cover, behind the date card.

Randall held it up to the light. "Too small to make out what it is," I said. "We need a magnifying glass."

"Hell with that." Randall threw his car into gear. "I'll get Jerry to make me a blowup." Jerry is the police photographer. "I'll drop you off at the library."

"Oh, no, Lieutenant. I'm mixed up in this. You said so yourself. I'm sticking until I see what's on that negative." He grunted.

Half an hour later I was in Randall's office at headquarters when the police photographer came in and threw a black-and-white 3½ by 4½ print on the Lieutenant's desk. Randall allowed me to look over his shoulder as he examined it.

Its quality was poor. It was grainy from enlargement, and the images were slightly blurred, as though the camera had been moved just as the picture was snapped. But it was plain enough so that you could make out two men sitting facing each other across a desk. One was facing the camera directly; the other showed only as part of a rear-view silhouette—head, right shoulder, right arm.

The right arm, however, extended into the light on the desk top and could be seen quite clearly. It was lifting from an open briefcase on the desk a transparent bag of white powder, about the size of a pound of sugar. The briefcase contained three more similar bags. The man who was full face to the camera was reaching out a hand to accept the bag of white powder.

Lieutenant Randall said nothing for what seemed a long time. Then all he did was grunt noncommittally.

I said, "Heroin, Lieutenant?"

"Could be."

"Big delivery. Who's the guy making the buy? Do you know?"

He shrugged. "We'll find out."

"When you make him, you'll have your murderer. Isn't that what you're thinking?"

He shrugged again. "How do you read it, Hal?"

"Easy. The kid you pulled from the river got this picture somehow, decided to cut himself in by a little blackmail, and got killed for his pains."

"And tortured. Why tortured?" Randall was just using me as a sounding board.

"To force him to tell where the negative was hidden? He wouldn't have taken the negative with him when he braced the dope peddler."

"Hell of a funny place to hide a negative," Randall said. "You got any ideas about that?"

I went around Randall's desk and sat down. "I can guess. The kid sets up his blackmail meeting with the dope peddler, starts out with both the negative and a print of it, like this one, to keep his date. At the last minute he has second thoughts about carrying the negative with him."

"Where's he starting out from?" Randall squeezed his hands together.

"The Starlight Motel. Where else?"

"Go on."

"So maybe he decides to leave the negative in the motel safe and stops at the desk in the lobby to do so. But Hazzard is in the can, maybe. Or has stepped out to the restaurant for coffee. The kid has no time to waste. So he shoves the little negative into one of Hazzard's library books temporarily, making a quick note of the book title and library number so he can find it again. You found the note in his shirt pocket. How's that sound?"

Randall gave me his half grin and said, "So long, Hal. Thanks for helping."

I stood up. "I need a ride to the library. You've wasted my whole afternoon. You going to keep my library book?"

"For a while. But I'll be in touch."

"You'd better be. Unless you want to pay a big overdue fine."

* * * *

It was the following evening before I heard any more from Lieutenant Randall. He telephoned me at home. "Catch any big bad book thieves today, Hal?" he began in a friendly voice.

"No. You catch any murderers?"

"Not yet. But I'm working on it."

I laughed. "You're calling to report progress, is that it?"

"That's it." He was as bland as milk.

"Proceed," I said.

"We found out who the murdered kid was."

"Who?"

"A reporter named Joel Homer from Cedar Falls. Worked for the *Cedar Falls Herald*. The editor tells me Homer was working on a special assignment the last few weeks. Trying to crack open a story on dope in the Tri-Cities."

"Oho. Then it *is* dope in the picture?"

"Reasonable to think so, anyway."

"How'd you find out about the kid? The Starlight Motel?"

"Yeah. Your friend Hazzard, the desk clerk, identified him for us. Remembered checking him into Room 18 on Saturday morning. His overnight bag was still in the room and his car in the parking lot."

"Well, it's nice to know who got killed," I said, "but you always told me you'd rather know who did the killing. Find out who the guy in the picture is?"

"He runs a ratty cafe on the river in Overbrook, just out of town. Name of Williams."

"Did you tie up the robbery squeal Hazzard mentioned when we were out there yesterday?"

"Could be. One man, masked, held up the night clerk, got him to open the office safe, and cleaned it out. Nothing much in it, matter of fact—hundred bucks or so."

"Looking for that little negative, you think?"

"Possibly, yeah."

"Why don't you nail this Williams and find out?"

"On the strength of that picture?" Randall said. "Uh-uh. That was enough to put him in a killing mood, maybe, but it's certainly not enough to convict him of murder. He could be buying a pound of sugar. No, I'm going to be sure of him before I take him."

"How do you figure to make sure of him, for God's sake?"

I shouldn't have asked that, because as a result I found myself, two hours later, sitting across that same desk—the one in the snapshot—from Mr. Williams, suspected murderer. We were in a sizable back room in Williams' cafe in Overbrook. A window at the side of the room was open, but the cool weed-scented breeze off the river didn't keep me from sweating.

"You said on the phone you thought I might be interested in a snapshot you found," Williams said. He was partially bald. Heavy black eyebrows met over his nose. The eyes under them looked like brown agate marbles in milk. He was smoking a fat cigar.

"That's right," I said.

"Why?"

"I figured it could get you in trouble in certain quarters, that's all."

He blew smoke. "What do you mean by that?"

"It's actually a picture of you buying heroin across this desk right here. Or maybe selling it."

"Well, well," he said, "that's interesting all right. If true." He was either calm and cool or trying hard to appear so.

"It's true," I said. "You're very plain in the picture. So's the heroin." I gave him the tentative smile of a timid, frightened man. It wasn't hard to do, because I felt both timid and frightened.

"Where is this picture of yours?" Williams asked.

"Right here." I handed him the print Lieutenant Randall had given me.

He looked at it without any change of expression I could see. Finally he took another drag on his cigar. "This guy does resemble me a little. But how did *you* happen to know that?"

I jerked a thumb over my shoulder. "I been in your cafe lots of times. I recognized you."

He studied the print. "You're right about one thing. This picture might be misunderstood. So maybe we can deal. What I can't understand is where you found the damn thing."

"In a book I borrowed from the public library."

"A book?" He halted his cigar in midair, startled.

"Yes. A spy novel. I dropped the book accidentally and this picture fell out of the inside card pocket." I put my hand into my jacket pocket and touched the butt of the pistol that Randall had issued me for the occasion. I needed comfort.

"You found this print in a book?"

"Not this print, no. I made it myself out of curiosity. I'm kind of an amateur photographer, see? When I found what I had, I thought maybe you might be interested, that's all. Are you?"

"How many prints did you make?"

"Just the one."

"And where's the negative?"

"I've got it, don't worry."

"With you?"

"You think I'm nuts?" I said defensively. I started a hand toward my hip pocket, then jerked it back nervously.

Mr. Williams smiled and blew cigar smoke. "What do you think might be a fair price?" he asked.

I swallowed. "Would twenty thousand dollars be too much?"

His eyes changed from brown marbles to white slits. "That's pretty steep."

"But you'll pay it?" I tried to put a touch of triumph into my expression.

"Fifteen. When you turn over the negative to me."

"Okay," I said, sighing with relief. "How long will it take you to get the money?"

"No problem. I've got it right here when you're ready to deal." His eyes went to a small safe in a corner of the room. Maybe the heroin was there, too, I thought.

"Hey!" I said. "That's great, Mr. Williams! Because I've got the negative here, too. I was only kidding before." I fitted my right hand around the gun butt in my pocket. With my left I pulled out my wallet and threw it on the desk between us.

"In here?" Williams said, opening the wallet.

"In the little pocket."

He found the tiny negative at once.

He took a magnifying glass from his desk drawer and used it to look at the negative against the ceiling light. Then he nodded, satisfied. He raised his voice a little and said, "Okay, Otto."

Otto? I heard a door behind me scrape over the rug as it was thrust open. Turning in my chair, I saw a big man emerge from a closet and step toward me. My eyes went instantly to the gun in his hand. It was fitted with a silencer, and oddly, the man's right middle finger was curled around the trigger. Then I saw why. The tip of his right index finger was missing. The muzzle of the gun looked as big and dark as Mammoth Cave to me.

"He's all yours, Otto," Williams said. "I've got the negative. No wonder you couldn't find it in the motel safe. The crazy kid hid it in a library book."

"I heard," Otto said flatly.

I still had my hand in my pocket touching the pistol, but I realized I didn't have a chance of beating Otto to a shot, even if I shot through my pocket. I stood up very slowly and faced Otto. He stopped far enough away from me to be just out of reach.

Williams said, "No blood in here this time, Otto. Take him out back. Don't forget his wallet and labels. And it won't hurt to spoil his face a little before you put him in the river. He's local."

Otto kept his eyes on me. They were paler than his skin. He nodded. "I'll handle it."

"Right." Williams started for the door that led to his cafe kitchen, giving me an utterly indifferent look as he went by. "So long, smart boy," he said. He went through the door and closed it behind him.

Otto cut his eyes to the left to make sure Williams had closed the door tight. I used that split second to dive headfirst over Williams' desk, my hand still in my pocket on my gun. I lit on the floor behind the desk with a painful thump and Williams' desk chair, which I'd overturned in my plunge, came crashing down on top of me.

From the open window at the side of the room a new voice said conversationally, "Drop the gun, Otto."

Apparently Otto didn't drop it fast enough because Lieutenant Randall shot it out of his hand before climbing through the window into the room. Two uniformed cops followed him.

* * * *

Later, over a pizza and beer in the Trocadero All-Night Diner, Randall said, "We could have taken Williams before. The Narc Squad has known for some time he's a peddler. But we didn't know who was supplying him."

I said stiffly, "I thought I was supposed to be trying to hang a murder on him. How did that Otto character get into the act?"

"After we set up your meeting with Williams, he phoned Otto to come over to his cafe and take care of another would-be blackmailer."

"Are you telling me you didn't think Williams was the killer?"

Randall shook his head, looking slightly sheepish. "I was pretty sure Williams wouldn't risk Murder One. Not when he had a headlock on somebody who'd do it for him."

"Like Otto?"

"Like Otto."

"Well, just who the hell *is* Otto?"

"He's the other man in the snapshot with Williams."

Something in the way he said it made me ask him, "You mean you knew who he was *before* you asked me to go through that charade tonight?"

"Sure. I recognized him in the picture."

I stopped chewing my pizza and stared at him. I was dumfounded, as they say. "Are you nuts?" I said with my mouth full. "The picture just showed part of a silhouette. From behind, at that. Unrecognizable."

"You didn't look close enough." Randall gulped beer. "His right hand showed in the picture plain. With the end of his right index finger gone."

"But how could you recognize a man from that?"

"Easy. Otto Schmidt of our Narcotics Squad is missing the end of his right index finger. Had it shot off by a junkie in a raid."

"There are maybe a hundred guys around with fingers like that. You must have had more to go on than that, Lieutenant."

"I did. The heroin."

"You recognized that, too?" I was sarcastic.

"Sure. It was the talk of the department a week ago, Hal."

"What was?"

"The heroin. Somebody stole it right out of the Narc Squad's own safe at headquarters." He laughed aloud. "Can you believe it? Two kilos, packaged in four bags, just like in the picture."

I said, "How come it wasn't in the news?"

"You know why. It would make us look like fools."

"Anyway, one bag of heroin looks just like every other," I said, unconvinced.

"You didn't see the *big* blowup I had made of that picture," the lieutenant said. "A little tag on one of the bags came out real clear. You could read it."

All at once I felt very tired. “Don’t tell me,” I said.

He told me anyway, smiling. “It said: Confiscated, such and such a date, such and such a raid, by the Grandhaven Police Department. That’s us, Hal. Remember?”

I sighed. “So you’ve turned up another crooked cop,” I said. “Believe me, I’m glad I’m out of the business, Lieutenant.”

“You’re *not* out of it.” Randall’s voice roughened with some emotion I couldn’t put a name to. “You’re still a cop, Hal.”

“I’m an employee of the Grandhaven Public Library.”

“Library fuzz. But still a cop.”

I shook my head.

“You helped me take a killer tonight, didn’t you?”

“Yeah. Because you fed me a lot of jazz about needing somebody who didn’t *smell* of cop. Somebody who knew the score but could act the part of a timid greedy citizen trying his hand at blackmail for the first time.”

“Otto Schmidt’s a city cop. If I’d sent another city cop in there tonight, Otto would have recognized him immediately. That’s why I asked you to go.”

“You could have told me the facts.”

He shook his head. “Why? I thought you’d do better without knowing. And you did. The point is, though, that you *did* it. Helped me nail a killer at considerable risk to yourself. Even if the killer wasn’t the one you thought. You didn’t do it just for kicks, did you? Or because we found the negative in your library book, for God’s sake?”

I shrugged and stood up to leave.

“So you see what I mean?” Lieutenant Randall said. “You’re still a cop.” He grinned at me. “I’ll get the check, Hal. And thanks for the help.”

I left without even saying good night. I could feel his yellow eyes on my back all the way out of the diner.

THE MUTILATED SCHOLAR

Originally published in* Ellery Queen's Mystery Magazine, *April 1976.

I was standing in the rear of a crowded bus when I caught sight of the stolen library book.

It was the wildest coincidence, the sheerest accident. For I don't ride a bus even twice a year. And normally I can't tell one copy of a particular library book from another.

I craned my neck to get a clearer view past the fellow hanging to a bus strap beside me. And I knew immediately that I wasn't making any mistake. That library book tucked under the arm of the neatly dressed girl a few seats forward was, without a doubt, one of the 52 library books which had been in the trunk of my old car when it was stolen six weeks before. The police had recovered my car three days later. The books, however, were missing—until I spotted this one on the bus.

Maybe I'd better explain how I recognized it.

As a library cop, I run down overdue and stolen books for the Public Library. I'd been collecting overdues that day, and about eleven in the morning I'd got back a bunch of books from a wealthy old lady who'd borrowed them from the library to read on a round-the-world cruise. She couldn't have cared less when I told her how much money in fines she owed the library after ten weeks' delinquency. And she couldn't have cared less, either, when I taxed her with defacing one of the books.

It was a novel called *The Scholar*, and she'd deliberately—in an idle moment on the cruise, no doubt—made three separate burns on the cover with the end of her cigarette, to form two eyes and a nose inside the O of the word scholar. I was pretty irritated with her, because that sort of thing is in the same class with drawing mustaches on subway-poster faces, so I charged her two bucks for defacing the book in addition to the fine for overdue. You can see why I'd remember that particular copy of *The Scholar*.

I scrutinized the girl now holding it under her arm on the bus. She certainly didn't look like the kind of girl who goes around stealing old cars and Public Library books. She was maybe 30 years old, well-dressed in a casual way, with a pretty, high-cheekboned face and taffy-colored (dyed?) hair, stylishly coiffured.

A crowded bus wasn't exactly the best place to brace her about the book, nevertheless I began to squeeze my way toward her between the jammed passengers.

I wanted to know about that book because I still winced every time I recalled the mirth of Lieutenant Randall of the Police Department when I called him that first day to report the theft of my car and books. First he had choked with honest laughter, then he accused me of stealing my own library books so I could make myself look good by finding them again, and finally he offered to bet I had sunk my car in the river somewhere so I could collect the insurance on it. The idea of a book detective being robbed of his own books sent him into paroxysms. It was understandable. I used to work for him and he's always needled me about quitting the police to become a "sissy" library cop.

The girl with the book was seated near the center doors of the bus. I managed to maneuver my way to a standing position in front of her, leaned over, and in a friendly voice said, "Excuse me, Miss. Would you mind telling me where you got that library book you're holding?"

Her head tilted back and she looked up at me, startled. "What?" she said in a surprised contralto.

"That book," I said, pointing to *The Scholar*. "My name is Hal Johnson and I'm from the Public Library and I wonder if you'd mind telling me where—"

That was as far as I got. She glanced out the window, pulled the cord to inform the bus driver of her desire to get off, and as she squeezed by me toward the center doors of the bus she said, "Excuse me, this is my stop. This book is just one I got in the usual—"

The rest of what she said was lost in the sound of the bus doors swishing open. The girl went lithely down the two steps to the sidewalk and made off at a brisk pace. I was too late to follow her out of the bus before the doors closed, but I prevailed on the driver to reopen them with some choice abuse about poor citizens who were carried blocks beyond their stops by insensitive bus drivers who didn't keep the doors open long enough for a fast cat to slip through them.

While I carried on my dispute with the bus driver, I'd kept my eye on the hurrying figure of the girl with *The Scholar* under her arm. So when I gained the sidewalk at last, I started out at a rapid trot in the direction she'd gone.

Being considerably longer-legged than she was, I was right behind her when she approached the revolving doors to Perry's Department Store. Whether or not she realized I was following her I didn't know. As she waited for an empty slot in the revolving door, a middle-aged, red-haired woman came out. She caught sight of my quarry and said in a hearty tone, loud enough for me to hear quite plainly, "Why, hello, Gloria! You here for the dress sale too?"

Gloria mumbled something and was whisked into the store by the revolving door. I hesitated a moment, then stepped in front of the red-haired woman and said politely, "That girl you just spoke to—the one you called Gloria—I'm sure I know her from somewhere—"

The red-haired woman grinned at me. "I doubt it, buster," she said, "unless you get your hair styled at Heloise's Beauty Salon on the South Side. That's where Gloria works. She does my hair every Tuesday afternoon at three."

"Oh," I said. "What's her last name, do you know?"

"I've no idea." She sailed by me and breasted the waves of pedestrian traffic flowing past the store entrance. I went through the revolving door into Perry's and looked around anxiously. Gloria, the hairdresser, was nowhere in sight.

After a moment's survey of the five o'clock crowd jamming the store's aisles, I turned away. I was due to meet Susan for drinks and dinner at The Chanticleer in half an hour. And I figured Susan, whom I hoped to lure away from the checkout desk at the Public Library into marriage with me, was more important than a stolen copy of *The Scholar*. Especially since I now knew where to find Gloria and the stolen book.

Some of my pickups next morning were on the South Side, so it wasn't out of my way to stop at Heloise's Beauty Salon. I went in, and, letting my eyes rove uneasily about the shop, feeling self-conscious, I asked at the reception counter if I could speak to Gloria for a minute.

"Gloria Dexter?" said the pretty black receptionist. "I'm afraid you can't. She's not here this morning."

"Her day off?"

"No. Yesterday was her day off."

"How come she's not here today?"

"We don't know. She just didn't show up. She usually calls in if she can't make it, but this morning she didn't."

"Did you try telephoning her?" I asked.

She nodded. "No answer."

"Well," I said, "maybe I can stop by her home. All I wanted to ask her about was a library book that's overdue. Where's she live?"

After I'd shown her my ID card, the receptionist told me Gloria Dexter's address. I thanked her and left.

The address wasn't fifteen minutes away. It turned out to be a single efficiency apartment perched on top of what used to be a small gatehouse to a private estate. The private estate was now two fourteen-story highrises set back from the street in shaded grounds. The only way up to Gloria's apartment was by a rusty outside stairway rather like a fire escape.

I was just starting up it when somebody behind me yelled, "Hey!"

I stopped and turned around. The hail had come from a burly man in dirty slacks and a T-shirt, who was clipping a hedge behind the gatehouse. "No use going up there. Mister," he informed me, strolling over to the foot of Gloria's staircase. "Miss Dexter isn't there."

I'd been expecting that. I said, "Do you know where she is?"

"At Memorial Hospital probably," he replied, "or the morgue. They took her off in an ambulance a couple of hours ago. I was the one who found her."

I hadn't been expecting that. "Did she have an accident or something?"

"She sure did. Fell all the way down that iron staircase you're standing on. Caved in her skull, it looked like to me."

I assimilated this news in silence. Then, "You found her at the bottom of this staircase?"

"Yep. Like a ragdoll."

"What time?"

"Eight thirty this morning when I came to work. I'm the yardman here. The ambulance boys said she'd been dead for quite a while, so she musta taken her tumble last night sometime." Remembering the pretty receptionist at Heloise's Beauty Salon, I said, "I stopped at the beauty shop where she works before I came here. They're worrying about her because she didn't show this morning. Maybe you ought to let them know."

"Never thought of that. Who'd you say you were, Mister?"

I showed him my ID card. "I wanted to see Miss Dexter about an overdue library book," I said. "Say, could I go up and get the book out of her place now? It'll save the library a lot of bother later on."

"Go ahead," the yardman said. "On second thought, I'll come with you, to see you don't take nothing but your library book." He grinned, exposing stained teeth. "Besides, you can't get in her place 'less I let you in. It's locked."

We climbed the rusty iron steps together. He unlocked the door at the top and we went into the Dexter apartment. It was as simple, pretty, and tasteful as Gloria herself. A daybed with a nubby red-and-gold coverlet stood against one wall, and over the bed there was a single hanging shelf filled with books.

I went straight to the bookshelf. "The book I want should be here somewhere," I said to the yardman. My eyes went down the row of spines. *The Scholar* wasn't there. Neither was any of the other 51 library books that had been stolen with my car.

"Take a look in her kitchenette and bathroom," the yardman advised me. "People read books in funny places."

A quick search failed to turn up *The Scholar* anywhere in the apartment.

The yardman was becoming impatient. "Tough luck," he said. "I guess you'll have to wait for the book and get it the hard way." He looked at the telephone on a dropleaf table near the kitchenette door. "I'll call her beauty shop from here," he said. "It'll be handier." He opened the telephone book, then hesitated. "What's the name of the place, anyhow?" he asked me. "Some fancy French name I can't remember."

"I'll look it up for you," I said. "Heloise's Beauty Salon is what it's called. With an H." I riffled through the telephone book and found the number for him. Another number on the same page was underlined in red. The yardman thanked me and I thanked him, and as I left, he was dialing the beauty shop.

* * * *

My car was stifling when I climbed back into it. I rolled down the windows and sat for a couple of minutes, trying to figure out what to do next. Finally I drove downtown, left my car in the parking lot behind Perry's Department Store, and went inside.

At the Lost and Found counter I asked the girl, "Has a Public Library book been turned in recently?"

She gave me a funny look and said. "Yes, the clean-up crew-found one in a trash basket."

"Mine," I said with relief. "May I have it, please?"

"Can you describe it?" she said.

"Sure. The title is *The Scholar*. There are three cigarette burns inside the O on the cover. Like eyes and a nose." When she looked prim I added, "Somebody else put them there, not me."

She was suddenly businesslike. "That's the book, all right. But we don't have it here. You'll have to claim it at the Security Office." She dropped her eyes. "I turned it over to them a few minutes ago."

"What did you do that for?" I asked curiously.

"Ask Security," she said. "Mr. Helmut."

"I will. Mr. Helmut. Where can I find him?"

She pointed toward the balcony that ran along one side of Perry's street floor. "Up there. Behind the partitions."

I mounted to the balcony and pushed open an opaque glass door with the word *Security Office* stenciled on it. An unattractive girl with dull eyes behind horn-rimmed glasses was sitting at a desk inside the door, typing.

She asked me what I wanted in a no-nonsense voice that didn't go with her bitten fingernails.

"You the Security Chief?" I asked, giving her my best smile.

"Don't be silly!" she answered sharply. "Mr. Helmut is our Security Chief."

"Then I'd like to see him for a minute, please."

"He's out in the store making his morning round. Maybe I can help you?"

"Your Lost and Found desk sent me up here to ask about a book from the Public Library that was found in the store last night."

She gave me a blank look. "I'm sorry. I don't know anything about any library book. Mr. Helmut ought to be back soon if you'd care to wait." She waved at one of those form-fitting chairs for which I understand the Swedes are responsible. I sat down in it.

Ten minutes later a burly black-browed man with long sideburns pushed open the Security door and came in. He paused abruptly when he saw me. He had my stolen copy of *The Scholar* in his hand.

"Mr. Helmut," his secretary fluted, "this gentleman is waiting to see you about a library book."

He shot me a sharp glance out of quick intelligent brown eyes and said, "Okay. Come on in." He held the door to his private office open and I preceded him inside. He motioned me to a straight chair and sat down behind a desk bearing a small metal sign that read *C. B. HELMUT*. He put my library book on the desk top and raised his black eyebrows at me.

"A library book?" he inquired. "This one?" He pointed at *The Scholar*.

I nodded. "That's the one. It was stolen from me some time ago, Mr. Helmut. The reason I'm here is that yesterday, on a bus, I saw a girl carrying it under her arm. I recognized it by those burns on the cover. When I tried to ask the girl about it, she ducked into your store—maybe to brush me off in the crowd of shoppers, or maybe to get rid of the stolen book before anybody caught her with it."

"The clean-up crew found it in a trash basket here last night," Helmut said.

"So your Lost and Found girl told me. She also told me the book was turned over to her first. Then she turned it over to you. Mind telling me why?"

"Routine security measure, that's all." Helmut ran a thick finger over the cigarette burns on the cover of *The Scholar*. He was enjoying himself, acting the important executive.

"Security measure?" I said. "How does store security come into it?"

Idly he opened the cover of *The Scholar* and leafed through the first 20 pages or so in a leisurely manner, wetting his fingertip to turn the pages.

Then suddenly he said, "Look here, Mr. Johnson," and held out the opened book for my inspection. *The Scholar* was a 400-page book, more than two inches thick. The copy Helmut held out to me was only a dummy book. The insides had been cut out to within half an inch of each edge, so that the book was now, in effect, an empty box, its covers and the few pages left intact at front and back concealing a cavity about seven inches long, four wide, and an inch and a half deep.

I said, "So that's it."

"That's it." Helmut echoed me. "A shoplifting gimmick. You see how it works? Shoplifter comes into the store, puts down her library book on the counter while she examines merchandise, and when our salesclerk isn't looking, the shoplifter merely opens the book and pops in a wrist watch or a diamond pin or a couple of lipsticks or whatever and walks out with them, cool as you please."

Helmut shook his head in reluctant admiration. "Can you imagine a more innocent-looking hiding place for stolen goods than a Public Library book? Why, it even lends class to the shoplifter, gives her literary respectability."

"Shoplifting!" was all I could think of to say.

"Pilferage ran almost a million bucks in this store last year," Helmut went on. "Most of it shoplifting. So we're pretty well onto the usual dodges—shopping bags with false bottoms, loose coats with big inside pockets, girls leaving fitting rooms with three or four sweaters under the one they wore going in, and so on. But this library-book trick is a new one on me. And it's a beaut!"

It was a beaut all right. I said, "You better watch out for more of the same, Mr. Helmut. Because that girl stole fifty-one other library books when she stole this one. Out of my car."

"Ouch!" he said. Then, "You're from the Public Library?"

I nodded and showed him my card.

"Well," said Helmut, "since you scared her yesterday, let's hope she'll think twice about using the library-book method again."

"Let's hope so. Can I have the book now?"

"Sure," he said. He handed me the book.

"I wish I hadn't lost the girl last evening," I said. "I might have got my other books back too."

"Wouldn't do you much good if she's gutted them all like that one," Helmut said as I went out.

* * * *

At two o'clock I was sitting across his scarred desk from Lieutenant Randall, my old boss. I'd just related to him in detail my adventures in recovering *The Scholar*, now considerably the worse for wear. The book lay on his desk between us.

Randall put his cat-yellow eyes on me and said. "I'm very happy for you, Hal, that you managed to recover a stolen book for your little old library. Naturally. But why tell me about it? Petty book theft just doesn't interest me." He was bland.

I gave him a grin and said, "How about first-degree murder, Lieutenant? Could you work up any interest in that?"

He sat forward in his chair. It creaked under his weight. "You mean the Dexter woman?"

I nodded. "I think she was killed because I spotted her with my stolen book."

"She fell downstairs and fractured her skull. You just said so."

"She fell downstairs, all right. But I think she was pushed. After somebody had caved in her skull in her apartment."

"Nuts," Randall said. "You're dreaming."

"Call the coroner," I suggested. "If the dent in her head was made by hitting one of those rusty iron steps, there could be some rust flakes in the wound. But I'll bet there aren't any."

"Jake hasn't looked at her yet. She only came in this morning. I've seen the preliminary report—fatal accident, no suspicion of foul play."

"Ask him to take a look at her now, then."

"Not until you give me something more to go on than rust flakes." He laced his voice with acid. "You're a showoff, Hal. So you probably think you know who killed her, right? *If* she was killed."

"Mr. C. B. Helmut," I said. "The Security Chief at Perry's Department Store. That's who killed her."

Randall's unblinking yellow stare didn't shift. "What makes you think it was Helmut?"

"Three pieces of what I consider solid evidence."

"Such as?"

"Number One: when I looked up the phone number of Heloise's Beauty Salon for the yardman in Gloria Dexter's phone book, there was another number on the same page underlined in red ink."

Randall frowned. "Helmut's?"

"C. B. Helmut."

"If she was a shoplifter," Randall said, "why the hell did she want to know the phone number of Perry's Security Chief?"

"Especially," I said, "since the underlined phone number was Helmut's *home* number, not the extension for Security at Perry's Department Store."

Randall's knuckles cracked as he curled his hands into fists.

"What's evidence Number Two?" he asked in a neutral tone.

"Helmut called me by name, although I was a perfect stranger to him and he to me."

Randall said, "Why not? You showed him your ID card."

"He called me Mr. Johnson before he saw my ID card."

"The Lost and Found girl or his secretary told him who you were."

"I didn't tell either one of them my name."

"Well." Randall stared past my shoulder in deep thought. "He knew who you were and what your job was before you told him, then?"

"Yes. And there can be only one explanation for that."

"Don't tell me. Let me guess. You think he stole your car and your books."

"Right. I'm sure he recognized me the minute he saw me today."

"I don't see what the hell that has to do with Dexter's murder."

"Dexter was in cahoots with Helmut," I said. "She told him I followed her and chased her into the store."

"Wait a minute," Randall said. "You've lost me."

I laid it out for him. "The girl was scared when I braced her about the library book. She ducks into Perry's to lose me, but has the bad luck to meet one of her hairdressing customers at the entrance. From inside the door she looks back and sees that I have stopped her customer and am obviously asking about her, about Dexter. So she panics. She steps into one of the store telephone booths, gets Helmut on the phone, tells him a Hal Johnson from the Public Library is hot on her trail and by now probably knows who she is on account of the hairdressing customer. What should she do?

"Helmut tells her not to come near the Security Office, just throw the library book into a trash basket and go on home. And deny she ever had the book if anybody asks her again about it. Helmut hopes the book will be burned in the store incinerator with the other trash, of course. But the book is turned in to the Lost and Found desk this morning, so Helmut's stuck with it. And I show up before he can dispose of it."

"You should have been a detective," Randall said, deadpan. "I still don't see how that gets Dexter murdered."

"Helmut knows I'll get to Dexter sooner or later, now that I know who she is. He knows I'll apply pressure about the stolen book and eventually go to the police. So he figures she'll blow the whole sweet setup he's got going for him, unless he takes her out of the picture completely."

"What setup?"

"Don't you get it? The guy's a modern Fagan," I said. "He's got a bunch of girls like Dexter shoplifting for him all over town! Using scooped-out library books—the books he stole from me—as containers. And reporting to him by telephone at home."

Randall took that without blinking. "Well, well," he murmured. He contemplated his folded hands on the desk top. "You said something about a third piece of evidence?"

I gave him a sheepish look. "I hesitate to tell you about that one. It's slightly illegal."

"So is your friend Helmut, you think. So tell me."

"I talked my way past Helmut's super and got into his apartment at Highland Towers—"

Randall blinked at last. "And—?" he said.

"I found twenty-seven of my stolen library books at the back of his clothes closet."

"Scooped out?"

I shook my head. "No, perfectly normal."

"So." Lieutenant Randall leaned back and put his hands behind his head, his elbows spread. "Twenty-seven, you said? You think he's got people using the other twenty-five books in shoplifting for him?"

I nodded.

"That he's recruited a gang of otherwise respectable people like Dexter to turn shoplifter for him?"

I nodded again.

Randall ruminated aloud. "He's store Security Chief. In the course of his job he runs into a lot of people who are *already* shoplifters, is that what you mean? So he blackmails some of them into working for him by threatening them with the police?"

"It could be, couldn't it?"

Randall looked at me with the air of a man who suspects his son of cheating on a geography exam. "Hal," he said, "you recently remarked, and I quote: 'The guy's a modern Fagan. He's got a bunch of girls shoplifting' et cetera." He tapped his desk top with a finger like a sausage. "How do you know they're *all* girls? You holding out something else?"

"I found a list of girls' names in one of the stolen library books in Helmut's place. Here's a copy." I tossed an old envelope on his desk.

He made no move to touch it. "That isn't evidence, Hal. It could be a list of his daughter's friends. Members of his wife's bridge club. Anything."

I said. "I *know* one of the girls on that list, Lieutenant. Ramona Gomez—she works in the library cafeteria. Couldn't you go and ask her in a friendly way if she's been blackmailed into shoplifting for Helmut? With what you know now, it shouldn't be hard to make her talk."

Randall stood up. "Yeah," he grunted, "I guess I could do that much, Hal. And a couple of other things too. Leave the book, will you?"

"Let me know how you make out," I said, "because the books in Helmut's closet still belong to the library, you know."

* * * *

I was at home having a lonely shot of Scotch after my delicious TV dinner when Lieutenant Randall phoned. Seven hours. He was a fast worker.

"How's the stolen library-book business?" he asked by way of greeting.

"Booming," I replied. "And how's it with the brave boys of Homicide?"

"Also," he said. "We've got your pal Helmut."

"For Murder One?"

"What else? That print we turned up under the dash of your stolen car, remember? It's Helmut's."

"Good," I said. "Does it match anything else?"

"Strange you should ask," said Randall. "It matches a thumbprint on the metal buckle of Dexter's dress. I guess Helmut dragged her to the iron stairway by the belt after he conked her."

"No rust flakes in her head wound?"

"None."

"What'd he conk her with?"

"Swedish ashtray. Glass. Hers. Weighs about two pounds. A perfect blunt instrument. His prints are on that too."

"Careless, wasn't he?"

"You might say so. He failed to reckon with the brilliance of the police is how I'd put it."

"You talked to Ramona Gomez?"

"Yep. We couldn't turn her off when we hinted that Helmut had knocked off Dexter. She spilled everything. Helmut caught her shoplifting at Perry's and blackmailed her into working for him, just as you figured. Same with the other girls."

"Poor Ramona," I said. "You're not going to take any action against her, are you?"

"Immunity," said Randall wryly, "in exchange for her memoirs about Helmut. Same with all the girls on the list."

I sipped my whiskey and asked, "Did Ramona say anything about fingering me to Helmut?"

"Yeah. She admitted telling Helmut he could get a whole load of books from the Public Library without any chance of their being traced if he just swiped your car when you had the trunk filled with overdues." Randall chuckled. "Your Ramona pointed you out to Helmut as a prime source for library books when he got his big idea about using them for shoplifting."

"That wasn't nice of Ramona," I said. "Maybe you better charge her with conspiracy or something, after all."

"We only picked up Helmut half an hour ago," Randall said. "He was taking a briefcase full of stolen goodies to the fence he's been using. We trailed him to the fence before we jumped him, and got the fence too. Isn't that clever?"

"Brilliant," I said. "Who's the fence? Anybody I know?"

"None of your business. You're a book detective, remember? Fences are for adult cops, my boy."

"As a book detective, then, I'm interested in whether any more of the library's books will turn up as shoplifters' tools," I said. "Bad for the library's image—you can understand that, Lieutenant."

"Don't fret yourself, Hal. Helmut called all his girls last night after killing Dexter and instructed them to discontinue using library books in their work. At least, that's what all the girls have told us."

"That means the library's lost twenty-five books, Lieutenant. Who wants to read a scooped-out novel, even for free? But you got the other twenty-seven for me, didn't you, out of Helmut's closet?"

"Evidence," said Randall. "You'll get them back after Helmut's trial."

"What!" I yelled. "That'll be months, maybe years!"

Randall sounded hurt. "You've got nobody but yourself to thank for that," he said. "If you're going to solve my murders, you can't blame me for collecting your library books."

THE SAVONAROLA SYNDROME

Originally published in* Mike Shayne Mystery Magazine, *October 1976.

CHAPTER I

Monday noon, when I got back to my office at the library, there was a note on my desk. "I'd like to see you when you have a minute," it said. It was signed "Ellen."

Anytime Ellen wants to see me, I have a minute. She's the girl on the check-out desk at the library. She has a face like a Botticelli angel and a figure like an Egyptian belly-dancer.

I didn't even sit down at my desk. I went down the corridor to the main library room, turned in through the double doors, and walked over to Ellen's desk with what is sometimes referred to as a spring in my stride.

I waited until Ellen had checked out a dozen books for a lantern-jawed, grizzled old man whose taste, judging from his book titles, seemed to run to the care and feeding of tropical plants. Then I stepped up to her desk and said, "Don't tell me, Ellen. Let me guess. You've decided to marry me."

She smiled and shook her head. "Don't nag me, Hal," she said. "I'm still thinking it over."

"You've been thinking it over for four months and eight days now," I answered. Which was true. "And I've only asked for an answer six times. Or is it seven? Do you call that nagging?"

"Borderline case, I'd say. Anyway, that isn't what I wanted to see you about. This is a professional matter."

Professional. That seemed an odd word to apply to my job. I'm the guy who chases down stolen and overdue books for the public library. Library fuzz. A kind of sissy cop. It's not exciting work, usually, but it's steady. And I suppose you *could* call it a profession of sorts. It pays a fair salary anyway—enough to marry Ellen on if she'd ever make up her mind to say "yes".

I said, "What is this professional matter that concerns you?"

"What it is," Ellen said, "is that there's something funny going on around here."

"Tell your favorite detective all about it," I said.

"Somebody's stealing books from my current fiction rack."

"What gives you that idea?" I asked.

"Well, a lot of people keep coming in and asking for The *Cult of Venus*, and complaining to me because they can't ever find a copy of it on the shelves. It's that novel by Joel Carstairs…"

"Whee!" I interrupted her. "That *Cult of Venus* book is a very warm item, baby. Have you read it?"

She flushed. "What difference does that make? Until this morning, I've just taken it for granted that all our copies of the book are out, and that's why there aren't any on the shelves recently. It's a very popular book, of course, a best seller."

"Bound to be," I teased her, "what with all decency thrown to the winds, explicit scenes of wild sexual abandon every other page and…"

"Be serious, Hal! I'm trying to tell you that this morning, after three more requests for the book, I decided to check our records on it."

"How many copies are we circulating?"

"Sixteen. Eight here and two each for our branches." She brushed her hair back from her cheek. "That's when I found something funny. When I checked the cards. Our records show that seven copies should be on the shelves. But they aren't. And they haven't been misfiled, either. I checked that. They've just disappeared, Hal. Don't you think that's funny?"

"Sure," I said. "Hilarious. Seven out of eight? That's a lot of copies for anyone to want of the same book. Even a dirty one."

"It's not really dirty so much," Ellen said primly, "as frank and realistic."

"Dirty," I said. "I read it." I thought for a moment. An acne-splotched teenager approached Ellen's desk with an armload of books. I said, "Here comes a customer, Ellen. I'll see what I can figure and see you later."

I went back to my cubby-hole behind the office of the library's business manager, sat down at my desk, pulled over my telephone and made four quick calls to our branch libraries. In each case, I asked the librarian to check on the two copies of The *Cult of Venus* her branch was circulating, and get back to me as soon as possible.

Twenty minutes later I had reports from all four branches. Of the eight copies of The *Cult of Venus* assigned to the branches, only three were accounted for as out on loan. The other five had been returned by borrowers and should have been on the current fiction shelves waiting to go out again. But they weren't. They had disappeared without the slightest trace.

Digesting that little nugget of information, I stood up and prowled around my closet-sized office for a couple of minutes before walking down the hall to visit Ellen again.

"Listen," I said to her when she was free for a minute, "is that the dirtiest book we're circulating right now? The *Cult of Venus*?"

She said, "Well, that's fairly outspoken all right, Hal, but..."

"We've got dirtier ones?"

She hesitated. "For my money, *The Parallel Triangle* is about as dirty as you can get—to use your word."

"You read that one, too?"

"Just skimmed it. Part of my job." She made a *moue* of distaste.

"Then check out our copies of *The Parallel Triangle* for me, will you, Ellen? When you get a few minutes free?"

She looked at me with raised eyebrows. "You think we've got some nutty thief here who loves dirty books?" she asked. "Somebody who's so enthusiastic that he collects all the copies he can get?"

"It's a possibility. Let me know what you find out, anyway. And you might take a look at your records on a few other dirty books, too, while you're at it. Even any you think are only frank and realistic."

Ellen sighed. "Okay, Hal."

I descended into the basement and grabbed a quick bite at the library cafeteria before setting out on my afternoon round of calls for overdue books and fines. When I returned to the library again at 5:30, Ellen had left for the day but there was another note on my desk. This one read:

The Parallel Triangle: Of our twelve copies, seven are missing. *Harrigan's Bag* (also very frank and realistic!): four of our eight are missing. How about that, Sherlock?

How about it, indeed?

CHAPTER II

Next morning, I checked our branches on their copies of *The Parallel Triangle* and *Harrigan's Bag*. More than half of the branch library copies were missing. They'd disappeared without a trace. As Ellen had said, something very funny seemed to be going on.

In my six years at the public library, I've had plenty of experience with book thieves. They come in all shapes and sizes. People who steal library books for the few dollars they'll bring from unscrupulous second-hand book dealers. Poor people who steal library books because they truly love books, feel compelled to own them, and can't afford to buy them. People who steal books just for the hell of it—sometimes to satisfy the urgings of deep-buried kleptomania, sometimes for no reason at all except the thrill of stealing.

Then there are the otherwise respectable book collectors who steal out-of-print, rare, hard-to-get books and special editions from the public library just to round out their collections.

And of course, there's a small but select group of secret pornography-lovers who steal salacious books from the library because they're ashamed to be seen openly buying or borrowing them.

Our current thief seemed to fit nicely into the latter category, judging by the type of books he was stealing. Yet if so, why would he want so many copies of each book? Even the most enthusiastic porno buff could only read one book at a time.

No, I decided, the thief I was after wasn't a secret lover of pornography. He had to be a market-wise practical thief who was conforming smartly to the law of supply and demand, interested only in the commercial benefits of his thievery.

For while our dirty books remained on the best seller lists, it figured that public demand for them would expand constantly. Therefore the second-hand dealers could resell as many copies of these particular titles as they could lay their hands on. And quite probably, they'd pay our thief a considerably higher price for his stolen goods than ordinary books would bring.

Well, good for you, Johnson, I told myself. You've figured out why the books are being stolen. So now figure out who is stealing them and how to get them back. That's what the library is paying you for, after all. Those books go for anywhere up to eight ninety-five retail, and that adds up to a lot of scarce library dough. So what are you going to do about it?

Simple, I answered myself. I'll set a little trap for the rascal.

I requested that all our remaining copies of *The Parallel Triangle* be withdrawn from circulation when they were returned by borrowers, and sent to me at the main library. As the lewdest and most popular book of the lot, that title would make the best bait, I figured.

When I had a reasonable backlog of copies, I would feed one copy at a time onto the current fiction rack at the main library and sit nearby, personally, and watch what happened to it. If a legitimate borrower selected the book and checked it out at Ellen's desk in the regular way, I would put another copy on the rack and watch *that*. If anybody smuggled *The Parallel Triangle* out of the library without checking it out at Ellen's desk, I figured the chances would be good that I'd caught our thief in the act.

By Thursday morning enough copies of the book had come in to my office to provide continuing bait for a couple of days, I hoped—at least during the heavy traffic hours in the library when the thief might be expected to operate.

It might take weeks to land him, I realized. On the other hand, I could get lucky in an hour. With no copies of the book available now at any of our branches, the thief would be forced to patronize the main library if he wanted to snag any more copies of *The Parallel Triangle*.

I decided to start the action. Not that I expected much action in the true sense of the word. I foresaw weary hours of sitting on a hard chair in a distant corner of the reading room, watching my bait in the fiction rack. Yet it was a welcome relief from collecting overdue books and fines.

So about eleven o'clock Thursday morning, I salted the rack with one copy of *The Parallel Triangle* and took up my vigil. It was really quite pleasant, I discovered, because I could see Ellen's desk, and Ellen herself, from my spy-chair. And I didn't know of any better way to rest tired eyes than to look at Ellen.

As it turned out, the third customer who picked *The Parallel Triangle* from the rack was my man. Out of the busy noon-hour crowd of library habitués who were browsing through the stacks, scanning the card catalog files, lining up before the checkout and check-in desks, he suddenly appeared at quarter after twelve, sidling up to the current fiction shelf so casually as to make it seem almost accidental.

Yet there was nothing accidental in the swiftness with which he plucked *The Parallel Triangle*, along with its nearest neighbor, from the rack, after only half-a-second's inspection of the shelf's contents.

With a nod of satisfaction he came at a brisk, decisive pace toward the reading room, where I was pretending to peruse a month-old issue of *National Geographic*.

As he passed me, I got a good look at him over my magazine. He was medium tall, strongly built, stooped a little with age but not much. His abundant shock of carefully-combed hair was pure white. He wore rimless eyeglasses. Deep-graven lines bracketed his thin-lipped mouth. And the reddish brown eyes, under brows which still retained some of the brown his hair coloring lost, held a curious half-desperate, half-resigned expression.

Altogether he was quite distinguished-looking. I couldn't easily imagine anyone looking less like a petty book thief. Yet there he was, two library books from the current fiction shelf in one hand, a black leather briefcase in the other. The leather briefcase looked expensive. So did the blue-checked slacks and navy blazer he was wearing.

He sat down in a vacant chair at one of the long reading-room tables and placed his briefcase on the table in front of him. Then he made a quiet business of reading the jacket-blurbs of *The Parallel Triangle* and leafing through it as though making up his mind whether he wanted to read it or not.

After five minutes of this, he raised his eyes without lifting his head, checked the other occupants of the reading room to make sure we were all absorbed in our books or magazines, then quietly lifted the lid of his brief-case three inches and slid *The Parallel Triangle* inside.

It was done as skillfully as a prestidigitator palms a card. One second, *The Parallel Triangle* was there, resting on top of his briefcase; the next, it had disappeared, and the white-haired gentleman was examining the sec-ond library book he had selected from the rack.

At length he rose from his chair, took his briefcase from the table, walked briskly into the main room and returned the second book to the fiction rack as though he had decided not to borrow it after all. He glanced briefly at Ellen's check-out desk and saw that her attention was fully oc-cupied by the half dozen people waiting in line at her desk. Immediately he swung about and walked confidently out the rear door of the main library room which led down a short corridor to our Technology Department. The Technology Department has an entrance of its own from the street border-ing the rear of the library.

I tossed aside my *National Geographic* and went right after him.

CHAPTER III

He disappeared down one of the narrow passages in the Technology Department between the ceiling-high shelves of books. I let him go and made for the librarian on the desk. She was a friend of Ellen's, and quite bored enough to exchange idle chat with anybody who came along—even me. Her name is Laura.

Laura and I had covered Laura's health, mine, Ellen's, the Oscar Awards on TV last week, and were just getting to the prospects for our local baseball club when my distinguished-looking thief, swinging his briefcase jauntily, appeared from the maze of bookshelves.

He cast a pleasant nod in our direction as he passed us before saunter-ing nonchalantly out the rear door of the library to the sidewalk.

I said, "You know that old bird, Laura?"

She nodded. "He's a steady customer. Comes here several times a week. He's a dear."

"Interested in science and technology, is he?"

"Of course. He's retired now, but he used to be a professor of electrical engineering at the University."

"Well, well," I said. I decided it wouldn't be necessary to follow him any farther right now. "What's his name, do you know?"

"Dr. Amos Satchell. Doctor as in Ph.D., not medicine."

"And why does he come to your Technology Department so often if he's retired?"

"He's still writing books," Laura said, "He has a lot of research to do for them naturally."

"I see," I said. But I didn't.

"Textbooks," Laura went on. "We have two or three of them here in the library as a matter of fact." She squinted at me. "Why are you so curious about Dr. Satchell, Hal?"

I was tempted to answer her by advising her to check her shelves to see how many technical works on sexual subjects were missing, but decided against it. Instead I said, "Just curious," and left her, returning to my own office.

There wasn't any great rush, now. I knew the identity of the thief, and I could get his address from his library card if he had one, or from the telephone book, for that matter. And I wanted to think about Dr. Amos Satchell for a bit before I braced him.

So it wasn't until the next morning that I drove my old Chevy out City Line toward the University and pulled up in front of a small but neatly-kept frame house, standing modestly well back from the street in a large lot, shielded from its nearest neighbors by high hedges. The Professor liked his privacy, apparently.

I left the Chevy parked in the street before Professor Satchell's house and walked up the long path of stepping stones, parallel to his gravel driveway, that led to his front door. I pressed the doorbell. Faintly I could hear musical chimes inside, announcing my arrival.

I was earnestly hoping the Professor himself would be at home and that I wouldn't have to deal with a loyal wife or daughter or son. For it's not my idea of fun to inform a nice woman that her husband or father is a dirty-minded old man who steals sexy books from the public library. If you know what I mean.

I needn't have worried. Dr. Amos Satchell himself opened the door to me, his thick white hair as smooth and neatly kept as his lawn and shrubbery outside. I felt suddenly unsure of myself. This venerable, respectable looking retired scientist *couldn't* be a book thief. I'd made a mistake somewhere. To cover my embarrassment I said, "Are you Dr. Amos Satchell?" I almost added a "sir." He was that kind of a guy.

He smiled cordially and nodded. "What can I do for you?"

I cleared my throat. "May I talk with you for a few minutes, Dr. Satchell? Alone?" I was still thinking about the possibility of a loving wife hovering around.

"Of course," he said easily. He stepped back and held the door open, inviting me in. I thought that was a trifle odd, asking a stranger to come in, until I remembered that he'd probably noticed me talking to Laura, the librarian, yesterday.

Just for the record, though, I got out my identification card and showed it to him. "I'm from the public library," I said. He peered at my ID through his rimless bifocals.

"Ah, yes, Mr. Johnson, is it? Come in, won't you?"

He led me through a center hall, richly carpeted, and into a small den, book-lined and cozy. I looked for copies of our stolen books among his volumes, but failed to locate any. He waved me to an easy chair and sat down himself behind a beautifully made desk of dark satiny wood. "I've rather been expecting you, Mr. Johnson," he said, "since yesterday afternoon." So he *had* recognized me.

I didn't say anything for a second or two. At that moment I was disliking my job intensely; I was reluctant to harry this harmless old fellow. At length I murmured, "I'm afraid I've come on a rather unpleasant errand, Dr. Satchell."

He went right on smiling. "It's about the books I've stolen from your library, isn't it?"

I swallowed. "That's right. You've...ah...appropriated quite a few of them, haven't you?"

He seemed to be making a mental calculation. "A good many, it's true. But only a few titles." No apology in his voice, no shame, no guilt, just a quiet statement of fact.

"The *Cult of Venus*," I said, "*The Parallel Triangle*, *Harrigan's Bag*."

Gravely he nodded his white-maned head. "Those are the ones, yes."

"Why did you confine yourself to those three titles? And why steal so many copies of each?"

"Because those three books are the latest and most blatant examples of the filth that is being foisted on us in the name of literature today!"

Satchell wasn't smiling now. His voice was sharp and high with angry passion. "I consider it immoral and disgraceful that a great public institution like the library should pander to the lowest tastes, should offer a free reading of lewd and obscene books to the citizens of this city!" So. A crusader. That's what Dr. Satchell was. I remembered Ellen's guess that our thief might be a nut who loved dirty books. He wasn't, obviously. He was a nut who *hated* dirty books.

I said, "What good did you think you could do by stealing those few books from the library?"

"I hoped I could get them all, Mr. Johnson, before I was apprehended. Get at least those three disgusting books off the shelves where teenagers and yes, even children, are exposed to their insidious corrupting influence! I stole them as a protest, I suppose. Against the careless, pernicious, permissive book selections made by our Library Board. In the hope that future selections might be more seemly and decent than those abominations I have stolen!"

Quite a speech. Dr. Satchell sank back in his chair. I said, as soothingly as I could, "You're absolutely right, Dr. Satchell. Some of the material our writers are turning out today is garbage of the worst kind. But surely you couldn't have hoped to do much to turn the tide of what you call 'filth' by stealing only a few books from the public library?"

He ran a thin hand across his forehead, puzzled and distraught. "I don't know," he said vaguely. "I don't know. Perhaps I *was* foolish to think I could accomplish anything in such a fashion. I…I realize that now…"

I interrupted him. "In that case," I said, "maybe we can make a deal, sir." I was feeling very sorry for the troubled old gentleman. And my own sympathies, I must admit, leaned toward his view of current fiction. "The library has no desire to be unduly harsh about your bookstealing, Dr. Satchell. To a certain extent, we can understand and sympathize with your views."

I took a list from my pocket and held it out to him. He made no move to take it. "As nearly as we can figure it, these are the books you've stolen from us. If you're willing to return them now, and pay a fine of ten cents per day per book for the period you've kept them, I think we can arrange to settle the matter without recourse to the police." I was struck by a sudden thought. "You haven't destroyed the books, have you?"

Dr. Satchell shook his head. "Oh, no. Not yet. I intended to gather them all together and burn them publicly in Woodhouse Square, as Savonarola did in Florence long ago. But I fully realize now that that would be an exercise in futility."

"Good," I said. "Then you'll return the books and pay the fine?

He sighed. "Rather than go to prison, yes, of course. I need my freedom to carry on the work, Mr. Johnson. I do not admit defeat, you understand. I merely realize that sterner measures will be required to dam the flow of prurient material you peddle to the public."

He stood up and turned toward a door in the corner of the den. "Your library books are here," he said. "I've kept them in my closet, out of sight. You can understand why."

I nodded and crossed the room to join him as he opened the closet door. "There they are, on the floor, Mr. Johnson."

It was dark in the closet. I stepped past him and stooped in the doorway, reaching out my hands for the books, and feeling a wave of relief that we wouldn't have to get tough, after all, with poor old Dr. Satchell, since he had turned out to be merely a pathetic crank and not a real criminal at all.

Poor old pathetic Dr. Satchell. I don't know what he hit me with. Later I figured it might have been a heavy onyx ashtray I'd noticed on his desk. But hit me he did—a good solid belt on the back of the head that tumbled me into the closet like a sack of wet sand and made me see a variety of fireworks before I blacked all the way out.

CHAPTER IV

The blackout was only temporary, although when I opened my eyes I couldn't see anything but blackness around me. Which meant that the closet door had been shut. And I knew I'd been out for only a few seconds because I heard the click of the key in the closet lock as Dr. Satchell turned it from outside.

Sounds reached me through the closet door, and my own returning senses told me what they were. Desk drawers being opened and closed in the den. Thumps as Dr. Satchell placed something on the desk or floor. The pad of footsteps then, leaving the room and returning after an interval. Then a repetition of the retreating and returning footsteps. I counted three such brief journeys out there before it occurred to me in my addled state to take any action myself.

I yelled through the door, "Hey, Dr. Satchell! Are you nuts?" Not a brilliant question to ask of a man who obviously *was* nuts. I wasn't tracking too well yet. Besides I was suffering from a king-sized case of chagrin at allowing myself to have been conned by the likes of Dr. Satchell.

Dr. Satchell didn't answer me, though the sounds of movement outside my door continued.

After several attempts, I stood upright in the dark closet and felt groggily around me with my hands and feet. My feet told me that there were no library books stacked on the floor of the closet as Satchell had claimed. And my searching hands told me that the rest of the closet was quite empty, too, except for Hal Johnson, the demon detective. There wasn't even a doorknob on my side of the door. And the door wouldn't budge, even when I leaned my weight against it.

I cleared my throat and bellowed, "Dr. Satchell?"

This time he answered me. "Yes, Mr. Johnson?" Deceptively mild.

"This is going to cost you a hell of a lot more than a fine! What's the idea of slugging me?"

"I told you I had decided on sterner measures."

"Knocking me on the head and locking me in a closet is what you call sterner measures?"

"No, no. Merely a necessary precaution. It is essential that I keep you… ah…safely incommunicado while I proceed."

"With what?"

"Sterner measures, Mr. Johnson. Aren't you listening?"

I felt a small bead of ice slide down my backbone. "What sterner measures?"

"They need not concern you." He kept silent for a moment. Then, "I *will* tell you one thing, however, Mr. Johnson. I intend to return your filthy books to the library at once. In fact, that is where I am going right this moment."

Did that explain his three sallies out of the den? To carry the stolen library books out to his car preparatory to returning them to the library? I could hear faint movement through the door before his voice came again. It was high, again, and thready with excitement. "Well, goodbye, Mr. Johnson."

"Wait!" I yelled. "How'sbout me? When will you let me out of here?"

"In exactly fifteen minutes," said Dr. Satchell. "You must try to be patient until then." And surprisingly, he laughed. A low snickering kind of laugh that chilled me, somehow.

And another bead of ice slowly slid down my spine. Because it suddenly occurred to me that if he was driving to the library or any of its branches to return the stolen books as advertised, he couldn't possibly be back home again in fifteen minutes to release me from the closet. Not even if he used a helicopter. And that funny laugh…

I decided not to be patient for fifteen minutes as advised. I decided I had to get out of that closet now. I shouted assorted threats and cajolery through the door at Satchell for several precious minutes without result. Then I shut up and listened. I heard a car start up at the rear of the house and scatter driveway gravel as it rolled out to the street. Satchell had departed. I attacked the closet door.

Maybe it was a thin door with an old rusty lock; maybe anger lent me extra strength; and maybe I was just scared stiff-legged. Whatever it was, my first kick at the door, in the region where the lock should be, split the wooden panel from top to bottom, ripped the lock tongue loose from the splintered door jamb, and catapulted me feet first into the den, where I brought up against Satchell's satinwood desk edge with a rib-shaking jar.

I paused an instant to rub my bruises and catch my breath before launching myself in eager pursuit of Dr. Amos Satchell. And that instant was long enough for me to take startled note of a curious object on Satchell's desk.

In the circumstances it seemed very curious to me. For there, lying beside the onyx ashtray Satchell must have used on my head, was a bright-jacketed copy of that dirty book to end all dirty books—*The Parallel Triangle*. I was sure it hadn't been there before I entered the closet.

It was one of the library's stolen copies. The library's identification was plainly discernible on cover and spine. Yet for a frozen moment, the significance of its presence there on Satchell's desk-top eluded me. I reached out automatically to pick it up. Then, as though arrested in midair by an invisible barrier, my reaching hand stopped dead. And I knew with sickening certainty what Dr. Satchell had meant when he spoke of 'sterner measures.'

The Parallel Triangle was ticking.

Fifteen minutes, Satchell had said. I'll let you out in fifteen minutes, Mr. Johnson. Oh yes, he'd let me out all right. By blowing his damned house down around my ears and killing me in the process. Very simple.

How many minutes were left of the promised fifteen? Not many, certainly. I'd dawdled for a good while in the closet before kicking my way out. And I'd dawdled away more precious time right here by this desk.

Besides, what if Satchell had been lying about the fifteen minute leeway? He'd lied about everything else, so why not? Maybe *The Parallel Triangle* would blow sky-high if I so much as touched it. Maybe Satchell had *counted* on my getting out of his rickety closet and seizing the book.

I shuddered. I tried hard to keep myself from panicking. For I can admit without shame that I've always been a practicing coward when it comes to explosives of any kind. And I'm all thumbs when it comes to anything electrical. So I didn't even consider trying to disarm Satchell's book-bomb. After all, he was an expert, an ex-professor of electrical engineering or something of the sort. I wasn't about to mess with his ticking bomb.

But I had to do something. A terrifying picture flashed into my mind and stayed there—a picture of Ellen Crosby, my possible future bride, being blown into gory bits when Dr. Amos Satchell returned his stolen books to the library. He wouldn't return them, of course, to the proper check-in desk; no, in all probability, if he returned them at all, he'd slip them quietly onto secluded library shelves where no one would hear them ticking until far too late to avert disaster.

He wouldn't overlook the branch libraries, either, I was pretty sure. After all, he had a whole car load of book-bombs to work with if he'd gimmicked every copy he'd stolen of those three novels.

So not only my Ellen, but all our librarians, our entire staff, and a lot of innocent men, women and children who would happen to be in the building when the books exploded, were probably in deadly danger, too.

The Parallel Triangle went on ticking merrily away, preventing me from thinking in my usual cool, logical, brilliant fashion. All I could think of to do at that moment was to grab the telephone sitting jauntily beside the book-bomb on Satchell's desk-top, and dial the police emergency number with a trembling forefinger, and pray a lot. I had Lieutenant Randall, my old boss at the Detective Bureau, on the line in thirty seconds. It seemed like thirty minutes with that ticking in my ears.

Randall said, "Yeah?" in his bland, bored voice.

"This is Hal Johnson," I said rapidly, "and I have only a minute or so to live, so don't interrupt me, for God's sake!" I jerked out my story to him in the fastest briefing anyone ever got, and when he snapped, "Okay, Hal, I got it," I hung up the receiver very, very delicately to avoid jarring the ticking book nearby, and then took to my heels as though all the devils in hell were after me.

CHAPTER V

I made a new sprint record getting through the front door of Satchell's house and down that long long path of stepping stones to the street where my car still stood at the curb. I jumped in, fired up the engine, made a U-turn and started south on City Line Avenue, heading for the main library.

It was not only closer to Satchell's house than any of the branch libraries, but I was confident he'd want to blow it up first anyway, it being, you might say, the main offender in purveying dirty books to the public. I hadn't covered half a block when I heard above the sound of my racing motor a kind of dull thumping boom behind me.

It took me twelve minutes to get downtown, even at my illegal rate of speed.

I screeched to a stop beside an unmarked car parked in the no-parking zone directly in front of the main library's entrance. I could see Lieutenant Randall sitting behind the wheel of this unmarked car, talking into a hand mike. I got out of my car, ran around behind it and stuck my head in the open window of Randall's command car and said, "Well?"

I must have looked and sounded somewhat tense because Randall switched off and grinned at me. "Calm down, Junior, everything's under control." He glanced complacently at the library. "We made it in nine minutes flat. That's not bad for a police department that gets more criticism than the President, is it?"

"Has Satchell showed yet?" I stuttered.

"Not yet. Not a sign of him. I've got a man stationed at the entrance of every branch library, just like you wanted. With instructions to hold any white-haired cat in rimless glasses carrying a briefcase or a copy of any of those dirty books you mentioned. Also, I've got a man at every entrance to the main library here with ditto instructions. And I've got another man in a squad car within sight of each door guard to call it in when your nut shows, so I'll know it quick. Relax. Wherever he goes, we've got him."

He looked at me narrowly. "You sure you're not just imagining all this? I notice you weren't blown up in the nut's house, after all."

"The bomb blew a minute after I left, Lieutenant. I heard it." I asked anxiously, "Couldn't you get the libraries evacuated?" I was still picturing Ellen in little pieces.

"Not enough time, Hal. We passed a goddam miracle to do what we've done! Besides, if your crazy friend shows up and finds a bomb scare going on, he's going to back off and come back with his bombs some other day when we're not ready for him. This way, we nail him now." He looked at his watch again. "He hasn't shown up yet, Hal. I'm sure of it."

"But he left his house more than twenty minutes ago! He could have got inside before your men were deployed."

"No way. How long did it take you drive here from his house?"

"About twelve minutes."

"See? Satchell wouldn't have made it in less than twenty. He'd drive slow and careful with a carload of bombs, right? And he'd drive by way of the quiet Park instead of by that traffic madhouse, City Line Avenue. Right?" I nodded doubtfully. "And he'll have to find a place to park, which is a fifteen minute project around any library unless you're lucky. Right? So relax. We've got him, I tell you."

I was only half-convinced. "How about the bomb expert?" Lieutenant Randall jerked a thumb over his shoulder. "Back there," he said. "Sergeant Kwalik, bomb squad."

I hadn't even noticed the cop in the back seat. I said, "Hi, Sergeant," and looked up the broad flight of steps to the main entrance of the library. A plainclothes detective named Corrigan was standing beside the door up there, keeping a sharp eye out—I hoped—for white-haired men with rimless glasses, briefcases and dirty books.

I had a sudden hunch. I said to Randall, "Listen, when this nut stole a book from this library yesterday, he left the library through the Technology Department exit on the back street. Maybe he'll go in that way now."

"I've got a man there, I told you. *Every* entrance. Shut up and let me listen to this." A subdued muttering came over the police band on his radio. "He hasn't shown up anywhere yet," he reported then.

I was too antsy to stay there doing nothing. I said, "I'm going around back and check that Technology entrance. Okay?"

Randall was talking into his mike again. He nodded to me. I ran up the front steps of the library, tipped a hand in greeting to Corrigan as I went through the door, then walked at a more sedate pace through the main library room past Ellen's desk, giving her a big smile as I passed. She returned the smile, not suspecting a thing.

I was enormously relieved to see her once again all in one beautiful piece, even if it might be the last time. I gave the library and reading room a hurried scrutiny as I sailed through them. No sign of Satchell. I was tempted to stop and look in the stacks, but my hunch was still driving me.

I went down the corridor to the Technology Department on the run. I didn't waste time casing the narrow aisles between bookshelves there, either, but went straight to Laura on the desk. I asked her as casually as I could whether her retired professor friend, Dr. Amos Satchell, had been in today. She said no, looking puzzled.

Without stopping to allay her curiosity, I stepped through the rear door by which Satchell had exited yesterday, and found Pete Calloway, an old friend from my days with the police department, standing guard outside.

I said, "Hi, Pete. Any action yet?"

"Nothing," said Pete.

"Nobody came in this way since you've been here?"

"One guy is all. No white hair, though. No briefcase. No rimless glasses. And no dirty books. I looked at them all."

"He was carrying books?"

"Sure. Six of them. Not the ones we want, though."

"You sure you looked at them all?" I felt uneasy suddenly.

Pete was hurt. "Hell, yes, Hal. One at a time."

"Just the covers?"

Pete stared at me. "What else? I wasn't told to read them all the way through, for God's sake?"

I discovered I was having trouble breathing. I said, "What color *was* this guy's hair?"

"Brown."

"And no glasses? Think about it, Pete."

"No glasses." Pete was positive. Then he gave me a startled look. "He blinked a hell of a lot, though," he said slowly.

I sucked in a deep breath and let it out again. "How long ago did this guy go in?"

"Couple of minutes. You must have passed him as you came out."

"I didn't. But he's got to be Satchell, Pete. The nut we're after. Even if he's nutty, this guy isn't stupid. The librarians here know him, he comes in all the time. And he knows we're on to him for stealing books. So he takes off his cheaters and wears a brown wig to disguise himself. And he disguises his dirty books, too."

"How?"

"Easy. With dust jackets from other library books. Make sense?"

"Could be," said Pete. He shrugged, then waved both arms over his head.

"What's that for?"

"Signal. It'll bring the Lieutenant here on the run with Kwalik."

"Good," I said. I was thinking frantically, trying to push down my first impulse, which was to rush into the library and yell for everybody to get out of the building instantly, especially Ellen. Which would no doubt cause a first class panic. And we didn't want panic now.

What we wanted was Satchell and his armload of books. If Pete's guy *was* Satchell, he'd been inside the library for less than two minutes. Had he seen me, perhaps, and ducked behind something as I went by him? I doubted it. He was probably already out of sight in the stacks of the main library when I came through it.

Because if he meant to deploy most of his six bombs in the main library, which seemed reasonable, he'd have gone directly there to start planting them. Especially if he meant to retreat through the Technology Department exit after his bombs were planted.

Now then, it would take a minute or two to arm each bomb before he left it on a shelf, wouldn't it? I hoped so. And Satchell would set the triggering mechanism far enough ahead so he'd have plenty of time to get safely out of the library himself before the first bomb exploded. Say ten or fifteen minutes, altogether, before he finished the job.

I said to Pete, "Stay here until Randall and Kwalik arrive, will you? Then bring them into the main library stacks. I'll go ahead now and try to locate Satchell. And when you come into the main room, keep it quiet and calm. This guy is crazy enough to blow his whole batch of bombs at once if he sees we're after him. Okay?"

"Okay"

I went at a quick walking pace through Technology, then at a run down the corridor to the main library room. There I slowed and turned into the stacks. At the end of each long, narrow book-lined aisle, I paused just long enough to see whether or not there was a brown-wigged, blinking Dr. Satchell in it anywhere before I went on to inspect the next aisle. Luckily I'm pretty tall. I could see over the heads of most of the people browsing in the stacks who might be blocking out my view of my quarry.

At the fifth aisle, I found him.

CHAPTER VI

He was alone in the aisle, standing perhaps twenty feet away with his back to me, his head bent over a book that was open in his hand. I drew back a couple of aisles, out of his sight if he turned. I was just in time to flag down Randall, Pete and Kwalik as they came quietly into the stacks. I made shushing signs at them. Randall nodded and raised his eyebrows, asking silently if I'd located Satchell.

I didn't say anything until they were beside me, hidden from Satchell by several aisles of head-high bookshelves. Then I pointed and whispered, "Twenty feet up aisle number five. Setting the timing gimmick on one of his book-bombs. I didn't see the others."

That's all Lieutenant Randall needed. Even speaking in a whisper, his command voice came through. "Go to the other end of that aisle, Hal, around the other cross aisle. Block him there. We'll go in from this end. Kwalik, you go for the bombs. Pete and I will take care of Satchell. When we've got him safe, Kwalik, disarm the bomb he's placing in that aisle. Ready?"

"Wait!" I whispered urgently. "Suppose he's already planted other bombs on some of these other shelves? We've got to know, if and where, before we take him. Because he sure as hell won't tell us afterward."

"How loud do the damn things tick?" Randall growled, momentarily at a loss.

"Not loud enough for Kwalik to find them quick among all these other books!"

Kwalik said, "How many books was the guy carrying?"

"Six," Pete said.

"That's it, then," said Randall, relieved. "Before we take Satchell, we locate and count the books he's still got with him. If he has five left, we know he's only planted the one so far. And Hal knows where that one is. All right? Let's go."

I walked to the far end of aisle one, where we'd been standing, found the cross-aisle, leading to aisle five, empty, and cautiously took my position just around the corner of aisle five in the cross-aisle. I peered through the gaps in the bookshelves between us and saw Satchell closing very carefully the cover of the book in his hand.

From where I was, I couldn't see what he'd done with his other books. He pushed the books on a middle shelf beside him tightly together, to make room for another book. Then he slid his armed bomb into the opening thus made, and turned away from me toward the other end of the aisle.

I risked a peek around my corner. Randall and his men were coming slowly down aisle five from the other end, Kwalik, the bomb expert, in the lead. Craning around my corner, I saw why Kwalik was leading instead of Randall. On the floor by Satchell's feet was a little pile of books with bright covers. I counted them with my heart in my throat. Five.

Satchell was beginning to stoop to pick them up when Kwalik reached him. The timing couldn't have been better. For Satchell, thinking Kwalik just another library patron browsing through the stacks, turned slightly sideways to allow Kwalik to pass him in the narrow aisle.

Kwalik didn't pass him. "Excuse me, sir," he said to Satchell in a polite, help-the-old-lady-across-the-street voice, "can't I help you with these?" He half knelt at Satchell's feet, and with a smooth, unhurried, sweeping movement of practiced hands, scooped up Satchell's five remaining book-bombs and backed quickly away on his knees, allowing Randall and Pete to pass him in the aisle and bracket a bewildered Satchell neatly between them.

By this time, I was approaching the huddle of figures from my end of the aisle. I saw the quick glint of metal and heard the clicks that told me Randall and Pete had each handcuffed himself to one of Satchell's wrists.

Poor Satchell couldn't go anywhere now without dragging two burly cops with him. Amazingly, Satchell still used the low tone of voice which old library custom demands when he said to Lieutenant Randall, "What do you think you're doing, may I ask?"

I didn't hear what Randall answered, if anything. I was watching Kwalik, the bomb boy, with those chills running up and down my spine again.

Kwalik cleared a space on a handy shelf behind him and gently placed Satchell's five books on it, flat side down. Then, with his fingertips, he delicately lifted the cover of one of the books a fraction of an inch, held it there with one hand, got out a pencil flashlight with the other, and shone the light into the crack. He peered inside, his head tilted slightly. He looked as though he was ready to run. I *know* I was.

At length Kwalik nodded to Randall. "Okay," he said, "these'll wait. Where's the live one?"

I said, "Here it is, Sergeant." I bent over and put my ear to the book Satchell had slipped in among the others on that middle shelf. And by God, it *was* ticking! Up to that moment, I hadn't quite been able to believe that Satchell really intended to wipe out five buildings full of books and people.

Six buildings, if you counted his own house with me in it. But that ticking book made a true believer out of me. "Hurry up, Sergeant!" I said to Kwalik, and backed off like a timid school girl to the end of the aisle. Have I mentioned that I'm scared of explosives?

Kwalik had nerves of ice, apparently. He removed the ticking book from the shelf, opened its cover, and disengaged, with a touch like a jeweler's, a wire somewhere inside the hollowed-out book. "Got it," he said calmly. Then, to Pete, "You sure he only had six books when he came in?"

"I'm sure," Pete said. "I may be dumb but I can at least *count*!" He was disgusted with himself for letting Satchell get by him at the door.

Satchell himself hadn't said a word since his first weak protest to Randall. Probably because he couldn't believe his eyes when he saw *me* coming down the corridor toward him. He thought I was dead. His face paled and his reddish brown eyes, a nice match for his brown wig, now contained more desperation than they had yesterday—and more resignation, too.

Randall said, "Pick up your goddam dirty books, Kwalik, and let's get the hell out of here. I never have felt comfortable in a library!" He turned to me. "I don't suppose you know what kind of a car the professor here drives? So we can collect the rest of his dirty books?"

"Sorry, I never saw his car."

Surprisingly, Dr. Satchell spoke up then. He said meekly, "The rest of the bombs are in my blue Ford sedan, parked on the street behind the library." He gave Lieutenant Randall the license number. Randall jerked on his handcuff and growled, "Show us where."

I followed them out of the stacks, down the corridor to Technology, through Technology to the rear exit. It was a regular parade. Kwalik went first with his armload of deadly books. Then came Randall, Satchell and Pete, shoulder to shoulder like old buddies, handcuffs hidden under jacket cuffs. Then me, bringing up the rear, lagging as far behind those bombs in Kwalik's arms as I respectably could. Laura, on the Technology desk, scarcely lifted her head from her book as we went by.

I looked at my watch. Incredibly, from the moment I'd first realized that Satchell might be inside the library till now, when he and his bomb-books were leaving it under guard, only four and a half minutes had elapsed. They were four and a half of the longest minutes I could remember.

Yet I knew I'd gladly go through a dozen more like them—or a hundred—to keep Ellen Crosby in one piece. Even if she decided *not* to marry me.

Girls with faces like Botticelli angels and figures like Egyptian belly-dancers aren't all that easy to find these days. You know what I mean?

THE HENCHMAN CASE

***Originally published ed in* Alfred Hitchcock's**
Mystery Magazine, *May 1977.*

My first stop on Monday morning was at a run-down duplex apartment in the West End, the abode of a Mr. Jefferson Cuyler. I parked my car at the curb under a plane tree that was shedding its bark in shabby strips, dodged through a cluster of pre-schoolers who, with intent faces, were playing some mysterious street game, and mounted the four steps to the door of Mr. Cuyler's residence.

Our records showed Mr. Cuyler was several weeks late in returning six books he had borrowed from the public library. He had neither renewed them nor heeded our postcard of reminder. So I had come in person to collect them.

That's part of my job. I'm Hal Johnson, book collector—or, as my former boss, Lieutenant Randall of Homicide, calls me, "library fuzz." I'm employed by the public library to chase down overdue and stolen library books. That sounds like a simple job, right? Well, it isn't. Not when you consider that in many public libraries (including ours) more than twenty percent of all the new books placed on the shelves vanish less than a year. *Every* year. We're doing everything we can to cut down on this enormous loss. We re installing book detection systems, hiring extra guards, refusing public admission to certain stacks of out-of-print or rare books, and hiring ex-cops like me to shove fingers in the dyke.

Anyway, there I was on Mr. Cuyler's cramped front porch. I rang the bell. After a minute, the door was opened by one of the handsomest men I've ever seen in my life. He was tall and relatively slender, a year or two past sixty at a guess. His iron-grey hair was crisp and inclined to curl although it was cut short. His complexion was fresh and healthy under a moderate suntan. His features were almost classically regular. And his eyes were cobalt blue, their gaze so candid and friendly that you felt you could trust him with your life if need be.

He said, "Yes?"

I introduced myself and showed him my ID card. "Are you Jefferson Cuyler?"

He nodded.

"I've come for your overdue library books," I explained. "You've kept them out too long without renewal. So you owe us some fines."

"I know it," he said, his friendly eyes not cooling in the slightest. "I'm sorry, I've been away for a spell. I meant to bring them back today." He gave me a half smile. "They're here. Come on in."

He led me into his living room and pointed to a battered coffee table. The six library books made a neat stack on one corner of it.

The books were all that was neat in the room. Everything else looked like the aftermath of a cyclone. Somebody had jerked up the faded carpet and tossed it into a crumpled heap in a corner. The cushions and upholstery of the sofa and chair had been slashed in half a dozen places with a sharp knife. The pictures were torn from their hooks, the draperies from their rods. A large TV lay on its side, shattered. The contents of the room's only closet had been dumped on the floor in disarray. Through an old-fashioned archway, I could see that Mr. Cuyler's dining room had been given similar treatment. And probably his bedroom and kitchen as well.

"What the hell happened here?" I asked.

His blue eyes brooded on the confusion around us. "Well, as I said, I've been away—fishing. This is what I found when I got home an hour ago. Somebody broke in through the back window."

"Have you called the police?"

"I guess I'd better, hadn't I?" He gave me a funny slanting look accompanied by a wry smile. "I've been checking out the mess. Lucky your library books weren't lost in the shuffle."

I gazed around me. "These weren't your ordinary friendly neighborhood burglars, Mr. Cuyler. I hope you realize that."

He shrugged. "I haven't had any previous experience."

"Well, I have. And I've never seen a more thorough job. Whoever turned the place over was looking for something special, I'd say."

Cuyler's handsome features shaped themselves into an expression of bafflement. "I don't know what it could be. It's not as though I owned the Hope Diamond."

"What's missing?" I asked. It wasn't my business any more, but old habits die hard.

"Nothing," Cuyler said, "as far as I can tell. Nothing here worth stealing, anyway."

"You're forgetting my library books," I said, keeping it light. "Did you know that it would cost the library an average of fourteen bucks apiece to replace these six books on the shelves if anything happened to them?"

"I had no idea a library book could be so valuable," he said. His cobalt eyes mirrored a new, nameless emotion for a brief instant. Anger? Uncertainty? Amusement? Triumph? Maybe a little of all of them. It wasn't until later that I recalled he'd said 'could be' instead of the more natural 'was.' "How much of a fine do I owe?" he asked.

I told him and finished checking the titles of his books against my list while he got his money and paid me. "Thanks," I said. "I'm sorry to bother you when you've got all this on your mind." I gestured at the chaos of the room.

"Forget it," he said. "You couldn't have come at a more opportune time."

Politely, he saw me to the door.

* * * *

That was Monday. The next time I heard anything about Cuyler, he was dead.

Lieutenant Randall telephoned me at the library during my lunch break on Friday.

"Listen, Hal," he said, "do me a favor."

"What is it?"

"A book called *The Henchman*. By somebody named Eugene Stott?"

"Yeah?"

"You got it in the library?"

"Yeah."

"You know the book?"

"Yeah. At least, the title rings a bell. It was on one of my overdue lists earlier this week."

"Good. Find out if it's in or out, will you? And if it's in, hold it for me."

"For what?" I said. "You know you can't reserve a book over the telephone, Lieutenant. Why are you interested in it?"

His voice held a note of weariness. "It may be a clue in a murder I'm working on." He put oral quotation marks around the word clue. "So move your tail, O.K.? Call me back at this number." He gave me a telephone number.

I moved my tail. Ten minutes later I called him back and told him that we had two copies of *The Henchman* circulating from the main library. Copy number one was on the shelves in its assigned place when I looked, and I'd taken it in charge for him. Copy number two had been borrowed on Tuesday by a lady named Carolyn Seaver.

Randall hesitated. "Could you drop the one you have off at Headquarters for me?"

"Sure, Lieutenant. On my way home. No trouble."

"Thanks. It may give us a lead, Hal. God knows we need one."

I had a cold flash of intuition. "Where are you now?"

"West End. Why?"

"I'm wondering if your murder victim could be a man named Jefferson Cuvier," I said.

Dead silence. Finally, "Still a show-off, aren't you? How'd you guess that?"

"He's the guy I collected the *The Henchman* from on Monday. I remember it now. He was a handsome…)

"He's far from handsome now." Randall paused. "Could you bring that book out *here*, Hal? If you saw this guy on Monday, you may be able to help us."

"Give me ten minutes," I said.

"I'll give you fifteen," Randall growled. "You're a private citizen now, remember? You can't break the speed laws with impunity anymore."

"Yes, Lieutenant," I said humbly. He's never forgiven me for leaving Homicide to become a sissy library cop.

* * * *

When I got to Cuyler's duplex, I told Jimmy Coogan, the Homicide cop on the door, that Randall wanted to see me, and Coogan, an old buddy of mine at the department, passed me inside with a friendly sneer about my present line of work.

I don't know what I was expecting to see on this second visit to Cuyler's house—maybe the same scene of chaos as the first time. Anyway, I was a little bit surprised at how quickly the place had been returned to a condition of normal bachelor neatness. The pictures and draperies had been rehung, the closet contents hidden away again, the rug replaced, the TV-set repaired. Even the slashed sofa and chair had been treated to ready-made slipcovers that hid their knife wounds.

Lieutenant Randall was sitting in the chair. "Come in, Hal. You got that book?"

I held it out to him. He took it without a word and leafed carefully through it. Then, with a frustrated shake of his head, he put the book aside and fixed his spooky yellow eyes on me and said, "Tell me about seeing Cuyler on Monday."

"I can't tell you much. It was just a routine call for overdue books. Except that this house was a howling mess when I arrived. Somebody had broken in and been through it with a fine-tooth comb while Cuyler was away fishing."

"I already got that much from Robbery's report. Nothing was stolen, they say."

"Well, it wasn't just a casual break-in, Lieutenant. Somebody was looking for something special. Couldn't Cuyler give Robbery any hints about who or what?"

"Apparently not. But it stands out a mile that Cuyler's murder ties in with it somehow."

I nodded. "Who found him?"

"His once-a-week cleaning woman. She has a key, and tripped over Cuyler when she walked in at seven-thirty. The M.E. guessed he'd been dead less than seven hours when he was here at eight-thirty. So it happened early this morning, probably, not long after midnight. And we haven't got anything on it yet. Zilch. None of the neighbors saw or heard anything out of the way last night or this morning. And the killers didn't leave calling cards." He sighed. "They never do."

"Who *was* Cuyler, anyway?" I asked.

"Cuyler? Jefferson Rhine Cuyler, born and brought up in the East End, a widower for eight years, sixty-three years old, retired with a bad heart from Crane Express over a year ago, took early Social Security and has been living here alone. He had only one living relative, out of town somewhere."

"He must have had something more valuable than a distant relative," I said.

Randall said, "That seems obvious. That's why I asked you to bring the book. Whoever killed Cuyler beat the hell out of him before he died. Cuyler had three broken ribs, multiple bruises all over, marks on his wrists and ankles where he'd been tied up. And his face was a disaster."

I remembered Cuyler's good looks and his warm friendly manner, and thought that he wasn't the type to withstand torture for very long, without cracking. Especially with a bad heart.

Randall seemed to sense my thoughts. "It's possible his killer didn't intend him to die. He may just have been trying to get Cuyler to talk. But the beating killed him, the medical examiner thinks. Caused heart arrest." Randall rubbed a big hand over his face and I could hear his whisker bristles rasp. "It must have been somebody he knew. There wasn't any sign of forced entry this time."

"The cleaning woman has a key, you said."

"She couldn't tie up a grown man and break his ribs with punches. She's seventy years old, four feet ten, and weighs 96 pounds!"

I grinned. "Just suggesting a possibility," I said.

He grunted.

I pointed to *The Henchman*, precariously balanced on the arm of Randall's chair. "So what did you want that for?"

In reply, Randall took an envelope from his pocket, and from it he carefully extracted a sheet of unlined memo paper, which he held out for me to see. "Ned Jordan found this when he was dusting for fingerprints. It's the top sheet of a memo pad Cuvier kept beside his telephone."

I leaned closer. The dusting powder had revealed faint impressions of handwriting on the paper's surface—indentations obviously made by a sharp pencil or pen pressing on the sheet above it. I could make out the smudged words quite easily:

The Henchman Eugene Stott Public Library

I looked at Randall. He nodded, somewhat sheepishly. "It's a chance in a million, I know that. But the handwriting doesn't match Cuvier's. So it might be that Cuyler's killers—or one of them—wrote the words on the memo pad."

"Making a note of information he'd beaten out of Cuyler, you mean?"

"Could be. Maybe the book stuff was all he got out of Cuyler before Cuyler cashed in. But then, I couldn't be that lucky. Your damned book doesn't seem to give us a thing."

"Let me look."

Randall passed me the book. I examined it carefully. Nothing. "Maybe this isn't the copy Cuyler had."

Randall said, "Check it, O.K.?"

I went to Cuyler's phone and called Ellen, the girl on the check-out desk at the library. I'm hoping she'll marry me someday. I usually propose to her every time I see her. "Listen, Ellen," I said, "find out which of our two copies of *The Henchman* by Eugene Stott I brought back on Monday from our card-holder, Jefferson Cuyler, will you?"

She recognized my non-courting voice. "Hold on," she said, all business. In a minute or two she was back on the line and informed me that copy number two of *The Henchman* was the one that Jefferson Cuyler had borrowed.

"Thanks." I hung up and turned to Randall who was standing beside my shoulder. "You hear that?"

He nodded. "Get me copy number two."

"It was borrowed on Tuesday," I reminded him, "by a Miss Carolyn Seaver."

"The day after you got it back from Cuvier?"

"Right."

"What's Carolyn Seaver's address? Do you know?"

"Prestonia Towers. On Clark Terrace."

"Let's go," said Randall.

* * * *

Our luck was out. So was Miss Seaver. She had left for a visit with friends at the shore and had taken *The Henchman* with her to read on the plane. The woman in the adjoining apartment gave us this information, but was unable to give us the name, address, or telephone number of the friends Miss Seaver was visiting. “She’ll be home Saturday afternoon—tomorrow,” the neighbor said. “Can’t you wait twenty-four hours? What’s so important about a library book?”

Randall was honest with her. “We don’t know ourselves. But it may turn out to be evidence in a crime. Will you ask Miss Seaver to get in touch with me the minute she returns?”

The neighbor’s eyes grew round. “Of course.” Randall gave her his phone number. We thanked her, left, and went back to Cuyler’s place, where I’d left my car.

As I climbed out of the police cruiser, Randall said, “Is *The Henchman* a popular book, Hal?”

Randall doesn’t know a best-seller from the *Encyclopedia Britannica.* I said, “Not any more, Lieutenant. The copy we have here hasn’t been borrowed for three months, as you can see from the last stamped date on the card envelope. And copy number two, borrowed, it seems, by both Mr. Cuvier and Miss Seaver in less than a month, represents a real burst of business, I should imagine.”

“Have you read it?”

“*The Henchman*? ’ I shook my head. “Historical fiction isn’t my dish.”

Randall pondered. “Listen. When you get back to the library, brief your librarians for me, will you?”

“On what?”

“Tell them to inform you—or me—immediately if anyone comes into the library and asks for *The Henchman*. And tell them to find out who’s asking, if possible.”

“O.K. And what about the book? Tell anyone who asks that we don’t have it?”

“Yeah. Until we check them out. And, Hal—”

“What?”

“Do one more thing for me. *Read* the goddamn book. Maybe something will jump out at you that seems significant.”

“How am I supposed to recognize anything, even if it’s there?”

Randall’s yellow eyes took on that bland amused look. “How the hell should I know? *You’re* the book detective, aren’t you?”

* * * *

The next day, Saturday, I stayed in the library all day, lining up my call sheets for the following week, so I was in my office when Ellen phoned me from her desk. "Hal?" she said. "Somebody just asked Joan for your book.

I snapped to attention. "*The Henchman*, you mean?"

"Yes. Joan gave her a song and dance and put her in the reading room."

"What song and dance?"

"Joan told her we have *The Henchman* but it's out for repair at the bindery. I'm supposed to be checking now on when it'll be back on the shelves."

"Good for Joan," I said, "and good for you. I'm on my way." Then, in belated surprise, "Did you say *her*, Ellen? Is it a woman?"

Ellen whistled lewdly under her breath. "Wait'll you see her!" she said and hung up.

She was a woman, all right. A blonde, beautiful young woman sitting with her hands clasped around her handbag in one of the reading-room chairs. I went over to her and said, "The librarian tells me you want to borrow *The Henchman*. It will be back in circulation in just a day or two. If you care to leave your name and telephone number, we'll be glad to call you when the book's available."

She stood up and I could see what Ellen's whistle meant. Her figure, which a modish pants suit did little to hide, was nothing short of spectacular. Every eye in the reading room, male and female, turned her way as though magnetized. Her face took on a look of disappointment. "I didn't want to *borrow* the book," she said, "I just wanted to look something up in it here in the library. I'm from out of town."

She didn't look capable of breaking a man's ribs and beating him to death, but maybe she had a friend who was. I said, In that case, perhaps we can help you, after all. "What did you want to look up in *The Henchman*?"

"That's the trouble," she said, "I don't really know.

That shook me a little. I said, "I've read *The Henchman* myself quite recently, Miss—"

"Elmore," she said. "Nancy Elmore."

"Miss Elmore, maybe if you cared to be a little more specific, I might be able to help you. I'm Hal Johnson. I'm on the library staff."

Miss Elmore looked around self-consciously. "Can we go somewhere and talk, Mr. Johnson? I'm sure we re disturbing the people here."

I didn't think the people in the reading room minded being disturbed by this Miss America candidate, but I said, "Good idea, I'll just tell the librarian and we can talk in my office, O.K.?"

Joan, the librarian, was hovering outside the door of the reading room, her curiosity showing. I told her in a library whisper to call Lieutenant Randall at Police Headquarters and tell him somebody named Nancy Elmore had asked for *The Henchman* and that I was about to interview her in my office.

Joan nodded and scurried off.

I had barely got Miss Elmore settled in the one chair in my tiny office when my phone rang. It was Randall. "Is the girl still there?" he asked.

"Yes."

"She says her name's Nancy Elmore?"

"Right."

"Ask her where she's from."

"What?"

"Are you deaf? Ask her where she's from."

"Why?"

"Because if she says Minneapolis, she's probably Jefferson Cuvier's niece. The one we notified of his death. Only living relative, remember?"

"Oh." I looked across my desk at Miss Elmore with new interest.

"Don't let her get away," Randall said. I'll be right over."

I hung up and turned to Miss Elmore. You said you were from out of town, Miss Elmore. Where do you live?"

"Minneapolis. Why?"

I said, "Nancy Elmore. Minneapolis. I *thought* that name sounded familiar. You've got to be the niece of the man who was killed here yesterday, Jefferson Cuyler. Right?"

She was surprised. "Yes, that *is* right. I flew in this morning to arrange for Uncle Jeff's funeral as soon as the police release...his body." She swallowed. "How did you know?"

"I collected some overdue books from your uncle on Monday, Miss Elmore, and he mentioned your name," I lied. "That's where I heard it before. Your uncle seemed very proud of you." 'As who wouldn't be?' I was tempted to add.

"Was *The Henchman* one of the books you collected from Uncle Jeff?" she asked. Beautiful, I thought, but definitely not dumb.

"Yes, it was," I answered carefully, "so I'm naturally curious to know why you're so interested in it now."

She gave me an uncertain smile. "You won't believe this," she said. "It's crazy. Really wild. But Uncle Jeff told me that if he died unexpectedly, I'd find something in that book he wanted me to have."

"Do you know what it is?"

"I guess it's a kind of a will or legacy or something. But I don't know."

"When did your uncle tell you this?"

"In a letter I got from him this past Tuesday."

"Do you have the letter with you?"

She took a new grip on her handbag, which was answer enough. "As I say, I thought it was crazy—until I was notified yesterday that Uncle Jeff had been killed. Then I thought I'd better do what he said. So after I checked in at my hotel I came straight here to the library to look for the book." Impatience or some other emotion roughened her smooth voice. "And now it's not even here! So what do I do now?"

"In your place, I'd tell the police about your letter," I began, just as Lieutenant Randall walked into the room. "Speak of the devil," I said. "Miss Elmore from Minneapolis, this is Lieutenant Randall of our very efficient Police Department. He's in charge of investigating your uncle's death."

Randall put his sleepy-looking, unblinking yellow eyes on her. "*If* she's really Nancy Elmore from Minneapolis," he said ungraciously.

Then to her. "Are you?"

Her answering smile took all of the official starch out of Randall. He appreciates a good-looking woman as well as the next man. "I'm sorry," he apologized gruffly, "but I have to be sure, you know." He checked the driving license and credit cards she handed him. Then, satisfied, he said to me, "What about the letter, Hal?"

I told him, making it short.

"Do you mind showing the letter to us, Miss Elmore?" he asked her, as bland as coffee cream now.

She dug in her handbag and came up with it. I read it over Randall's shoulder:

MONDAY

Dear Nancy,

This is to tell you that the fishing trip of which I wrote you in my last letter went off very well. You'll be glad to hear that my ailing heart performed splendidly throughout.

I must tell you, however, that upon returning home this morning, I have noted certain disquieting signs that my spell of good fortune may be nearing an end. I won't go into detail but I'll be frank with you: I feel I may suffer an attack at any time now. An attack which might even prove fatal.

I don't want to frighten you, Nancy. But I do want you to be aware that you are my sole heir. Hence this hasty letter, just in case.

You see, my dear, there are reasons, which I won't go into, why I can't just draw up a will in the usual way. So if anything happens to me, I suggest that you visit the main branch of our local public library and ask for a book written by Eugene Stott called *The Henchman*. In it, you will find my legacy to you for what it's worth. It will puzzle you, I'm afraid. So I further suggest that you consult our local police about it, showing them this letter. I am confident they will help you locate my estate, and will see to it, I trust, that you get what is coming to you.

Affectionately, as always, Uncle Jeff

Randall didn't say anything for a few seconds after he finished reading. Instead he looked at me and raised his eyebrows.

I nodded. "I think she ought to know the score," I said.

Randall gave her the story: the attempted robbery, the murder, the memo-pad writing, the whole thing. Including where copy number two of *The Henchman* was at the moment.

She listened quietly. At the end of his recital, she sighed. "Poor Uncle Jeff. I honestly thought he might be turning senile when I read that letter. But he wasn't, was he? The 'disquieting signs' in his letter was the attempted robbery. And the 'attack' he feared wasn't a heart attack, but an attack on him by the people who killed him. Do you think he knew who they were?"

"Yes."

"Then why didn't he tell the police?"

"I don't know," said Randall, brooding. He tapped the letter with a forefinger.

I put my oar in, just to avoid being forgotten. "So what do we do now? Wait till Miss Seaver gets home from the shore with *The Henchman*?"

"No." Randall was emphatic. "You two are interested primarily in what's in the book. I'm interested in catching a murderer. So we put copy number one of *The Henchman* back on the shelves, Hal. And its file index card back in the cabinet. And we hope very hard that the murderer will still come in today and try to get the book." He reached for my phone. "I'll put a man in the library to nab anybody else who shows interest in it."

* * * *

When I got back, Randall and Nancy Elmore were leaving. "When we hear from Miss Seaver," Randall was saying to her, "I'll be in touch."

She thanked him and gave him the name of her hotel. He said he'd drop her off there on his way back to Headquarters. Then she thanked me too, and they left.

"Jimmy Coogan is on his way over to babysit with the book," Randall said over his shoulder. "Will you watch it until he gets here?"

"Sure," I said.

I went to the reading room and took a seat to the right of the double-door entrance. From there I could see the shelf where I'd put *The Henchman*, could even make out the crimson cover of the book itself.

It was just as well I took up my vigil when I did, because it wasn't five minutes after Randall left that the action started.

A massive chunky man with shaggy hair and a drooping mustache hove into view at the far end of the aisle of bookshelves I was watching. He had the muscular sure-footed look of a pro fullback. His big shoulders strained the seams of the windbreaker he wore. As he came toward me, I caught a brief glimpse of his face: blunt features, small eyes sunk in deep sockets, a thin slash of a mouth under the mustache. Unlike the beautiful Miss Elmore, I thought, this specimen would be capable of breaking a man's ribs and beating him to death. He carried a battered black briefcase in one hand.

He moved unhurriedly up the aisle of bookshelves, his eyes turning from side to side as he scanned the numbers on the spines of the books, obviously seeking a certain number and a certain book.

It was warm in the reading room, but cold fingers touched my spine.

I got the tight feeling in my stomach I used to get at the start of action when I was a real cop. After my relatively peaceful time as a library detective, the old sensation, oddly enough, was almost pleasant, a reminder of more exciting times. From behind a copy of *Newsweek*, I watched the man.

Suddenly he halted, reached out a hand, and plucked a book from the shelf. The book with the crimson cover. *The Henchman*. At the same time he gave a nod of satisfaction, as though congratulating himself on a stroke of good luck.

He raised his eyes to look around him. I dropped mine to the magazine. Evidently he saw nothing to alarm him, because when I risked a surreptitious look he was in the act of opening the book.

While I watched, he gave the book a superficial examination, first leafing rapidly through it, then holding it upside down by its covers and shaking it to dislodge anything that might be lying loose between its pages. Finding nothing, he pried up with his fingernail one corner of the card envelope in the front of the book and peered beneath it. Again nothing. He paused, considering his next move.

I was fairly sure what that move would be—a more thorough inspection of the book in a more private place. And I was right. After another quick survey of his surroundings, he casually opened his briefcase, put *The Henchman* in it, and turned to leave.

I stood up and followed him toward Ellen's check-out desk, knowing with absolute certainty that he didn't intend to stop for Ellen to check out the book in the usual way. Ellen, busy with a half dozen customers, didn't even look up as he strode past her desk.

I caught up with him in the lobby before he was able to push through the glass doors of the exit. I tapped him on the shoulder from behind.

For the space of half a breath, he kept going. Then he halted and swung around, his eyes mean. "What?"

"You've forgotten something, haven't you, sir?' I asked in my smoothest library voice.

"Forgot what?" His knuckles tightened on the handle of the briefcase.

"I believe you forgot to check out the library book in your briefcase."

He blinked. "Who the hell are you?"

"A member of the library staff. I must ask you to check out your book in the usual way before removing it from the library."

"I don't have any book of yours, buster. Get lost." He began to turn away.

"I saw you put it in your briefcase," I said. I was beginning to sweat. What was I thinking of, bracing him before Jimmy Coogan arrived to back me up? For I knew after tapping that iron-solid shoulder that I couldn't take this gorilla alone the best day I ever lived.

He gave me a tight grin, displaying yellow teeth with a gap between the upper fronts. "You got it all wrong," he said. "I'll tell you one more time. I don't *have* a book of yours. So drop dead."

"Let's just have a look in your briefcase," I suggested mildly. "That ought to settle it."

"Not a chance, pal. This briefcase is private property. *My* private property. That means it ain't open to the public. So goodbye." He turned his back and started for the exit doors again.

I let him go, deciding with a feeling of immense relief that discretion in this case seemed the better part of you know what. That is, I let him go until I caught a glimpse of the cheerful Irish countenance of Jimmy Coogan climbing the library steps. It was a heartening sight—so heartening that I grabbed the book thief by one arm—the arm with the briefcase—and whirled him around again. I said sternly, "I can arrest you, you know. So why not cooperate?"

"*Arrest* me?" He laughed out loud. "You and who else, junior?"

"Me and Detective Coogan of the Police Department," I said with a touch of smugness, "who is now coming through the door behind you." I raised my voice. "Hey, Jimmy! Here's a customer for you."

The man snarled like an animal and swung around, poised for flight. Coogan blocked his way. "Hold it!" he advised in a quiet tone that snapped like a whip. "What's going on here?"

"This guy's stealing one of our books," I said, giving Coogan a meaningful look. "It's in his briefcase."

"Is that so now?" Coogan murmured. "Would you mind opening the case, sir?"

"Why should I? There's no book in it."

"Yes, there is," I insisted. "A book called *The Henchman*." Another meaningful glance at Coogan.

Coogan clicked his tongue reprovingly. “In that case, sir,” he said cheerfully, “I’m afraid you’ll have to come downtown with me until we straighten this out. I’ll just take charge of your briefcase in the meantime.” He held out his hand, giving his prisoner a flash of his ID.

I could almost see the wheels going around in the thief’s head. This is no big deal, he was telling himself. At the most they’ve got me for book theft—a crummy misdemeanor that I can settle by returning the book or paying for it.

After a moment’s hesitation, he nodded sullenly and handed the briefcase to Coogan. I said, “Get him out of here, Jimmy, O.K.? Before we upset the whole library. I’m glad you showed up when you did.” I winked at Coogan. “I don’t think I could have handled him alone.”

Coogan beamed at the thief. “But you won’t give *me* any trouble, will you now?” he asked politely. Coogan can afford to be polite. He stands six feet five and weighs in at 260 on the police scales.

* * * *

At four o’clock, Randall called me. “Thanks for Slenski,” he said.

“Slenski? Is that his name?”

“Yeah. Truck driver based in Detroit. He could be our man, Hal. Although he denies it, of course.”

“Both for the break-in and the murder?”

“We’ve already checked him out in Detroit. The trucking outfit he works for says his schedule put him here in town both last weekend and this.”

“But he has airtight alibis for both nights, no doubt.”

“Certainly.” There was a shrug in Randall’s voice. “When he’s in town, he always stays with a waitress at the Radio Bar, name of Ellie Slack. And Ellie Slack tells us that Slenski was with her both of the nights in question. All night.”

“Lying in her teeth?”

“Probably. Slenski also claims she recommended *The Henchman* to him as a good yarn to kill time with between runs.”

I said, “That ought to prove she’s a liar. Even a bar waitress would know it’s no kind of book for a truck-driver.”

“Slenski says he thought he’d just ‘borrow’ it from the public library and return it the next time he hits town—less trouble than all the red tape of applying for a non-resident library card and so forth. Obviously a crock. But we can’t prove he’s lying. At least not yet.”

“He’s lying,” I said. “Take my word for it.”

Randall laughed. He seemed in high good humor. “He’s offered to pay for your damned book, so don’t bad-mouth him.”

"Well, that's generous. You're holding him all the same, aren't you?"

"Sure. At least until we find out what's in Miss Seaver's copy of *The Henchman*. I'm hoping that'll point us toward some sort of a connection between Slenski and Cuvier. So far, we can't find any."

"How about Miss Seaver?" I said. "Is she home yet?"

"That's why I called. She's home. Are you free to go with us to pick up the book?"

"I wouldn't miss it for the world, I said.

"We'll meet you at the library's main entrance in twenty minutes."

* * * *

Miss Seaver didn't mind in the least giving up her copy of *The Henchman*. "I didn't even finish it," she said. "It's a poorly written, predictable story, and I can't imagine how it could possibly be connected with a crime…)

Randall suggested that she watch the newspapers to see if it actually *was* connected with a crime, and we left.

The Lieutenant pretended to be calm and properly official about the book, but he was just as anxious to learn its secret, if any, as Miss Elmore and me. Or else Miss Elmore's Christmas-morning look of anticipation won him over. He handed me the book as we settled into the police car for the ride back to town and said, "Here, Hal, you're the book expert. Give it a look while I drive."

I obliged. And of course, once you knew there was something to find in the book, finding it proved to be easy. What we were looking for wasn't in the book at all, as it turned out; it was *behind* the book. When I bent the covers back on themselves and held the book up against the light and peered through the opening between the spine and the binding, I could see it plainly. "There's *something* here, Lieutenant," I said, keeping my voice level for Miss Elmore's benefit, although I felt excitement quickening my pulse.

Randall took his eyes off the road briefly. "What is it?"

"It looks like a key," I said. I shook the book hard. "It's glued, I guess—to the inner surface of the spine."

"Well, get it out," Randall directed.

Easier said than done. The key must have been cemented to the inside of the spine cover with epoxy or something of the sort, because it stubbornly refused to be pried loose. In the end, I cut the book cover through with my pocket knife and jimmied the key loose with the screwdriver from the toolkit of the police car.

When I had the key free, Lieutenant Randall pulled over to the curb and parked, leaving the motor running. "Let's see it," he said.

I handed the key to him. Flat, about two inches long, with a rounded head, it looked something like a standard safe-deposit-box key; yet the notches cut into only one edge of the flat shank were far too simple and uncomplicated for that. The number 97 was stamped into the head.

Randall grinned at Miss Elmore. "Well, here's your legacy," he said.

"What do you suppose it's a key to?

Randall turned the key in his fingers. "A locker of some sort, I'd guess."

I thought he was right. "Bus station, maybe?" I suggested.

He shrugged. "Could be. Or bowling alley, country club, railroad station, city club, almost anywhere. So all we'll have to do is try the key on number 97 of every bank of lockers in the city."

I didn't say anything because I knew he wasn't serious. Miss Elmore said, "But I know poor Uncle Jeff didn't belong to any kind of club, so that should narrow it down, shouldn't it?"

"How about the YMCA?" Randall asked.

"Yes!" Miss Elmore cried. "He *did* belong to the YMCA! He went swimming twice a week in the YMCA pool. How did you guess that?"

"Just routine police work," Randall answered, deadpan. Then, "Look under the cement." He handed her the key.

Peering over her shoulder, breathing her carnation scent, I could see too, through the hardened gob of transparent cement still adhering to the key head, four small letters stamped into the metal: YMCA.

When Randall and I went into the locker room of the YMCA fifteen minutes later, Miss Elmore remained in the police car outside. All she said as we left her was, "Please hurry! I'm dying of curiosity!"

The locker room was sparsely populated: maybe a dozen men, mostly young, dressing or undressing, none of them in the aisle of lockers we wanted. We stopped in front of locker 97 and had our first surprise.

Locker 97 wasn't locked. What's more, there wasn't even a keyhole in the door to show that it *could* be locked. "Ouch!" I murmured.

Randall swore under his breath, grabbed the door handle, tripped the latch, and pulled the locker door open wide.

We breathed easier. The lower left segment inside was a locker within a locker—a little built-in safe in which you could leave your valuables, I guess, while you were swimming, playing basketball, or working out in the gym. The inner locker *was* locked. It had a keyhole. And Uncle Jeff's key slid into it smooth as grease.

Randall took a breath, raised his eyebrows at me, turned the key, and opened up.

We found ourselves looking at three bulging canvas bags crammed together into the three cubic feet of locker space. The bags had the words

"Crane Security Express" stenciled on them. And they contained, as Randall told me later, three hundred and eleven thousand dollars in cash.

* * * *

A few days later, over a pizza and beer which he insisted on paying for, Randall told me the rest of the story. I suppose it was his way of thanking me for my help in what he was already calling The Henchman Case.

"Cuyler was working for Crane Security when he had his heart attack and had to retire a year or so ago. But he only had his Social Security payments to live on because he hadn't been with Crane long enough to qualify for a pension. So there he was, a widower, a semi-invalid with an uncertain future, and all alone in the world except for a niece in Minneapolis."

"Yum," I said.

"Shut up, Hal," he said. "Do you want to hear this or don't you?"

"Continue, I urged him, "please."

"Cuyler is bitter at his rotten luck in being so poor so suddenly. He decides he'll try to steal enough money from his old firm to live high on the hog for whatever time he has left. After all, they wouldn't even pay him a pension, the ungrateful tightwads."

I said, "Where does your truck driver come in?"

"Cuyler hired him to do the actual robbery. He hadn't the nerve to do it himself."

"I remember the heist," I said. "A Crane Security Express van loaded with cash for three or four payroll deliveries was cleaned out in the parking lot of some diner while the guards were having lunch inside."

"Slenski did the cleaning out. Cuyler waited around the corner in the getaway car. It was a cozy set-up. Cuyler knew all about the routes, schedules, pick-ups, and deliveries of the Crane vans; he also knew the guards on that particular van always stopped for lunch on Fridays at that diner and left the van unattended in the parking lot. He also managed to get keys to the van's door-locks."

Something was bothering me. I said, "Two questions, Lieutenant. You told me we recovered the entire loot from the van robbery in Cuyler's YMCA locker. So why hadn't Cuyler spent any of it since the robbery? And what did the truck driver get out of the caper?"

Randall said, "Cuyler was probably waiting for the heat to die down a bit before he began spending hot money. As for Slenski's cut, it was five thousand dollars—a good hunk of Cuyler's savings—paid to Slenski half beforehand and the other half when Slenski turned over the loot to Cuyler. Slenski went off home to Detroit, apparently pleased with his windfall. But he didn't stay pleased very long. When he had a chance to think things over, he realized he'd been taken. And he decided not to hold still for it."

"So he tried to help himself to a bigger cut when he broke into Cuyler's house that Sunday night?" I said.

"Sure. Who else would make such a shambles of the place?"

"So Cuvier figures he'll try again. Maybe right away. And telling the cops is out for obvious reasons. Even though he suspects Slenski may cut up pretty rough on his next visit."

"That's when he decided to write that letter to his niece, and to hide the key to his YMCA locker in your library book. He wanted his niece to know the score if anything happened to him."

"It seems to me it would have been simpler all around to send the key to his niece in the letter."

"It would. But Cuvier definitely intended to enjoy that money himself if he had the chance. And he was afraid, maybe, that his niece would get so curious about the key that she might find out he was a thief while he was still alive. And he didn't want that."

I finished off my pizza and drained my beer mug. I said, "Come on, Lieutenant, you used to lecture me about the rules of evidence. What evidence—*hard* evidence—do you have that Slenski actually beat up Cuvier and caused his death? As far as you know and can really prove, Slenski is just a petty out-of-town thief who snitched a book from our public library here. Isn't that right?"

"No, it isn't right." There was honey in Randall's voice. "Didn't I tell you, Hal? We found a memo in Slenski's wallet the day you turned him in. Oddly enough, the memo said: '*The Henchman*. Eugene Stott. Public Library,' and was in the very same handwriting as *our* memo from Cuyler's house. We knew we had him cold for Cuyler's killing before we found the Scott loot."

"Mercy," I said, "you do play them close to your vest, don't you, Lieutenant?"

"When we showed him we had him all wrapped up for murder, he sang like a canary to get his rap reduced. How do you think we learned all this jazz about the robbery?"

"Routine police work," I said, grinning. I was quiet for a minute, thinking. Then I said, "The real screwball in the whole mess was handsome Uncle Jeff, if you ask me."

"I'm not asking you. But why?"

"That nutty letter to his niece for one thing. Telling her he was leaving her a legacy in a library book, then telling her to go to the *police*, for God's sake, to be sure she got it. That was a great legacy to go to the police about! Three hundred thousand *stolen* dollars!

Randall laughed. "Old Cuvier wasn't so dumb, Hal."

"No?"

"No. You're forgetting the reward."

I was. It had been widely advertised at the time of the robbery. Twenty-five thousand to anybody supplying information leading to the arrest of the thieves or the recovery of the money. I said, "You mean Nancy Elmore gets the reward?"

"Sure, said Randall. "The least I could do was to see she collected it. He paused. "Of course, Miss Elmore did see fit to write a big fat check for the Police Widows and Orphans Fund before she left for Minneapolis."

"How peachy for the Widows and Orphans," I said. "But *I* found the key in the book, remember. *I* snagged the murderer for you. Don't I get something for that?"

"Sorry," said Randall, his cat's eyes showing amusement, "but you're neither a widow nor an orphan, Hal. Will you settle for another beer?"

"I guess I'll have to," I said sadly.

THE YOUNG RUNNERS

Originally published in* Ellery Queen's Mystery Magazine, *July 1978.

It was the worst kind of tenement. In the 1200 block of Gardenia Street. I checked my list to be sure I had the address right. Then I went inside, looking for a young man named Jasper Jones.

In my capacity as a library cop, I'd been in the neighborhood before, trying to trace books that had been stolen from the public library. This time, however, I was on Gardenia Street merely to collect an overdue book. A routine call.

Gardenia Street. The littered filthy hallway of the tenement didn't smell like gardenias, believe me. Luckily the room I was looking for was on the ground floor. I rapped lightly on the door.

It was cautiously opened a few inches by a once-pretty woman with a pale face and a do-it-yourself blonde dye job. She peered out at me with tired-looking eyes.

"Yes?"

"I'm looking for Jasper Jones," I said. "Is he here?"

Sudden concern made her tired eyes even more tired. "Jasper? He's not home from school yet. What's he done?" she asked. "Has Jasper done something? Who are you?"

I told her, and showed her my ID card from the library.

"Oh," she said, relieved. "Well, Jasper isn't home yet, like I said. I'm sorry."

"You're Mrs. Jones? Jasper's mother?"

"That's right." She perked up a little, fluffing her hair with one hand. She didn't invite me in, though.

"Maybe you can help me then. Mrs. Jones. If you can find Jasper's overdue library book and pay me the small fine he owes on it, I won't need to bother Jasper at all."

She said, "Jasper's really a terrific reader for an eleven-year-old, Mr. Johnson." There was pride in her voice. "And consequently, he gets so many books from the public library that I can't even begin to keep track of them. So...)

"He borrows a lot of books, all right," I agreed. "Our children's librarian told me that. But this is the first time Jasper's ever failed to return a book on time. So it's no big deal, Mrs. Jones. With his excellent record I'll even forget the fine if you'll just give me the book."

"I'm sorry, Mr. Johnson." Mrs. Jones sounded harried. "I'm trying to get dressed to go to work and I'm late, okay? Can't you find Jasper and ask *him* about your book? I haven't got time to look for it right now."

"Sure," I said. "Where'll I find him?"

"Well, you can either wait here till he gets home, or you can probably find him in the park two blocks down. He usually stops there on his way home from school."

"Thanks, Mrs. Jones." I left her and went out and took a deep breath of the polluted outside air. It smelled as fresh as gardenias compared with the air in the tenement hallway.

I walked the two blocks down Gardenia to Mrs. Jones's "park." It turned out to be a playground. No trees, flowers, grass, or rustic benches. Just a sun-baked expanse of bare beaten earth, enclosed by a chain-link fence eight feet high. At one end of the enclosure was a mounted basketball hoop, and I could make out the faint markings of old softball bases in the dust. A bunch of kids, some black, some white, all ages up to about 15, was having a high old time in a pickup basketball game beneath the single basket. There was a lot of yelling, jumping, and juvenile cursing, and a lot of wild set and hook shots that never came near the basket. Another bunch of kids was standing around offering comments and waiting for a chance to get into the game.

It was evident that Jasper Jones wasn't the only ghetto kid to stop here on his way home from school, because schoolbooks, homework papers, and bulging book bags were scattered on the ground along the inside of the wire fence. Three battered old bicycles, and one that looked almost new, were leaning against the fence went into the playground and walked along the fence past the books and bicycles toward the knot of nonparticipants in the game. They watched me come in unfriendly silence. I didn't know whether their unfriendliness was because I was dressed so well for this neighborhood, or because they smelled cop on me. Probably the latter. I'd been a Homicide cop for quite a few years before I switched to the public library, and I knew that these street-wise ghetto kids could smell fuzz a mile off—even harmless library fuzz like me.

I went up to a tall gangly black boy who had outgrown his windbreaker by six inches and said politely, "Can you tell me if Jasper Jones is around?"

He treated me to a long thoughtful stare before he replied, "Who wants to know?" He wasn't being arrogant or nasty, just cautious.

"I'm from the public library and Jasper has an overdue book I want to collect," I said. "Is he here?"

"Yeah," said the boy in the windbreaker, making up his mind. He turned and shouted toward the players, "Hey, Jazz! Guy to see you!" I could feel the hostility around me subside.

The youngster who responded to this summons was small for his age. He had a shock of black unruly hair, a thin face with a pointed chin, and two of the brightest blue eyes I've ever seen. The eyes were older than the kid. He said to the tall black boy who had called him out of the game, "Go in for me, will you, George?" I thought Jasper's team would benefit by the change. For tall George was obviously better equipped as a basketball player than this short eleven-year-old that faced me.

He was panting a little from his recent exertions on the basketball court. He led me away from the other kids a few steps and said, "Yeah? You want me?" His blue eyes looked me over.

"If you're Jasper Jones, I do. I came to get a library book from you, Jasper."

"Call me Jazz," he said cockily. "Everybody does." Then, "A library book?" he repeated. "I never saw you before, did I?"

"Not that I know of. What difference does that make? I still have to collect the library book from you. It's four weeks overdue." I showed him my library identification card.

"Oh!" he said. In some curious way his steady blue eyes seemed to be reassessing me. "Overdue? What's the name of the book, Mister? You must be wrong. I never keep a book out too long."

"We sent you an overdue notice, Jazz. Didn't you get it?"

He looked blank. "Nope. I suppose Mom didn't bother telling me. Anyway, what's the book?"

I said, "*The Robber of Featherbed Lane*. Remember it?"

He shook his head. "Naw. I read 'em so fast I don't even bother to look at their names, half the time."

"Well," I said, letting some of my impatience show, "I've come all the way out here to get that book, Jazz, so let's go back to your place and find it, huh?"

Jasper looked over my shoulder into the distance. "No use going to my place," he said uncomfortably. "It's not there."

"How do you know till you look?"

"I just know, that's all, man." He raised his eyes to mine.

"That's no answer. How do you know?"

He frowned in thought. At length he said, "I guess I'll have to tell you." His expression was half hang-dog belligerent, half proud. "I've got this little business going on the side with your library books, man, and that particular book—"

I interrupted him. "A little business on the side? What kind of business? Are you *selling* our library books?"

He was scornful. "You're not too sharp, are you, Mister? If I was selling your crummy books, how come none of 'em ever turned up missing before?"

He had me there. "So what is this business of yours?" I asked.

"I don't sell your books, I rent them," explained Jasper Jones blandly.

I couldn't keep from grinning at him. A rental library operated by an 11-year-old businessman with somebody else's books was something I'd never run into before. I said as severely as I could, "You mean you rent all those books you get from the public library to other kids?"

"Sure." Unrepentant. "After I've read 'em myself, why not?"

"Can't they apply for library cards and borrow their own books—free?"

"I save 'em a lot of time and trouble by letting 'em read mine. They pay me a nickel apiece and promise to put 'em in the library book-drop before the date on the card. And that saves *me* a lot of trouble. I don't have to keep track of the dates and return 'em myself."

"Some racket," I said. "Do you make much money at it?"

He beamed. "I made enough the last coupla years to buy me that set of wheels over there." He pointed proudly at the almost new bicycle leaning against the fence. There was a big book bag on the flat luggage rack above the rear wheel. Jasper, suddenly cautious, asked anxiously. "It's okay for me to do that, isn't it? Rent library books, I mean? Long as the books are back on time?"

I laughed. "As far as I know, there's no law against lending—or renting—public library books to other people besides the cardholder. Always providing, of course, the library gets its books back in good shape." I fixed him with a stern look. "Which brings us back to *The Robber of Featherbed Lane*. Do you know which of your—ah—customers you rented that one to?"

"Yeah." He hesitated. "Solly Joseph. That's why I didn't tell you. Solly's the class behind me at school. And Solly's old man got drunk and tore your library book all to pieces because he didn't want Solly reading anything about robbers, see?" Jasper sighed heavily. "So I guess I got to pay for the book, right?"

"Right," I said. "Or your mother or father or somebody."

He said, "I'll pay for it myself. Mom never has any bread. She's only working part time. And my old man went off somewhere a coupla years ago."

"Okay," I said. "Three fifty. Kids' books run kind of high these days. I'm sorry."

"Forget it," he said with a chopping gesture. "I'll collect it from Solly, don't worry." He took an old-fashioned coin purse from his jeans, opened it, and counted out $3.50 into my hand—two one-dollar bills and the rest in small change. "Is that it?"

"That's it." I grinned at him. He was quite a kid. "Now you better get back in that basketball game, Jazz. Your friend George just missed an easy layup."

Everybody at the library got a big kick out of my story about Jasper Jones and his book-rental operation. And about Solly Joseph's old man getting drunk and destroying one of our children's books because it might have a bad influence on Solly. Olive Gaston, head children's librarian, was especially amused. "That little Jasper Jones goes out of here every Saturday morning as regular as clockwork," she said, "with so many books in his book-bag he can hardly carry it. So *that's* why he takes so many. He rents them. He always tells me it's because he's such a fast reader."

I turned in the kid's $3.50 along with the day's fines, and forgot about Jasper Jones until several weeks later when Lieutenant Randall, my former boss at the Police Department, brought the incident back to mind.

We were having a pizza and beer together in Tony's Diner, having met there at Randall's suggestion. He made it clear, however, that I was not his guest; I could pay for my own pizza out of the princely salary the library paid me for being what he called a "sissy" cop. Randall has never forgiven me for leaving him and the Department and seeking a more literate, not to mention more literary, association.

I started on my pizza and opened with my usual query, "Well, how many murders did you solve today, Lieutenant?"

Normally he'll answer this with a sour glance from his spooky eyes and a contemptuous belch if he's drinking beer. Tonight, however, he replied promptly, as though on cue. "One," he said.

"One?" I raised my eyebrows. "A new record. Congratulations."

"Don't knock it," he said. "It lets me do you a little favor."

"A favor?" I stared at him. "You feeling all right?"

"I feel fine," he said, chomping on a large section of pizza to prove it.

"Then for God's sake," I said, "tell me about it."

He shrugged, obviously pleased that I'd given him the lead. "Nothing much to it," he apologized. "Routine stuff. Fellow got stabbed in a bar in a quarrel with a former girlfriend about his present girlfriend. He made it home and quietly bled to death. You remember that kind, don't you? From when you were a real cop?" He underlined the word *real* with his voice.

“Yeah,” I said, “I remember.” And I did. It made me a little homesick for Homicide, but not much.

“When they discovered the stiff about midnight,” Randall went on, “they called me and I went out there. Ghetto room on South Wildflower.”

“And you solved the case instantly?”

“Took about half an hour. Three witnesses in the bar saw the stabbing and could identify the stabber. We’ve got the murderess sewed up tight.”

“Where does a favor for me come into it?” It’s hard for me to tell, even after all these years, when Lieutenant Randall is kidding and when he’s serious.

“That’s the real reason I called you tonight, Hal. Kind of a curious thing, but I saw right away last night that I could do you some good.”

“You going to tell me how?”

“Certainly. But answer a question first. You probably think of me as a tough, unappreciative, demanding type who asks for favors but never returns one, right?” Randall’s unwinking cat’s eyes gleamed in the fluorescent lights of the diner.

“Right.” I agreed heartily, playing along.

“So I go out to where this fellow bleeds to death and look over the scene, and to my utter amazement,” said Randall, grinning like a chimpanzee with a banana in view, “I discover something that makes me think of you immediately.”

“What? Either tell me or shut up.”

He took a long swallow of beer. “You wouldn’t have dared talk to me that way in the old days,” he complained.

“That’s one reason I left you.”

He wiped beer foam off his lips with a paper napkin. Then he said with dignity, “You’ve done me several favors since you left the Department, Hal. I’ll admit it. You’ve helped me solve a couple of my major cases. So now I’m going to help you solve one of *your* major cases. Tit for tat. And prove that I’m not as unappreciative as you think.”

“Hurry up,” I said, “before I start to cry or sing ‘Hearts and Flowers.’”

He grinned. “What I’m going to do for you, pal, is to save you a lot of time and trouble—and an unnecessary trip to South 1 Wildflower Street.”

I sat up. Despite himself, Lieutenant Randall was beginning to interest me. “Yeah?” I said.

“Yeah.” He was enjoying himself.

“How come?”

“Well, when I got out there and the M.E. had taken a gander at the stiff, I kind of cased the dead guy’s room a little bit.” Randall made a face. “It was a dump. Filth, stench, a real pigsty, you know?”

I nodded. I remembered that from my cop days, too.

"But the surprise was, I found a book under the guy's bed," said Randall, smirking. "The only book in the whole joint. Like he'd thrown it under the bed and forgotten about it. And you know what it was?"

"A library book?" I guessed.

"Right. And I looked at the card in it, and you know something? That book was way overdue, Hal. Think of that! Overdue! That's a pretty heinous crime in library circles, I said to myself. So what did I generously decide to do? I decided to bring the book in for you, thus saving you the arduous job of tracking the damn thing down and bringing your criminal to justice!" He leaned back and made an expansive gesture.

I said, "You're all heart, Lieutenant. Where's the book?"

"I've got it. Don't fret yourself, son. But there's a couple of funny things about it that probably call for the attention of an expert book detective like yourself."

"Such as?"

"Such as the fact that it says inside the front cover of the book that it's intended for kids from ten to fourteen years old. And this murdered man of mine was twenty-seven if he was a day." Randall snickered into his beer glass.

"A kid's book? Well." I paused. "Maybe your murder victim was what we call a reluctant reader. There's no disgrace in reading kids' books, you know, even if you're grown up."

"I understand that. And you think he may have been one of your reluctant-reader types, is that it?"

"Maybe."

He shook his head solemnly. "No way, Hal. This guy was a cheap hood with a record as long as your arm. The only reading he ever did was the sports page and the racing form. And what's more, he was a junkie. Hooked like a mackerel, judging from all the mainline needle marks on him. So what's with the children's literature under the bed?"

I shrugged. "Beats me."

"No solutions from the famous book detective, Hal Johnson?"

"Not tonight," I said. "Now you've pulled your gag, let's have the book."

Right then was when I suddenly recalled my eleven-year-old friend Jasper Jones. For the book Randall handed to me over the table was *The Robber of Featherbed Lane*. I looked at him. "Was the name of your stabbing victim Joseph, by any chance?"

"Yeah. How'd you guess that? Although he was better known as Joe."

I relaxed a little. "Joe what?"

"Joe Sabatini," Randall said.

* * * *

More out of curiosity than anything else, I checked the book against our records the next day to see if it could possibly be the copy that Jasper Jones had reported destroyed by Solly Joseph's drunken father. With four or five copies of most juvenile books circulating through our library system, it was unlikely this could be Jasper Jones's overdue book.

But it was.

My first thought was that Solly Joseph had told Jasper Jones a big lie about what happened to the book he'd rented. My second thought was that if so, Jasper had probably taken $3.50 out of Solly's hide by this time. My third thought was that I ought to return Jasper's money now that our book was recovered. My fourth thought was that the fines on the book almost equaled $3.50 by now, anyway, so why bother? And my fifth thought was, belatedly enough, that maybe Jasper Jones was the one who'd been lying.

I stopped counting at that point and just let my memory of Jasper's conversation with me slosh around in my head. Right away several curious angles occurred to me that I hadn't noticed at the time. For one thing, I now found it rather puzzling that when I'd told Jasper I'd come to collect a library book from him, his initial reaction was to ask me a strange question: "I never saw you before, did I?" Then, when I'd explained it was an *overdue* library book and identified myself, his whole manner had undergone a subtle change. And while claiming not to remember *The Robber of Featherbed Lane* at first, he'd later remembered exactly what had been done to that particular book by Solly Joseph's intoxicated father.

I didn't want to believe that an eleven-year-old ghetto kid had been able to con an old pro like me so easily. But the conviction grew. During my rounds that day doubts about Jasper Jones kept flagging at me.

I got back to the library about three in the afternoon, and after sitting in my office for ten minutes, looking at the wall, I reached for the phone and dialed Gardenia Street Grade School. I explained to the secretary in the principal's office who I was, telling her the truth. Then I embroidered it a little. "A couple of kids from your school have applied for cards at the public library," I told her, "and we're checking them out before we issue the cards." Nonsense, of course, but the secretary didn't know that. "Would you be good enough to confirm that they're bona-fide students in your school?"

"Certainly," she said. "What are their names?"

"Jasper Jones," I said. "Probably in the fifth or sixth grade. Maybe seventh. And Solly, or Solomon. Joseph, around the fifth grade, I guess."

She went off to check their rolls and when she came back on she said, “Jasper Jones is in our sixth grade. But we have no Solly or Solomon Joseph in any grade that I can find. Does that help you?”

“Enormously,” I said. “I had doubts about Joseph myself and you’ve confirmed them.” I thanked her and hung up.

So there was no Solly Joseph in the class behind Jasper Jones at Gardenia Street School. How about that? Solly had been made up out of whole cloth for my benefit, apparently. And Solly’s drunken father, too.

On my way home that evening I took *The Robber of Featherbed Lane* with me to Police Headquarters, and without stopping first at Randall’s office I paid a visit to my old side-kick, Jerry Baskin, who heads up the police laboratory. I handed him the book and asked him as a personal favor to give it his best going over, and let me know if he found anything out of the way about it. And not—repeat not—to say anything about it to anyone at the Department until I gave him the word.

He agreed, for old times’ sake. And for the fifth of J & B Scotch which just happened to be peeking out of my carcoat pocket. “What am I supposed to be looking for?” Jerry asked me, uncapping the Scotch and taking a luxurious sniff of its rich aroma.

“Anything,” I said. “Or nothing. I don’t know. But give it your best shot, will you?”

“Okay,” said Jerry. “I’ll call you.”

He called me the following afternoon. “Your library book, Hal,” he said without preamble, “I found something.”

“What?” I asked.

“Traces of heroin in the card pocket.”

“Heroin?” My heart gave a sickening lurch. “You sure?”

“Mexican, I’d guess. Not enough to analyze for quality. But definitely heroin, Hal.”

“I was afraid of that.” I paused, thinking. I wanted to be sure. I said, “Will you give some other books the same treatment for me, Jerry?”

“Why not?” Jerry said. “At a bottle of Scotch per book, what can I lose?”

I went to the children’s library and took from the shelves half a dozen of the books borrowed by Jasper Jones and recently returned. Olive Gaston dug them up for me without comment and I took them over to Jerry Baskin. With only one more bottle of J & B, however, not half a dozen. I can’t afford to be a spendthrift on my anemic library expense account.

Jerry reported his findings on the additional books two days later: three of the six books I’d given him showed traces of heroin in the card pockets. “Anything else?” I asked him.

“A shred of glassine paper in one card pocket, Hal.”

That's when I went to see Lieutenant Randall. Facing him across his scarred desk, I said, "You remember that library book you found under Joe Sabatini's bed?"

"What about it?"

I told him the whole story. Throughout my recital he didn't move, he didn't blink his cat's eyes once. I finished up by saying morosely, "I'm sure the kid isn't on smack himself. So all I can come up with is that he's a pusher. That he's not renting library books to his pals, but passing them out to his customers with packets of heroin in the card pockets. What's more innocent-looking than a kid's library book? This is an eleven-year-old kid, Lieutenant! I can't believe it!"

Randall lit a cigarette. "You've been out of touch too long, Hal. Messing around with your library books. The Narc boys are arresting kids as young as Jasper Jones every day. Didn't you know that?"

"No."

"They are. And even younger. The kids are recruited to the drug trade primarily because they *are* kids, Hal. Juveniles. If they get caught possessing or selling heroin, they're treated leniently by the courts as juvenile delinquents. But if *adults* get caught doing the same thing, they get a mandatory life sentence under state law. See how it works? The kids run all the risks of handling the dope while their bosses, the older pushers, just hang around on the edges, picking up the money and dodging that life sentence. They call the kids their 'runners' or 'holders.' And half the time the kids don't even realize what they're doing."

I remembered Jasper Jones's old-young blue eyes and the facility with which he had improvised the story about Solly Joseph. "I'm afraid my kid knows what he's doing," I said.

"Well, they all know they're doing something not quite legal, put it that way. But they usually don't realize the enormous street value of the stuff they're handling. Most of them work for peanuts, or a new bike, or for kicks, or because somebody they admire—like an older pusher, say—asks them to."

I could understand how that would happen. The pusher's a big man in the neighborhood. He wears fancy clothes, drives luxury automobiles, is always flashing money. The kids look up to him, want to be like him. They gladly do what he asks. I said, "So the kids take the heat? And the adult pushers go free?" I felt very depressed.

Randall nodded. "Usually."

"Lieutenant," I said grimly, "will you do me a favor? A real one this time?"

"Another?" Randall smiled tightly. "What did you have in mind?"

"I want you to turn my Jasper Jones information over to the Narcotics Squad downstairs for action. But I'd like you to insist on one thing for me to Lieutenant Logan: that they identify and get the goods—possession, peddling, the works—on Jasper's adult pusher before they arrest Jasper Jones."

Randall said, "I guess I can promise you that much, Hal."

* * * *

A couple of weeks later, after the Narcs had wrapped it up, Randall bought me a pizza and told me how they did it.

"It wasn't too tough with what you gave them, Hal. To identify and locate the kid's boss, the Narcs figured their best bet was to put a tail on the kid on Saturday morning, after he'd picked up his weekly load of books at your library. They reasoned that whoever the adult pusher was, he'd certainly want his personal possession of the heroin to be as short a time as possible before handing it over to his holder. So it seemed a good bet that the pusher got his weekly supply of smack from his dealer at about the same time on Saturday morning that the kid would show up with the books to distribute it in. And that's the way it worked. The kid led them right to the pusher."

"Great!" I said. "Who was it?"

"A flashy twenty-year-old who lives in the same tenement as Jasper and his mother. On the top floor. Kind of a local idol with the ghetto kids. Turned out later he's Jasper's cousin."

"That's all there was to it?" I asked incredulously. "Just follow the kid and pick up his cousin?"

"Not quite. The Narcs couldn't be absolutely sure the cousin was their man. The kid could have stopped to see him for any number of reasons, of course."

I nodded.

"After about fifteen minutes in his cousin's place, the kid comes out and goes back downstairs to his own pad. And believe it or not, Hal, the kid sits down and starts to read his new library books right through, one after the other. Outside in the alley, the Narc is watching him through the window. By lunchtime the kid's finished reading maybe five or six books. He puts them in his book-bag, makes himself a Dagwood sandwich—his mother was out working—and goes off to the playground down the street."

"With the book-bag?"

"With the book-bag. The Narc trailed along. When Jasper got involved in a basketball game, the tail went back to the tenement and—ah—managed to examine the library books the kid hadn't taken with him to the playground."

I said, "He had a warrant, I hope."

Randall shrugged. "Anyway, he found a glassine envelope of heroin in the pocket of every book—about a ten-dollar packet, he said. So that put the finger on the cousin with no possibility of mistake. You see? No heroin in the books when they left the library. And every book stuffed with it after Jasper's visit to his cousin."

I nodded again. "Then what?"

"Then the Narc went back to the playground and kept a cozy eye on Jasper Jones. Three times during the afternoon the kid was called out of the basketball game by men who passed him a coin and some code name, probably, and received, in return, one of Jasper's library books. The cousin never showed at all."

"Directing traffic from a distance."

"Right." Randall continued placidly. "At six o'clock it's getting dark. The kid goes home and eats dinner with his mother, who's now home from work. And that's what the pattern was like all week for Jasper Jones—passing out library books on demand to users at school, at the playground, or at home."

I shook my head. "An eleven-year-old kid!"

"Listen," Randall said softly, "don't feel too bad about Jasper Jones. Lieutenant Logan told me that while his man was staked out at the Gardenia Street playground, he saw a guy take delivery of two bundles of smack from a little girl who was jumping rope on the sidewalk. She couldn't have been more than six or seven years old. And when this guy called to her, she rolled up the sleeve of her sweater and revealed a lot of packages of heroin taped to her arm. He took what was needed and the little girl rolled down her sleeve and went back to jumping rope."

I found myself hoping with an almost feral ferocity that somehow, some way, justice would be visited on the depraved animals who recruited little children to do their dirty work for them. I said harshly, "Did they nail Jasper's cousin?"

"Yeah. Relax."

"When did they make the arrest?"

"Last Saturday morning. The Narcs hit him after he'd got his supply from his dealer and before Jasper arrived with his library books to take it off his hands. The cousin's going up for life, Hal."

I sighed. "I hope to God he gets the whole treatment!" I hesitated. "What about the kid?"

"Jasper?" Randall's sulphur-yellow eyes held a spark of something that could have been sympathy. "Lieutenant Logan, at my request, released Jasper Jones in the custody of his mother."

Suddenly I felt fine. "Let me buy you a beer, Lieutenant."

He gave me a calm cool stare. “Gladly,” he said, “and you can pay for the pizza, too, if you feel all that grateful.”

I paid for the pizza.

THE HONEYCOMB OF SILENCE

Originally published in* Alfred Hitchcock's Mystery Magazine, *August 1978.

I found a public telephone booth on the apron of a gas station two blocks away from Benton's house. I pulled into the service station, parked out of the way of possible pump traffic, and entered the stuffy booth, groping in my pocket for change.

It was a hot bright morning in August—a Tuesday, I remember—and I was sweating even before I closed myself into the booth.

Instead of dialing the emergency number, I called Headquarters and asked for Lieutenant Randall of Homicide. He was my former boss. I hadn't seen him or heard from him in several months, so I figured this was a pretty good chance to say hello.

Randall picked up his phone and said, "Yeah?" in a bored voice. "Lieutenant Randall."

"Hal Johnson," I said. "Remember me?"

"Vaguely," he answered. "Aren't you that sissy cop from the public library?"

"You *do* remember me," I said. "How nice. Are you keeping busy these days, Lieutenant?"

"So-so." He paused. Then, with an edge of suspicion, "Why?"

"I think I may have stumbled across a job for you, Lieutenant."

"You always were papa's little helper," Randall said. "What kind of job?"

"I think a man's been murdered at 4321 Eastwood Street."

"You *think* a man's been murdered?"

"Yes. I went there just now to collect an overdue library book, and when nobody answered the doorbell I took a quick look through the living-room curtains, which weren't drawn quite tight, and I saw a man lying on the floor in front of the TV set. The TV was turned on. I could hear the sound and see the picture through the window."

"Did you go inside?"

I was shocked. "After all you taught me? Of course not. I didn't even try the door."

"So the guy didn't hear you ring the doorbell on account of the TV noise," said Randall hopefully. "He's tired. He's lying on the floor to relax while he watches his favorite soap opera."

"Face down? And with all that blood on the back of his shirt?"

Randall sighed. "4321 Eastwood?"

"Right."

"I'll send somebody to check it out. What name did you have for that address?"

"Robert Fenton. I hope he's not the guy on the floor, though."

"Why?"

"Because if it's Fenton, he owes the library a fine of two dollars and twenty cents on his overdue library book."

"You're breaking my heart," Randall said. "Where are you calling from?"

"A pay phone two blocks away. Do you want me to go back and wait for your boys?"

"No. Thanks all the same." His voice became bland. "If it's a murder, we'll try to handle it all by ourselves this time, Hal. Aren't there some kids somewhere with overdue picture books you can track down today?"

* * * *

Randall telephoned me back at home that evening. His call came just as I was taking my first sip of my first cold martini before dinner. I hadn't even decided yet whether to go out to eat or to finish up the meatloaf left over from the pitiful bachelor Sunday dinner I'd cooked for myself two days before.

Randall said, "The guy wasn't watching a soap opera, Hal. He was dead."

"He looked dead," I said. "Was he murdered?"

"We think so—the lock on the back door had been forced and he'd been shot in the back and there wasn't any gun around."

"Oh," I said. "And was he Robert Fenton?"

"According to the evidence of his landlord, his neighbors, and the bartender at Calhoun's Bar down the street, he was. The bartender ought to know because she went out with him a few times. It seems he was a bachelor, living alone."

"A lady bartender?"

"Yeah. Not bad looking, either," said Randall, "if you go for bottle blondes with false eyelashes."

I didn't rise to that. At this point, I'm still waiting for Ellen Crosby, the girl at the library's check-out desk, to tell me she'll marry me or else to get lost.

"How about Mr. Fenton's library book, Randall?" I said. "Can I have it?"

"Which one was it? There were several library books scattered around the living room."

"I'll have to look up the title. Fenton probably borrowed the others recently, and they're not overdue yet. Anyway, can I have them back to clean up his library record?"

"Why not?" Randall agreed. "Stop by tomorrow and I'll have them for you."

"Thanks," I said. "I'll be there."

Lieutenant Randall was as good as his word. When I got to his office next morning about eleven, he had a stack of library books waiting for me.

"You have any suspects yet?" I asked him.

He shook his head. "Fenton had only lived there for a year, according to his landlord. And nothing in the house showed where he'd been before. As far as we've been able to discover, he has no relatives or friends in town except the blonde bartender in Calhoun's Bar."

I said, "Who's looking for friends? It's an enemy who killed him, presumably."

Randall grunted. "We haven't turned up any of those, either."

"Funny. No friends, no relatives, no enemies?"

"And no job either."

"Fenton was unemployed?"

"A gentleman of leisure. With private means. That's what he told the blonde bartender, anyway."

"Hell, that's what *I'd* tell a blonde bartender too," I said. "That doesn't mean it's true."

Randall lit a cigar—if you can call those black ropes he smokes cigars. He said, "Exactly what did you see through the crack in Fenton's draperies yesterday?"

"Just what I told you. Fenton lying on the floor looking very dead, blood all over the place, the TV set going."

"You didn't notice anything else?"

"No. I went to call you after one look. Should I have noticed anything else?"

"The joint was a shambles, Hal. Somebody had tossed it. Almost a professional job."

"The killer?"

"We're guessing so. Looking very hard for something."

"A prowler," I suggested, "looking for dough. Interrupted by Fenton."

Randall shrugged. "Maybe. Fenton's wallet was missing. But if so, the prowler overlooked five one-hundred-dollar bills in Fenton's money belt."

"You wouldn't usually hang around long enough after shooting somebody to make a thorough search of his body, would you?"

Randall shrugged again. I stood up. "Well, anyway, Lieutenant, thanks for salvaging my library books." I gathered them up.

"Do you need any help?" he asked. "You could rupture yourself."

I ignored that. I said, "Have you looked through these books?"

"Sure."

"Whoever killed Fenton was searching for something," I said. "Books make dandy hiding places."

"We looked. Hal. There's nothing in them."

"They haven't been searched by an expert until *I* search them," I said, knowing it would infuriate Randall.

He snorted. "Well, don't do it here. Get lost, will you?"

I grinned at him and took the books and went on about my business, which is tracing down lost, stolen, and overdue books for the public library. It's a quiet life after working for Randall in Homicide for five years. But I like it. Almost as much as Randall resents it.

When I got back to the library that afternoon about four. I turned in the fines and the books I'd collected on my rounds—all except the books Randall had found in Fenton's living room. These I took with me to my minuscule office behind the Director's spacious one, and began to examine them carefully, one by one.

I examined the card pocket of each book, the space between spine and cover, the paper dust-jackets. I checked each book painstakingly for anything hidden between the pages, either loose or attached.

There were eight books in the stack. I was holding the seventh book by its covers, shaking it pages down over my desk to dislodge anything that might possibly have been inserted between the pages, when I struck pay dirt.

Under the fingers of my right hand. I felt a slight irregularity beneath the dust jacket.

We protect the dust jacket of every library book with a transparent jacket cover made of heavy cellophane with a white paper liner. We fit this transparent cover over the book jacket, fold it along the edges to fit the book, and attach the end flaps to the book with paste. It was under one of these end flaps that my fingers encountered a slight ridge that shouldn't have been there—a suggestion of extra thickness. The book was called *Mushroom Culture in Pennsylvania.*

Feeling a tingle of excitement. I worked the pasted edge of the fold-over flap loose from its moorings, pulled it clear of the book cover, and found myself staring down at a crisp fresh one-hundred-dollar bill.

I looked at it for a second or two without touching it, surprised and, yes, mildly elated. As an ex-homicide cop, I knew enough not to handle the bill and chance destroying or smearing any recoverable fingerprints. Yet as a curious library cop, I couldn't resist using a pair of stamp tweezers from my desk drawer to tease the bill aside enough to count the others under it. There were ten of them—all hundreds—crisp, fresh, deliciously spendable-looking. A thousand dollars.

I won't say I wasn't tempted. Funny thoughts ran through my head. Nobody knows about this money but me, I thought. This is a library book, so it's kind of like public property, I told myself, and I'm certainly one of the public. And wasn't there a section of the criminal code that said something about Finders-keepers? However, after a couple of minutes, I'm proud to say that I picked up my telephone and asked the switchboard operator to get me Lieutenant Randall.

* * * *

I was eating lunch in the library cafeteria the next day when Lieutenant Randall appeared in the cafeteria doorway. He spotted me at once, walked to my table, and slid into a chair.

I said, "Welcome, Lieutenant. You're just in time to pay my lunch check."

Randall said, "Why should I? Because you turned that money over to me? You probably figured it was counterfeit, anyway."

I stopped a spoonful of chocolate ice cream halfway to my mouth. "And was it?"

He shook his head. "Good as gold. So finish up that slop and let's get out of here where we can talk."

I went on eating very deliberately. "First things first," I said. "I should think out of common gratitude the police department would pay my cafeteria tab for the help I've given you. It's only a dollar and twenty-three cents."

"Subornation of a witness," Randall said. He ostentatiously got one of his black cigars from his pocket and felt for matches.

I said, "No smoking in here, Lieutenant. Don't you see that sign?"

He gave me a cold stare. "Who's going to stop me? I outrank the only other cop I see anywhere around."

"O.K.," I said with a sigh, "I'll go quietly."

I paid my check and we went upstairs to my office. The Lieutenant sat down in a straight chair facing me across my desk. I said, "All right, Lieutenant, you need more help, is that it?"

Randall gave what for him was a humble nod. "This book business has us talking to ourselves, Hal. We did find out something this morning that has a bearing, we think. Fenton was a man who had a lot of hundred-dollar bills, apparently. His landlord says he always paid his rent with hundred-dollar bills. The bartender at Calhoun's Bar says he sometimes paid for his drinks by breaking a hundred-dollar bill. And he had five hundred-dollar bills in his money belt when we find him."

"So the fact that the money in the library book was in hundreds too makes you think they were intended for Fenton?"

"It seems likely. And possibly they were from the same source as the others he had."

"And also transferred via library book?"

"Could be." Randall frowned. "But I can't figure out how whoever hid the money in the book could be sure Fenton got it. Anybody could borrow the damn book once it came back to the library with the money in it…)

"Not if Fenton had put in a reserve for it." I said. "Then, when it came back to the library, we'd send him a postcard and hold the book for him for three days."

"Well," said Randall, "that could explain Fenton's end of it. But how about the guy *paying* the money? How'd he know what library book Fenton wanted him to put it in?"

I leaned back and thought about that. At length I said, "There's only one way I can see. Fenton could call the library and put in a reserve on that book in the other guy's name. Then, when the book was available, we'd automatically notify the other guy that the book he'd reserved was in. And he'd know that was the book Fenton meant for him to put the money in."

Randall nodded. "And meanwhile Fenton calls in his own reservation on the same book so he'll be sure to get it when it's returned to the library?"

"Yeah," I said. "That could work."

"It's pretty complicated. Who knows enough about how a library operates to dope out a system like that?"

"I do, for one," I answered modestly. "And maybe Fenton did too."

Randall brooded. "Say you're right about it. Then how come the money was still in the book? Why didn't Fenton take it out as soon as he got home from the library'?"

"What time does the M.E. figure he was killed?"

"Sixteen to eighteen hours before you found him.

"O.K. That's about the time he might have got home from the library with his books, around cocktail time let's say. So maybe he mixed himself a drink and turned on the TV before he removed the money from the book? And he was killed before he had a chance to retrieve it."

Randall made a noncommittal gesture with his hands. He fiddled with his unlit cigar. "The whole thing smells more and more like blackmail to me," he said. "There's only one reason I can think of for Fenton to devise this crazy pay-off method, Hal. To conceal his identity from whoever he was blackmailing. It's a more elaborate scheme than the usual trick of renting a post-office box under a false name and having your blackmail payments mailed to you there."

"You can stake out a post-office box and see who comes to collect mail from it," I said. "But there's no way you can tell who's going to borrow a library book from the public library after you return it. Besides, we circulate more than one copy of most of our books. How are you going to keep track of the particular copy you hid your money in?"

In a deceptively innocent voice, Randall asked, "How many copies of *Mushroom Culture in Pennsylvania* does the library have in circulation?"

"One," I admitted, grinning at him. "There are *some* books we have only a single copy of. And maybe that's worth noting. For *Mushroom Culture in Pennsylvania* was the only one of Fenton's library books that doesn't have two or more copies going."

"So what?"

"So by reserving an unpopular one-copy book for his blackmail victim, Fenton made sure there wouldn't be a long wait before he got his money."

"The devil with that," said Randall irritably. "All a guy would have to do to find out who borrowed a certain book is ask your librarian to look it up for him. Right?"

"Wrong. That's against the rules—as is giving out information about who's on the waiting list for books that have been reserved. Our system works on card numbers, not names."

"I know that, but when you issue a library card to somebody you take a record of his name and address, don't you?"

"Sure," I said easily. "But matching the names to the numbers is the trick. Once a book you've borrowed is returned to the library by its next borrower, you can tell by the date card in its pocket the card renumber of the person who borrowed the book after you did, but not the person's name."

"There must be plenty of ways to crack *that* crummy system," Randall commented acidly.

I shrugged. "Our master file of cardholders' names and numbers is kept out at the main desk."

"Locked up? In a safe?"

"Just a simple file cabinet," I said, deadpan. "I suppose somebody might gain unauthorized access to it."

Randall said with contempt, "Child's play."

"For example?"

"I could hide in the stacks some evening until the library closes and the staff goes home. Then I'd have all night to locate your damn file and milk it."

"That's very good," I complimented him. "Right off the top of your head too."

The Lieutenant jumped up. "Let's stop fooling around, Hal. Lead me to this master file of yours. *You* have authorized access to it, right? So if we can nail down the name and address of the person who borrowed *Mushroom Culture* just before Fenton, we may have our killer."

"Wait a minute," I said. "Say we're right about this being blackmail, and your blackmailee figures out Fenton's identity through his card number. He goes out to Fenton's house Monday afternoon, breaks in through the back door, and is turning the joint upside down looking for whatever blackmail evidence Fenton is holding over him. O.K. Fenton comes home from the library unexpectedly, interrupts him, and gets shot for his pains. His killer is sure to see *Mushroom Culture* among the library' books Fenton is bringing home. If he'd hidden a thousand bucks of his money in that book just a day or so before, wouldn't he take his money back? Why did he leave it in the book for me to find afterward?"

Randall said impatiently, "How should I know? Give me his name and I'll ask him! Come on, Hal. Move!"

I reached into the center drawer of my desk and pulled out a card.

"I just happen to have the information you want right here. Lieutenant. I looked it up this morning."

"Why didn't you say so?"

"I wanted you to ask me, nice and polite," I said. "Because you assured me last Tuesday morning that you wouldn't need any help from me this time. Remember?"

Randall didn't give an inch. "How was I supposed to know the murdered man would turn out to be another damn library expert?" he said.

He took the card and read the name out loud. "Samuel J. Klausen." And the card number: "L-1310077."

When he left, he had the grace to throw a "Thanks, Hal" over his shoulder.

I felt smug.

* * * *

My smugness vanished when Randall called me at the library the following noon. "Is this the resident library expert?" he greeted me.

"It's too late for compliments. Did you arrest Mr. Samuel J. Klausen?"

"No way. He was a washout, Hal. He's no more a murderer than I am."

I was disappointed but not surprised. "Not even a blackmailee?"

"Oh, yes, he admits to being blackmailed. He broke wide open when I told him we'd found his fingerprints on the money in the library book."

"Did you find his prints?"

Randall coughed. "We found fingerprints, yes. We didn't know they were his until he admitted the blackmail payments." Randall coughed again. "Anyway, he readily admitted he was paying off somebody in hundred-dollar bills concealed in library books—but until we told him, he didn't know it was Fenton. He claims he didn't know Fenton from Adam's off ox."

"Did he tell you how the book thing worked?"

"About the way we worked it out. A year ago, Klausen got a print of a very compromising photograph in the mail, no return address, then a phone call from a man threatening to send the picture to Klausen's wife unless he paid him hush money. When Klausen agreed to do so, the man asked him if he had a library card, and set up the library-book pay-off system."

"What did Fenton have on Klausen?" I asked curiously.

"None of your business."

"Excuse me," I said. "Is it any of my business why you're so sure Klausen didn't kill Fenton, despite his denials?"

"Klausen has a cast-iron alibi for Monday evening when Fenton was shot."

I clicked my tongue against my teeth. "Too bad. Cast-iron, you say?"

"Klausen was making a dinner speech to a gathering of insurance brokers in Baltimore, five hundred miles away, when Fenton caught it. We've checked it out."

"That's pretty cast-iron, all right," I said. "So what's next?"

"Back to the drawing board, I guess. Unless you've got some more brilliant suggestions."

"Let me think about it," I said.

"Nuts to that. *I* do the thinking from here in. You just give me the library jazz when I need it, O.K.? So here's something to start with. Suppose Fenton was blackmailing somebody else besides Klausen, which seems fairly likely, and using the same library-book method of collecting his money? Would he use the same books he did for Klausen, or different ones?"

"Different ones," I said promptly. "Even if he didn't screw up his timetables, our people would think it was queer if he reserved the same books for himself more than once."

"Check. Now here's another little thought for you. Did you happen to notice, Hal, that none of the eight books we brought in from Fenton's house was overdue?"

He whistled a few bars from "Tea for Two" under his breath, while he waited for me to realize the full enormity of my oversight. Then, "You did tell me, didn't you, Hal, that you were calling on Fenton last Tuesday to collect an overdue book?"

I abased myself. "Yeah, I did. And Lieutenant, I'm sorry. I guess finding the money in *Mushroom Culture* drove everything else from my mind, including that overdue book."

"Well, well," Randall said softly.

I said, "You want me to go out and jump off a bridge or something?"

"Not just yet." The more apologetic I became, the more cheerful Randall sounded. "Not till you tell me the title of that overdue book."

"Hold on," I said. "I'll look it up." I checked my overdue lists. "It's a book called *The Honeycomb of Silence* by somebody named Desmond."

"Another one I'm just dying to read," Randall cracked. "So I'm on my way right now out to Fenton's house to find it. It might tell us something if we're lucky."

"You want the name of the person who borrowed it before Fenton?" I offered.

"Not till I find the book." He hung up with a crash.

I got back to the library after my afternoon calls about five-thirty. There was a message on my desk to call Randall. I called him and he said, "I'll take that name now, Hal."

"You found the book?"

"Between the back of the TV set and the wall. It obviously slipped down there after Fenton took the money out of it, and he forgot to return it to the library. Hence, it was overdue."

"After he took the money out of it," I repeated. "So it was another of Fenton's pay-off books?"

"Shut up and give me the name of the cardholder before Fenton. And let's hope he doesn't have an alibi like Klausen's."

I read him the name and address from the master file card: W. G. Crowley, 1722 Plumrose Street.

* * * *

I knew everything had worked out all right because on Tuesday of the following week, Lieutenant Randall called and offered to buy me a dinner at Al's Diner, provided the total cost of my repast didn't exceed a dollar and twenty-three cents.

At Al's Diner, he was seated in a back booth waiting for me. He had a look of work-well-done on his face and a beer on the table before him. "Sit down," he invited me expansively, "and join me in a beer. I hope you don't want a salad with your hamburger, however. Salads are thirty-five cents in this joint."

"Never touch them," I said, sliding into the seat across from him. "But I'll take the beer." He signaled to the waitress. When she brought my beer we told her we'd order dinner later.

I took a sip of my beer and said to Randall, "Did you snaffle W. G. Crowley?"

He nodded.

"And he's your murderer?"

He nodded again. "Murderer, bank robber, dope pusher. And also, I'm sorry to say, an ex-cop.

I stared at him. "Are you serious?"

"He used to be a member of the narcotics squad of the Los Angeles Police Department, under a different name—his real one—James G. Crawford. He's a security guard at the First National Bank here. And that's where the bank-robbery charge comes in. The guy had the nerve to steal the hundred-dollar bills he was paying Fenton from his own bank! How do you like that for resourcefulness?"

"If he's all that resourceful," I suggested, "he's probably resourceful enough to walk away from your murder indictment too. You did say he was Fenton's killer, didn't you?"

"No question about it. Open and shut, as the TV cops say. And don't worry, we've got him hogtied. He'll never walk away from anything again."

"Good," I said. "What do you mean again?"

"He was suspended from the LAPD, charged with pushing the dope that his own narc squad appropriated in raids. And before the grand jury could come up with an indictment, he jumped bail and left town permanently. Disappeared. Now he's a bank guard here in town calling himself Crowley."

"And you're certain he killed Fenton?"

"With his very own police positive," said Randall. "The .38 he carries under his arm every day as a guard at the First National." Randall held up a hand as I opened my mouth to speak. "And how, you are about to ask," he said, "do we know that? Well, we found three of his fingerprints *under* the flap of the book about honeycombs. And the same three prints on one of the hundred-dollar bills in Fenton's money belt. And the same three prints again among those on the butt of Mr. Crowley's gun. Isn't that enough?"

"Not enough to convict him. And you know it."

His yellow eyes emitted a gleam of satisfaction. "Well, then, how about this? Our ballistics boy tells us the bullets taken out of Fenton's body were fired by Crowley's gun. And Crowley has zilch in the way of an alibi for the time of Fenton's murder. And he also, of course, had a good solid motive for killing Fenton."

"What did Fenton have on him?" I asked.

"Probably just the knowledge that Crowley was really Crawford, the indicted, dope-pushing LA cop who disappeared without leave. Fenton could have landed him in jail for quite a spell by disclosing his whereabouts to the LA police."

I said, "I don't get it. If that was the case, what was Crowley looking for when he searched Fenton's house? All he needed to do was kill Fenton to protect himself."

"I've got two theories on that." Randall said. "One: he was trying to make the murder look like what we originally thought it might be—the work of a casual prowler. Or two"—Randall's unblinking sulfur-colored stare was amused—"maybe Crowley was thinking of taking over Fenton's customers, and *collecting* a little blackmail money for a change instead of paying it out."

He paused and I said, "The first theory might be possible. But what gave rise to the second? Your overactive imagination?"

"We found something interesting in Crowley's apartment," Randall replied.

Dutifully I asked, "What?"

"The negative of the compromising photograph that Fenton used on Klausen," Randall said, "all neatly labeled with Klausen's name and address."

"Well, well," I said, "For an ex-cop, Crowley was pretty bright, wasn't he?"

"You can't insult me tonight," Randall said comfortably. "Finish your beer and let's order."

"Not yet. I still don't get it."

"Get what?"

"How Fenton knew that Crowley was the fugitive Crawford."

Randall shrugged. "What difference does that make? Accident, I imagine. Fenton just happened to see Crowley in the bank one day probably, and recognized him."

"You mean Fenton knew him in Los Angeles?"

"Maybe. Or at least knew what he looked like."

"All right. My next question is the real puzzler to me. How did you find out that both Crowley and Fenton came from Los Angeles? You didn't know fact one about Fenton *or* Crowley the last I heard."

He gave a negligent wave of his hand. "Just good solid routine police work, sonny. After Klausen pointed us toward Los Angeles."

"Klausen!" I said, confused. "He pointed you toward LA?"

"Didn't I mention it?" Randall was complacent. "The—ah—indiscretion for which Klausen was being blackmailed by Fenton occurred at a convention Klausen attended last year in Los Angeles."

"Oh," I said.

"LA gave us a rundown on Fenton too. They'd had him up out there for extortion once, and for peddling porno films twice, and he walked away each time without a scratch. A very cagey fellow. Incidentally, his Los Angeles record showed that he worked summers while he was in high school at the public library."

I finished my beer. "Very, very neat, Lieutenant. May I offer my congratulations? And we may as well order now."

As he signaled for the waitress, he seemed so pleased with himself that I couldn't resist saying, "All the same, you'd never have got to first base on Fenton's murder, may I modestly point out, if I hadn't found that money in *Mushroom Culture*."

"That's not necessarily so," said Randall judiciously. "But it's possible you're right, of course."

"Wherefore," I said, "may I please have a tossed salad with my hamburger?"

Randall grinned. "Well—O.K. Just this once I guess I can throw caution to the winds."

"And speaking of financial matters," I went on, "what are you planning to do with that five hundred bucks you found in Fenton's money belt?"

"In default of any known relatives or heirs, I thought I'd turn it over to the Police Benevolence Fund."

"You can't do that," I said. "At least not all of it."

"No?" He bristled. "Why not?"

"Because part of that money is mine."

He looked at me as though I'd lost my mind. "Yours? What do you mean, yours?"

"Now whose memory is failing?" I said. "Didn't I tell you last Tuesday that Fenton owes me an overdue fine of two dollars and twenty cents on *The Honeycomb of Silence*?"

THE JACK O'NEAL AFFAIR

Originally published in* Alfred Hitchcock's Mystery Magazine, *May 1979.

You'd think that chasing down missing and overdue books for the public library would be pretty dull and unexciting work, wouldn't you? Most of the time, it is. But occasionally my job gets me into situations that are very far from dull and unexciting, believe me.

Like the Jack O'Neal affair.

It started off like any other call to collect an overdue book. The address was 1218 King Street. King Street's in the East End, a couple of blocks south of the Crossroads intersection, in a still-decent but deteriorating neighborhood of sixty-year-old houses. Number 1218 seemed to be better cared for than the houses that flanked it on either side. Its small lawn was neat and close-cropped and the house had been freshly painted quite recently.

I parked my car at the curb, walked up the short cemented driveway to the house, and rang the bell. A white-haired, pleasant-faced woman answered the door.

I said. "Is this the O'Neal residence?"

She gave me a big smile and said, "Yes, it is," and waited for me to explain myself.

"I'm Hal Johnson from the public library, Mrs. O'Neal." I showed her my identification card. "I've come to collect an overdue library book that was borrowed five and a half weeks ago by John C. O'Neal. Is that your husband?"

She shook her head. "My son," she said. "Jack. I'm sorry, but he's not here right now, Mr. Johnson. He's at work. Then she added with a note of pride, "He's a city fireman, you know."

"Oh," I said, "that's what I wanted to be when I was a kid. A fireman. I never made it, though. I—"

She interrupted me. "Yes, Jack's a fireman. And he really loves the job. It's his whole world, really. He never showed the slightest interest in getting married or anything like that, can you believe it? He mopes and sulks around here every Friday—that's his day off—as though he'd much rather be working down at the firehouse. But you can't work-seven days a week, I tell him, you have to have free time."

"I need all the free time I can get," I said, trying to head off any further comment about John O'Neal the fireman. "For instance, if you could just give me your son's overdue library book, Mrs. O'Neal, I wouldn't have to make another trip out here for it. You son has forgotten that he has the book. I suppose, although we did send him a postcard reminding him it's overdue."

Mrs. O'Neal stepped back and held the door open wider. "Oh," she said, flustered and apologetic, "please come in, Mr. Johnson. I'll see if I can find it for you. Jack would forget his head if it wasn't t fastened on."

I followed her into a living room that was as neat and manicured as the lawn outside. An expensive television set stood in one corner, next to a built-in bookcase. Avocado shag carpeting stretched from wall to wall. The overstaffed sofa and easy chairs wore tasteful slipcovers in harmonizing prints. The lampshades looked almost new.

"What's the name of the book?" Mrs. O'Neal asked.

I consulted my list. *"War and Peace* by Tolstoy."

"Sit down for a minute," Mrs. O'Neal said. "I'll see if it's in Jack's bedroom upstairs. That's where he usually does his reading." Her voice faded as she ascended the stairs to the second floor.

Instead of sitting down, I wandered over to the bookcase beside the TV set and scanned the titles on the shelves, thinking that Jack O Neal might have absent-mindedly stowed *War and Peace* there after he finished reading it.

War and Peace wasn't there. As I turned away, an outsize scrapbook lying horizontally on top of the books on the bottom shelf caught my eye. It had the word 'FIRES' lovingly hand-lettered on its cover in old English script. Evidently the work of Jack O Neal, the fireman who loved his work.

Idly I picked up the scrapbook and leafed through it while I waited for Mrs. O'Neal to return with War and Peace. *FIRES* was an apt title. The scrapbook contained nothing but clippings from local newspapers describing a number of newsworthy fires that had occurred over the past few years in the city. The newspaper articles were illustrated with photographs of the fires in progress and of the smoking ruins afterward. Most of the fires in the book—only half a dozen—I remembered reading about. A furniture warehouse. The fancy home of a local lawyer. A dry-goods store. A tenement. An Italian restaurant on the North Side that had once been famous for its gnocchi. A florist's warehouse on City Line.

I heard Mrs. O'Neal's thumping footsteps descending the carpeted stairs and returned the scrapbook to its place in the bookcase, thinking it was only to be expected that a fireman who loved his work as much as Jack

O'Neal evidently did would keep a record of his most dramatic encounters with the enemy. Personally, I was very glad that I hadn't realized my boyhood dream of becoming a fireman, although it was bad enough to have become a cop. A sissy library cop at that.

"I found it," Mrs. O'Neal said, handing me the overdue copy of War and Peace. "My, it's a long book, isn't it? Maybe Jack hasn't finished it yet. He isn't a fast reader." She shook her head fondly. "But I expect he really just forgot about it, as you say. It was on the floor by his bed, out of sight under the telephone stand."

"If he hasn't finished reading it," I said, "he can borrow it again the next time he comes to the library. So far, he owes us a small fine on it, Mrs. O'Neal. Do you want to take care of that for him?"

"Of course." She went into the kitchen and reappeared with her purse. "How much is it?"

I told her and she counted out the exact change. "I'm sorry Jack's caused you so much trouble, Mr. Johnson. He's so forgetful." She laughed indulgently. "He even writes notes to himself to help him remember things."

"I do that myself." I smiled at her, holding up my penciled list of overdues. "Thanks, Mrs. O'Neal."

I bid her goodbye, put *War and Peace* under my arm, and went down the driveway to my car.

* * * *

Three days later, I dropped into police headquarters downtown. Since I'd worked there for five years as a homicide detective before switching to library cop, I knew my way around. I climbed the stairs to the gloomy cramped office of Lieutenant Randall, my former boss, and entered without knocking.

Randall was in the act of lighting one of his vicious black stogies, in blatant disregard of the Surgeon General's warnings. He held the flaring match in midair and gave me a dirty look out of his sulphur-colored eyes. "Well, look who's here," he greeted me without enthusiasm. "The famous book detective himself."

"Hi, Lieutenant," I said and sat down without being asked.

Randall puffed on his stogie till it was well alight, then waved out the match. "What do you want? And make it quick, Hal. I'm busy."

"Yeah," I said. "I can see that." There wasn't a paper of any kind on his desk.

"What do you want?

"I'm a public-spirited citizen," I answered. "And as a public-spirited citizen with the community's good at heart, I have come here this morning to help you clean up some unsolved crimes." I gave him my public-spirited grin.

He gave me his you've-got-just-one-more-minute grin. "*You* can help *me?"* he asked. "How?"

"By bringing to your attention a couple of murders you completely missed last year. And by pointing out the murderer to you."

Randall snorted, peering unblinkingly at me through a cloud of rank tobacco smoke. "How careless of me to miss a couple of murders," he said blandly. "What were they?"

"Two derelicts," I said, "who had sneaked in out of the freezing weather last November to sleep in an empty building. At least that's what the newspapers called them. Derelicts."

Randall came to attention. "You mean the bums who were burned to death in that empty Ross Street tenement?"

"Yeah," I said.

"They weren't murdered. They were trespassing in a building that happened to catch fire and incinerate them."

I shook my head. "I don't think the building happened to catch fife. I believe somebody deliberately put the torch to it."

"Arson?" He was patronizing.

I nodded. "And murder." He didn't say anything so I went on. "Even if the arsonist didn't know the bums were holed up inside when he set fire to the building, he's their murderer all the same, isn't he?

"If there *was* an arsonist, yes. Nobody has ever suggested that there was one, though," Randall sighed, "except you."

"I'm ninety-nine-percent sure that there was, Lieutenant. Do you want to get Sandy Castle up here to hear the rest of this?" Sandy Castle heads up the Department's arson squad.

In the old days, when I worked for him, if I was ninety-nine-percent sure about anything, that was usually enough to convince Randall, and it still was, I guess. He picked up the phone and called Sandy.

While we were waiting, the Lieutenant smoked in noncommittal silence for about three minutes. Then he asked casually, "And who was this murderer, Hal? You said you knew."

I replied with equal casualness, "A city fireman named Jack O'Neal."

That shook him a little. "A fireman? For God s sake!"

"Ironic, isn't it?

The door opened and Sandy Castle came in and took the other chair. "How are you doing, Hal?" he greeted me. "Back at the old stand?"

"Only temporarily. I've got something I think will interest you, Sandy."

"So I hear. I'm listening."

I quickly filled him in on what I'd told Randall. "I think that tenement fire was set," I finished.

"He even claims to know who set it," Randall murmured. "Don't ask me how."

"You want it from the beginning?" I said. "O.K. Last Wednesday I went to collect an overdue library book from a city fireman named Jack O'Neal, who lives with his mother at 1218 King Street. Jack wasn't home, but his mother found the library book for me—on the floor under the telephone extension beside the bed in Jack's upstairs bedroom. While she was upstairs looking for the book, I came across a scrapbook in the living room and glanced through it while I waited. The scrapbook had the word 'FIRES' on the cover, and contained six illustrated newspaper clippings about local fires. The Ross Street tenement fire was one of them."

Castle looked puzzled. "Nothing funny about that, Hal. A fireman could keep a scrapbook of fires like a writer keeps a scrapbook of reviews. I've personally known a dozen—"

I held up a hand. "Wait a minute, Sandy. I'm not finished."

"Let him talk," Randall interjected. "He loves to talk."

"There were only six clippings in the scrapbook, Sandy. The fires were spread over a period of about three years. And we've had a lot more than six newsworthy fires in this town in the last three years, haven't we?"

"So what?" Castle still looked puzzled. "Your fireman Jack O'Neal just keeps clippings on the fires that *he* helped to fight. It's natural."

I shook my head. "That's what I thought at first too. Until I found out that Jack O'Neal works at Station 12 and Station 12 wasn't called for any of the fires in his scrapbook."

Castle said, "How the hell did you find *that* out?"

"A telephone call to O'Neal's mother. Reading O'Neal's fire clippings in the back issues of the papers. The fire companies involved in fighting each fire were mentioned. No Station 12. Don't you find that odd?"

"Maybe," Castle admitted. "You got anything else?"

"Yes. All the fires in O'Neal's scrapbook happened on a Friday."

"What's that got to do with anything?"

"Friday is O'Neal's day off."

They both looked at me as though I'd lost my mind. "You think that's significant, I take it," Castle said.

I shrugged. "When taken in connection with some other suggestive items."

"Like what?" Randall said.

I said with false humility, "I know how you feel about library cops and library books, Lieutenant, so I hate to bring up the subject. However, I will this time because I think there's an interesting inference to be drawn from the books Jack O Neal has been reading."

"Stop with the fancy talk," Randall grunted. "Just tell us."

"I'm trying to. The book I collected from O'Neal was *War and Peace.* Combined with what I saw in O'Neal's scrapbook, it gave me an idea. I looked up the titles of the books O'Neal has borrowed from the library since he got his card several years ago. There were only five of them, so I guess I have to believe his mother that he's a slow reader. Can you guess what the five books were?"

Randall said sardonically, "I can't wait to hear."

I ticked them off on my fingers. "*War and Peace. Gone With the Wind. The Life and Death of Joan of Arc. Slaughterhouse-Five. The Tower.* You see what I'm getting at?"

Randall looked blank.

Sandy Castle said, "Let me guess. I saw *War and Peace* on television. And *Gone With the Wind.* The books all have one thing in common, right? A big fire scene?"

"You amaze me, Sandy," I said. "But you're dead right. For his light reading at home, Jack O'Neal chooses books with graphic fire scenes in them. And his mother told me he's so nuts about his job that he wishes he could work seven days a week." I looked at them quizzically. "Wouldn't you say the man is definitely queer for fires?"

"Maybe," Castle conceded, "but that doesn't make him a torch, Hal."

"Granted."

"Nor a murderer," Lieutenant Randall put in. He fixed his yellow eyes on me and said, "Come on, Hal, what hard evidence do you have? You must have something better than this jazz you've been feeding us. You wouldn't have worked your dainty fingers to the bone reading all those newspaper clippings because of a mere passing suspicion. So what is it?"

"Let me ask you a question first. Didn't a big hardware store burn to the ground last Friday on the South Side?"

"Sure. Bartlett's Hardware," Castle said promptly.

"And what was last Friday's date?"

"That's two questions," Castle said. "Last Friday was the eighteenth. Why?"

"Because I found a penciled note in O'Neal's overdue library book," I replied.

Randall pounced. "Saying what?"

"Saying, and I quote, 'O.K. Bart's 18th.' Which meant absolutely nothing to me until I read about the Bartlett fire in Saturday's paper."

Randall said brusquely, "Let's see it."

"The note? I can't. I threw it away. But that's what it said: 'O.K. Bart's 18th.'"

"Why didn't you tell us about this note right off, instead of going through all this other drivel?" Randall demanded testily.

My real reason was just to needle Randall. So I lied a little. "I wanted to give you the sequence and the coincidences just as I got them," I said sweetly. "So you'd be able to put together just as I finally did, all the little facts that seem to add up to one big fact: namely, that Jack O'Neal is an arsonist and a murderer." I turned to Sandy Castle. "Is there any suspicion of arson in the Bartlett fire?"

"Not so far. The investigation is still going on, Hal. The fire marshal is certain that the fire originated in a paint storage closet in the store's basement. Spontaneous combustion. And I'm inclined to think he's right."

"Was the owner of the hardware store in town last Friday?" I asked Castle.

"Bartlett?" He gave me a slanting look. "No. He was with his family at the seashore for the weekend. You're thinking alibi, aren't you, Hal?"

I shrugged. "Here's the list of the other fires in O'Neal's scrapbook." I handed it to him. "I wonder where the owners of those buildings were when their property burned."

"I'll check," said Castle.

Lieutenant Randall's mind began to click, smooth and easy and well-oiled as usual. I could almost hear it. He said, "This note was in O'Neal's library book, you say, which his mother found beside his bed. Did you say there was a telephone extension beside his bed?"

"That's what his mother told me."

He nodded. "So you figured somebody phoned O'Neal to torch Bartlett's store last Friday, and O'Neal wrote down the instructions and put them in his library book."

"I think that's what happened. O'Neal's mother said Jack had such a rotten memory he often wrote notes to himself as reminders."

Castle said slowly and heavily, "My department runs into a dozen wild-eyed nuts a year who get their jollies out of fires instead of sex or drugs. They usually act on their own, though, and on impulse, setting fires indiscriminately. This O'Neal of yours, if you're right about him, isn't like that. He's torching buildings to *order* on certain specified dates."

"Ah," I said. "Now you've got it. But to whose order? That's the question."

Randall broke in. "Thanks for the tip, Hal," he said, rising from his battered swivel chair and crushing out his stogie in his ashtray. "We'll take it from here."

"Good," I said, standing up too. "Don't be too rough on O'Neal's mother if you can help it, O.K.? And let me know how you come out, will you? I'm keeping a scrapbook of my own."

"On what?" asked Castle.

"On the crimes I solve for Lieutenant Randall," I said.

The newspapers called it the biggest arson racket in the history of the state. Thirteen of our local citizens, including merchants, property owners, a lawyer, a real-estate agent, a fire marshal, and, of course, Mrs. O'Neal's son Jack, were ultimately tried and convicted on charges of conspiring to burn property with the intent of defrauding insurance companies. When all the figures were in, they indicated that the arson ring cheated insurance companies of some half million dollars over a period of three years by having properties appraised at inflated values, overinsuring them, then burning the buildings down and filing fraudulent insurance claims.

"I'm sorry we have to go light on your boy O'Neal," Lieutenant Randall told me. "He's crazy as a bedbug when it comes to fires, Hal, just as you figured. But he's plenty smart in other ways. Smart enough to plea-bargain himself into a maximum ten-year term for his part in the arsons by agreeing to rat on everybody else in the ring."

"How did you nail him in the first place?" I asked. "Nothing I gave you was strong enough to prove he's a torch.

"Well," said Randall complacently, "we didn't have too much trouble. On the presumption that his note in your library book meant what you thought it did, we persuaded Judge Filmer to issue us a search warrant, and we went through O'Neal's home with a fine-tooth comb while he was at work. We turned up a couple of interesting items there."

"Besides his scrapbook?"

Randall nodded. "Yep. Item one: a diary that he kept locked in the drawer of his bedside telephone stand."

"How lucky can you get?" I said. "Don't tell me it mentioned the arson jobs?"

"It did. Twice. Sandrini's Florist warehouse. And Bartlett's Hardware. On the exact dates the fires occurred."

"What did the diary say about them?"

"*Handled S job today for TX.* And *Handled B job today for TX.*"

"That's pretty convincing. But not legal proof. Who's TX?"

"The lawyer whose fancy house burned down."

I remembered it now, the name I'd read in the newspaper clipping. "Thomas Xavier! Of course. How many people would have the initials TX?"

"Nobody else connected with *this* case anyway. Knowing that name gave us a little leverage when we braced O'Neal."

"Xavier is pretty important people." I ventured.

"Important enough to be the respectable front for the arson ring. The ringleader, in fact. He arranged the torching dates with the property owners, saw that they all had unshakable alibis, gave O'Neal his orders, and set up the insurance claims."

"Paymaster too? I asked.

"Yeah. O'Neal says he got five thousand dollars from Xavier for every fire he set. We found his pay for the Bartlett job in O'Neal's locker at the firehouse."

"Five thousand a job. Not bad. What else did you find beside the diary?"

"A key." Randall paused ostentatiously to light a cigar. I sighed and asked the question he wanted.

"A key?"

"Yeah. A key to the rear delivery door of Bartlett's Hardware Store."

"Bartlett's burned to the ground, including that door. How could you tell it was *that* key?"

"There was a little tag tied to it saying 'Rear door, Bartlett's.'" Randall's smile was smug.

I said, "My God, the guy must have *wanted* to be caught! Where'd you find the key?"

"In a pocket of the slacks his mother told us he wore on the eighteenth, his day off. The eighteenth, get it?"

"I get it. But it's still not enough to have made him sing. Everything against him is purely circumstantial."

"Not quite," said Randall. "As a matter of fact, we kind of implied that an off-duty fireman who knows O'Neal was smooching with his girlfriend in a parked car behind Bartlett's store the night it caught fire. And that this fireman saw Jack O'Neal enter the store by the back door, disappear for a few minutes, then emerge and make tracks away from there just a little time before the fire broke out."

I clicked my tongue and gave the Lieutenant a shocked stare. "You mean you told him you had an eyewitness?"

"We didn't tell *him* exactly." Randall's tone was as bland as cream. "We merely suggested the possibility in a way that made Jack think it was true. *That's* when he broke wide open."

"Well," I said, "congratulations, Lieutenant. I suppose you've got a solid case against each member of the ring?"

"Airtight." Randall's cat's eyes regarded me without blinking for a moment. Then he said, "I told O'Neal about your part in this mess, Hal. About the note you found in his library book that made you suspicious, and so on. And you know what he said?"

"No idea."

"He said he was sorry we'd caught up to him before he torched just one more building."

I played straight man again. "What building?"

"The public library," said Lieutenant Randall, "with you in it."

THE REWARD

Originally published in* Alfred Hitchcock's Mystery Magazine, *October 1980.

I didn't want to waste my time on another fruitless call at Annabel Corelli's home, so I telephoned her at eight-thirty Friday morning.

After two rings, I heard the receiver lifted and a voice said, "Hello." The voice was unmistakably female and it sounded like contralto coffee cream—rich and very, very smooth. It gave me such a jolt of pleasure that for an uneasy moment I felt somehow disloyal to Ellen Corby, one of our librarians, whom I'd been assiduously courting for over a year.

I said, "Is this Miss Annabel Corelli?

"Yes. The way she said it painted an instant image of a tall, Junoesque creature in a string bikini walking along a tropical beach.

"My name is Hal Johnson," I said, "and I'm calling about your overdue library book, Miss Corelli. I stopped at your house yesterday to collect it, but you weren't home."

"I'm almost never home in the daytime, Mr. Johnson. I'm an Argyll Lady. I'm just on my way out to work now." That figured, I thought, a door-to-door cosmetics lady. With that voice, she ought to be able to sell skin lotion to a porcupine. "I'm sorry about the book, she said. "I'm afraid I let a friend borrow it and then forgot all about it.

"It's six weeks overdue, I said, "and it's a one-week book, so it's costing you a bundle in fines."

"I'm really sorry, Mr. Johnson." Her voice caressed me. "How much do I owe on it?"

I told her.

"Well, how about if I leave the book and the fine in my carport for you so you can pick it up today while I'm out?

I said, "Today? But if you've lent the book to a friend—"

"No, today'll be fine," she said with a laugh. "The friend I lent it to lives here with me."

Lucky friend, I thought as I hung up.

* * * *

I stopped at Miss Corelli's house in the Last End in mid-morning. Sure enough, there was the library book—*The Hong Kong Diagram*—on a shelf in the carport, with the exact amount of the fine neatly stacked on top of it. A cornerpost concealed the book and money from anyone not specifically looking for it.

As I put the book on the back seat of my old Ford, it occurred to me that Annabel Corelli must do pretty well as an Argyll Lady. Her house was nothing elaborate, but it was no hovel either—two-story white clapboard with green shutters and a neat yard attractively planted. And the carport was a two-car job. Maybe Miss Corelli's friend contributed to the budget. I felt a vague sense of regret that I hadn't been able to meet the lady and her exciting voice in person.

That Friday was a busy day for me. By the time I'd made the last call on my overdue list, the hot August afternoon had already gobbled up my usual cocktail hour and was shading rapidly toward dinnertime. I was tired and out of sorts, and I felt sticky. I wanted a long shower and an ice-cold martini, straight up. So instead of returning to the library to check in my books and fines before I knocked off for the day I went straight home, luxuriated for twenty minutes in the shower, and had not one but two ice-cold martinis before dining in bachelor loneliness on a double package of frozen chicken chow-mein.

I cleaned up the dishes, listened to the news on television, then turned it off, feeling fidgety and restless and wondering how long it was going to be before Ellen agreed to marry me—or at least let me see her more than two evenings a week, which was my present ration.

Thinking about Ellen reminded me of Annabel Corelli's sexy voice, and that in turn reminded me of her overdue library book, *The Hung Kong Diagram*. It was a relatively new novel of the stolen-nuclear-device-endangers-the-world school, and a suspense blockbuster.

It was full dark now. I went out the back door of my garden apartment into the garage, unlocked the car, and, by the light in the dome, rummaged through the stacks of books in the back seat until I found *The Hong Kong Diagram*.

Have I mentioned that I'm an avid reader? Well, I am. I'll read anything—from coffee-table art books to paperback gothics. I've found that reading's the best way to educate yourself beyond the few basic disciplines you get in college. When I was working as a homicide detective under Lieutenant Randall, before I decided to become a library cop, I d taken courses in speed reading and memory development. You know how an ambitious rookie in any new job can be an eager beaver? That was me. But, as a matter of fact, the speed reading and memory training come in very handy in my present work, which, as you've probably gathered by now, is to run down overdue and stolen books for the public library.

I figured I could probably zip through *The Hong Kong Diagram* in a few hours. At the very least, it would amuse me until bedtime. I relocked the Ford and went back inside, riffling through the book, looking for anything that might inadvertently have been left between the pages. The shakeout is standard procedure with me when I collect overdue books, and you'd be surprised at some of the items I've discovered. I once found a brand-new hundred-dollar bill in a library book borrowed by an offset printer on the South Side. From the alacrity with which he grabbed the bill and thrust it out of sight, I've always suspected it might have been one he'd printed himself.

There wasn't any hundred-dollar bill in *The Hong Kong Diagram*. There was, however, a list of addresses written in a careless scrawling hand on the back of a sales slip that carried the heading Argyll Cosmetics. A memo, I concluded, to herself from Miss Annabel Corelli.

I ran my eye down the half-dozen addresses. They didn't mean anything to me. But they might he important to a door-to-door Argyll Lady. At the very least, I thought, they gave me an excuse for further exposure to Annabel Corelli's golden voice. I dialed her number and waited eagerly for the sound of rich contralto. What I got, after two rings, was a harsh, impatient baritone, "Yes?"

I said, "Is Miss Corelli there?"

"Who's calling?"

"Hal Johnson from the public library. I spoke with Miss Corelli this morning."

"Hang on."

I hung on, reflecting on the sad fact that Miss Corelli's live-in friend, judging from the depth and proprietary sound of his voice, seemed to be a man—and not another woman, as I'd imagined. Probably a Fuller Brush Man, I thought sourly.

"Hello, Mr. Johnson. Didn't you get your book O.K.? It was gone from the carport when I got home."

"I got it, Miss Corelli. And thanks. But I found a memo in it and I thought maybe you'd need it.

"A memo?" she said with a puzzled lift to that gorgeous voice.

"Yes. A list of addresses written on the back of an Argyll Cosmetics sales slip. Maybe a list of calls you plan to make or something."

She hesitated a moment. Then, "Oh, yes, Mr. Johnson. I recognize if. It *is* a call list, but I don't need it any more. You can throw it away."

"OK I just wanted to be sure it wasn't important."

"It was terribly nice of you to call about it."

"Not at all, Miss Corelli," I said. "Good night."

I hung up, tossed the list in the wastepaper basket, and started to read *The Hong Kong Diagram*.

The ads were right; it was a suspense blockbuster. It made me so nervous I couldn't get to sleep until after midnight.

* * * *

Wild coincidences do happen occasionally in library work like mine, just as I suppose they do in other businesses. I was at my desk in the library the next morning, working on my weekly records, when I got a telephone call from my old boss, Lieutenant Randall of Homicide.

"Hal," he said, "do me a favor." It sounded more like an order than a request, but that was in character for Randall when he was in a hurry.

"Like what? I asked noncommittally.

"Like saving me a trip to the library. You can get me the information I need quicker than I can—if there is any."

"What do you need?

"Any information you can dig up about one of your card-holders named Josephine Sloan. A twenty-seven-year-old woman. Single. A live-in maid. One of your best customers, judging by the stack of borrowed library books in her room.

"Who has she killed, if I may ask?"

"Nobody that I know of. She was reported missing on the eleventh of this month by her employers, a Mr. and Mrs. Gaither. When the Gaithers got home from a weekend at the shore on that date, she was missing."

"Along with the family's jewels and silver?"

"No. Nothing was missing except the maid."

I said, "Since when have you been switched from Homicide to Missing Persons?"

"I haven't. Josephine Sloan's body was found yesterday afternoon by some kids playing in Gaylord Park. The body, with a badly cracked skull, was stashed under an overhang along the creek bank. It could be a hit-run, murder, or any other damn thing except a natural death."

"Well, in that case," I said, "sure. I'll nose around for you. But her employers ought to be able to tell you a hell of a lot more about her than any of our people here."

"Her employers can't give us anything that helps. We've tried. Since they were away, they don't know anything about her activities that weekend. To hear them tell it, she was a model maid—industrious, efficient, quiet, honest, no known boyfriends." Randall cleared his throat. "Which figures, I suppose. She was quite unattractive."

“I still don t get why you think we can help you, no matter how many library books she read.”

“The post-mortem shows her death had to have occurred that weekend. And we’ve only got one lousy lead to her movements that weekend.”

A pause.

“Something to do with the library.”

“Right. Apparently one of the last things she did before she went missing was to borrow eight books from your library on Saturday, the eighth—two weeks ago today. You and your people are probably the last ones to have seen her alive.”

“O.K.,” I said with a deep sigh. “What do you want me to do?”

“Ask around about her among your Saturday stall and volunteers, find out if anybody knows her. Does anybody remember her coming in on the eighth? Has anybody ever noticed her with a boy friend at the library. Did she, by some freak of chance, say anything to anybody about her plans for that weekend? Or about her employers being away? You know what I want, Hal. A starting place, that’s all.”

“I’ll try, Lieutenant,” I said, “but don’t hold your breath. I took out a pencil. “Josephine Sloan. Twenty-seven years old. A spinster. Unattractive. Address?”

“Same as her employers’, said Randall. “The R. C. Gaithers. Thirty-four North Linden Drive.”

I took it down. “I’ll be in touch.”

“Thanks, Hal.” We hung up.

That’s when the coincidence showed up. As I looked at the address I’d just jotted down on my pad, I realized I’d seen it before very recently. In fact, only last night. On the call-list bookmark left in her overdue library book by Annabel Corelli, the Argyll Lady.

* * * *

After plenty of questioning, what I got for Randall out of our Saturday staff and volunteers was exactly zero. We have four girls on the check-out desk of the main library, including Ellen, and only one of them had. Anything of even remote interest to reveal about Josephine Sloan, and that was Ellen herself, who, after much thought, said she vaguely remembered checking out some books for the name Sloan on the Saturday morning in question. Beyond that, nobody could remember anything at all. In fact, though two of the other girls and one of our men volunteers were familiar with Josephine Sloan through her frequent visits to the library, not one of them had ever exchanged any more words with her than were necessary to check her books in and out.

Before calling Lieutenant Randall with the bad news, however, I decided, on the basis of that odd coincidence of addresses, to take another look at Annabel Corelli's call list, which should still be reposing in the wastebasket at my apartment. The library closes early on Saturdays. I went straight home, dug the list out, and was pleased to see my memory hadn't let me down on the Sloan address. It was there all right, along with five others—34 North Linden Drive.

There was something else there too, something that hadn't registered with me the night before when I'd found the list and telephoned Annabel Corelli. I stared at the tiny figures for a moment, then reached for my car keys.

* * * *

Twenty minutes later, I was sitting across the desk from Lieutenant Randall at Downtown Police Headquarters. "You got something for me," he asked hopefully.

I shook my head. "I'm sorry. One of the girls remembers Sloan checking out her books on that Saturday, but that's all. And you already knew that."

Randall sighed. Then he shot me a sleepy look from his cat-yellow eyes. "So why are you here?"

I told him about the Argyll Lady—about her overdue library book, her live-in boy friend, her bookmark memo with Josephine Sloan's address on it. He snorted. "Your Argyll Lady probably called on the Gaither woman to sell her some cosmetics."

"Right, Lieutenant. But look at the tiny figures under the Gaithers' address there." I handed him the list and pointed.

Randall peered at them. "Eight dash eleven," he read aloud. "The other addresses all have numbers too. Probably order numbers. Or appointment dates." He paused and his eyes narrowed. "Dates," he repeated softly. He lit one of his vicious stogies and puffed acrid smoke across his desk in my direction. I coughed. "Dates," he murmured again. "The eighth of the month is approximately when the Sloan girl was killed. And the eleventh is when the Gaithers came home from their weekend and reported her missing. Is that what you're getting at, Hal?"

"Could be," I said.

"Let's find out."

Randall was never one to waste time. He called a police clerk into his office, gave him the list of addresses, and told him to get the names and telephone numbers that went with them. While we waited, Randall smoked in silence and I sat on the hard chair and remembered to be grateful I was no longer a homicide cop. Sissy library fuzz or not, it was a lot more restful collecting library books than murderers.

The clerk was back in eight minutes. Randall grunted his thanks, picked up his phone, asked the switchboard for an outside line, and dialed one of the numbers the clerk had just handed him.

After a short wait, a woman answered. "Mrs. Symons?" Randall said. "This is the Police Department." His tone was as bland as vanilla pudding. "Maybe you can help us. We're investigating a mugging that occurred on your street on the night of—" he read the tiny numbers under the Symons' address from the call list "—either the twenty-seventh or the twenty-eighth of last month. Were you at home those evenings, can you remember?"

Mrs. Symons voice squawked in the receiver. Randall held the phone far enough from his ear so I could catch her words. They were heavily freighted with indignation. "A *mugging*!" she said. What's the *matter* with the police in this city? It wasn't a mugging at all, as you ought to know very well since you spent a whole morning here at my house investigating it!"

"Oh-oh." Randall was abject. "We must have our wires crossed here, Mrs. Symons. If it wasn't a mugging, what was it?

"Our burglary here! They stole every bit of sterling silver we had in the house!"

While she paused for breath, Randall repeated his question. "Were you at home that weekend, Mrs. Symons?

"At home? Of course not! If it hadn't been Parents Weekend at our daughter's college, we wouldn't have lost our silver. The house was empty." Her voice went shrill. "But I've already *told* all this to one of your men named Leroy! And we haven't heard a *word* from him in almost a month now! *Some* police department! Lucky for us we were insured!"

Randall soothed her. "I'll ask Detective Leroy to get in touch with you at once. I can't understand this mix-up, Mrs. Symons. I'm very sorry—please believe me." Mrs. Symons gave the Lieutenant an unladylike raspberry and hung up abruptly.

Randall grinned. "Remind you of old times, Hal?" he asked. He picked up the phone again and asked for Detective Leroy in Burglary. While he waited, he talked to me around his stogie. "We'll take it from here, Hal. Thanks for the lead—

It was a dismissal. I stood up. "Thanks aren't enough," I said. "I want a reward."

"Reward?" He glared at me.

"Reward." I repeated. "If you decide to interview the Argyll Lady any point during your investigation, I want to be there."

"What for?"

"So I can see what goes along with that sexy voice," I said.

* * * *

The following Friday night, Randall called me after midnight. I'd just come in from a dinner and movie date with Ellen. Randall said, "You in bed yet?

"Almost," I said. "Why?"

"We've got your Argyll Lady here. If you want to collect that reward come over to headquarters."

"Now? Its after midnight!"

"So your Police Department never sleeps. You coming?"

"What happened?"

"I'll tell you when you get here." He hung up with a crash.

I sighed. I was tired and sleepy. I wanted to go to bed, not downtown—not even to meet the girl with the sexy voice. After Ellen, Farrah herself would be an anticlimax. But I'd asked for it. I put my jacket and tie back on and went out to the car.

The Lieutenant was alone in his office when I got to headquarters. He smirked at me, and waved me to a chair.

"Couldn't this wait till tomorrow?" I asked.

"You said you wanted to meet her. She may be out on bail tomorrow."

"I said, Don't tell me *she* killed Josephine Sloan."

"I won t tell you anything unless you shut up." He was enjoying himself. "O.K.," I said meekly.

"The minute Detective Leroy in Burglary saw that list of your Argyll Lady's, Randall said, we were practically home free. It was just routine from there on."

"Let me guess. All those addresses had reported burglaries too?"

He nodded. Four out of six. All committed when the owners were out of town and the houses were empty. On the dates indicated by the little figures under each address."

"And silver was stolen from all of them?"

He nodded again. "With the price of silver today, did you know you can get several grand at the smelter for a set of sterling flatware that retailed for only a few hundred bucks ten years ago? Silver's very big in the B-&-E business these days."

"Even a library cop is aware of that," I said sarcastically. "So what about Annabel Corelli?"

"In each case, she'd made a sales call at the burglarized house shortly before the burglary took place."

I grimaced. "So she *did* set them up. A crooked Argyll Lady. She makes a call and during a friendly conversation learns when the lady of the house and her family will be away. She notes the best prospects for a large silver haul, and the dates when no one should be at home."

Randall blew smoke. "A neat operation. You got to admire it."

"I do. But I still don't see how it gets you anywhere with the Sloan murder."

Randall treated me to one of his unblinking yellow stares. Then he said "In each of the four burglaries, entry into the house was effected the same way. By means of a hydraulic jack." I must have looked puzzled, because he went on to explain in a patronizing tone.

"You cushion the pushing head and the footplate of a jack with foam-rubber and position it horizontally against the edges of a door frame about the level of the lock. When pressure is applied, the jack spreads the door-posts apart enough so the lock and deadbolt tongues are drawn out of their sockets and the door can swing open. When you leave the house with your loot, you release pressure on the jack and the door frames spring back to vertical again, reseating the bolts in their sockets as though they'd never been touched. And the only sign of a break-in having occurred is a couple of shallow pressure marks on the doorposts made by the jack."

"Well, well," I said, "what'll they think of next? I still don t see—" But as I uttered the words I did see. "You found the same jack marks on the doorposts of the Gaithers house."

"The very same," said Randall. "Exact match of the marks on the other four break-ins. Although nothing was reported stolen at that address, remember. Only the disappearance of the maid. Yet a break-in had obviously taken place. Are you beginning to get it now?"

"Yeah. Corelli set up the jobs, and she and her boyfriend probably worked them together. But when they broke into the Gaithers' house, it wasn't empty, as they expected it would be. The maid was there. She probably caught Corelli and friend at the silver chest and recognized Corelli as the Argyll Lady who called on Mrs. Gaither. So the fat was in fire, unless—"

Lieutenant Randall nodded. Unless something was done to keep the maid from talking. So they did something. They killed her and, leaving the silver behind, they relocked the door, packed the maid into their ear, and hid her body in Gaylord Park, six miles away.

"Do you have any proof of all this?" I asked.

"Some circumstantial stuff. And when their lawyer gets here and we can interrogate them, I'm hoping for more. Anyway, we sure as hell have proof they're silver thieves if nothing else. We caught them red-handed, about two hours ago, burgling the last house on your list." Randall yawned cavernously. "A blackjack in the boyfriend's pocket could be the Sloan murder weapon. It's at the lab now. And the boys have found a few faint bloodstains on the upholstery of the back seat of Corelli's car that may give us something."

Randall noted my sour expression and said cheerfully, "Hal, my boy, you were dead right about your Argyll Lady. She's a real dish. Wait'll you see her."

He picked up the phone and spoke into it.

* * * *

Two minutes later, Annabel Corelli appeared in the doorway escorted by two uniformed cops, one holding each arm. Even without makeup, her auburn hair in a tumbled mess and her clothing in disarray, she was something to see. She was really impressively beautiful—and big. She must have stood almost six feet tall and tipped the scales at a good hundred and sixty-five pounds—every one of them distributed in the proper place.

Randall stood up politely. I also got to my feet. The Lieutenant said, "Miss Corelli, let me present Hal Johnson from the public library. I promised him he could meet you in person if that list of addresses he found in your library book should help us with this case."

She seemed momentarily taken aback when she heard my name. Then she smiled at me very sweetly. In that unforgettable voice, she said, "I *am* glad to meet you, Mr. Johnson."

Trying to hide my embarrassment, I started to mumble something fatuous, I don't remember what. But I didn't get a chance to finish it. Annabel Corelli pulled sharply away from her guards, took two steps toward me, drew back her right arm, and slapped me so hard I fell back against Randall's desk, my head ringing like a church bell.

They hustled her out but I could tell by the frown on Lieutenant Randall's face it was all he could do not to laugh himself sick.

THE SEARCH FOR TAMERLANE

Originally published in* Ellery Queen's Mystery Magazine, *May 1981.

I was engaged in my bi-weekly proposal of marriage to Ellen Thomas when I got the call.

"I simply can't understand," I was saying flippantly to Ellen, "why I am so attractive to other women but not to you. Here I am, a man not too old, not too bad-looking, not too immoral, and probably the best library detective in the business, and my chosen bride, Miss Ellen Thomas of the Public Library, treats me as if I were Joe Unknown from Patagonia. Why is this?"

"I like you, Hal," Ellen said, not at all flippantly, "I like you very much indeed. More than I've ever liked another man. But I'm not sure I like you enough to marry you. And spend the rest of my life with you. Even though you *are* a good library detective."

"And a fine homicide detective before that," I said.

She began to eat her pineapple upside-down cake. "Please run that by me again," she said, her tone changing, "that bit about your being so attractive to other women."

We were eating lunch in the cafeteria of the Public Library where we both worked. I took a spoonful of my vanilla ice cream and said with some dignity, "It's quite true."

"Name one other woman who finds you all that attractive."

"Tessie Troutman," I said. "A very perspicacious waitress at Carmody's Bar and Grill."

"Oh, the blonde with the—" Ellen hesitated. "The one built out to here?"

"The very same. She's willing to marry me at the drop of a hat."

"How do you know? Have you asked her?"

"No. And I won't—not until *you* give me a definite answer. But by her ingratiating manner when she brings me my martinis, I can tell. If I *were* to ask her, she'd swoon with pleasure while saying 'Yes' at the top of her lungs."

"Why?" asked Ellen, scraping industriously at the glutinous remains of her cake. "Because of your overpowering charm?"

"Not at all," I said. "Admittedly, I have no overpowering charm. It's my good looks she fancies. She likes what she sees, you might say."

"What I might say," said Ellen, "is that Tessie—and it's true—has a cast in one eye and sees things slightly out of perspective. Instead, I shall merely be lady-like and tell you that I am honored by your—what is it now?—eighteenth proposal of marriage. And shall deliberate further on my response, with your kind permission."

I groaned. "I don't know why I want to marry you, anyway!" Ellen, unperturbed, licked her fork daintily. And that's when I saw the cafeteria cashier waving to me and holding up her telephone receiver. I went over to her counter, took the telephone from her, and said into it, "Hal Johnson here."

The voice of our switchboard girl murmured into my ear, "You about finished lunch, Hal?"

"Yeah. Why?"

"Two men here to see you. Jerry Coatsworth from the University Library and another one. A cute one."

"Send them to my office and tell them I'll be up in a few minutes. Jerry knows where my office is." Jerry Coatsworth, the assistant librarian at our biggest local university, bowls on my team at the College Club every Thursday night. We're good friends.

I went back to the table where I'd left Ellen. "You can have the rest of my ice cream, baby," I said generously. "I've got another date." I left and went upstairs to my office.

My office is a tiny cubicle behind the Library Director's spacious quarters. It contains only my desk and swivel chair, two visitors' chairs (castoffs from our Reading Room), a filing cabinet, and a patterned rug masquerading unconvincingly as a worn but genuine Sarouk.

Jerry and his "cute" friend were occupying the two visitors' chairs when I came in. I had to squeeze past them to reach my desk. "Hi, Jerry," I said, seating myself, "you come to find out how a real man-sized library is run?"

"No way," he replied, grinning. "And not how to bowl a perfect score, either." He said to the man in the other chair, "This is Hal Johnson," and to me, "Shake hands with Perry Kavanaugh, Hal."

I did so, across the desk. Kavanaugh was somewhere in his late twenties, I judged—blond, fresh-faced, with rumpled longish hair and a drooping mustache. He reminded me of the sun-bleached types you see riding horses in the cigarette ads. Cute, all right. He was smiling, but his eyes were anxious-looking and he had been sitting on the edge of his chair even before he leaned forward to shake hands with me.

I sent an inquiring look at Jerry. "What can I do for you?"

"We're in trouble, Hal," Jerry said, "and I promised Mr. Kavanaugh I'd ask you to help us get out of it."

"What kind of trouble?"

"Mr. Kavanaugh," said Jerry, "is the executor of his uncle Ralph's estate. His uncle died a few days ago. His uncle's will leaves a number of his books to us—to the Brightstone University Library—to form the nucleus of a collection of rare books for his alma mater that he hoped would ultimately bear his name. Like the Beinecke Rare Book Library at Yale. You with me so far?"

I nodded. "The books your uncle left to the library were rare books?" I asked Kavanaugh.

"It seems so," he replied. "First editions and so on. I don't know a rare book from Adam's off-ox myself, but Mr. Coatsworth here tells me—"

Jerry broke in, "They're listed and described in the will, Hal, and yes, they'd qualify as rare books. Yes, indeed."

"So where's the trouble?" I asked.

"The trouble is," said Jerry, "that Mr. Kavanaugh gave the books away six months ago."

Kavanaugh flushed in embarrassment. "Before I *knew* they were rare books," he hastened to defend himself. "And before I knew they were to be a legacy to Mr. Coatsworth's library."

Already guessing the answer, I asked, "Who'd you give them to, Mr. Kavanaugh?"

"To you," Kavanaugh said. "To the Public Library."

"And you want them back?"

"Yes. So I can carry out the provisions of my uncle's will."

Jerry added inelegantly, "And *we* want those books so bad we can taste them!"

I sat back in my chair. "How'd you happen to give them to us, Mr. Kavanaugh?"

He seemed glad of the chance to explain. "My uncle was an old man living here alone in a rented apartment since his retirement. He's been ailing for years, nothing too serious until six months ago when his friends and neighbors and doctor began to worry about his deteriorating health and frequent mental lapses, and his doctor decided he ought to go into a nursing home. I was uncle Ralph's only living relative, so his doctor called me in New York to see if I'd come down here and help him make the move. So I got a leave of absence from my job and came down to do what I could to help him. I got him admitted to Cedar Manor Health Center, helped him move in, and cleaned out his old apartment. Actually, I gave away most of his belongings just to get rid of them."

"Including his books?"

"Right. Seven big cartons of them. I offered them to you—the Public Library—and you seemed happy to take them off my hands." Kavanaugh smoothed his rumpled hair with one hand. "It was only after my uncle's death two days ago, when I came down to make the funeral arrangements, that I discovered I had inadvertently given you the rare books he wanted the Brightstone Library to have."

"Didn't you know he owned some rare books?" I asked. "Hadn't he ever mentioned them to you or told you he was a collector?"

"Never."

"Not even when he knew you were going to clear out his old apartment?"

Kavanaugh shook his head. "He was suffering from advanced arteriosclerosis, Mr. Johnson. He wasn't even aware he was living in a new place when he entered the nursing home. He didn't remember much of anything about himself or his past or—or me, for that matter. So I just went ahead on my own and did what I figured ought to be done—cleared out his apartment, terminated his lease, arranged with his bank to take care of his expenses, and so on."

Jerry said, "He gave you the books by mistake, Hal. So what do you think? Is there a chance you still have them?"

"Maybe fifty-fifty," I said. "Depends on what they were and what shape they were in when we got them. Any donated books we can't use, we usually sell off at periodic book sales." I turned to Mr. Kavanaugh. "Did we give you a receipt for the books when you donated them?"

"Yes, and at least I was smart enough to save that!" Kavanaugh got it out of his pocket and handed it to me. It was one of our regular receipt forms which merely acknowledged a donation of 193 hardcover and 55 paperback books to the Public Library by Ralph Kavanaugh of the Crest View Apartments. No book titles or anything specific. The receipt was dated the twentieth of the previous October and signed by Mary Cutler, our chief librarian.

"Okay," I said. "May I keep this temporarily?" Kavanaugh nodded. "And I'll need a list of titles—the rare book ones—to check on. The ones mentioned in the will."

Kavanaugh handed me a typed list. "We came prepared," he said. "There are only six."

The list read:

Ulysses by James Joyce. 1922

The Adventures of Huckleberry Finn by Mark Twain. 1884

Psalterium Americanum by Cotton Mather. 1718 (Autographed)

The Sun Also Rises by Ernest Hemingway. 1926
For Whom the Bell Tolls by Ernest Hemingway. 1940
Tamerlane and Other Poems by A Bostonian. 1827

"Are these the publication dates?" I asked.

"Yes," Jerry said.

"Okay." I stood up. "That's it for now, then. I'll check and let you know how I make out. I can't promise anything, of course. But I'll give it a whirl."

"We sure appreciate it, Hal," said Jerry. "Thanks a million."

Kavanaugh added his thanks to Jerry's.

I waved a deprecatory hand. "I'll be in touch," I said, and they left.

Ten minutes later I had given the whole story to Dr. Forbes, our Director. He listened in silence. At the end of my recital he said, "If we've still got the books, Hal, we'll have to return them to Mr. Kavanaugh. Legally, they're the rightful property of the Brightstone University Library."

"They must be worth a bundle," I ventured, "if they're really rare books. Dr. Forbes. We could be giving up a potential fortune, couldn't we?"

He smiled. "Yes, but it's a fortune to which the library has no reasonable claim, I'm afraid. Since the books are in our possession, if they still are, only because of a misunderstanding, we must return them to their proper owner. I suggest you consult Mrs. Cutler to see if we still have them."

Mary Cutler, our chief librarian, listened to my story, not in silence, like Dr. Forbes, but with frequent interjections of dismay, regret, and indignation. Books are a passion with her—all books, whether rare or common or neither; she loves and treasures them, and she disliked intensely the idea that her dear Public Library might have to relinquish any of the precious volumes on our shelves to that "stuck-up" University Library across town.

However, she promised to look into the matter at once. And with the aid of our computer, and that of the assistant librarians who are normally charged with sorting, cataloguing, and preparing donated books for circulation or sale, it didn't take her long. By the following afternoon I was ready to report to Mr. Kavanaugh and Jerry Coatsworth.

Their eyes went instantly to the small stack of books on my desk as they settled themselves into my visitors' chairs.

"Hey!" cried Jerry exuberantly. "You found them, Hal!"

"Thank God!" was Kavanaugh's devout comment.

I said, "Some of them, Jerry. I found five out of six."

That calmed them down a little. But Kavanaugh exclaimed, "Five out of six is wonderful, Mr. Johnson! Just great and in only one day! Doesn't that mean you may still find the sixth?"

I shook my head. "I'm afraid not. We have no record at all of the missing book, whereas these five here were simple to trace. One of the five, the *Psalterium Americana* by Cotton Mather, had been put in our special section, where the books may be consulted with the librarian's permission here in the library, but not borrowed or taken out of the building. The other four books here were circulating as three-week books in the regular way. Both the Hemingways had been checked out, and I had to collect them from the borrowers this morning."

Kavanaugh said anxiously, "What about the missing one, Mr. Johnson? The one you couldn't trace?"

"It must have been sold at one of our used-book sales. That's all we can figure—that the sorter who went through your uncle's cartons of books decided it was too fragile, or old, or unpopular or something to be of any use to us. It probably went for a buck or two to some member of our reading public. As I say, we don't have any record of it, and we don't have it among our uncatalogued books. We looked."

Jerry groaned. "A buck or two!"

Kavanaugh said, "I was a complete damn fool!"

"Anyway." I said, patting the books at my elbow, "our records show these are five of the six rare books you gave us by mistake. I'll need a receipt from you, Mr. Kavanaugh, stating that we have returned them to you." I shoved the books over to him.

"Wait a minute!" Jerry said. "Which book didn't you find? Which one is missing?"

I consulted their list. "This *Tamerlane* thing by A Bostonian," I said.

Jerry groaned again. "Wouldn't you know? This *Tamerlane* 'thing,' as you call it, is the most valuable book of the whole lot! I was planning to make it the centerpiece of our new rare-book collection!" He looked deeply distressed.

I stared at him. So did Mr. Kavanaugh. "What's so special about *Tamerlane*?"

Jerry said, "Only that in 1827 when it was published, a certain famous American writer wasn't well enough known yet to get his name on a book, so he used that pseudonym, 'A Bostonian,' instead. You know who 'A Bostonian' really was?"

"Who?" asked Kavanaugh and I together.

"Edgar Allan Poe," said Jerry in a dismal voice. "The last time one of these *Tamerlane* 'things' was auctioned off, you know how much it fetched?"

"How much?" said Kavanaugh and I, again as one voice.

"A hundred and forty thousand dollars."

Nobody said anything for a minute. Kavanaugh and I were too shocked and Jerry was too depressed, then I pointed to the five books on my desk. "How about these?"

Jerry spread his hands in a belittling gesture. "They're rare books, and they're worth a good deal, of course. But peanuts compared to *Tamerlane*. The Cotton Mather, with his signature on the flyleaf, and the Mark Twain, might go at auction for five thousand apiece. The two Hemingways at maybe two thousand apiece. Ditto for the *Ulysses*." He paused. "Do you think there's *any* chance of recovering the missing book, Hal?"

"We'll give it another try, but I can't hold out too much hope."

Jerry stared gloomily at his feet. Finally he lifted his head. "Anyway. Hal, it's no skin off your nose. You've been great to get these five back and we appreciate it. Mr. Kavanaugh, how about giving Hal his receipt?"

I pushed a form over to Kavanaugh, already filled out and requiring only his signature. While he was groping in his pocket for a pen, I said to Jerry, "I didn't know you were a rare-book buff."

"I'm not. I read up on the six books after we were informed of the contents of the will."

I said, "I can see why the Cotton Mather, with his signature on it, would be a rare book. But what about these others?"

Jerry managed a grin. He took the copy of *The Adventures of Huckleberry Finn* out of the pile and leafed through the book for a minute, then put it down on the desk in front of me, opened to an illustration of an old man. "Look at that fellow," he said.

I looked. Then I did a double-take and looked again. "His fly's open!"

"Right. In this 1884 edition a disgruntled pressman altered the engraving of the illustration so that this guy's fly was open instead of closed. They call this the 'open-fly copy,' and it's worth much more than a correct copy of the edition would be."

I laughed. Kavanaugh said, "You're joking!"

"No, I'm not. The *Ulysses* is a first edition, published in 1922, but the Hemingways are a little unusual." He leafed through the copy of *The Sun Also Rises*. Then, like a proud child playing "show and tell" at kindergarten, he placed the open book in front of Kavanaugh and pointed. "Page 181," he said. "Do you see that word 'stopped'?"

"Yes," Kavanaugh said. "What's rare about that?"

"How is it spelled?"

Kavanaugh looked again. "With three p's!"

Jerry nodded. "Part of the first run had that misspelling before it was caught and corrected. So this uncorrected copy is considered by rare-book buffs to be the genuine first edition." He held up *For Whom the Bell Tolls*. "This is a first edition, 1940. For most of the first run of this one the photographic credit line under Hemingway's picture on the back of the dust jacket was mistakenly omitted. See? Like this copy. Consequently this is more valuable than the corrected first-edition copies with dust jackets."

"Well, well," I said. "You learn something new every day, don't you?"

Kavanaugh handed me my receipt. "What do we do next?" he asked helplessly.

"Get together with your lawyer," I suggested.

"We tried to," Jerry said, "but he's in Washington at a meeting of the Bar Association. Back Monday."

"You need him," I said to Kavanaugh. "You need him bad. For what you've done by giving those books to us was to dissipate some of the valuable assets of your uncle's estate, of which you are the executor. That's a real no-no to the legal boys. Your lawyer will have to figure out a way to persuade the probate court to accept your uncle's will for probate in spite of the missing assets."

"Can he do it?" Kavanaugh was suddenly downcast.

"I don't know. The receipt we gave you when you donated the books may help. Your recovery of these five books here will be reasonable proof that you gave the rare books to us by mistake. You will probably need an affidavit from us stating that we unknowingly sold the missing book at public sale to an unknown buyer. And you'll certainly have to advertise for the missing book, offering a reward, as reasonable proof that you made all possible efforts to get it back for the legatee."

Jerry wagged his head. "What are you, Hal?" he asked. "A lawyer as well as a cop?"

"No. But I'm surrounded by about a million reference books here."

Kavanaugh sat up and said with more enthusiasm now, "I'll place the ads this afternoon, Mr. Johnson. How much reward shall I offer?"

"Don't name an amount. Just say 'generous reward.' And don't mention rare book, for God's sake. You just want to get the book back for sentimental reasons."

"Okay," Kavanaugh said. He stood up and Jerry followed suit. "And thanks for your help, Mr. Johnson. I don't know what we'd have done without you."

He gathered up his five books and they left, trailing expressions of gratitude as they went.

* * * *

That was Wednesday. I waited until Friday evening before I called the telephone number listed in Mr. Kavanaugh's advertisements.

I draped a handkerchief over the mouthpiece of my telephone.

When he answered, I said through the handkerchief, in as hoarse a voice as I could manage, "Are you the one who's been advertising for a book?"

"Why, yes," said Kavanaugh promptly. "*Tamerlane and Other Poems*. Why do you ask?"

"I've got it," I said.

A sharp intake of breath and a long moment of silence at the other end of the line told me all I wanted to know. I went on, "How much is the reward?"

Kavanaugh said, "Are you sure you have the book I advertised for?"

"Yep." I said. "So how much is the reward?"

A hesitation. Then Kavanaugh said, "Do you mind telling me who you are? And how you happen to have the book?"

"Never mind that until we get the reward settled. Books are the way I make my living, and I just got lucky when I spotted the one you want."

"Lucky?" Kavanaugh sounded thoroughly bewildered.

"Yeah. The book's worth a lot of money, isn't it? So the reward should be pretty big, shouldn't it?"

"I—hadn't settled on a specific amount. You'll get whatever seems fair, of course."

"How about ten thousand dollars?" I said. "The *Tamerlane* thing is worth that much reward, isn't it?"

"Well, that's pretty steep, don't you think? The book has only a sentimental value to me."

"How about if we talk it over before you decide. Are you free now?"

"Yes, but—"

"Great. Come over to my place. You can make sure my book is the one you want. And we can bargain a little about the reward. I live in apartment twelve at Pennfield Gardens."

"Where's that?" asked Kavanaugh. "I'm pretty much a stranger in town."

"Your cabbie will know the way. I'll look for you in about twenty minutes."

* * * *

Actually, he made it in seventeen, which is pretty good going. At his knock I opened the front door without turning on the light in the vestibule, so he was inside before he got a good look at my face.

Then he stood stock-still and stared. "Mr. Johnson!" he exclaimed. "Was it *you* who telephoned me about the missing book?"

"Yeah," I said. "Come on in and sit down where we can talk this whole thing over."

He advanced into my living room and, dazed, sat down stiffly in an armchair with his back to my bedroom door. I sat opposite him on the sofa. "I don't understand this at all, Mr. Johnson. Why did you call me and pretend to have found my book?"

"Because," I said quietly, "I decided you are a rank amateur and need some professional help."

"Such as yours?"

"Exactly. Such as mine."

"What professional help can you offer me, for God's sake?" asked Kavanaugh a little wildly.

"I can tell you where your missing book is, for starters."

Kavanaugh blinked. "Where?"

"In New York. Either in your safety-deposit box or squirreled away in your home."

He drew a deep breath and ran a hand over his blond hair. "Now I think I understand," he said. "You're trying to blackmail me, aren't you, Mr. Johnson?"

"Call me Hal," I said. "And let's not talk about blackmail. I'd rather consider it a reward for locating your missing book. I think about half of what you get for it at auction would be a fair reward. Say, roughly, seventy thousand dollars, if we can trust Jerry Coatsworth's figure."

He said matter-of-factly, "It probably won't bring that much. Anyway, what makes you think I'll split with you? You can't prove anything against me. I can destroy the book, then it would be merely your word against mine. And whose word do you think the probate court would take?"

I slid in the clincher very gently. "They'd take mine," I said, "unless you had that affidavit from the Public Library that I mentioned to you."

That stopped him for a few seconds. Then, "My lawyer could get around that, Johnson, and you know it as well as I do." But his voice held uncertainty.

"You're dreaming. Your goose is cooked, Kavanaugh, unless you agree to cooperate with me."

"Well…) he hesitated. Then he sketched a tight smile. "Do you mind telling me how I gave myself away? Why you think me such an amateur?"

I ticked the points off on my fingers. "First, I found it slightly odd—and thought-provoking—that the only book we couldn't locate was the most valuable one. Second, I didn't believe for a minute that you never knew your uncle owned rare books or had willed them to the Brightstone Library. It seemed much more likely that as his appointed executor under his will, you'd been given a copy of the will long ago, with the rare books listed in it. And third, I couldn't quite accept the presumed fact that our people, who sorted your uncle's books, would be dumb enough to discard a book like *Tamerlane* without first checking with our chief librarian."

Kavanaugh said nothing. His expression, by rights, should have been sheepish after my little lecture. Instead he looked thoughtful. I asked him, "Why did you decide to steal your uncle's books anyway? As his only living relative, you're probably the heir to everything he had *except* the books, aren't you?"

He nodded. "Yes. But I knew when I moved him into that nursing home that if he lived for more than a year at those prices, he wouldn't have a nickel left to his name except his Social Security. So I was merely trying to salvage a little bit of his estate for myself before it was too late."

I said, "Well, you had a good idea, Kavanaugh, but you handled it like an amateur." I grinned at him. "Which is where I come in."

With the air of a man asking a very important question, Kavanaugh said, "How many other people have you told about this?"

I gave him my you-must-be-out-of-your-head look. "Cut anybody else in on this sweet little setup? The only chance to get in on some big money I'll ever have? I haven't breathed it to another soul. I'm telling you the truth."

"Good," Kavanaugh said, in what sounded like a relieved tone to me. He put his hand inside his jacket and pulled out a dainty little automatic and pointed it at me.

I was dumfounded.

Kavanaugh stood up, took two paces toward me, and directed the round cold eye of his gun in the general area of my mid-section. No doubt aiming, I thought, to slaughter some of the butterflies that had suddenly come alive there.

I swallowed hard, like taking a big pill without water. "Hey!" I got out in a squeak. "Hold it!"

Kavanaugh's gun hand was trembling, I saw, but not enough to make much difference to me if he pulled the trigger. He said, with a thread of smugness in his voice, "I knew it was you who telephoned me tonight. So I brought this with me in case you got any big ideas. He waggled the gun and sweat broke out on my normally placid brow.

"You knew it was me on the phone?"

"Of course. You're not as professional as you seem to think, Johnson." He was thoroughly enjoying my discomfiture.

"How did you know it was me?"

"Because you referred to the *Tamerlane* book as the *Tamerlane* 'thing,' just as you did in your office when you discussed it with Coatsworth and me."

I winced. He had a point. An amateur he might be, but he was not a complete fool. I said. "You figure to shoot me? In cold blood? Right now?"

"Why not? Without you around to interfere with my handling of the *Tamerlane* 'thing,' my little scheme could still work."

I looked down at the gun menacing my stomach and said, "If I were you, Kavanaugh, I wouldn't shoot me." I fed him the old cliché. "You'd never get away with it."

He said tauntingly, towering over me, "Why not, Mr. Professional?"

I looked over his shoulder toward my bedroom and said loudly, "Come on in, Jerry. Did you hear it all?"

Startled, Kavanaugh took his eyes off me long enough for me to twist the gun out of his hand, after which I thrust it, none too gently, into *his* stomach.

He gasped.

I said, "You *are* an amateur, Kavanaugh. That looking-over-the-shoulder trick is as old as the hills. And I see you even forgot to take the safety off your gun. Now sit down and listen to me." I emphasized my request with another stiff prod of the gun barrel.

Slowly he backed up and sagged into his chair.

"I deliberately rigged this whole affair tonight," I informed him. "And you're now tied up so tight you better stop squirming or you'll really get hurt."

Kavanaugh said sullenly, "You rigged it?"

I nodded. "I've got our entire conversation on tape. How does that grab you?"

His eyes widened. He lifted his gaze from the gun in my hand to my face.

He didn't say anything, however, so I went on quickly, "I don't intend to use the tape against you, even though the police, your lawyer, the probate judge, and the Brightstone University Library would find it very interesting indeed."

"Why did you tape it then?" he asked.

"An anchor to windward," I answered, "in case you refuse to cooperate."

"I don't believe you taped anything."

"The mike's under the arm of your chair." He ran his fingers along the underside of his chair arm and found the mike. He still didn't say anything, just sank a little deeper into his chair. I allowed him a silent minute to think things over.

At length he said, "Cooperate. What the hell do you mean, cooperate?" He frowned, the sullen look replaced now by a contemplative one. "What do you want from me, Johnson?"

"The book," I said. "The *Tamerlane*."

"Half the loot isn't enough for you? You want it all, is that it?"

"Who are you to complain?" I said. "After all, you just tried to kill me to hang onto the whole bundle for yourself." I shook the clip out of his automatic and tossed the empty gun into his lap across the few feet separating us. I said, "What I want you to do is to give the book to the Brightstone Library, just as directed in your uncle's will."

That wiped the contemplative look off his face and replaced it with one that was half puzzled, half astonished, and wholly ludicrous. It was all I could do to keep from laughing.

"You're not going to sell the book at auction?"

"No way, buster," I said firmly.

"Then what's in it for you?"

"Look," I said, "Jerry Coatsworth is going to be in charge of the Brightstone new rare-book collection. And Jerry Coatsworth is a friend of mine. I'm not going to stand around and see him cheated out of his rare books by an amateur crook who doesn't know any more about stealing than I do about playing left field for the Cubs. Especially when you try to make *my* library the fall guy in the sketch. Does that answer your question?"

He had the grace to look embarrassed. "Yeah," he murmured. "I guess so."

"So here's what I want you to do. Get the book from wherever you've hidden it. Tell your lawyer and Jerry Coatsworth that some guy who bought it at a local used-book sale saw your ad in the papers and returned it to you for the reward."

"I can't just say 'some guy'," protested Kavanaugh. "And how much reward?"

"How about five hundred dollars? Could you scrape up that much? Not from your uncle's estate, but from your own funds?"

"Sure."

"Okay. Then you write a check for five hundred bucks to the Public Library Building Fund. We're opening a new branch on the

South Side. And you tell Coatsworth and your lawyer and the probate court that the guy who returned the book wanted to remain anonymous, and asked you to give his reward to the Public Library. You got it?"

Kavanaugh began to perk up. "Sure, I got it, Hal. And if I do it that way, you'll never say anything about what really happened? You'll never—ah—?"

"Never breathe a word?" I gave him my biggest trustworthy grin. "You'll have to hope so, won't you?"

Kavanaugh got out of his chair, put his little gun away, and held out a hand to me. "It's a deal," he promised solemnly. Then he added impulsively, “And a better one than I deserve, Hal. Thank you for making me keep my amateur status.”

That night I took Ellen out for dinner, made her swear a sacred oath of secrecy, and told her the whole story. “So you see, Ellen,” I finished up, “I’m not only nice-looking but I’m intrepid in the face of danger, loyal to our library, and compassionate to amateurs. Don’t you think you should make up your mind to marry me?”

Ellen put down her knife and fork. After a minute she said, “Since you’re such a paragon, Hal, I think I ought to confer an honorary degree on you.”

“An honorary degree would be nice,” I said, pleased. “What degree did you have in mind?”

Ellen dimpled. “How about B.L.S.—Bachelor of Library Science?”

“Bachelor?” I said, regarding her sorrowfully. “You’re turning me down again, aren’t you? For the eighteenth time.”

“Nineteenth,” said Ellen. But she reached across the table and squeezed my hand hard, which I took for a hopeful sign.

SIDESWIPE

Originally published in* Ellery Queen's Mystery Magazine, *June 1982.

As my car struck broadside against the low curb and, already beginning to roll, slammed across the bridge's walkway and crashed through the flimsy steel railing, my most intense emotion was one of raw anger rather than fear.

Not that I'm a particularly fearless character, or too slow of mind to recognize instantly the imminence of my own death. No, what caused my outrage was simply a long-standing pet abomination of mine—it had marked my years as policeman and civilian alike—for anybody, young or old, man or woman, who drove a car while under the influence of alcohol or drugs and blithely played Russian roulette with other people's lives.

I took a flashing lopsided look through my tilted windshield at the car that had forced me off the bridge and through the railing. And I suspected at once that whoever was driving it was either drunk or high or both, because the car showed no sign of stopping. It was drawing rapidly away at speed.

Then I was too busy for further thought about the departing car. My own old Ford, carrying shards of steel railing with it, was falling rapidly, end over end, toward the river thirty feet below. I thanked God fervently for my seatbelt. It held me sturdily in place, kept me oriented enough to permit me to do the little things that might possibly save me from drowning—roll up my driver's window to the top, unlock both front doors, and pray a bit. The prayer was only a quickie, of course, but I hoped it might help a little. I also thought fleetingly of Ellen Thomas, the girl on the checkout desk at the library, whose hand I had been vainly seeking in marriage for lo, these many months.

Then the car hit the water with a resounding splash and slowly, inexorably carried me with it beneath the surface.

* * * *

I called Lieutenant Randall, my old boss at Homicide, from the hospital early the next day. "Lieutenant," I asked querulously, "did you hear what happened to me yesterday?"

"Yeah, Hal, I heard." Randall's voice was as gruff as usual. "Somebody forced you off the Wolf Hollow Bridge, right? And you made it to shore okay. So congratulations. You should be dead."

"I know it," I said. "But thanks, anyway."

"What were you doing on Wolf Hollow Bridge, for God's sake? Nobody uses it any more except a few farmers."

"I was going to collect some books from a farmer's wife out at Dell Corners," I said, "and it was a farmer who found me beside the road when I crawled out of the river, so don't knock it."

"You always did make friends easy. What do you want from me?"

"I want that SOB who sideswiped me on the bridge and left the scene of the accident. I want to find out who's responsible for my bath. And for the total loss of my car. And for the destruction of the forty-two library books that were in the trunk when we went overboard."

Randall said, "You and your library books. You're a little confused, aren't you? Hit-and-run, leaving the scene, DWI—you don't want me, you want Traffic. Aside from that, how you feeling?"

"I got a knot on my head, a sprained thumb, and a cracked rib. But the doctor says I can leave here today if I promise not to breathe deep and don't go bowling for a while."

"Great," said Randall. "Get lots of rest. And hold on. I'll switch you to Traffic."

"Wait a minute! That guy could have killed me!"

"You *aren't* dead, though, are you? So it's none of my business." There was a click in my ear and a new voice said, "Traffic. Sergeant O'Rourke."

I said, "Jerry, let me talk to Lieutenant Henderson. This is Hal Johnson." I knew Jerry from the old days.

"Hey, Hal, we heard you got dunked. You okay?"

"Yeah," I said, "but boiling mad. I hope Henderson can find my H-and-R driver for me. I'd like to say a few choice words to him. Is Henderson there?"

"Hold on."

Henderson came on the wire. "How you doing, Hal?"

I said, "Okay, Lieutenant. But I'm mad as hell. Will you please find out for me who the joker was who ran me off Wolf Hollow Bridge yesterday?"

"I wish I could," said Henderson regretfully. "There's not much chance, though, with no witnesses and nowhere to start."

"Listen," I said, "I'm going to *give* you a place to start. I saw the license number of the car that knocked me off the bridge."

"Oho!" Henderson sounded suddenly cheerful. "Let's have it then, Hal. Maybe we can get you some raw beef for dinner after all." They were just gathering up the breakfast trays at the hospital when Henderson called back. "Hal?"

"Quick work, Lieutenant. Any luck?"

"Not much. I'm sorry. The car that sideswiped you is registered to a man named Frank Shoemaker at 818 Northway Road, Apartment #3."

"Frank Shoemaker, 818 Northway Road, Apartment #3. I got it. Thanks, Lieutenant." I felt my anger beginning to build anew. "Did you take him in?"

"No. Shoemaker reported his car stolen from the Haas Brothers parking lot downtown at twelve noon yesterday. Shoemaker's on the Haas security staff. Cruiser 23 found his car abandoned in the East End at 6:30 this morning. With the right side pretty well bashed in."

"Hell's bells!" I said, seething. "Just my luck! I'm forced off a bridge and nearly killed by a drunken thief who'll get away with it scot free—and the next time he gets high and feels like a joyride in a stolen car he'll go right out and endanger the lives of other innocent citizens!" I tried to calm down, contain my fury.

"Look at it this way," said Henderson. "You're still in one piece, Hal. And that ain't bad for starters. So take it easy. I'll see you around."

* * * *

They released me from the hospital about eleven o'clock. I took a taxi to the rent-a-car office nearest the library. There I rented a Chevy Citation to get me around on my collection routes until the Ford was either dragged out of the river and repaired or declared a total loss and replaced by the insurance company. Meanwhile, my insurance covered the rental of the Chevy, which helped. Library detectives like me, who track down stolen and overdue books for the public library, aren't the highest paid people in the world, and I needed all the money I could muster if I was ever going to set up housekeeping with Ellen Thomas.

If. She hadn't said yes yet, but I thought she was weakening a little. Why else would she have telephoned twice after she found out I was in the hospital and sounded so pleased when I assured her I was still my usual handsome, carefree self with no arms or legs in splints and no bandages around my head?

I drove my rented car to the library, reported in to the Director, and picked up the overdue-books list from my office. Then I went about my business as usual, trying to ignore the occasional sharp pain from the cracked rib and the throbbing of the sprained thumb.

About three in the afternoon I made a call at an apartment just around the corner from Haas Brothers Department Store and it occurred to me that as long as I was in the neighborhood I'd go and have a little chat with Frank Shoemaker.

Leaving the Chevy—locked up tight—in the parking lot, I went into the store and asked at the Information Desk where I could find Shoemaker of the-security staff.

The pretty blonde at the desk said, "He's around somewhere. I saw him only a few minutes ago. Try back toward the book department. That way," she pointed. "Do you know him?"

"No, I don't."

"Well, you can recognize him by his hair and mustache," she said. "They're almost pure white. And his skin is almost black right now, he's so tanned. He's just back from a Florida vacation."

"Thanks," I said. "I'll have a look."

I headed for the book department, keeping a sharp eye out for a man with white hair and mustache and a tan. I was only halfway there when the possible significance of the girl's words struck me. I'm sure the clerks at the nearby perfume counter must have thought I had experienced a sudden revelation of some sort, like St. Paul on the road to Damascus or something, because I stopped dead in my tracks and stood stock still in the middle of the aisle while busy shoppers side-stepped around me.

When at length I got moving again and located Shoemaker at the jewelry counter, I inspected him carefully and decided I wouldn't speak to him after all. At least for now.

* * * *

An hour later I was facing Lieutenant Randall across his cluttered desk. "It wasn't hit-and-run," I said, "and it wasn't DWI, and it wasn't leaving the scene of an accident, Lieutenant. It was attempted murder. And that *is* your department."

Randall kept his cat-yellow eyes on me without blinking. "What makes you think so?"

"Mostly a hunch—with a few bits of evidence to back it up. Want to hear?"

He nodded.

"Okay. I got this sudden idea that somebody had been trying to kill me only an hour ago. I dropped into Haas Brothers to see the guy who owns the car that knocked me off the bridge yesterday."

"Fellow named Shoemaker, right?" said Randall. "But he wasn't driving when you were pushed," Peterson said.

I was touched. That meant Randall had been interested enough in my welfare to follow up Traffic's investigation. I said, "What started me thinking was that Shoemaker has a heavy Florida tan."

Randall gave me a kind of look you give people who have lost their minds. "A tan."

"Yeah, Lieutenant, a tan." And I told him about Mrs. Radcliffe.

* * * *

She had been the fifth name on my list—Mrs. John H. Radcliffe, 1272 Highland Drive, North Side. She had, according to my records, six books from the public library that were three weeks' overdue. She hadn't paid any attention to our written notice and she hadn't answered the telephone the two or three times I called her. So I went there, hoping to retrieve the books and collect the fines due on them.

It turned out to be a boxy white clapboard house in the middle of a row of seven others exactly like it, each separated from its neighbor by a narrow gravel driveway leading back, I assumed, to a garage at the rear.

I parked the Ford in front of 1272, went up the porch steps, and rang the doorbell. No answer. After waiting a few moments, I rang again. Still no answer.

After a moment's thought, I went and rang the doorbell of the house to the left. A plump lady in a dressing gown and flat bedroom slippers answered my ring at once. She had pink plastic curlers in her hair.

"Yes?" she said.

"I'm looking for the lady next door," I replied. "Mrs. Radcliffe. I've been trying to reach her for two weeks."

"What do you want with her? Who are you?"

"I'm from the public library," I explained. I showed her my ID card. "Mrs. Radcliffe has some overdue books I'm supposed to collect."

"In that case I can tell you why you haven't been able to reach her. She and her husband have been in Florida for three weeks. They just got home last night."

I had a suspicion this sharp-eyed lady was aware of most of what went on with her neighbors, so I asked, "Do you happen to know where she or her husband are now? I'd like to get in touch with one of them."

She nodded complacently. "Her husband left for work at eight this morning as usual. And Dora went marketing over an hour ago."

"Well, maybe I can stop by later this afternoon."

"She ought to be home any minute. She goes to the supermarket around the corner."

"In that case, I'll wait a while. Thank you very much, Mrs.—"

"Jones. And you're welcome." She closed her door.

I went back to the car and crawled inside. The day was cold enough to see your breath, but I was quite comfortable inside the car.

After perhaps fifteen minutes a vintage Volkswagen Square-back—one where the back seats fold down flat to form-a small station wagon—turned into the Radcliffe driveway and crunched over the gravel toward the back of the house, the driver giving me a curious look when she saw me parked in front of the house. The tops of numerous grocery bags showed through the rear window. I got out and followed the white car up the driveway on foot. By the time I made it to the rear, she had pulled into a rickety carport and was already out of the VW and lifting the back panel to get at the groceries. I called to her, "Are you Mrs. Radcliffe?"

When she turned and I saw her face, I hoped she was. She was a genuine brunette beauty with blue eyes under fine black brows and the smoothest, loveliest mahogany tan I've seen in my life. The rounded contours of her slim figure were pleasantly revealed by the slacks and windbreaker she wore.

"Yes, I'm Mrs. Radcliffe." Her voice was as nice as her face and figure.

I introduced myself, showed her my credentials, and told her what I wanted. "Oh," she said with a smile, "they're in the house. I took them to Florida with me during our vacation. I'm sorry to have caused you this trouble. If you'll wait just a minute, I'll get them for you, Mr. Johnson."

"Let me help you carry these groceries in," I offered. "You have quite a load there."

"Thanks," she said. "I'll open the door." She hefted a paper bag in one arm and started for the back door. I grabbed up two more bags and followed her.

The door opened directly into the kitchen, which was small but well equipped with modern appliances. She put her grocery bag down on the work surface between the sink and the refrigerator and pushed a lock of shiny black hair back from her eyes. I placed my two bags beside hers and said, "I'll get the rest of your stuff, Mrs. Radcliffe, while you get me the library books."

"Okay," she said, disappearing through a swinging door toward the front of the house. I returned to the Volkswagen and got the remaining bags of groceries out of the back. I was just about to slam the lid down when a glint of sunlight on metal caught my eye under a loose corner of the rubber mat that covered the VW's engine hatch.

Curious, I flipped back the mat. Lying half under its edge was a gold ring—a plain heavy band with a couple of green stones set in it. I picked it up and carried it into the house with the groceries. As I set my burden down in the kitchen, Mrs. Radcliffe's voice reached me through the swinging door. "In here, Mr. Johnson. I've got the books."

"Right." I went through the swinging door and found myself in the dining area of an L-shaped living room. I rounded the corner of the L and saw

Mrs. Radcliffe depositing a stack of books on a coffee table before a gaily upholstered sofa.

"Six?" she said.

"Six is right." I approached the coffee table, admiring the graceful curve of her back as she straightened up. "Have you lost any gold rings lately, Mrs. Radcliffe? I found this one just now in the back of your car." I held the ring out to her.

Her silken brows drew together in a brief puzzled frown. Then she laughed. "Oh, *that* dumb ring! I wondered where I lost it." She took the ring from my fingers and dropped it carelessly into a side pocket of her windbreaker. "Thank you."

"Dumb?" I said idly. "It looks pretty nice to me. Almost like an antique."

"Antique?" She laughed again, a nice little cascade of sound. "Some antique. It's a gag gift from my husband. He gave it to me when we left for Florida." She held out her ringless left hand. "I don't wear a wedding ring, so Jack thought it would be fun to have me wear one on our vacation so folks would realize we were respectable married people. It was a dumb idea. And the ring was too big for me, so I promptly lost it." She smiled at me. "How much is the fine?"

I consulted my list. "Six dollars and thirty cents."

She dug into her purse, murmuring, "Antique ring. That's good. What made you think that?"

I shrugged. "I saw some that looked like it last winter at a Spanish-treasure museum near Cape Kennedy, Florida. With a lot of stuff recovered from a Spanish treasure ship. Rings and bracelets and necklaces and stuff. You should have seen it. There were even some pieces of ancient Chinese porcelain."

"Sounds fascinating," she said. "I'd like to see it on our next visit to Florida. This time we spent our two weeks on the west coast, near Clearwater." She handed me a ten-dollar bill and I made change for her. Then I went through my regular routine of holding the library books upside down and riffling through them to make sure no bookmarks or forgotten papers were between the pages. A receipted bill from a Holiday Inn fell out of one-of them and fluttered to the floor. I stooped over and recovered it and handed it to Mrs. Radcliffe.

She went to open the door for me since my arms were full of books and said, "Thanks again, Mr. Johnson. I'm sorry I caused a bother."

* * * *

"That's it?" asked Randall when I'd finished. "That's all? You want me to slap an attempted murder charge on Shoemaker on the basis of *that*?"

"That's just the background. It didn't mean anything to me either—until I saw the tan on Shoemaker."

"He wasn't driving his car when it pushed you, Hal."

"That's what he says. How do you know it's true?"

"How do I know it's not?"

"The coincidence of his having a heavy tan and owning a car that almost wasted me made me think about Mrs. Radcliffe some more. And a couple of other things that might mean something too."

"Such as?"

"The vague impression I saw—a white Volkswagen Squareback like Mrs. Radcliffe's behind me every once in a while as I finished my morning rounds yesterday morning."

"You think she may have been following you?"

"Maybe. I put the library books in the trunk of my car when I left her and crossed her off my list and checked the list for my next stop. I was in front of her house long enough for her to slip into her VW and follow me if she felt like it."

"Why should she feel like it? You're paranoid, Hal."

I grinned at him. "Maybe. All the same, that 'dumb' gold ring I found in her car *did* look like an honest-to-God antique, Lieutenant. Heavy yellow gold with a setting of rough-cut emeralds."

"You couldn't tell a rough-cut emerald from a cake of green soap," Randall hooted. "What do you know about women's jewelry?"

"Not much. But I do know how to remember pretty good, you'll admit that, won't you?"

Randall waved a hand. "So you've got a photographic memory. What's it got to do with this?"

"I remembered something about that hotel bill that fell out of one of Mrs. Radcliffe's library books. I didn't think anything about it at the time, but later, when these other things began to hit me—"

"What about the hotel bill?"

"It was from a Holiday Inn at Titusville, Florida."

"And?"

"That's just a hop, skip, and a jump from Cape Kennedy, where that sunken-treasure museum is."

Randall began to look thoughtful.

"Mrs. Radcliffe told me she and her husband spent their vacation on the west coast, near Clearwater. She was lying. Why? And why did she follow me around in her car until I stopped for lunch at Johnny's Cafeteria? If she did, that is."

Randall wasn't smiling condescendingly at me anymore. "What time did Henderson tell you Shoemaker's car was reported stolen?"

"Twelve noon."

"And what time did you stop for lunch at Johnny's?"

"About quarter of twelve."

"Plenty of time for Radcliffe to telephone Shoemaker and tell him you'd seen the ring and the Holiday Inn bill. Plenty of time for him to report his car stolen before he used it to come out to Johnny's and pick up on you when you left? And maybe follow you to Wolf Hollow Bridge where he saw his chance and pushed you off it? Is that what you mean?" When Randall's brain started ticking it ticked fast. "And therefore whatever Radcliffe thought you'd learned from her ring and her hotel bill was important enough to be worth killing you for?"

I said, "I *know* what they were afraid I'd learned, Lieutenant. I went right from Haas Brothers to *The Examiner*'s office and went through the back copies of the newspaper for the last two weeks. I found this item that I missed when it came out last week." I put the copy I'd made of it down on the desk before him. It had an inconspicuous two-column headline followed by a brief block of copy. It had been on page 4 of the first section four days ago.

GUARD SLAIN IN MILLION-DOLLAR ROBBERY

> Cape Kennedy (UP) Police intensified their search today for the thieves who fatally shot a museum guard while stealing nearly a million dollars' worth of old coins and jewelry from the Museum of Spanish Treasure here last Friday.
>
> Cape Kennedy Police Chief George Boniface said he had alerted smelting firms throughout Florida about the theft, hoping to head off any attempt to melt down the irreplaceable artifacts.
>
> The thieves broke into the Museum early Friday morning, bypassing burglar alarms with apparent ease, smashed plate-glass display cases, and helped themselves to the eighteenth-century Spanish treasure recovered from the sea floor.
>
> The lone security guard on duty, Lancelot Frederick, was shot by one of the thieves when he attempted to prevent the robbery. He later succumbed after informing police there were two men and a woman involved in the theft, all wearing ski masks to conceal their identity.

Lieutenant Randall didn't bother to read the item all the way through. He grabbed the phone and barked into the mouthpiece, "Get me the Police Chief of Cape Kennedy, Florida, Jerry, name of George Boniface—in a hurry!" He turned toward me, slamming the receiver down. "We'll take it from here, Hal. I'll be in touch."

I stood up. "Go easy on Mrs. Radcliffe," I said. "I feel like a heel for even suspecting her."

* * * *

A few weeks later the affair had been wrapped up with Randall's usual neatness and dispatch. Shoemaker and the Radcliffes had been returned to Florida to stand trial for murder, armed robbery, and grand theft, with enough solid evidence to put them away for a long, long time.

Item: Shoemaker's Police Positive .38 revolver, which was found to have fired the bullet that ended the life of the museum guard. Item: a penciled diagram of the intricate burglar-alarm system of the Spanish Treasure Museum, obviously made on the spot during preliminary visits to the museum by John Radcliffe, who turned out to be not only an electrical engineer employed by a local firm called Continental Alarms, Inc., but a college classmate and the oldest friend of Frank Shoemaker. Item: a taped confession by Mrs. Radcliffe, recounting the robbery and designating Frank Shoemaker as the guard's killer. And item: two suitcases full of the Spanish treasure stolen from the Museum, discovered by police in the bedroom closet of Frank Shoemaker at 818 Northway Road.

I told Ellen all about it over dinner at the Lotus Bud, one of the poshest restaurants around. I was mellow enough from two martinis and a half bottle of Mateus rosé to boast a little. "Aren't you proud of me, Ellen?" I asked her. "Figuring out the entire plot from a ring they just happened to drop when they were stowing their loot in the back of Radcliffe's VW for their trip home?"

She said, "Of course I'm proud of you. But they almost *killed* you, Hal."

"Would you have cared?"

"Of course." She flashed me a smile. "It would have been very bad publicity for the library."

"Well," I said, sighing, "that brings me to the reason I've told you all this. The Florida authorities were so glad to get their treasure back and catch the thieves, they suggested a small reward might be in order for the alert, honest library fuzz who solved the case for them."

"A reward!" Ellen exclaimed. "How exciting! What is it?"

"I have it right here in my pocket." I pulled out the antique gold ring I'd found in the back of Mrs. Radcliffe's car. The dull-gold band looked bright and polished under the restaurant lights; the rough-cut emeralds glistened. I held it out to Ellen.

She took it and said, "Oh, how lovely," and turned it this way and that, tilting her head to examine it from different angles. At last she said, "It's very beautiful, Hal, but what in the world do they think you're going to do with a fancy thing like this, a man of your simple ascetic tastes?"

I shrugged. "It would make a nice wedding ring," I suggested.

"For me?"

"For you."

She slipped it on her ring finger. "It's too big for me."

"I'll have it made smaller."

She protested. "It would cost us a fortune to waste any of this gold."

Cost *us*? My heart began to hammer. "Does that mean you'll take it?"

She said, "Is Mrs. Radcliffe really all that gorgeous?"

"A knockout," I said. "A dish. Black hair, blue eyes. With that sexy tan she's the best-looking woman I've seen in my life. Except for you."

"I could wear the ring around my neck on a chain," Ellen said. "Would that be all right with you, Hal?"

I took a deep breath and my cracked rib responded with a brief stab of pain. "Wear it anywhere you want to," I said, "just as long as you wear it."

She leaned over and kissed me, ignoring the other diners around us. I felt a wave of euphoria wash over me—a blessed mixture of triumph, love, tenderness. "Are you saying we're engaged?" I said, having trouble with my voice.

"You better believe it," said Ellen.

THE BOOK CLUE

Originally published in* Ellery Queen's Mystery Magazine, *February 1984.

It wasn't one of your ordinary hit-and-run, in-and-out bank robberies.

It was, in fact, a real work of art, a model from which any earnest young apprentice in the bank-robbing trade could have learned plenty.

It took place over the frigid New Year's weekend—a three-day holiday, since New Year's Day fell on Saturday—so the thieves had three full days and nights to knock a hole through the rear wall of the bank, disarm the bank's elaborate alarm system, cut open the vault with acetylene torches, and rifle two hundred private safe-deposit boxes of their contents.

Later, when the owners of the stolen valuables came to the bank and reported the extent of their losses, the bank estimated that the thieves had made off with roughly three and a half million dollars' worth of cash, securities, jewelry, antiques, coin collections, and whatnot.

Not a bad haul for three days' work—especially since the looters made a clean getaway, leaving behind them, aside from the shambles of empty deposit boxes and a hole in the wall, only a few traces of their three-day visit. A small pile of rubble from the shattered wall. A thin film of plaster dust on the floor of the bank inside the hole, marked with hundreds of indecipherable footprints. Scattered crumbs of crackers and cheese and some coffee splashes on the vault floor. The crusts of several peanut-butter sandwiches on the vault custodian's desk. And nothing else. Except for embarrassed bankers, puzzled policemen, and rueful insurance adjusters.

About noon on the fourth of January, I was at my desk at the Central Library working on my next overdue-list, when the girl on the switchboard rang through and said a police officer wanted to talk to me.

"Lieutenant Randall?" I asked. Randall was Chief of Homicide and had been my boss for five years before I joined the Public Library staff.

"No, Hal. Somebody named Waslyck."

Waslyck, Head of the Robbery Detail. Jake Waslyck. Sure, I remembered him from the old days. "Put him on," I said.

"Hal?" His voice came through like gravel on a tin roof. "How you doing, Hal?

"Can't complain, Jake. You?"

"I can complain," he said. "Plenty."

"The First Federal Bank job, right? I read about it in the papers."

"Who didn't? I want to ask a favor of you, Hal."

"Any time," I said. "What?"

"I need advice. Can you stop in here or shall I come out there?"

"I'll be downtown this afternoon. I'll stop by headquarters. Advice about what?"

"One of your library books. See you about three?"

"Two-thirty would suit me better."

"See you then."

* * * *

At two-thirty, I was in Jake's office. The place is cramped, smells strongly of stale cigar smoke, and is furnished in police-station modern: a battered steel desk, worn linoleum on the floor, a scratched filing cabinet in one corner, an old-fashioned hat rack in another, two uncomfortable straightback chairs, and a grimy Venetian blind over the unwashed window.

Jake sat behind his desk, his squat body overflowing his chair, his bulgy eyes red and puffy. His bushy ginger mustache was badly in need of trimming. And he didn't seem to have any neck at all.

Same old Jake. He looked a lot like an oversized bullfrog crouching there. But I remembered there was nothing wrong with his brain.

I sat down gingerly in one of his straight chairs. It trembled under my weight as I reached across the desk to shake hands. I said, not entirely sincerely, "Nice to see you again, Jake. It's been a while."

In a frog's croak of a voice he said, "Thanks for coming in, Hal." He paused.

"You look shot," I said. "The First Federal job getting to you?"

He nodded. "We got nothing to go on. ID's still comparing fingerprints, trying to find some that aren't those of safe-deposit-box holders or bank custodians. Absolutely no luck so far."

"It's probably hopeless," I said sympathetically. "It was below zero that weekend. They needed gloves, for the cold if nothing else."

"Yeah. So we got zilch. No leads. No suspects. We're going around in circles on a three-million-dollar robbery!" He cleared his throat. "It's a hell of a feeling, believe me."

"Frustration," I said. "I know what you mean, Jake. I've been there."

"So that's why I called you. I'm clutching at straws."

"Like the library book you mentioned?"

He gave one sharp nod, up and down.

"Tell me about it."

"It's a book we found in our search of the bank vault after the heist. You know those little booths where they let you gloat over your treasures in private?"

"Yeah."

"Well, we found this book from your library under the table in one of those booths."

"And you think it's a *clue,* maybe?" I underlined the "clue" with my voice. Cops hate the word.

"Not really. But a million-to-one chance. See, we figured, considering where the book was found and all, that some box-holder had left it in the booth by mistake when he stopped in last week to count his fortune or whatever."

"Doesn't the vault custodian always come in afterward and check out the booth to see you haven't left anything behind? Mine always does."

Jake said, deadpan, "You mean you rent a safe-deposit box?"

"Sure. But not at First Federal, thank God."

"What do you keep in it?" He was needling me.

"I skim a little off the top of the fines I collect."

"That must come to—let's see, maybe forty cents a week?"

"In a good week," I said. We both laughed. My laugh had a little edge in it, I'm afraid. "You're saying that a vault custodian might not notice a library book under a booth table?"

"It's possible. Those guards are only checking the booth to see if you've left a thousand shares of IBM or something like that lying around."

"So?"

"So last night when I couldn't sleep, it suddenly occurred to me that the library book just possibly might be something the *thieves* took into the vault when they broke in."

"You mean so they'd have something to read during coffee breaks?" The idea tickled me.

"Why not? They're in there for three days and nights, remember. They bring in cheese and crackers, thermoses of hot coffee, sandwiches—we even found some bits of fabric the lab says could be from a sleeping-bag lining. So why not something to read during their rest periods? Maybe one of them is a book nut. You know, queer for books."

"It's a long shot," I said, grinning. "But possible, I suppose. Let's see the book."

Jake yelled "Josie!" at the top of his voice and a minute later Detective Second-Class Josie Evans came into his office from the squad room across the hall. I remembered Josie from old times, too. She's black, slender, and very attractive in her navy-blue skirt and white blouse. To look at her you'd never guess she can toss a two-hundred-pound man over her shoulder without even mussing her hair.

She recognized me. "Hi, Hal," she said.

I said, "Hi, Josie. What's a nice girl like you doing in a place like this?"

"Defending my virtue most of the time," she answered tartly. "What is it, Jake?"

"Bring me the library book we found in the bank vault. He turned to me. "Josie's a book nut, too. She's reading the damn thing."

"I've finished it," Josie said. "It's a swell story." She went out and returned shortly with it. After she left I said to Jake, "You think this book may be evidence in the biggest bank robbery this state ever had, and you're letting Josie *read,* it, for God's sake?"

"Relax, Hal. Relax. The book's been put through the works by the lab already and gives us nothing. Except about two hundred sets of smudged latents from former readers. That's why I asked you to come in. Maybe you can get more from it than we can."

I picked up the book. "It's from our Central Library."

"I can read, Hal. I saw the stamp."

"There's no return card in the pocket."

"I noticed that, too."

I grinned at him. "And furthermore," I said, not averse to needling *him* a little, "It's a hell of a good yarn, like Josie said." The book was a popular novel by Wilbur Smith called *The Eye of the Tiger.* "It takes place in Africa," I said, "just like the old-time goodies by Rider Haggard."

Waslyck grunted. "Can you find out who borrowed the book from the library?"

"Sure. Name, address, and library-card number. Simple. Our computer coughs that stuff up on demand. But—" I held up a hand as he started to speak"—wait a minute, Jake." Another small jab of the needle wouldn't hurt, I thought. I had it on good authority that Jake Waslyck was one of my many former colleagues in the police department who had been known to refer to me slightingly as Library Fuzz Hal, the sissy ex-homicide cop who now spent his time tracking down library books instead of murderers—and although this was perfectly true, I didn't like them patronizing me. My work's a lot quieter than theirs, it pays just as well, and I can sleep better at night. So I said, "Our computer coughs up what you want only if the book happens to be overdue."

"Why the hell's that?"

"Invasion of privacy," I said. "Until a book is overdue, it legally belongs to the borrower. Our library is a *public* library. It's none of our business who has a book until it goes overdue. Then it belongs to us again."

Waslyck swore. "Listen, this is an official request from a police officer—a *public servant*—for the name and address of a suspect who may have been involved in the commission of a major felony." He glared at me.

I smiled. "In that case, our computer might be conned into making an exception. You see, Jake, we have this nifty secret code to bypass our computer's compunctions about breaking the privacy laws. We feed in the first three letters of the author's name—his last name—then we feed in the middle two digits of the book's Zebra patch number. Then comes the middle initial of the city's current Democratic mayor—"

"Knock it off, Hal. This is serious. Can you get me the information I want?"

"I'll try." I stood up. "I'll have to take the book with me, okay?" He made a dismissing gesture.

I took the book and left.

I called him back within half an hour. "I've got it," I said. "The book *is* overdue. You ready?"

"Shoot."

"The address is 1221 Bookbinders Lane."

He wrote it down. "What's the name?"

"You won't like this, Jake. The name is Adelaide Westover."

Jake swore. "A woman!"

"Seems like it," I said. "I'm sorry. It kind of blows your theory, doesn't it?"

"Not necessarily," said Jake, but his disappointment was evident in his tone. "I've heard of woman bank robbers before. Like Clyde's lady friend, Bonnie."

Trying to cheer him up, I said, "This Adelaide Westover may have wanted to spend the long weekend with *her* boyfriend, so she went along with him on the bank job and curled up with a good book while he worked."

Waslyck ignored that. After a moment's silence, he said, "I think we'll give it a whirl anyway, Hal. We might get lucky."

* * * *

Ten minutes later, my phone rang and it was Jake Waslyck. He said harshly, "You sure that's the name and address your computer came up with?"

"Sure I'm sure."

"Then your computer has a slipped disk. There's no such street as Bookbinders Lane in this city or any of its suburbs. And there's no such person as Adelaide Westover listed in the City Directory or the phonebook."

I sighed. "Then the book was borrowed on a phony card, Jake—a card issued to a fictitious person at a fictitious address. Sometimes people lie about their names and addresses when they apply for a library card and show us fake references. We can't check up on every citizen who applies for a card. But it doesn't happen often."

"I thought it was your job to prevent that sort of thing."

"It is. I'll see what I can do about this. If I come up with anything, I'll let you know, Jake…)

Four days later I telephoned Waslyck. It was around five o'clock in the afternoon and he'd gone off duty. I called him at home.

His wife answered the phone. "Hello?" she said in a rich creamy contralto that made me wonder how she ever came to marry a cop with a voice like a bullfrog.

"I'd like to speak to Jake if he's there," I said.

"Who's calling?"

"Hal Johnson from the public library."

"Hold on."

"Hi," he said when he came on the line.

I said, "I think I've got something for you on that library book, Jake. It's complicated for the telephone. I better see you."

"Okay. Be in my office at noon tomorrow."

"Right," I said. I hung up, feeling unappreciated and put upon.

* * * *

I was in his office at noon, sitting on the same shaky chair. Jake greeted me with a short question.

"What you got?"

"Well, our library thief might possibly—just possibly—have something to do with *your* problem. I think I'm onto his real identity. But I'm not sure. I need your advice this time."

Waslyck sat back in his creaking swivel chair. "Make it short. Okay?"

I said, "I questioned all the check-out people at Central Library about Adelaide Westover. Did anybody remember anybody checking out a book called *The Eye of the Tiger* by Wilbur Smith on a card made out in that name on that date—it didn't have to be a woman. Nobody remembered anything."

"Figures," said Jake.

"So then I thought, what if this Adelaide Westover, whoever she really is, borrowed other books by Wilbur Smith with her phony library card? Your library card is good," I explained parenthetically, "at any of our branches. And you can return borrowed books to any branch you want to. Did you know that, Jake?"

"To my shame, I didn't." Jake tapped his fingers impatiently on his desk.

"Well, I checked out all our Wilbur Smith titles, both at Central and all our branches—no easy job, since Smith has had six or eight successful books published in this country and some of our branches have as many as six copies of each one circulating. Thank God for our computer."

Jake said an unpleasant word.

I went on blithely, "Which is how I found out that three other Smith titles have gone overdue—although not long enough overdue to have been brought to my attention just yet."

Jake was following me closely now. "And the three overdue Smith books were checked out to Adelaide Westover?" he guessed.

"No, only one of them. A book called *The Delta Decision*. The other two titles—*A Sparrow Falls* and *Hungry As the Sea*—were checked out at our North Side and East Gate branches by two different people entirely. The book from North Side branch was checked out to Alexander Warfield. 15101 Quarto Avenue, the book from East Gate was checked out to Alan Woolfolk, who supposedly resides at 6225 Doubleday Drive."

"But doesn't?"

"But doesn't. Nor does any Alexander Warfield reside at 15101 Quarto Avenue. There are no such people and no such addresses in the city."

"More phony library cards?"

"Seems like."

Jake mulled it over for a few seconds. "And you figure the three phony library patrons are one and the same person? Because they all borrowed Smith's books?"

I nodded. "Sometimes people borrow a book by an author they've never tried before and they like it so well they want to read all the other books the author has written."

"And this joker who uses fake library cards has gone ape over Wilbur Smith."

I shrugged. "Could be. If the three phony names and addresses are the same person."

"You think they are?"

"Yeah," I said.

"Why?"

"Look at the names." I passed him my notebook. "Look at the addresses."

"The names have the same initials—Adelaide Westover, Alexander Warfield, Alan Woolfolk."

"Right. And as I remember my homicide work, a lot of people use their own initials when they're dreaming up an alias."

"Are you saying your book borrower's real initials are A. W.?"

"It seems reasonable."

"I'll buy that. But what about the addresses?"

"All three street names have something to do with books. The kind of phony names a guy who likes books might come up with. Bookbinders Lane. Quarto Avenue. Doubleday Drive."

"Okay. So what's the phony's real name then?" Waslyck leaned forward in his chair.

"Don't you want to hear how I nosed him out?" I asked innocently.

"No, I don't. But you're going to tell me anyway."

"All three phony library cards were issued at our South Side branch," I said. "That narrowed things down. But naturally nobody at South Side remembered anything about issuing them, so I pulled the application files of all the library volunteers who work at South Side and are authorized by our librarian to issue new library cards. Did you know we have twenty-seven volunteers working an average of four hours a week without pay at the South Side branch?"

"I know it now."

"So after examining the applications of volunteers over the past few years at South Side, I talked with the librarian and her assistant—and came up with a really hot-looking suspect for you."

"Who?" asked Jake.

"A volunteer named Arthur West. Sixty-nine years old, authority to issue new library cards, ready access to the check-out and check-in machines, considered a compulsive reader by his associates. He works twelve hours a week at our South Side branch without pay, has a pleasant personality, a minuscule income from Social Security, and a negligible pension from his former employers."

Waslyck interrupted. "But what's this Arthur West got to do with the First Federal Bank job?"

"That's what I wanted to ask your advice about," I said. "He's got a small checking account at First Federal, for one thing."

"So have hundreds of other people."

"Our South Side branch is right next door to the bank."

That got me nothing but a blank look.

"Arthur West often brings his lunch to the library in a paper bag—and the lunch invariably consists of peanut-butter sandwiches."

"Half the people in the world eat peanut-butter sandwiches for lunch," Jake said wearily.

"But Arthur West doesn't eat his crusts," I said. "Just like one of your bank robbers."

"The world's full of people who don't eat their crusts."

"True, Lieutenant," I said, "but the world's *not* full of library volunteers whose names begin with the letters A and W, who are peanut-butter-sandwich fiends who don't eat their crusts, who are living on inadequate incomes and who—" I paused for dramatic effect "—were employed before their retirement by the Universal Security Company of Chicago, whose specialty is the manufacture and installation of sophisticated alarm systems for banks."

Waslyck acted as though a bomb had exploded under his chair. He shot to his feet. "Why the hell didn't you tell me that in the first place? Where can I find this Arthur West? You *do* know *his* address, I take it?"

"He lives in a rented room over The Corner Cupboard Bar and Grill out in Lake Point. You know The Corner Cupboard, Lieutenant?"

"Who doesn't? It's a dive. Some very hard characters hang out there."

"Well, that's where Arthur West does his beer-drinking and eats most of his dinners," I said. "And maybe it's where he recruited his help for the bank job."

Waslyck yelled for Josie. When she showed up in the doorway, he said, "Get your coat on and check out a car for us—I'll meet you down in the garage." He took his own overcoat off the hat rack in the corner. The thermometer was still flirting with zero outside.

I said, "Aren't you going to get a search warrant before you go out there? You want to keep things legal, don't you?"

Jake gave me an exasperated look. "You know something, Hal?" he asked. "I'm really glad you don't work here anymore." He turned for the door. "So now get lost, will you? I'll let you know how this turns out."

* * * *

The morning newspaper next day told me all I needed to know—under a front-page headline. The police, the story went, acting on a tip from an informer, had arrested an elderly man named Arthur West in The Corner Cupboard Bar and Grill the previous afternoon and charged him with complicity in the sensational robbery, ten days ago, of First Federal Bank on the South Side. According to police Lieutenant Jacob Waslyck, other arrests were imminent. A search of West's rented room above the bar led to the recovery of almost a third of the loot stolen from First Federal's safe-deposit vault. The stolen valuables had been found hidden in a sleeping bag under West's daybed. The police reported that West's room also contained seven hundred and forty-two books bearing the identification stamp and card pockets of books from the Public Library.

That last item, I knew, was a direct message from Lieutenant Waslyck to me. His way of saying thanks—or a malicious reminder that I wasn't any better at my job than he was at his.

* * * *

I found a message on my desk when I got to the library that morning. Dr. Forbes, the Library Director, wanted to see me in his office right away. His spacious office is right next to my cubbyhole. He could have yelled for me and usually does. But this morning the message was formal. Dr. Forbes must be upset. And I thought I knew why.

He looked at me over the newspaper he was reading. Before he could say anything, I blurted out, "Dr. Forbes, I know what you're thinking and I don't blame you. But that newspaper article didn't mention two important facts. One, that Arthur West, the bank robber and library-book thief, is also a trusted volunteer who works at our South Side branch. And two, the informant who tipped off the police to him was me."

His expression went from stormy to partly cloudy. "Tell me about it, Hal," he said.

I told him everything. When I finished, his expression had gone from partly cloudy to fair and warmer. He said, "No wonder we didn't realize the books were missing. West checked them out to himself on spurious cards, and before they were overdue he checked the cards back in again without actually returning the books."

"Exactly. We were lucky he forgot to check those Smith titles in before they showed overdue on our computer."

"Why do you suppose he forgot to do it?"

"Maybe he was too busy planning the bank robbery—or more likely, after over seven hundred book thefts he began to think his system was foolproof and we'd never get onto him. He got careless."

Dr. Forbes smiled.

"So am I fired, or not?" I ventured to ask him.

"Not," he said.

* * * *

Two weeks went by. Two weeks during which I carried out my duties as usual. Two weeks during which Arthur West plea-bargained himself down to a charge of petty book theft in return for naming his accomplices in the bank robbery and agreeing to testify against them when their trials came up. Two weeks during which said accomplices—an apprentice plumber and a backhoe operator, both local citizens and regular patrons of The Corner Cupboard Bar and Grill—were duly charged with bank robbery. Two weeks during which, to everyone's relief, the other two-thirds of the missing loot was recovered almost intact, the plumber's share from a beat-up suitcase in a locker at the Greyhound Bus Station, the backhoe man's share zipped into one of his wife's drip-dry pillow-covers and stashed in the crawl space between his garage ceiling and roof.

On Saturday night of the second week I took Ellen Thomas out to dinner at Jimmy's Crab House. Ellen is the girl who holds down the check-out desk at the Central Library. She has promised to marry me as soon as we can acquire an adequate nest egg to see us through any rainy days in the future.

We were facing each other across a narrow table in a booth. Ellen looked at the prices on the menu and said, "Are you out of your mind, Hal? This place is too fancy for us."

I said, "I'm going to have Maine lobster, myself."

"Maine lobster?" She hesitated. "If you say so." Another pause. "Me, too."

The waiter took our orders and in due course brought in the lobsters. They were delicious. Not worth the price, but delicious.

Between bites, Ellen said, "What's the occasion, Hal? It is one, isn't it?" She gave me her up-from-under keen look.

"Yeah," I said, "a celebration of sorts."

"What sort? A celebration of what?"

"Wait till dessert," I said. "I want to surprise you."

"Okay. I'll wait." She worked on her lobster for a bit. Then she said, "I can't wait any longer, Hal. Tell me now. Why are we blowing a week's wages at this elegant restaurant?"

"Because," I replied, "the First Federal and their insurance people got together and decided to give the Police Benevolent Fund and Hal Johnson from the Public Library a small reward in recognition of their services in solving the robbery and recovering their loot."

"Hey!" cried Ellen, her eyes shining. "My hero! How much?"

"Ten thousand for the PBF, ten thousand for me."

She was stunned. She stared at me, her eyes wide with outrage. "Ten thousand dollars," she said indignantly. "Ten thousand dollars for saving them three and a half million!"

I agreed. "But ten thousand is better than nothing."

She brightened.

"It's pretty wonderful when you think about it. We've got our nest egg in one fell swoop. Now we can get married."

I said, "On ten thousand dollars? You call that a nest egg? It's hardly enough for a decent honeymoon. Not nearly enough to pay the obstetrician for the sixteen children we're going to have. Think of the college tuition for only one of the sixteen." I shook my head. "No way, Ellen. Suppose I lose my job or you lose yours? Suppose one of us has to spend a couple of weeks in a hospital sometime? Or we get divorced and I have to pay alimony and child support? Where would the money come from?"

Ellen leaned across the table and gave me a buttery kiss. "Well," she said, "we could always rob a bank, couldn't we?"

THE VAPOR CLUE

Originally published in* Alfred Hitchcock's Mystery Magazine, *December 1961.

If you want to go to Washingtonville, Pennsylvania, you go east from Pittsburgh on Route 78 for about twenty miles toward the Riverton entrance to the Pennsylvania Turnpike. As you approach Washingtonville, you dip down past a big new shopping center and run along the bottom of a shallow valley past seven gas stations, three roadside markets, two branch banks, a yard full of trailer rigs waiting for assignment, and several fairly clean cafes that cater largely to truck drivers.

Just before you lift out of this shallow valley over the western ridge, you can quickly look to your left and see the huddle of houses just off the highway that is Washingtonville itself. And because the accident happened on Highway 78 within shouting distance, almost, of Washingtonville City Hall, it was the Washingtonville Police who had jurisdiction and Lieutenant Randall who was largely responsible for handling the case. Randall would never have caught up with the killer without the help of a waitress named Sarah Benson.

* * * *

At 5:30 A.M. on December 16th, a 1954 Plymouth sedan, following Route 78 east, labored heavily up the slope of the ridge that formed the western boundary of Washingtonville's little valley. The car had engine trouble; the motor was running very unevenly and the car jerked and hesitated in its progress. The road had been plowed clean of yesterday's five-inch snowfall, but piles of snow edged the highway and the still-dark morning was bitter cold.

Inside the sedan, Hub Grant said to his wife, "If I can coax her up this hill and over, maybe we can find a gas station or garage open on the other side. We've sure got to get something done to this baby before we can make Connecticut in it."

His wife nodded anxiously. "It's so early, Hub. I'm afraid nothing will be open yet. We should have stopped at one of those motels back there."

"I wish we had," Hub admitted.

The car topped the ridge. Washingtonville's valley lay before them, snow-covered, silent, and marked by only a few lonesome-looking lights along the highway ahead.

Hub said, "There's a gas station. Let's try it."

He urged the reluctant car toward Amos White's gas station halfway down the gentle slope of the hill. And the Plymouth's engine chose that moment to conk out completely.

Hub took advantage of his downhill momentum to pull to the edge of the highway, where the car buried its right wheels in a bank of plow-piled snow and came to a cushioned stop. Hub opened his door and got out into the chilly darkness. No sign of dawn showed yet. He walked into Amos White's service station and saw that it was deserted. Amos didn't open up until seven o'clock these winter mornings.

Hub came back to the car. "Nobody there." He looked down the road toward Washingtonville's sparse lights. "Guess I'll try down in the valley. Looks like something might be open." He beat his arms against his sides. "Boy, it's cold out here! You sit there and wait for me, honey, and keep the doors locked. Okay?"

"Okay," she said. "I'll wait here."

"I won't be long, I hope." He slammed the car door and walked down the road toward the shopping center. It was 5:41.

At that moment, Sarah Benson was walking from her home on Washingtonville's outskirts toward the concrete ribbon of Highway 78 where it touched the periphery of the town at the shopping center. Sarah was bundled up in a heavy plaid coat and wore a green scarf over her titian hair. It was her week to open up Wright's Truckers' Rest and prepare the first enormous urn of coffee for the sleepy, chilled truck drivers who would soon begin arriving. They were regular customers, most of them; they knew that Wright's opened at 6:00 A.M. sharp, that Wright's coffee was good and hot, and that Sarah Benson was the best-looking waitress between New York and Chicago.

When she reached the highway, Sarah walked toward Wright's cafe, a hundred yards down the road from the shopping-center parking lot. It was awfully cold, must be near zero, she thought. And still dark. No one was about. Only an occasional car or truck swished past her on the concrete. She was reaching into her bag for the key to Wright's cafe when she heard a man's footsteps on the road behind her.

She turned in surprise and saw a dark form approaching from the west, his lanky figure silhouetted for her against the snow bank that edged the highway. He saw her at the same time, apparently. For he lifted an arm and called, "Hey, there...!"

Whatever he intended to say, he never finished it. A car rocketed down the highway toward him, coming fast on the outside right-hand lane of Route 78, the one he was walking in. He was suddenly caught in the beam of the approaching car's headlights. Sarah could see him make a startled move toward the snow bank beside him to avoid the onrushing vehicle. But he was too late.

Transfixed by horror, Sarah watched the car swerve wildly as the driver applied his brakes with a scream of rubber against the road; she saw in slow-motion detail the heavy, pinwheeling arc described by the pedestrian's body after the sickening sound of its impact against the car's bumper; she saw the body come to rest in grotesque, spread-eagled limpness on the snow bank not twenty yards from where she stood.

It was only as a dazed after-thought that she looked at the car again. It slowed almost to a halt, its stoplights glowing red, and Sarah thought it would stop. But then, with a snarl of desperately applied power, it gathered speed and made off down the highway toward the eastern ridge of the valley.

Sarah couldn't believe her eyes. "Stop!" she shrieked after the vanishing car. "Stop!" She thought she was going to be ill. "You hit a man!" Even while she screamed, the taillights of the murder car winked out over the eastern ridge.

Sarah tried to control the trembling of her legs and the heaving of her stomach. She ran to the motionless man in the snow bank. When she saw that nothing could be done for him, she returned to the cafe, opened the door with her key, switched on the lights inside, and telephoned the Washingtonville police.

It was 5:55.

* * * *

Lieutenant Randall and the police ambulance arrived at the scene of the accident at 6:05, just as the first faint glimmer of daylight showed. By then, a lot of cars and a truck had stopped beside the snow bank, drawn by the sight of the spread-eagled body and the bloodied snow, and by Sarah Benson's slim figure standing beside it, waiting for the law.

When Randall arrived, he detailed a policeman to send the curious on their way when it was certain none of them had witnessed the accident, and dispatched the hit-run victim to Washingtonville Hospital, where he was pronounced dead on arrival of multiple external and internal injuries, including a smashed skull.

Randall sat down at the counter of Wright's Truckers' Rest and talked earnestly with the only witness to the accident, Miss Sarah Benson. She was being as helpful as she could, though she was still pale from shock and wisely sipping a cup of her own coffee, black, to settle her nerves.

Randall was full of driving urge to get a description of the murder car as quickly as possible, but even so, he couldn't help noticing with approval how pretty Sarah Benson was—how well her titian hair set off her creamy skin and level blue eyes.

"What kind of a car was it?" he asked her.

"I don't know, it was dark. And coming toward me, the headlights blinded me. I couldn't tell anything about it."

He sighed. "I was afraid of that. But after you saw the car hit the man, you looked at the car again, you say…as it was going away from you?"

"Yes, I did."

"And you didn't recognize its make?"

"No. It seemed to be a dark-colored sedan, all one tone. That's all I can be sure of. And that its stoplights were on, bright red, before the driver decided to run away."

"Those stoplights," Randall said. "What shape were they?"

"Round, I guess," Sarah said.

"You guess? Don't you know?"

"No, I can't be sure."

"Big and round, or small and round?" Randall insisted.

"Medium and round, I guess," said Sarah. "I didn't really notice. I was so shocked…)

"You saw the back of the car," Randall interrupted her rudely, "with the stoplights on and nothing between you and the car. Surely you saw the license number or at least the license plate. Think hard, please."

"I'm thinking, Lieutenant."

"Well, was it a Pennsylvania license? Or New York?" He was still hopeful. "Did you see it?"

She shook her head slowly. "I'm afraid not."

"Damn it," Randall said, "you *must* have!"

She smiled at him sympathetically, conscious of how anxious he was to elicit a description of the car from her. "No," she said very quietly, "I didn't see any license plate."

He flushed. "I'm sorry, Miss Benson. But a description of the car, *some* description, is essential if we're to have any chance at all of catching this man. You understand that, don't you? If you didn't see the license plate, did you notice anything else about the car? A dent in the rear fender, maybe, a cracked back window, luminous tape on the bumper, anything at all?"

She closed her eyes and conjured up the horror of fifteen minutes ago. She was silent for a long time. Then she opened her eyes and said, "I can't remember anything more. There was this cloud of white steam coming out of the car's exhaust pipe and it sort of hid the back of the car, I guess."

Randall stood up. "Well, thanks very much. We'll have to do the best we can with a general description. There is evidence of damage to the front end of the car. We found a piece of metal in the road that broke off the grill." He turned to go, then paused. "Could you come down to headquarters sometime today and sign a statement? It will be helpful to have an official eyewitness record."

Sarah finished the last of her coffee and reached for her coat on a hook behind the counter. "I'll come now," she said. "Jenny can handle things here until I get back." Jenny was a sallow-complexioned bottle blonde already serving coffee and doughnuts to four drivers at the far end of Wright's long counter.

"Good," said Randall, "I'll drive you in. Come along."

It was 6:24.

* * * *

When Amos White arrived at 6:45 to open up his gas station for the day, he found a Plymouth sedan stuck in the snow right beside the apron to his place with a young woman sitting alone in the front seat, her chin in her upturned coat collar for warmth and a very worried look in her eyes.

Amos unlocked his service room. The young lady climbed out of the car and came in and asked in a timid voice if she could use his telephone. Amos said yes, and heard her call the police. And he kindly helped her over the first awful moments when she discovered from the police that she was a widow...that Hub Grant, her husband, had been killed by a hit-run driver, identity so far unknown.

Amos' watch said seven o'clock.

* * * *

All these events occurred in a little more than an hour in Washingtonville on the morning of December 16th. Then, for the subsequent six hours until one o'clock, nothing happened at all.

At least, it seemed that way to Lieutenant Randall. Of course, he flashed his meager description of the wanted car to state, county and turnpike police and asked their cooperation in spotting and holding the car and driver. And he fine-tooth-combed the stretch of Highway 78 between the shopping center and the eastern ridge in the forlorn hope of locating another witness who could come up with a better description of the hit-run car than Sarah Benson had been able to supply.

But he had no luck.

That is, he had no luck until one o'clock, at which time he was eating a ham-on-rye at his desk at headquarters waiting for some word on the car. The desk sergeant downstairs called him and said there was a woman to see him. When she came into his office, it was Sarah Benson.

He hastily swallowed the bite of sandwich he was working on and stood up awkwardly. "Well," he said. "You again, Sarah."

She raised smooth brows at his use of her first name but didn't comment on it. She sat in a straight chair across from his desk. "Me again, Lieutenant. I've thought of something that may prove helpful."

"Good for you," he said. "What is it?"

"You remember my statement about the car…) she began tentatively.

"Sure." He took the typed statement off his desk and handed it to her. "What about it?"

She read slowly from the statement: "A cloud of white steam was coming out of the car's exhaust and I couldn't see the license plate or any other identifying marks."

Randall stared at her. "So what? You told me that this morning. The car smoked. Probably needs a ring job. I've already given the boys that information."

A lively animation marked her manner now. "That cloud of steam," she said, leaning forward in her chair, "wasn't an oily kind of smoke. It was whiter, like mist, as I told you. Or the white vapor that your breath makes on a cold morning."

Randall said, "Yes? And what about this white vapor?"

She replied indirectly. "You know Wright's, where I work? It's right across the highway from Jensen's trucking depot, where all his trucks stand waiting for loads."

He nodded.

"Well, I've watched those trucks go out on cold days. And it occurred to me that after they've sat in the yard all night in the cold, their exhaust smoke looks just like what the hit-run car was giving out this morning." Randall merely stared at her in puzzlement.

"And when trucks drive into our place after running all night, they never give out that white exhaust vapor." Randall's eyes widened and he sat bolt upright in his chair. "Hey!" he exclaimed.

She smiled at him. "That's right," she said. "I called my brother on the phone to check it. He's a mechanic in a garage in Pittsburgh. And he says that's right."

Randall swung around in his chair, grabbing for his phone. Over his shoulder he said, dismissing her, "Thanks a million, Sarah. I'll call you."

* * * *

When he called her later, at her home, she answered herself. "Oh, hello, Lieutenant Randall," she greeted him. "Any news?"

"Plenty," he said with satisfaction. "The state police picked him up outside of Allentown an hour ago, thanks to you, Sarah. His car has a dented front end, a broken grill that ought to match up with the piece of metal we found in the road, and traces of blood and hair. We've got the whole thing lined out." He hesitated in unaccustomed embarrassment. "I'd like to tell you about it, Sarah."

"Go ahead, Lieutenant," she answered. "I'm listening."

"Well, I mean…) He rubbed a hand over his hair irritably. "Personally."

She ignored that. "Then the clue of the white vapor *did* help?" He thought he detected a teasing note.

"Sure it helped." His own voice was laced with chagrin. "Until you called it to my attention, it never occurred to me that white steam from an exhaust pipe in cold weather usually means that the car motor has only very recently been started. I kept thinking of the hit-run car as one from a distance, passing through here without stopping. But the white exhaust vapor made it clear that the guilty driver was either a local, or somebody who had stayed here all night. Because it showed that his car engine had just been started before the accident…and had been sitting in the cold for some time quite close to the accident scene, I tried the simplest thing first, and hit pay dirt right away."

"Where *did* the car start from?" she asked.

"The Buena Vista Motel. The fellow pulled in there at three yesterday afternoon from the west, slept till five this morning and started out again. His was the only car that left any of our local motels or hotels that early this morning. He was driving a dark blue Ford sedan, Pennsylvania license number VN 167. It was all on the record at the Buena Vista. After I fed that information to the boys, they had him in twenty minutes."

"Good," she said.

He changed the subject abruptly. "Why did you go to all that trouble—to telephone your brother and so on—just to be helpful to the police?"

"Because I wanted to help you catch that hit-run driver." Remembered horror was in her voice. Then she laughed a little. "And besides," she added, "I took a liking to you, Lieutenant."

"Good," said Randall. "Fine. I hoped that might be part of it. I've got another idea I'd like to check with you now."

"If it's the same idea that my truck drivers get about me, you can forget it," she said.

He cleared his throat. "I think you have a flair for police work, Sarah. Can't I take you to dinner tonight so we can talk it over?"

She hesitated only long enough to worry him slightly. Then she said softly, "That would be lovely."

Randall cradled his phone and glanced at the round, discolored police clock on his office wall. It said 5:45.

THE MISOPEDIST

Originally published in* Alfred Hitchcock's Mystery Magazine, *April 1968.

I don't like kids. You wouldn't either if you were in my shoes, which happen to be size ten, prison issue.

Until the South Side job, I could take kids or leave them alone. I had nothing particular against them. On the other hand, I wasn't exactly on the point of tears because I had none of my own, especially with me not married.

Anyway, kids were the farthest thing from my mind when Lieutenant Randall came over to me in Tasso's Tavern that night, where I was sitting at the bar beside a girl named Sally Ann.

I didn't know who he was then, of course. He had on a dark blue suit, a striped tie and a white button-down shirt. He also had on a bland friendly manner that promised nothing but kindness and understanding. Nobody would have thought he was a cop.

He was, though. I found that out right away when I he flashed a badge on me and told me his name. "And you're Andrew Carmichael, aren't you?" he asked me politely.

Without thinking, I said, "Yeah."

He nodded. His odd yellow eyes looked at me with what could only be gentle affection. "Good," he said. "Then I'd appreciate it if you'd come downtown with me for a little talk, Mr. Carmichael. Would you mind?"

Mind? Who wouldn't mind under the circumstances? I was only half-way through my second martini; my left hand was resting companionably on Sally Ann's thigh beneath the bar. "Now?" I said. Surprisingly, a certain hoarseness roughened my voice. I cleared my throat.

"Now would be fine," said Randall. He leaned forward and looked past me along the bar at Sally Ann. "Will you excuse him for a while, Miss?"

Sally Ann brushed my hand off her thigh, said, "With pleasure. Whatever he's done, I had nothing to do with it. I just met the jerk fifteen minutes ago for the first time."

That's how it goes. Romance dries up fast when a cop appears.

Randall said, "You want to finish your drink?"

I'd lost interest in my martini. "No," I said, and stood up. Randall towered over me. "I'm ready, but it would be nice to know what you want to talk to me about"

Randall grinned. It was a boyish, happy grin despite the unblinking yellow eyes above it. "No reason to keep it secret," he said, and herded me out of Tasso's Tavern ahead of him to a police cruiser parked at the curb. Randall held the back door open for me. When I got in, he climbed in beside me and nodded to the uniformed driver up front. The police car surged away from the curb. "What we want to talk to you about," Randall said, "is a little matter of counterfeiting, Mr. Carmichael."

Counterfeiting. I exhaled a long breath, said, "I thought counterfeiting was a federal thing, Lieutenant?"

"It is. Except there's a local angle in this case, and we're handling that. See what I mean?"

I didn't, but it wasn't important now. The skim of ice that had formed over my nerve centers when I first felt Randall's big hand on my arm began to melt. If it was counterfeiting Randall had on his mind, that let me out. I was home free, and I'll tell you why.

I know a little bit about most things. My fund of general knowledge is perhaps bigger than average, if you want the truth, but when it comes to counterfeiting, I'm nowhere. I don't even know how to spell it.

Phony bills and coins never had the slightest attraction for me. In fact, the very idea of fake money has always repelled me. I'm too fond of the real stuff to mess around with cheap substitutes. That's why I was able to breathe easy again the minute Lieutenant Randall mentioned counterfeiting. It just couldn't be me they wanted—not for counterfeiting.

If the lieutenant had said "armed robbery" now, I might have been worried. For armed robbery, especially the bank variety, was something I *did* know about. I'd robbed eighteen branch banks in the last couple of years without a hand being laid on me or even a breath of suspicion drifting in my direction.

I was proud of my success. After all, bank robbery is a demanding line of work. It takes careful planning, courage, intelligence and a fine sense of timing—in addition to a system, of course. For bank work, you need a system, one that takes a million little things into account but stays simple and uncomplicated just the same. That isn't easy; not when you have to think about armed guards, silent alarms, concealed cameras, patrolling police, hysterical tellers, and a whole potful of unpredictable factors like that; not to mention the big decisions, like which teller in the target bank will be easiest to intimidate; which bank to knock over at what time of what day; and even—this may strike you as strange—how big a score you want to make.

Yes, that's important. At least, it is in my system, I confine myself to a relatively modest take on each job. Just the contents of a single teller's cash drawer, that's all, no more, no less. It's quick, it's clean, it's unimportant to the banks and their insurance companies. A few hundred bucks stolen? A couple of thousand even? Forget it, Charlie. It's peanuts. Just be damn sure you lock up the vault tonight where the big stuff's kept!

See what I mean? You can toss a lot of little pebbles into a pool without stirring up much fuss, but heave in one two-ton boulder with a big splash and all hell breaks loose.

My system, what the cops call an MO, was good, I admit it. Our local newspapers and broadcasters had been calling me The Whispering Bandit for two years now, and nagging the police to do something about catching me, so far without result because I stuck to throwing those little pebbles, the frequent small hauls. They suited me fine. Who needs a fortune? Not me. A few hundred a month besides my honest pay kept me comfortably supplied with all the martinis and Sally Ann's my heart desired.

So you can see why Lieutenant Randall's mention of counterfeiting relieved me. You can understand, too, why I was calm and unworried when I faced him across the battered desk, in his dingy office at headquarters. Since my conscience was clear, I leaned back in my wooden chair and waited for him to open the ball.

He offered me a cigarette. When I refused, he lit one himself and leaned down beside his desk to drop the paper match into his wastebasket. Then he said, "It's very good of you to cooperate like this, Mr. Carmichael. Believe me, I appreciate it."

I shrugged. "Am I cooperating, or am I under arrest? Are you charging me with anything, Lieutenant?"

He seemed genuinely shocked. "Under arrest? Charged with anything? You've misunderstood me, I'm afraid."

"You said you wanted to talk to me about counterfeiting, didn't you?"

"Sure." He puffed smoke. "And so I do." He coughed. "I don't inhale," he informed me virtuously. "About this counterfeiting thing, I got a call from Tasso's Tavern this evening. They reported that a counterfeit bill had been passed at their bar so I naturally took a run out there to check into it. Sure enough, somebody had laid a phony bill on Tasso's bartender."

"That's tough on Tasso," I said, "but what's it got to do with me?" I was getting fed up with this foolishness.

"You were there," he said reasonably, "weren't you? Sitting at the bar with your young lady?"

"You know I was. Is that any excuse for making me waste my evening like this?"

"I'm not 'making' you waste your evening." The lieutenant's voice was hurt. "I asked you—politely—if you'd mind coming downtown for a talk, and you agreed quite readily. Is that coercion? Or is it voluntary cooperation?"

"All right, it's cooperation—but a damn waste of time all the same."

"I'm glad that's settled," said Randall.

"Nuts." I blustered a little. "Do me a favor, will you? As long as I'm here, pump me dry quick and get it over because this is the last cooperation you'll ever get from me, and you better believe it. Don't you know that you can't push honest citizens around as though we were criminals?"

Randall grinned. "I've got news for you, Mr. Carmichael. We can push honest citizens around as much as we like. It's the criminals we have to treat with the utmost gentleness and respect. If you don't believe me, ask the Supreme Court." He ground out his cigarette in a stained tray on his desk, then he lifted his eyes to me. "The bartender at Tasso's Tavern," he said, "pointed you out to me as the customer who passed the counterfeit bill."

That really surprised me. It disturbed me some, too, and I thought back to my interrupted session at Tasso's bar with Sally Ann. I remembered paying for our drinks with a used fifty—President Grant's picture on the bill had been wrinkled and dirty—and the bill could have come into my possession in only one way. To Randall I said incredulously, "Me?"

He nodded. "The barman said it was the only fifty buck bill he's handled this week."

I know now that I should have owned to the fifty; told Randall I won it in a floating crap game or at the racetrack or some place equally untraceable. Instead, I made a bad mistake. I put on an air of amused relief and said, "A fifty! Then the bartender has to be dead wrong about who gave it to him. I haven't even *seen* a fifty buck bill for ten years, let alone spent one, Lieutenant!" I called on the truth to convince him. "I'm a short-order cook in MacDougal's all-night restaurant, working the midnight-to-eight shift. You know many short-order cooks with fifty buck bills to throw around?"

"No," Randall murmured, "can't say I do. The barkeep was pretty sure he remembered you giving it to him though."

"He couldn't have remembered if his own grandmother gave it to him, not in Tasso's tonight. The joint was really jumping. You see it yourself. They were lined up three deep at the bar. The bartender was too busy to remember anything."

Randall gave a reluctant shrug. "Could be," he said. "Anyway, that's why I asked you to come down for a talk."

I said, "Sure, Lieutenant. No hard feelings, now that you've explained. If you want to know for the record, I paid for our four drinks, Sally Ann's and mine, with a five buck bill and gave the barkeep half the change for a tip." I said this boldly; it would be the bartender's word against mine. Leave Sally Ann out of it. When she was drinking, she never noticed anything except her own reflection in the backbar mirror.

Randall dropped his eyelids over his cat eyes and sighed. I think it was the first time I'd seen him blink. His face looked entirely different with those yellow eyes covered. "Well, then," he said, "if you didn't pass the fifty, maybe you can still give me a little help, Mr. Carmichael."

"I'll try."

"Give me the names of anybody else you knew at the bar in Tasso's tonight. *Somebody* passed that fake fifty and I've got to find out who it was. If you can give me a couple of names to start on…) He paused hopefully.

I shook my head. "Only one I knew was that girl Sally Ann, and she didn't even tell me her last name. You know how it is. Go into a bar for a drink and ask a babe to have one with you, just for company? Maybe the bartender can help you."

Randall gave another sigh. "I hope so."

I stood up. "All right if I blow now?"

He waved a hand. "Sure. But I'll drive you back. It's the least I can do." He glanced at his watch. "I'll be free to leave in about five minutes, if you want to wait."

I didn't want to wait. I wanted to get away from Randall's yellow eyes and his false politeness just as soon as I could; and I certainly didn't want to go back to Tasso's Tavern. I said, "Never mind, thanks. I'll catch a cab."

"Suit yourself," he said. Then, on a different note, "I'm really counting on that *particular* fifty buck bill, Mr. Carmichael, do you know it?"

"Counting on it?" I said. "For what?"

"To lead me to The Whispering Bandit," Randall said.

I stiffened all over. For a second I was afraid to turn my head for fear it would creak. "The Whispering Bandit? You mean the bank robber the papers keep talking about?" The words were hard to get out.

"That's the one," Randall said. "A two-bit thief who's got crazy-lucky eighteen times in a row."

I eased myself back into my chair, interest and animation in my face. With not a trace of his insult to me and my system showing, I asked casually, "How could a counterfeit fifty dollar bill lead you to a bank robber, Lieutenant? That doesn't make sense to me."

"Oh, it does in a way, considering the off-beat scheme we're trying right now…out of desperation, you might say." He sucked his lips, fixed his eyes on a cobwebbed corner of the ceiling. I waited for him to go on, trying not to look anxious.

Finally he said, "It's a childish scheme. Really childish. It probably won't work at all. How could it? In the first place it was dreamed up by an amateur, not even a cop. A nosey reader sent the idea in a letter to the president of the last bank The Whispering Bandit robbed."

I kept quiet, not doing much breathing.

"A nutty idea," Randall went on, "but I was willing to try anything to get the newspapers off my back." He shot an uncertain look at me. "As long as you've been inconvenienced by it, Mr. Carmichael, I guess maybe you're entitled to hear what the deal is—if you're interested."

"I'm interested," I said. "Everybody in town's interested in The Whispering Bandit."

"Don't I know it! Well, the thing is, that fake fifty dollar bill at Tasso's is a kind of a trap."

I felt cold on the back of my neck. I turned to see if the office door behind me was open. It wasn't.

"A trap?" I repeated.

He nodded. "You've got to understand that we know the MO of The Whispering Bandit pretty good by this time."

"What's an MO?" I thought I ought to ask.

"Method of operation. Like The Whispering Bandit always speaks in a whisper to disguise his voice during holdups, for instance. Always works alone. Changes his appearance for every job. Takes only one drawer of cash at each heist. Makes his raids during the noon hour at small isolated branch banks in a geographical suburban pattern that's pretty well defined now, after eighteen robberies. Stuff like that, that's part of his MO. Do you follow me?"

"Yes, but not about the counterfeit fifty."

"I'm coming to that. Once we know the regular MO of The Whispering Bandit, we can kind of figure ahead of him a little, can't we? Take a rough guess at what banks he'll be hitting next and, even more important, what teller in any bank he's likely to point his Woodsman target pistol at, and ask for the money in her cash drawer."

"You're kidding," I said.

"No, I'm not. It's all part of his pattern. It's always a girl teller that he holds up, never a man; and it's always the *prettiest* girl teller in the bank."

I stared at him. He was telling me things about my system that I didn't even know myself. "How come the prettiest teller?" I asked, fascinated.

Randall laughed shortly. "The guy's probably a psycho, gets his jollies from scaring pretty girls with a gun. How do I know? Anyway, that was the basis of our counterfeit money trap for him."

"The pretty teller bit?"

"That, and the list of branch banks we figured he might hit next. See, we just picked out the prettiest teller in each of those possible branch banks; or the teller, rather, that The Whispering Bandit would think the prettiest, judging from his past selections. Then we fixed up a little bundle of money for her to keep in her cash drawer at all times, separate from her regular cash. It was just a few genuine tens and twenties, with two counterfeit fifties we borrowed from the Treasury boys mixed in. Used money, understand; not banded, just loose in the drawer, but never to be touched unless The Whispering Bandit showed up. Too, we fixed it with every one of those girl tellers that *if* The Whispering Bandit showed up at her window some noontime, she was to give him all the money in her cash drawer immediately and without arguing—especially the stack that had the two fake fifties in it. You begin to see the plot, Mr. Carmichael?"

"Sure," I said out of a dry throat. "Then I suppose you passed the word that counterfeit fifty dollar bills were showing up around town, and warned stores and bars and places to watch out for them. Right?"

"Right."

"Well." I managed a small grin. "So that's why Tasso's bartender called you so quick tonight."

"Yep. That fifty he took in rang all the bells. I thought we had The Whispering Bandit at last, because there were two fake fifties in the loot he lifted two weeks ago from the South Side branch of the Second National and this was one of them. No doubt about it."

I felt sick. Two fake fifties; then the other one was still under the mattress in my room at the fleabag hotel where I lived. I've got to get out of here, I thought in a panic, I've got to get home quick, I've got to burn that damned bill, I've got to leave town…

Randall's telephone rang. He picked it up and listened to a tinny voice on the other end, nodding his head from time to time. When he hung up, he said, "That call concerned you, Mr. Carmichael."

"Me?" I said.

"Couple of my boys have been visiting your room," the lieutenant's tone was almost apologetic, "and I'm afraid Tasso's bartender was right about who passed the fifty, Mr. Carmichael."

Words of doom! Casually said, but doomsters all the same. I flipped. My voice went up three notches. "Visiting my room!" I yelled.

Randall held up a hand placatingly. "All in order," he said. "They had a proper warrant for the search. In fact, we've had the warrant ready for a month—all except for filling in your name." He coughed.

"Tasso's bartender came up with that when he called to report the fake fifty. He knew your name, it seems, because somebody called you on the bar telephone at Tasso's once, and when the bartender asked if Andrew Carmichael was in the house, you took the call. Remember that?"

All too well. The cold feeling on the back of my neck was spreading downward between my shoulder blades. I tried to think.

Randall didn't give me much chance. He went right on. "Once we had your name, it didn't take us five minutes to find out where you lived, fill in the blank warrant, and start my boys over to your hotel. Then I came out to Tasso's."

"You said I wasn't under arrest!" I sounded shrill, even to myself. "You said I wasn't charged with anything."

"You weren't. Not then, but you are now."

I did the best I could. "You got me here under false pretenses, Lieutenant. You've questioned me without my lawyer being present or informing me of my rights. You've deprived me of my constitutional—"

Randall closed his eyes again. "I did nothing of the sort."

"You did. You've questioned me. You've accused me, at least by implication, of being The Whispering Bandit. You've tried to trick me into confessing."

"Oh, no." He reached into a desk drawer and brought out a compact tape recorder. "I think this tape will confirm that most of the questioning was done by you, and most of the confessing, if any, done by me, when I told you about our little trap for The Whispering Bandit."

When had he switched on that tape recorder, the smooth devil? When he reached to discard his first burnt match in the wastebasket?

I gave it another try. "You were deliberately holding me here while your men searched my room."

"That I admit," he said, bland as cream. "And don't you want to know what they found there?" I didn't answer, so he went on, "I'll tell you. Item: one counterfeit fifty dollar bill stashed with genuine currency under the mattress and with a serial number that identifies it as one of the two false fifties stolen two weeks ago from the South Side branch of the Second National Bank. Item: three pairs of contact lenses, various colors. Item: three hair pieces, three sets of false eyebrows, two sets of false mustaches and beards, matching colors. Item: one Colt Woodsman revolver. Item: a complete file of local newspapers detailing exploits of The Whispering Bandit, going back more than two years." He looked at me sadly, and clicked his tongue. "Shall I go on, Mr. Carmichael?"

Miserably I shook my head.

"*Now* you get your lawyer," Randall said. "*Now* we charge you with multiple armed robbery offenses. *Now* the Supreme Court steps in to assure you tender loving care. Because now, Mr. Carmichael, you're sure as hell going to spend a little time in the sneezer as The Whispering Bandit!"

I didn't doubt it. I said, "Very smart, Lieutenant. Very clever. Quite a gag you've pulled on me, I'll admit."

"It's not my gag. I told you that." He opened the middle drawer of his desk, making a show of it. "I've got the original letter here that suggested the idea."

He pulled out a single sheet of paper. "Here it is. Would you care to see it?"

He held it out to me. Automatically, I took it and read the few lines scrawled on it in pencil:

Dere Mr. Presidant of the bank:

I know a way to fool The Whispring Bandit. When he holds up your bank, you could give him play money instead of reel money. Thank you.

Richard Stevenson, Age 9

I tossed the letter back on Randall's desk. He looked at me and his expression was hard to read. "The bank president started an account at his bank for young Richard Stevenson in the amount of five dollars," he told me. "Wasn't that nice?"

"Great," I said. Then I began to laugh.

Do you blame me for not liking kids?

CAUSE FOR ALARM

Originally published in* Ellery Queen's Mystery Magazine, *April 1970.

It is well known that while a criminal is engaged in the commission of a crime, and during the period immediately following, he is a veritable bundle of nerves. He is drawn up so tight that any trifling occurrence of an unexpected nature can send him into a blind panic, with his nerves twanging like guitar strings. And his reaction to such an event—to anything which, in his highly nervous state, seems to him to be a cause for alarm—often takes unpredictable forms. Sometimes his panic makes him more cunning, more dangerous; sometimes it has just the opposite effect.

Lieutenant Randall of the robbery detail was well aware of this basic psychological truth. He had even, in his early days as a patrolman, been its victim. A thief, emerging from a jewelry shop with considerable loot and a sweet certainty that there wasn't a cop within three blocks, was rudely startled by a sudden yell from Randall who, off duty and merely passing by, happened to spot him.

As a result. Randall took a .32 caliber bullet through the calf of his right leg from a usually prudent and peaceful lawbreaker who had never before so much as raised his voice to an officer of the law. As the thief explained later in court, if he'd *known* a cop was in the vicinity he would have surrendered meekly on being challenged, but Randall had so startled him that he had instantly begun to shoot, a reflex action occasioned entirely by blind panic.

After that experience Randall believed he knew pretty well what to expect when a crook was given sudden cause for alarm. He had the scar on his leg to prove he had earned the knowledge the hard way. Yet he had acquired only half the lesson. The other half he learned from a young bank teller named Harry Oberlin.

Harry Oberlin worked at the Citizens National Bank. And it was through his teller's window that a bank robber, one day in early summer, relieved the bank of $3200.

Randall got the call at headquarters about a half hour after noon. The bank's cashier, in the usual half-coherent state of bank officials who call the police to report a bank robbery, wasn't very helpful. "No, I don't know what he looked like or how much he stole. It happened only minutes ago. At Harry Oberlin's window—he's the one who touched the alarm. I haven't had a chance to—"

"Hold everything," Randall said sharply. "I'll be there in five minutes." He figured he could get the information more quickly on the spot than he could over the phone. He went himself.

The bank was only a block from headquarters, so Randall was as good as his word. Five minutes later, the cashier, a Mr. Dangerfield, met him at the front entrance of the bank, recognizing him as a police officer, no doubt, by the unbanking-like speed with which Randall came through the revolving door.

Leading Randall into the railed enclosure where the bank's officers sat quietly behind impressive desks, Dangerfield said, "We haven't made any fuss, of course. Our patrons don't even know there's been a robbery." He jerked a thumb at the dozen or so customers lined up before the two tellers' windows opposite.

"Where was your guard during the stickup?" Randall asked.

"In the Men's Room." There was anger in Dangerfield's tone. "I think perhaps the thief waited for that moment."

They reached Dangerfield's desk. A young man of mild appearance was waiting for them in a chair beside it. The cashier sat down behind the desk and invited Randall to have a chair. "This is Harry Oberlin," he introduced the young man. "He's the one who had the—ah—bandit at his window."

"Then you're the one I want to talk to," Randall said. "Tell me exactly what happened."

The teller cleared his throat. "This fellow came up to my open window. He was alone, nobody behind him. He handed a canvas sack through to me along with this note." Oberlin passed Randall a slip of brown wrapping paper.

It was the usual thing: THIS IS A STICKUP. EMPTY YOUR CASH DRAWER IN THIS BAG. It was printed in block letters, with a ballpoint pen.

"What did he look like?"

Oberlin shrugged. "Medium height, medium weight, white man, brown hair, maybe twenty-four or five. Gray slacks, gray windbreaker. He kept one hand inside his jacket as if he had a gun. Anyway, our cameras probably got him."

The cashier broke in, "Oberlin managed to trigger our security cameras."

"Good," Randall said t o Oberlin. "Then what?"

"I did what he said. We have standing instructions to do that, since we're insured and the bank doesn't want any of us murdered." Mr. Dangerfield waved his hands.

"Never mind that, Harry." Randall said, "How much money was in your cash drawer?"

"About thirty-two hundred, I think. Bills and silver. I haven't had time to check the precise amount."

"Didn't anybody else notice what was going on?"

Oberlin shook his head. "I guess not. The bandit looked around the bank several times while I was filling his bag, but nobody seemed to pay any attention to him. He was plenty nervous, though."

"And after you filled his sack?"

"He took it and walked out the side door to the street and turned south. Then I hit the alarm bar to alert Mr. Dangerfield."

"And that was it, eh?" Randall had heard the story so many times before. "Disappeared in the lunch-hour crowds, I suppose?"

"Well," Oberlin said, "I followed him to the door as soon its l could get around the counter and I saw him duck into a dark-blue Plymouth sedan, 1968 model, that was parked down Ward Street, and drive off like a shot."

"For God's sake!" said Randall. "Why didn't you say so before? A dark-blue 1968 Plymouth sedan?" He reached for the telephone on the cashier's desk, then paused. His respect for Harry Oberlin was mounting. "You didn't by any chance see the car's license number?"

"Not all of it. Just the last two digits—39."

Randall got an outside line, dialed headquarters, and asked for Hennessy. "Randall," he said crisply when Hennessy came on the line. "Take a look at your Auto Theft list and see if there's a dark-blue 1968 Plymouth sedan on it with a license number ending in 39."

After a brief wait Hennessy said, "Here it is, Lieutenant. Reported stolen last night from the North Side Shopping Center. Full license number is—"

"Don't tell me," Randall interrupted, "Put it on the air. All points, urgent. I'm at Citizens National Bank. Ten minutes ago a guy robbed this place and he's using that Plymouth as a getaway car." He gave Hennessy a quick recap of the bandit's appearance, quoting Oberlin. Then he hung up.

He turned to Mr. Dangerfield. "I'm afraid he has a good start. He'll probably abandon the stolen car as soon as he's well away from this neighborhood. But we'll do what we can. I'd like to see what your camera got as soon as the film's developed, and I'll have this note checked for fingerprints. Meanwhile, can l get a definite figure on the amount of money actually stolen, Mr. Oberlin? Can you find that out for me now?"

"Sure," Oberlin said, and stood up.

Randall left Dangerfield sitting disconsolate at his desk and followed Oberlin to his cage. The teller pulled open his cash drawer and showed it to Randall. It was empty as a school house on Saturday morning.

"Lieutenant," said Oberlin hesitantly, "I didn't want to say anything to Mr. Dangerfield, but I was kind of prepared for this robbery."

Randall stared. "Prepared?"

"I mean, there are so many holdups of banks and savings and loan companies these days that I figured it might happen to *me* sometime, too, you know?"

Randall nodded.

"So what I did, I tried to figure out how I could kind of surprise any bandit who held me up. You know, without running too much risk of getting hurt myself."

The phone on Oberlin's counter rang. The teller picked it up and answered it. "It's for you, Lieutenant."

Randall took the phone. "Randall," he said.

"Hennessy, Lieutenant. We've picked up that Plymouth sedan of yours."

Randall couldn't believe his ears. "Already?"

"Yep." Hennessy tried to keep from sounding complacent. "Not too far from the bank. Abandoned."

"That figures. No sign of the man?"

"No sign of him." Hennessy laughed a little. "But the car wasn't empty, Lieutenant. There was a bagful of money on the front seat."

"Well, well." Randall stole a look at Oberlin. "How much?"

"No details yet. Lieutenant. Car 36 just this minute called in that they'd found the Plymouth and a sackful of money. I thought you'd want to know about it right away."

"I do. Fast work, Hennessy. And thanks." Randall hung up slowly. "Did you hear that?" he asked Harry Oberlin.

"No," said Oberlin. "You haven't caught the bandit already, have you?"

"Not quite. But we've found the money. At least some of it. He left it behind in the car."

It was Oberlin's turn to laugh. He laughed out loud and his pleasure was infectious. The teller in the adjoining cage looked over and grinned in sympathy. "You mean the robber not only abandoned his getaway car but the money, too?"

"Seems like it." Randall fixed the young teller with a stern eye.

"Now, just before the phone rune, Oberlin, you were saying something about being prepared to surprise any bandit who might hold you up. What did you mean?

"I guess it did surprise him!" Oberlin said. "But it must have scared the daylights out of him if he went off and left the money behind." The best part of it is the teller was practically chortling. "All I did was exactly what he told me to do—to put everything in my cash drawer into his bag. Including the little surprise I always kept in the drawer in case of bandits."

Randall said, "All right. Oberlin. I'm asking again. What was it?"

"A smoke bomb, Lieutenant," Oberlin said with the air of a David who has just bested a Goliath. "A smoke grenade, timed to go off three minutes after I pulled the pin. I put it in the bandit's bag with the money."

HELL IN A BASKET

Originally published in* Mike Shayne Mystery Magazine, *December 1972.

Lieutenant Randall thought there was something fishy about the whole thing right from the beginning when Captain Forbes, his superior, told him on Wednesday morning to go out to Capucino's Carnival and get the facts about the death of one Ram Singh. A call had just come in; an ambulance and the medical examiner were already on their way.

"An Indian?" Randall asked.

"A Hindu I suppose, with a name like that," said Captain Forbes acidly. "He was the snake charmer in the side show."

"How'd he die?" Randall asked.

"The man who called said his snake bit him."

Randall, already on his way out, paused. "Snake-bit? Then where do we come in? Why the Homicide Bureau?"

"How do I know?" Forbes growled at him. "Don't stand there asking me questions. Get out and ask the Carnival boss, Capucino."

Capucino, owner and manager of Capucino's Carnival, was a short, beefy, bushy-browed specimen with the fast-paced talking habits of a circus barker. Randall found him on the lot.

"It was the worst shock ever I had," Capucino said as he led Randall toward a small house trailer that was parked behind the deserted side show tent. Randall could see the police ambulance standing beside the trailer. "I go into Whitey's trailer half an hour ago, to see why he don't show up for breakfast, and I practically stumble over him. He's lying there on the floor right next to the basket where he keeps King, and he's dead as a last year's hollyhock!"

"I thought the guy was a Hindu," Randall said. "Name of Ram Singh."

"Whitey Whitaker was his real name. He just put on a body stain and a turban and a beard for his snake-charming act, see? He was an American, Whitey was. But we billed him as The Great Ram Singh, Ruler of Reptiles."

"Oh," said Randall. They were approaching the trailer. "And I gather that King, who lives in a basket in Whitey's trailer, is his snake?"

"Sure, sure." Capucino nodded. "King's his snake." They reached the trailer. "Only one he had."

They went into the trailer. Christy Huneker, the M. E., was just getting up from a squatting position beside Whitey's body.

"Ah, Randall," Huneker said pleasantly. "Nothing here for you, I'm afraid. This guy died of snake bite."

"What kind of snake?" Randall asked curiously.

"Cobra," Capucino said. He pointed. "He's in there."

Their eyes went to a shallow, pot-bellied, covered basket of woven straw that stood in one corner of the room.

Randall asked, "Isn't there some kind of serum you can take when you're bitten by a snake, Doc?"

The doctor nodded. "Antivenin. But you've got to have it handy when needed. How about that, Mr. Capucino? Wouldn't a man who handled a poisonous snake keep a supply of antivenin handy, just in case?"

"Yes," Capucino said. "I'm sure Whitey had it around some place. Andy always did, I know. And Whitey took over from Andy."

Capucino went to a small wall cabinet above the bed and rooted through it.

"Here's the serum," he said, holding up a sealed phial, "and the hypodermic to inject it with."

"Probably too drunk to use it when the snake bit him," the doctor said. "He'd been drinking. You can still smell it on him." He tipped a hand to Randall. "I've got to get back to town. You coming?"

Randall said, "Not for a minute. I'll call you later to verify, Doc." The ambulance men came in and carried Whitaker's body from the room on a stretcher. Dr. Huneker left, too.

"Let's see the snake," Randall said.

Capucino approached the basket in the corner, cautiously reached out a hand and took the weighted cover off. He jumped back. Nothing happened immediately, although Randall could hear a dry stirring, as though of disturbed leaves, in the basket. Then a nightmare triangular head emerged sleepily from the basket, and two yellow, lidless eyes regarded them solemnly, while a black forked tongue flicked questingly in and out of the armored mouth.

Randall, whose own eyes were the joke of the department because they were of a strange, sulphur-yellow color and seemed seldom to blink, was stared down immediately by the snake. It was no contest at all.

"Put the lid on, Capucino," he said in a nervous voice, "before the damn snake bites us."

"Call me Cap," the carnival man said. "Everybody does." He took a long pole from another corner of the room, slid it through the loop on the basket lid, gingerly reached out and dropped the lid down over the basket opening. The snake's head disappeared. Capucino came back and sat down on the unmade bed.

"Look, Lieutenant," he said in a neutral voice, "I called you because I think there's more to this than a snake biting a guy who's had too much booze. Whitey always drank a good deal when he went to bed. Every night. He claimed it helped him sleep. He had an old bayonet wound in his gut from Korea that ached him pretty bad, and the whiskey eased it up, he said."

"What's on your mind then?" Randall asked.

"The snake," Capucino said, leaning forward and putting his elbows on his knees. "King's on my mind. King couldn't have bit Whitey and killed him."

Randall slowly lowered himself into a straight chair. "Give me that again," he said.

"King couldn't have bit Whitey," Capucino repeated doggedly. "It sounds nutty as hell, but it's true. I think that's another snake over there in the basket, Lieutenant. Another snake entirely."

"What!" Randall stared.

"King couldn't have bit Whitey. He was de-fanged."

"He was what?"

"De-fanged. Had his fangs pulled by a vet. Like you go to a dentist and have your wisdom teeth pulled out. Sort of the same thing."

Randall felt suddenly out of his depth. "You mean Whitey's snake didn't have any fangs left to bite with?"

"He still had teeth, understand. So he could eat the rats and mice and things that Whitey fed him, but his poison fangs was gone. So he was harmless, see?"

Randall looked at the snake basket in the corner. "Can you tell if it's a different snake from its appearance?"

"Not me. I'm no snake expert. And I ain't about to examine him close-up. Hell, I never had a snake act in my show at all until two years ago, and now I wish I never had one."

"Isn't there anybody around here can tell for sure whether that's King over there in the basket?"

Capucino hesitated. "I can't think of anybody much," he said, "now that Whitey's gone. Gloriana, maybe. Or Andy Grissom. But he's not around any more, either."

"Who's this Gloriana?"

"One of my tumblers. Acrobat. A great kid, Lieutenant. Pretty as hell, and built like a brick outhouse. I never could get to first base with her, though." He sighed, profoundly saddened by his memories. "First it was

Andy, and then Whitey that she went for. But just let me, the boss, make a pass, and it was 'aren't you ashamed of yourself, Mr. Capucino!' You know how that goes?"

Randall grinned. "Not me," he said. "I got a wife and two kids."

Capucino said with dignity, "So have I. But that don't mean I can't like an acrobat, too."

"You say Gloriana spent a lot of time with Whitey?"

"Yeah. They played house a good bit in his trailer here."

"And this other fellow, Andy Grissom. Was he Whitey's predecessor?"

"Yeah, he used to be our snake charmer before Whitey. Andy was the original Ram Singh, the first snake act we ever had in the show. And King was his snake. Andy's, I mean. Andy trained him, and worked up the act and I hired them for my side show a coupla years back. It wasn't much of an act, really, but the marks went for it big.

"Andy dressed up like a Hindu and squatted down in front of King's basket on the platform, and tottled a little tune on a whistle he had. When he played on the pipe, King sticks his head up out of the basket and blows out his hood like he's mad, and kind of waves himself around like dancing. And every once in a while, he tries to strike at Andy, but he never gets out of the basket. It's a smash with the yokels, Lieutenant, a real draw."

"And this is the same act that Whitey has been doing?" Randall asked.

"Sure. Same thing. Andy taught Whitey the routine before he left."

"Left?"

"Andy left the show. But he turned over his snake and his act to Whitey, so we'd still have a Ram Singh."

"Pretty big-hearted, wasn't he? Was Whitey a good friend of his?"

"Not exactly. Whitey was just an ambitious helper on my Ferris wheel when Andy gave him his chance to be snake charmer."

"Then how come he picked out Whitey for the job?"

Capucino blinked several times and shrugged. "Because of Gloriana, maybe."

"Gloriana was Andy's girl friend before she was Whitey's?"

"Yep. Whitey kind of took her away from Andy." He grinned. "She changed trailers, you might say. You know the way girls are. She decided she'd rather play house with Whitey than Andy. Perfectly simple, Lieutenant. Happens all the time. Even with married folks." He squinted at Randall.

"And how did Andy Grissom take that?"

"Oh, normal, I'd say. He was pretty burned at first, but he got over it quick. It broke up his little family." Capucino chuckled at his own euphemism. "Some family," he said raising his bushy eyebrows humorously. "A snake and an acrobat, and a fake Hindu."

Randall said, "He didn't seem specially sore at Whitey Whitaker?"

"Naw."

"But Andy could have had it in for Whitey all the same. Maybe he just kept it hidden," Randall said.

Capucino shook his head. "The hell with that. What you want to know, Lieutenant, is who changed the snakes in Whitey's basket over there."

"Tell me some more about this de-fanging deal. If a vet did it, he ought to be able to identify King, and be able to testify that this is a different snake, oughtn't he?"

"Sure."

"So who's the vet?"

"I never heard his name. And he's five hundred miles away, anyhow. In Indianapolis. That's where my Carnival was playing when Andy took King to be de-fanged."

Randall brooded. Capucino said, "Damn, I wish Andy hadn't give his snake to Whitey and didn't leave the show at all. Or I wish he'd of taken the snake with him. Poor Whitey. He was a good kid, coming along fine, going to be a real carny hand before long. I liked him:"

Capucino lit a cigarette with a kitchen match and flicked the match stick toward the snake basket. Randall stared at the little wall cabinet where Whitey had kept his antivenin.

"He kept his antivenin in that cabinet," Randall said. "Only a few feet from where he collapsed. Seems funny he wouldn't have been able to make it just those few feet and give himself the shot."

"Not if you remember Whitey was a little tanked. And maybe he didn't even realize he'd been bit. Or maybe the poison paralyzed him too quick."

"Cobra venom paralyzes you quick, does it?"

"Don't ask me. I'm only telling you what Andy used to say. Cobra bites go after your nerve centers. Rattlesnake bites go to work on your blood corpuscles and are slower. Maybe Whitey never even thought of the antivenin when King bit him. Drunk and excited and all, like he was."

"If he's a snake charmer and knows his business, the antivenin would be the first thing he'd think of, Cap."

"He didn't know his business so damn good," Capucino said. "He was still pretty new at it. He'd only been doing the Ram Singh bit for a few days, remember."

Randall's yellow eyes narrowed. "What!" He sat forward in his chair.

"Sure. I told you. When Andy left the show last week—"

"You didn't say last week!"

"In Indianapolis, I said. Last week. Where Andy had King de-fanged. Didn't I tell you that?"

"Never mind," said Randall. "You told me now." He looked at Capucino curiously. To Capucino, the passage of time expressed itself only in the places where his traveling Carnival played. To him, Indianapolis meant last week. And Terre Haute probably meant the second week of August.

"Sure," Cap was saying, "that's when Whitey took over as Ram Singh. Last week in Indianapolis. That's why Andy got King de-fanged there, see?"

"Wait a minute." Randall tried to keep his irritation from showing. "You mean King has been de-fanged only since last week?"

"Sure. What did you think?"

"I thought Andy had him de-fanged when he started to train him, naturally. To make him safe to handle. Before he even joined your show."

Capucino laughed. "Oh, no. Andy didn't need him de-fanged. Andy always milked him. He had him de-fanged to protect *Whitey* when he took over the act."

Randall had the curious feeling that he was slowly sinking out of sight in a morass of irrational facts that refused to allow him a secure hold on any of them. He made an effort and inquired, "Andy milked King?"

"Sure. Andy knew how to force King's jaws open and press out the poison from his poison sacs into a saucer, so he'd be without poison for long enough to be safe during the afternoon and evening performances. That's all milking is, drawing out the poison."

"That I know," said Randall sardonically. "But it's the only damn thing I do know about this whole mess, so far."

"Andy was a real snake man," Capucino said. "He milked the poison out of King every day instead of having him de-fanged, because he thought the sight of those big fangs in the front of King's mouth made the act that much better for the marks. They get a kind of morbid jolt out of seeing the fangs."

"So why didn't Andy show Whitey how to milk King when he took over?"

Capucino shrugged. "Too dangerous for the kid, he said."

"You're sure King really was de-fanged when Andy said so?"

Capucino stared at him, startled. "Why, I think so. You want to be absolutely sure, whyn't you ask Gloriana?"

"I will," Randall said.

Gloriana's trailer was an altogether different proposition from Whitey's. It was larger. Its interior was as frilly and feminine as the frosting on a pink birthday cake. When she wasn't visiting with Whitey, Gloriana shared it with three other female members of the Carnival troupe. And when Capucino led Randall up the steps and into the trailer, Gloriana's roommates were variously engaged in trying to comfort the grief-stricken acrobat.

Randall stood in the doorway while Capucino introduced, him. He picked out Gloriana instantly, and after his first inclusive glance, he had eyes for no-one else. She was worth looking at. Even Capucino's enthusiastic description had failed to do her justice. She had tear stains on her cheeks; her face, innocent of make-up, had the clean, scrubbed look of a little girl's after a hot bath. Her short blonde hair was in disarray, her pale blue skirt was twisted over her swelling hips, and her pullover sweater had come adrift from its moorings at her waist, exposing an inch-wide gap of milky white flesh. She was one of the most breathtakingly provocative women Randall had ever met.

At his request, her trailer-mates withdrew with Capucino, leaving him alone with Gloriana. She sat down on the daybed. Randall took a chair against the wall, trying not to look at the girl's legs.

"Mr. Capucino told me you might be able to give me a little information, Gloriana," he began. "You were pretty friendly with Ram Singh, the snake charmer, he tells me."

She nodded un-selfconsciously. "Yeah. Whitey and I got along." Her voice was breathless music.

"Capucino says there was a little more to it than just 'getting along.' Is that right?"

"That's right. Whitey was a doll. Is it a crime?" She was quickly defensive.

"No." He smiled at her. "I don't blame Whitey and you a bit."

She softened. "He was wonderful, Mr. Randall," she said. "I feel terrible to think he's gone. And how could it have happened? King had no fangs."

"Do you know he had no fangs? For sure, I mean?"

"Of course. Andy brought King home from the vet's and showed King's mouth to both Whitey and me that same afternoon, so we'd know King was harmless."

"Why did Andy have King's fangs drawn?"

"So Whitey'd be safe putting on the act with King. Whitey was real new at the snake business. He was a Ferris wheel operator before—" Her voice trailed off miserably and her eyes filled.

"I know all about that," Randall said hastily. "Did Whitey take care of King himself?"

"Yes. Andy always did, and he recommended Whitey do it, too. The snake will do his act better for the man who feeds him and takes care of him, Andy said."

Randall cleared his throat. "When you changed your affections from Grissom to Whitey, what did Grissom think about it?"

She waggled one incredibly graceful shoulder. "What did he think? He thought I was giving him a dirty deal at first."

"And weren't you?"

"Look here, Mr. Randall." The tears were out of her eyes now, replaced by a flash of independence. "I pick out my own boy friends. And who I pick out is nobody's business but mine. Andy had his time with me before I met Whitey."

"And he didn't carry a grudge when you left him?"

"Not after his first jealousy wore off."

"When did you shift from Andy to Whitey?"

"About three weeks ago, I guess. In Fort Wayne, it was."

"Only three weeks? Then it's perfectly possible, isn't it, that your change of boy friends had something to do with Andy's deciding to leave the Carnival?"

"It's possible, I suppose. But he'd been talking about leaving for a long time before I met Whitey. He wanted to get into something more dignified."

Randall said, watching her, "You'd be pretty hard to let go of, once a fellow had you."

"Thanks," she said, "if that's supposed to be a compliment."

"You say Andy didn't carry a grudge. How do you know?"

"He gave Whitey his snake, didn't he? For free? King was Andy's favorite possession, next to me." She giggled. "He told me he liked Whitey and that's why he wanted Whitey to take over his act when he loft. He said if Whitey had a good job in the Carnival like that, maybe Whitey and me could get married."

"I see." Randall fidgeted in his chair. "When was the last time you saw Whitey alive?"

"Last night, just after the last side show performance. About eleven o'clock. I was going into the city for awhile, and I stopped off in the side show tent to tell Whitey about it."

"And you didn't go to his trailer after you got back from town?"

"No. It was pretty late. And Whitey needs his sleep. He usually takes a big dose of whiskey."

"Cap told me about that." Randall considered silently. On a hunch, he asked, "Did Grissom happen to tell you the name of the vet in Indianapolis who pulled King's fangs?"

Surprisingly, she nodded. "Yeah. A Dr. Sachs."

Randall wrote it down in a little notebook.

"How about Andy Grissom? Did he leave any address with you?"

"Sure," she said. "He's right here in this city, Mr. Randall. I had a date with him last night."

Randall, who thought he was used to surprises by now, almost did a double-take on this one. "You had a date with Grissom? Last night?"

"Why not? This is his home town. It's where he decided to settle down when he quit the Carnival last week. He's living at a boarding house on Spruce Street he told me. Mrs. Marion's."

"How come you have a date with him when you're Whitey's girl now?"

"I didn't want to," she said solemnly. "But he called up yesterday morning and asked me to come in and have a late supper with him after the show last night, just for old time's sake. What he really wanted, I found out, was to ask me how Whitey was getting along with King, and how I was getting along with Whitey." She looked deprecatingly at Randall, staring into his yellow eyes as innocent as a three-year-old in the Sunday school pageant.

"And you went?"

"Sure. I couldn't refuse him a little thing like that. He'd been nice to me, you know. And I still *like* him, for heaven's sake!"

In two days time, Randall thought morosely, she'll have forgotten all about Whitey. He wrote in his book: Mrs. Marion's. Spruce Street.

He got out of his chair. "Would you recognize King from any other snake?" he asked.

She shook her blonde head. "He's just a snake. I didn't look at him any more than I had to!"

Randall hesitated. "You've been very helpful," he said.

She rose from the daybed with the undulant grace of the acrobat she was. "And you're kind of sweet for a policeman, Mr. Randall. You know that?" She moved toward him, every curve an invitation.

"Thanks," said Randall in confusion. He backed out the door.

He returned at once to Headquarters. By three-thirty that afternoon, he had accumulated these facts.

From Dr. Huncker, after post mortem examination: that Whitey Whitaker had, in fact, died of a snake bite on his right hand; that the snake almost certainly was a cobra, since the victim's symptoms were all neurotoxic; that Whitey had been bitten between midnight and one o'clock in the morning.

From the police laboratory: that the snake putatively guilty of biting Whitey—brought from the Carnival lot to the lab, cooled to torpidity in the cold chamber, and then examined very gingerly by a technician—did, indeed, possess poison fangs capable of inflicting the fatal bite.

By long distance telephone: that Andy Grissom had paid an Indianapolis vet named Dr. K. L. Sachs to draw the fangs of a cobra called King, in order, as he made plain to the vet, to protect a new snake charmer who would be handling the snake.

From a Tri-state police broadcast: that no cobra had been reported lost, strayed or stolen within the past three days in the Tri-state area.

And from personal interviews: that Andy Grissom did, in fact, reside at the boarding house on Spruce Street; was planning to enter college in the Fall; had indubitably spent the hours between eleven and two A.M. the preceding night in a place called The Purple Angel, where he had met at eleven-thirty and had eaten supper with a girl enthusiastically described as "blonde, beautiful and stacked."

Contemplating this meager information without, pleasure. Randall swore and lit a black cigar whose bitter taste and evil odor suited his mood. At 3:35 he left his office and walked two blocks to the public library.

There, for the first time, he became convinced beyond doubt that he was dealing with murder.

At four o'clock, he was asking Mrs. Marion, at the front door of her boarding house on Spruce Street, whether her lodger, Andy Grissom, was in. She said he was in his bedroom, would the gentleman like to go up? The gentleman would.

He found Grissom in a small cheerful room on the second floor. The former Ram Singh was, surprisingly, a slender, small-boned man with a thin, almost ascetic face, level blue eyes, a gentle voice, and an unruly shock of black hair. He was younger than Randall had pictured him, too—not more than twenty-six or seven.

Randall introduced himself. "May I come in, Mr. Grissom? I'd like to talk to you."

"What about?" asked Andy Grissom. He was cool.

"Your snake, King," Randall said.

"King!" In concern, Grissom held his door wider immediately, and Randall walked in. "Last night, Gloriana, a girl I know from the Carnival, said King was fine."

Randall sat down without invitation. "Nothing's happened to King, Mr. Grissom. But something kind of permanent has happened to your friend. Whitey Whitaker."

Grissom shut the door and leaned back against it. "Whitey? Gloriana said he was great, too."

"He was. Until last night. Then your old buddy King bit him, and Whitey couldn't seem to keep from dying of it."

For a moment, Grissom seemed struck dumb. He stared at Randall with shock and incredulity in his level blue eyes. Randall, who was watching him closely, had to admit that incredulity seemed to predominate. Grissom finally sputtered, after several unsuccessful efforts to speak, "Whitey's dead?" He swallowed. "And King bit him? What are you trying to hand me, Lieutenant?"

"Nothing but the truth. Gloriana told Whitey she was coming in town to see you last night, Grissom. So after the show, he went to the trailer with your snake, put the basket down in its regular corner and turned in, feeling a little sorry for himself, no doubt. He took his usual jolt of whiskey, maybe more than usual to forget Gloriana's absence. But before he sacked out for good, he decided to say goodnight to the only companion he had left, your snake. He lifted off the basket lid and King stuck his head out and struck at Whitey like in the climax of your act. Only this time Whitey's reactions are slowed down by liquor. He's standing too close to the snake, too, probably. Anyway, King bites him in the hand."

Grissom was slowly shaking his head. "Not King," he said in a positive voice. "Poor Whitey. He was a nice kid."

"Wasn't he? Nice enough to sweet-talk Gloriana away from your trailer to his. And you hated him for that, didn't you?"

"No. He took Gloriana away from me, sure. But I never did kid myself I was a permanent fixture with her. Evidently you've seen her, so you must know—"

"I have."

"So nuts," Grissom said. "What I want to tell you is that King couldn't have bitten Whitey. It was impossible. King doesn't have any fangs."

"Here we go again," Randall said ironically. "I know the touching story of how you took King to the vet's and had him de-fanged for Whitey's protection. I've talked to Dr. Sach's office about it on the phone."

"Well, then, you know I'm telling the truth. King couldn't bite." Grissom sat down quietly on the edge of his neatly-made bed. "Were you asking Mrs. Marion about me earlier this afternoon?"

Randall nodded. "Yeah. And I know you weren't anywhere near the Carnival lot last night. When King bit Whitey."

"You keep saying King bit Whitey. Do you suspect that I had something to do with Whitey's death?"

"Maybe."

"Well, I'll be damned!" Grissom laughed, a gentle cascade of amusement. "Why didn't you say so? Aren't you reaching pretty far, Lieutenant? I did everything possible to protect Whitey. You've proved it. I made him a present of my girl and my snake and my act. And I had an alibi, it seems, for the time some strange snake bit Whitey and killed him." His eyes widened. "Say! How about my antivenin? I gave it to Whitey with the snake."

Randall's yellow eyes blazed briefly at Grissom. "Why didn't you teach Whitey to milk King, the way you did, instead of having him de-fanged?"

"Too dangerous for the kid. There's a trick to it. And the snake doesn't relish it much, of course."

Randall stood up, feeling defeated. "Will you come down to Headquarters and take a look at the snake that bit Whitey?"

"Sure, Lieutenant," Grissom agreed readily. "I'd like to see him. But I'm warning you in advance that it won't be King." At the police laboratory in the basement of Headquarters building, Randall gestured toward the pot-bellied basket the lab men had consigned to the farthest corner of the big room. The lid was wired down.

Grissom put on heavy leather gauntlets offered him by the lab man. "I wouldn't need these if it was King," he apologized. "He knows me. But with a strange snake—"

Without hesitation, he unwrapped the wire that held down the basket lid. Then he lifted the lid with one hand, stepped back, and began to whistle a shrill tune, trying to imitate the flute sound, Randall guessed.

Nothing happened.

"Still sluggish," the lab man hazarded, "from our cold treatment."

Grissom nodded and bent over the basket. With a sudden stab, he reached into the basket and brought out a foot and a half of snake, thick-bodied, dully shining, the evil head held away from him by a tight grip on the back of the snake's neck. Randall could see the reptile making a half-hearted attempt to expand his hood, but he was very sluggish.

Grissom turned the snake; this way and that, examining his markings. He looked up at Randall then, startled and bewildered.

"This is the snake that bit Whitey?" he asked tensely.

Randall nodded.

"But this is King!" Grissom exclaimed then, almost shouting. "This is my snake, Lieutenant! Fie couldn't have bitten Whitey!"

Grissom dropped the basket lid on the floor and brought his other hand around forcing open the snake's jaws. Plain to be seen were the two needle-like fangs, incurving, set at the forward end of the upper jawbone.

"I told you," said the lab man to Randall. "Fangs."

But Randall wasn't watching the snake's fangs. He was watching Grissom. And as Grissom exposed King's fangs to view, Randall could have sworn a Bible oath that the only sign of emotion detectable in the snake charmer's gentle blue eyes was a glimmer of amusement. *Amusement.*

Grissom dropped the snake back in the basket and clapped on the lid. He turned accusingly to Randall, then said in a heavy, dumfounded kind of way, "For God's sake, what is this. Lieutenant?" He held out a hand in appeal.

"I'll tell you," Lieutenant Randall said "Come on up to my office."

They went to Randall's office on the third floor and sat down, Randall behind his scarred desk, Grissom on the edge of a straight chair opposite him. With a negligent movement of his hand behind the desk top, Randall switched on the little tape recorder he had arranged. Its mike was concealed very cleverly in the paper-piled "out-going" basket not far from Grissom's lips.

"I'll tell you what it is," Randall went on as though he had never paused at all. "You murdered Whitey, Grissom. Because he took Gloriana away from you. And you did it with a brand new weapon. Ignorance."

Grissom stared uncomprehendingly. "You said King killed him, Lieutenant."

"King did kill him. But only because you kept Whitey in ignorance of one little fact about poisonous snakes. A fact that hardly anybody but a herpetologist, or a snake charmer, would know. Not even the city veterinarian who takes care of dogs and cats for the most part. It was very clever of you." He waited.

Grissom was the picture of injured innocence. He said, "I don't need to sit here and take this kind of talk from you, Lieutenant. And you know it. But I want to know how King could bite Whitey when I had him defanged."

"I'll tell you that, too. I didn't know it myself until an hour ago, but any poisonous snake has a number of extra fangs in reserve in ease he breaks off a fang in capturing his prey." Randall's voice rose grimly "Or in case his good-hearted owner takes him to a vet and has his fangs pulled out to protect a trusting fool like Whitey.

"I can remember what the book said, Grissom, word for word: 'by the side of each functional fang is a series of new ones in different stages of development, hidden in special pockets of the mouth lining. As soon as a fang is lost or broken, one of the successional series moves into its place and is fused to the jawbone.'" He turned his yellow eyes on Grissom's blue ones. "You get the picture, don't you, Grissom?"

Grissom's mobile face expressed horrified disbelief. "You're kidding, Lieutenant!"

"Like King was kidding when he bit Whitey. Yeah."

"But that's fantastic! I can't believe it. You mean that after I had King's fangs drawn last week and told Whitey King was harmless, another new set of fangs grew in right away?"

Randall's tone was bitter. "Having King de-fanged was a deliberate deception on your part. You did it to give Whitey and Gloriana a false sense of security with the snake, set them up for the kill. And you didn't give a damn whether it was Whitey or Gloriana that King bit after he got his new fangs. You hated them both. Didn't you?"

Grissom didn't seem to hear him. He dropped his face into his hands. "My God!" he said, agonized. "And I thought I was making sure Whitey couldn't get hurt!"

"You didn't know anything about this extra fang business, is that it?"

"Of course I didn't, man! What do you take me for?"

"A murderer," said Randall simply. "What else? By remote control you murdered the guy that stole your girl." If I'm ever going to get anything damaging out of him, he thought, this is about the time.

But Grissom merely shook his head, his face still covered by his hands. He wouldn't look at Randall. At length he mumbled, just above a whisper, "I didn't know, Lieutenant Randall. I give you my solemn word I didn't know that snakes can replace their fangs."

Randall lit one of his black cigars viciously. Did the guy know there was a recorder in the room?

He puffed his cigar. Then he gave it one more try, thinking he might prod Grissom into admitting something by insulting him. He said in a quiet voice, "You knew about the fang replacement, Grissom. And you also know there's no way in the world I can prove it. So get out of my office, will you? You're stinking it up, scum. You're all yellow. I'm not a bit surprised that you arranged for a dumb, dirty brainless snake to do your killing for you. Get out Grissom, before I lose my temper and feed you to your own snake!"

Grissom's eyes were still mild, still bland, still contrite-looking. But Randall was sure he saw that spark of sardonic amusement in them again. Grissom stood up.

"If that's the way you feel, I'll go," he said mildly. "I've got to get in touch with Gloriana, anyway. She must be feeling pretty low about poor Whitey."

He put on his hat and turned toward the door. "And thanks for the snake lecture, Lieutenant. It's to learn exactly that kind of thing that I'm entering college this Fall. I don't want to be a square all my life, you know, like you."

He went out.

Randall blew acrid smoke from his mouth and slapped the tape-recorder switch shut in a fury.

Then he reached for his telephone. Capucino was eating dinner in the restaurant tent on the carny lot, but he came to the phone at once. "Any news. Lieutenant?" he asked, his voice sounding very cheerful.

"What are you so happy about?" Randall barked at him.

Capucino chuckled. "I kinda tried my luck with Gloriana again after you left this morning," he said in his fast, fruity voice. "With Whitey gone, and Andy gone and all, I thought maybe she might be in a better mood, you know? And guess what?"

Randall sighed. "What?"

"She was. In a softer mood, I mean."

"Well, well. Congratulations, Cap. But watch yourself. Except for her, Whitey would still be alive."

"What's that?" Capucino said. "How come?"

Randall told him. Capucino listened in amazed silence. "I been in the carny business all my life," he finally said, "and I never heard that about a snake before."

"Neither did Grissom," said Randall. "He says."

"Don't you believe him!" Capucino was incensed. "He's a snake man! A specialist. He knew it, for sure. If he didn't it's funny as hell!"

"It's funny, all right," said Randall sourly. "Can't you hear me laughing?"